SHATTERED ICE

Printed in the United States of America.

First edition May 2024

Cover art by Ethemos (Manon Auclair)
Edited by Alison Cherry and Emily Klopfer

ISBN 979-8-9899572-0-0 (Paperback)
ISBN 979-8-9899572-2-4 (Hardcover)
ISBN 979-8-9899572-1-7 (eBook)

Published by Rebekka Strand
www.rebekkastrand.com

SHATTERED ICE

The Origins of Kaia
BOOK ONE

REBEKKA STRAND

CONTENT WARNING

Shattered Ice is a Fictional Action Adventure about a female character who is forced to flee an unknown adversary while learning about herself and her past. While fast-paced and exciting, the story might include elements that might not be suitable for some readers. Mentioned death/illness to a parent, mentions of self-harm and suicidal thoughts (past, off-page), reference to abuse by an ill parent (past, off-page), violence toward fictional animals and robots, and graphic violence are present in the novel. Readers who may be sensitive to these elements, please take note.

For your information, Shattered Ice is a novel inspired by both Scandinavian culture and the Sámi. As a Norwegian, I must preface that I am not the right person to write a Sámi story, but I believe a Nordic-inspired world cannot be true to its roots if it does not also highlight the Sámi. Please take some time to learn about their culture and history here: https://nordnorge.com/en/tema/the-sami-are-the-indigenous-people-of-the-north/

To those who never dared,
it is never too late to start your journey.

CHAPTER 1

Kaia had learned three things living under a glacier: it was terribly boring, she would never see the sky, and if the cold didn't kill her, her shift leader would.

Ice and gravel crunched beneath Kaia's boots as she charged forward. She heard the familiar hum of her heat converter as it struggled to keep the temperature inside her monosuit above freezing. It was old and tired, like everything she owned. Her breath was loud inside her helmet as she ran. Green flames in copper lanterns lit her path. Sweat trickled down her neck. She was late *again*.

Swearing, she left the small ice tunnel and sprinted into the central hub of Kaldwell. The cave, carved from the glacier, protected them from the surface. In seconds, she crossed the distance between the tunnel and the large metal door of the domed miner's shift building.

Catching her breath, she patted the work pack strapped across her stomach. She felt the weight of her ice axes on her hips. Her thermos, filled with her favorite drink Sizzler, hung against her back. Hoping she hadn't forgotten anything at home, she stepped forward. The massive slab of metal slid to the side, and the familiar screech of unoiled hinges and old gears rippled through her. She tried not to make a face as the door closed behind her with another shriek.

Kaia unfastened her helmet from her suit and pulled it off. Her brown curls fell forward, and a corkscrew swung into her eyes. Annoyed, she tucked the curls back under the thermal hood that was supposed to keep them in place. Moving to the next door in the antechamber, she rolled her shoulders back and breathed in deeply. With her helmet tucked under her arm, she took another step. The brown door slid open.

Kaia looked up at the frozen ceiling—an incredible sight at odds with the labyrinth of rusted metal cubicles below. Like most structures in Kaldwell, the shift building was carved from ice. Sighing, she moved through the first row of stalls toward the row of cubicles at the back of the building, her boots thudding against the floor.

Chairs scraped against metal, and murmurs drifted between stalls. Someone coughed in a cubicle to Kaia's right. She pulled the collar of her suit higher. After a few more turns, she stood in front of Ulla's booth. She paused, squared her shoulders, and walked in.

"Good cycle, Ulla."

The old woman raised an eyebrow as Kaia sat on the empty three-legged chair. The cubicle was small, fitting only a desk, two chairs, and a broken cabinet. The rusting metal desk looked child-sized next to the woman's large frame. The chair under Ulla squealed as she leaned forward, her elbows on the desk. Kaia had learned early not to ask about the creepy metal doll beside Ulla's organizer.

Ulla stared at her, not answering her greeting. *Oh no!*

Kaia straightened in the chair. "Where in L3 should I start my shift this cycle?"

"Your shift?" Ulla's dull blue eyes didn't blink as she stared Kaia down.

Kaia knew better than to answer.

"You're late." The sharpness in Ulla's voice could cut through reinforced steel. "Again."

Kaia pressed her lips together. She'd been running behind

because she had forgotten to turn on the dryer for her only thermal underwear set that morning. Preparing for the worst, she met Ulla's eyes.

Ulla took a deep, raspy breath. "Kaia. Dear girl." Her voice was softer now, almost sweet. "You want to work, do you?"

Kaia didn't *want* to; she had no other choice. But arguing with Ulla was useless. She nodded, waiting.

"Are you sure?"

Kaia nodded again.

"Well, that surprises me. Why do you think that is?" Ulla tapped a finger on the desk, her voice dropping into a deeper register.

Kaia kept her mouth shut and tried not to look at her hands.

"When someone doesn't show up for their shift, I assume they have better things to do. Wouldn't you?" Ulla smacked her lips. "I guess I can't expect more from someone like yourself. You're your father's daughter, after all. Too bad you don't have a mother. That excuse for a man tried to cover for you again, so I sent him back down into the mines."

Clenching her jaw, Kaia put her hands behind her back, lacing her fingers together tightly so she wouldn't punch the woman. She was used to the comments, used to people mocking her for never having met her mother, for knowing nothing about her. She focused on her breathing as she waited for Ulla to finish.

"You Framnes people believe you're above everyone else, with your new technology and your fancy soups."

"We're from the Killdreson caves, not Framnes." The words fell out of Kaia's mouth before she could stop herself. They had lived in Kaldwell since she was four rotations old. She was now eighteen, but Ulla never forgot that they were immigrants.

Ulla's eyes narrowed, and she continued as if Kaia hadn't spoken. After saying something about *such scum* and *good for nothing*, she finally got to the point.

"Go to Area Two in L3. They are reinforcing a new cave opening. I'm docking half your pay for being late."

Ulla's voice cracked with disapproval, which launched her into a coughing fit. Kaia leaned as far back in her seat as she could and held her breath. The cough was a constant reminder of cystic effusion, or CE. The illness had spread through Kaldwell when Kaia was ten. It began with a dry throat, then progressed to a cough, and in the end, people went mad before their lungs collapsed. There wasn't a cure. Either you got lucky and survived, or you didn't.

Ulla hunched over as the cough forced itself through her, giving Kaia a minute to think. Her dad was in Area Two this cycle. She would have to explain that she had lost half the money from the week's best-paying shift. She pressed her lips together and shifted her weight on the chair, which threatened to tip over.

Ulla stopped coughing, still gasping for air. Then, meeting Kaia's eyes, she slammed a hand on the desk. "Go! Do you want to be fired?"

Biting back a retort, Kaia shook her head.

"Well, what are you waiting for? GO!" Ulla barked.

No matter how much she wanted to slap the woman, she couldn't risk her job. Kaia pulled on her helmet and ran out of the cubicle without saying a word.

Kaia kicked a chunk of ice as she walked over to the shafts that led to L3. It slid across the ground, the sound drowned out by the large ventilation fans whirring above. The suits filtered out copper dust but could do only so much about the carbon dioxide. The fans were, like everything else in these caves, necessary for survival.

She wanted to blame Ulla for docking her pay, but she knew it was her fault. She *had* been late, and for a stupid reason. Keeping clothes dry and warm was an elementary survival skill. She had planned to use the money from this shift to surprise her dad with a new helmet.

She opened her work pack with a rough tug and pulled out her harness, then pressed the capsule to the center of her chest.

Nothing happened. She punched the capsule once, twice. With the third hit, the harness shot out of it and wrapped itself around her. It was standard-issue mining equipment, nothing fancy, but it did the job. She rubbed her throbbing gloved hand and sighed, then took a deep breath and held it. Took another step and breathed out, as her dad had taught her. There was no time to dwell on her mistake.

Her head was cool by the time she reached the L3 shaft. Not entirely collected, but she was focused enough. The shaft, a pitch-black hole, disappeared into the glacier. She clipped her harness onto the trolley. The wire it attached to would need to be replaced soon; patches of rust ran along the metal.

Kaia ensured that the braking mechanism aligned with the wire. Going down a zip line without a functioning brake was not a good idea, though she had considered how fast she could travel without it constantly dragging along the wire. She checked the trigger mechanism for the brake and leaned out over the dark chasm, making the wire groan. Then she turned on her helmet light, took one last deep breath, and plunged headfirst into the darkness.

Her helmet lit up the carved ice walls around her. They whooshed past in greens and blues, and she smiled, the familiar lightness of flying through the tunnels consuming her. The trolley hissed behind her as she accelerated. She wrapped her arms across her chest and braced for the upcoming turn, her smile turning into a grin. Her harness dug into her shoulders, stomach, and thighs as the wire threw her around the bend. The trolley made an awful sound against the cable, and sparks flew from the point of contact. The yellow drops of light sizzled as they hit the ice. Kaia laughed as she shot out into another straightaway.

She knew she should slow before turns, but that would be boring. The tug on her core and the rush of adrenaline that surged through her veins were like warm hugs. Her laughter echoed around her, then faded into the rush of air as she shot around another bend, a spray of golden light behind her. At least she was making up a little bit of time now.

After another turn, the tunnel plunged straight down once more. Kaia tapped the harness in the center of her chest. The octagonal capsule flashed once. A loud shriek filled her ears, her helmet muffling the dangerous decibels as the brake closed around the cable. Her momentum decreased, and only experience kept her head from snapping forward. Slowing down, Kaia stopped perfectly at the opening of the shaft, her feet dangling only a few centimeters above the ground. She smiled. It had been one of her best descents yet. Still, she had once stopped so close to the opening that the tip of her boot had touched the ground. This was one of the many competitions she had with herself. There wasn't much else to do in these tunnels except for iceboarding, which she had little time for these cycles, so she was thankful she could zip-line at work. It was one of the reasons she had applied to be a scavenger in the first place.

Kaia tapped the octagon on her chest three times and dropped to her feet. She adjusted her harness before looking around the cave. It was a small space used as a hub to transport smaller things, like replacement gears and tools, lost items, and people. Her job was to retrieve those lost items and transport them where they needed to go.

This hub, one of her favorites, was relatively high up in the mines. Carved from ice and mountain rock, the floor, dark and solid, stood in stark contrast to the glacier above. Large chunks of black stone rose from the ground and up through the ceiling. Three lanterns hung in the cave. Their green flames danced on the ice, making the ceiling glow.

Kaia glanced over to the other side of the cave. There on a black rock sat her wide-shouldered coworker Biorki. She still remembered the first time they'd met. Biorki had found her sitting outside her house, crying. Though he was two rotations older than she, he had looked younger, scrawnier, as if he were about to collapse. Kaia had expected him to walk away once he'd realized what she was—an immigrant.

To her surprise, he had asked her what was wrong. She had choked out that some kids from school had broken the magnets on her iceboarding boots. Boots her dad had spent rotations saving up for. Boots three sizes too big so she could grow into them.

Biorki had sat down with her, examined the boots, brought out a mini tool kit, and fixed them, just like that. Later, Kaia had learned that Biorki was also a genius with robotics. However, that didn't help him in the mines; it was too cold for anything to work that wasn't specially insulated. No one in Kaldwell could afford such luxuries anyway. So when he'd turned seventeen, the age at which everyone had to pick jobs in the mines, he had signed up to be a scavenger. Two rotations later, she had done the same.

"Biorki." Kaia's voice echoed through the hub.

Biorki looked up from the gadget he was fixing for one of his neighbors and grinned. His blue eyes shone, reflecting the lantern light like the ice behind him. His suit, a patched-up thing, was all faded greens and grays.

"Kaia. What made you late this time? Did you forget to put on socks?"

Heat rose in her cheeks. She had been late because of that once, and Biorki still hadn't let it go. She was grateful her helmet hid most of her face as she shrugged.

"I forgot to turn on the dryer." Wanting to avoid his commentary, she changed the subject. "The black, red, and white rider is incredible—I watched one of his iceboarding reruns at breakfast. Have you seen the bit where he uses the tip of his board to jump over an obstacle?"

Biorki put the gadget in his work pack and rose to his feet. Lately, she had noticed how tall he was, how he rose above her by a few centimeters. Which said a lot, considering that she was abnormally tall for a mine worker.

Biorki grabbed his harness and snapped it onto his chest. "You have shown me that clip a hundred times. He is pretty good. But what about you?"

She was thankful he wasn't harping on why she was late, but she knew what he would say next, and she grimaced.

Biorki stared at her, lifting an eyebrow. "Are you ever going to enter the contest? We both know you're good enough."

She looked at one of the lanterns, watching as the flame licked the oil-soaked wick in its center. "I can't afford to go. You know that."

It wasn't entirely true. She could save up. It would take her rotations, but she could do it. The real reason she hadn't tried was partly because her dad disapproved but mostly because she was afraid—afraid to lose, to have someone tell her she was horrible. She didn't want to face the possibility that she couldn't do anything right.

Biorki tapped his harness, and the straps wrapped around his large frame. "I know," he said, inspecting the harness. "Speaking of affording things, we better get started."

Kaia cringed, remembering that she would get only half her pay this shift. She nodded. "Yeah, let's go."

"The boxes won't find themselves." Biorki winked at her and gestured to the shaft that led to Area Two. "You first."

The shaft was a straight drop used for quick travel between mines. Smiling, she stepped to the edge and attached her harness to the cable. She looked over at Biorki, and her grin widened. "Try to keep up."

Biorki's laugh faded behind her as she dropped into the shaft that led to Area Two, this time feetfirst. There was a rush of air and exhilaration. Then, halfway down, a deafening sound burst through the shaft. Before she could identify it, a pressure wave threw her back, slowing her descent. The harness groaned against the force and cut into her shoulders. Biting down against the pain, Kaia scrambled to engage her brake. That's when she heard it—a scream. It filled the shaft, and within seconds, a chorus of primal cries engulfed her.

Kaia's blood ran cold. She looked up. Biorki hung above her, his eyes wide.

"We need to get down there *now*." His voice rang through the tunnel.

Dad. Ulla had sent him down to Area Two. She disengaged the brake and descended at an alarming speed. She smelled it before her feet hit the ground: burned flesh.

CHAPTER 2

Kaia unlatched from the wire and took a few shaky steps forward, absorbing the horrible scene. Pieces of helmets and suits were strewn around the cave. Red-stained lumps of ice rolled across the floor in a low rumble that mixed with the screams that still echoed around them. Large stone slabs pierced the cave floor and walls as if hurled by a giant. Diggers lay on their sides, crushing anything and anyone in their way. A dark chasm of sharp angles remained where parts of the roof had caved in. Only one thing could have done this much damage. A miner's worst enemy: an explosion.

Above the main cave entrance, there was an open sore in the mountain, confirming Kaia's suspicions. Dying flames licked the raw copper exposed by the blast. Smoke and ash filled the air. The beams of helmet lights cut through the swirling soot. Kaia stepped back and ran into something on the ground. Behind her lay a pile of gray fabric—a body without a head.

Her stomach twisted; her lungs tightened. She gasped for air, then immediately regretted it as ash mixed with the smells of blood and burnt flesh filled her nose and mouth.

Biorki landed just as she buckled forward. She tore at her helmet, barely getting it off before the contents of her stomach poured onto the ground. Her breakfast, brown pieces of dried meat, slid across the frozen cave floor and mixed with the blood. Her stomach clenched again, sending another spasm through her.

Kaia wiped her mouth on her sleeve and pulled her helmet back on. The bitter taste of acid stung her mouth as she straightened.

"Kaia." Biorki's voice shook behind her.

She turned to see his eyes bulging as he attempted to open his work pack, his hands shaking. She stared at him, unmoving.

"I will go up and deploy a rescue beacon." His hands finally found the piece of metal that would signal an emergency to Kaldwell from the hub above. "Find a breathing body and administer the emergency protocol."

Biorki clipped himself back onto the cable while Kaia stood still, staring. The world tipped and blurred as the thumping in her head grew. *A breathing body.* How many had died in the blast? How many were still breathing but dying from their injuries? How many were buried by the collapsed ceiling or crushed by the slabs of rock that had shot from the center of the explosion? Where was her dad?

She spun around, back toward the screams. The zip line screeched behind her as Biorki shot back up the shaft. Trying not to breathe too deeply, she scanned the cave, searching each lump of fabric. She tried not to linger on their faces; some she recognized, and she had to force herself to look away. She had to find him.

Then, at the back of the cave, she saw it: a pair of legs sticking out from under a large slab of stone balancing precariously against the cave wall. A gash ran across the right thigh, the blood already freezing in the cold. And below the gash was an iceboard-shaped patch—a patch she had helped sow on when she was seven rotations old.

She didn't remember moving, but she found herself pulling him out from beneath the stone. His visor was covered in blood, but she would recognize that helmet anywhere. Her dad lay still on the ground, stiff and cold.

She fell to her knees next to his left arm, which was bent in an unnatural direction. Her breath lodged in her throat; her hands shook as she lifted them to her face. She had done this. He was down here because she had been late for her shift.

Tremors ran through her body, her hands fell to her sides, and her scream twisted through the air, braiding itself in with the others, a chorus of pain. Then it became nothing, and she became nothing. She stared straight ahead, her body still as the mountain, her blood cold as ice, her mind filled with ash.

A hand on her shoulder, a warm presence behind her, a voice. At first it was just a murmur, and then the hand shook her. It snapped her back to the present, and she heard the shouts for stretchers, bandages, and patches. And then a familiar sound cut through the fog in her brain.

"Kaia! Why didn't you administer the emergency protocol? He is barely breathing." The voice reminded her of late cycles by the fire, hot drinks, and reprimands.

"Who is breathing?" Her voice was like gravel in her mouth.

Ingá, a friend of her dad's and the rescue team leader, shook her again. "Your dad. Lu. He is losing too much blood."

He's breathing? Kaia jerked upright, tried to move toward him, and failed. Her arms were stiff, her legs heavy as solid rock. *He's alive?* But he hadn't moved.

Ingá let go of her shoulder, turned around, and yelled, "Over here! Bring a stretcher. We might be able to save him, but be quick!"

Kaia watched, still paralyzed, as Ingá pulled a set of patches and bandages from her work pack. Ingá lifted her dad's leg and looped one of the bandages under it. She tied it around the upper part of his thigh, placed a small metal rod on the bandage, made another knot, and twisted—a tourniquet. With practiced fingers, Ingá administered a layer of gauze to the gash and patched up the hole in his suit. She inspected his bloody visor, sighed, then turned back to Kaia, who was still staring at the patches and tourniquet.

Ingá grabbed Kaia's helmet with both hands and forced her to meet her eyes. Ingá's face was usually hard and sharp, her brows tight with disapproval, but now she softened.

"Kaia." Her voice was calmer now. "Why didn't you administer the emergency protocol?"

"I…I thought he was dead. And I couldn't—I couldn't move." Kaia's eyes widened as she realized what Ingá was asking. "Is he going to die because I didn't administer the protocol?"

A tremor ran through her, then another, constricting her movements, her breathing. She gasped for air as white spots danced in her vision. The world threatened to fall out from beneath her.

Her teacher's words filled her mind. *Act first, think later. Workers are useful only if they can patch a suit so they don't freeze to death before treatment.*

She stared at Ingá's tourniquet as the tremors intensified. *Useful only if…*

Ingá grabbed her shoulder and squeezed. Two figures moved across Kaia's field of vision. Ine and Kjartan placed a stretcher beside her dad. They wore patches with red crosses on their chests. Kaia hadn't known that Ine had joined the rescue team.

Ingá squeezed Kaia's shoulder again. "He is not dead yet. We'll do everything we can for him. But you're in no shape to be down here." Her voice took on its familiar sharpness. "Ine, he's losing less blood now, but he might have hit his head or neck. Make sure you handle him with care. Kjartan, when you get to the sick bay, tell whoever receives him to have a look at his head. It's top priority. His arm and leg can be dealt with later. Understood?"

Kjartan and Ine nodded and moved to pull Kaia's dad onto the stretcher. Ine held her dad's neck steady, her hands under his jaw. Kjartan pulled until her dad rested on the cloth stretched between two metal rods.

Ingá let go of Kaia's shoulder. "Come back with the stretcher when you have dropped him off. There are many more wounded. Yes?"

The two rescue workers lowered their heads a little and answered in unison, "Yes."

"Good. Now, go."

Ine's blue eyes rested on Kaia briefly, then slid to Kjartan, who nodded. They gripped the stretcher by the handles, lifted it, and moved away. Kaia knew she should follow them. She should do something. *Do something!* But her arms and legs wouldn't move, and her eyes wouldn't close as she tracked the stretcher. Away, away, until Ine and Kjartan attached it to the shaft wire between them and it ascended out of sight.

"Here." Ingá pushed a hard object into Kaia's hand. "Hold on to this and try to drink something. I will be right back."

Kaia looked down. Ingá was already running away, yelling orders, before Kaia registered what she held. It was her thermos cup, unscrewed and filled with her favorite drink. Steam rose from the cup, and heat seeped through her gloves and into her shaking hands.

A cup of flavored hot water could ease pain, could make a bitter miner smile after a long shift and make her dad grin after a fight with Ingá. There was nothing special about it—an artificial flavor, sweet at first, then sour. She stared, expecting it to do something. Nothing changed. Nothing happened. And by the time someone spoke to her again, it had frozen into a solid block of purple ice.

"Are you sure you're okay?" Biorki stepped back as she waved him off at the door to her house.

Ingá had ordered him to take her home. "She is in shock. She needs to get some rest," Ingá had told him over Kaia's head as she sat on the ground, still bent over her frozen drink, in Area Two. "She will only be in the way or freeze to death here."

She will only be in the way. The words echoed in her mind as Biorki grabbed her hand, trying to get her attention. She looked down, and he sighed.

"Someone will come and get you when Lu is stable. There is nothing you can do now. You have to rest." He moved closer, then thought better of it and stepped back. "I have to go back down and help Ingá. Please rest."

Biorki turned to go. She grabbed his sleeve. He didn't move, didn't pull away. They stood there in silence until she managed to form words.

"How do you do it?" Kaia gripped his sleeve harder. "How do you walk around as if nothing happened? I saw your hands shake. How are you not afraid?" *Why am I the only one who froze?*

Biorki turned back to her and waited until she was able to lift her head, until she met his eyes. And when she did, he smiled a sad smile.

"I'm terrified." Biorki's voice was weak, not at all like he appeared, tall and unshakeable. "When I got to the shaft crossing, I almost ran home. I considered clicking the beacon and leaving you behind." His smile fell, and he looked at something above Kaia's head. "Then I remembered what my mum told me before she passed away. *Eaten is eaten, lost is lost, hurt is hurt—we can't change it. But we can change what we do right now.*"

Biorki looked back down at her. "I focused on those words, and…well, it helped." The corners of his lips lifted, and he leaned closer. "You know, your eyes are similar to my mum's. Although hers were a deeper brown and less green."

The words hung between them. Biorki's mother had died from CE, and his father had disappeared soon after. Yet Biorki always seemed so carefree, so cheerful.

Kaia let go of his arm and looked at her boots again. "Thank you for helping me home."

"Don't worry about it. You would do the same for me."

Her gut twisted at his words. She didn't know if she would but didn't correct him as he turned and ran back to Ingá.

When he disappeared around the tunnel bend, she opened the door, stepped into the entryway, and collapsed on the floor. The automatic heater turned on above her, blowing warm air into the room. She didn't scream or howl. She didn't cry. She felt nothing, nothing at all. Not the metal floor, hard against her knees. Not the cold leaving her, replaced by needles of pain. A minute ticked by on her helmet screen. Fifty-five minutes had passed since she and Biorki had rappelled into Area Two. Not even one hour, and her whole world had crashed down around her.

She was useless. Useless. The worst of the worst. Here she was, sitting at home while others were patching up the injured, saving lives, burning the dead. And she…she was hunched over in the puddle of water that had melted from her suit.

"Pathetic." She punched the metal floor.

"Useless." She struck it again. Her dad was lying in the sick bay, fighting for his life, thanks to her. She threw her helmet against the wall and screamed.

Her voice echoed off the metal floor. Her lungs burned. She couldn't stay here, couldn't sit inside and wait for someone to tell her that her dad had passed, that they had burned him without her. She released another scream, this one louder, her voice bouncing around the small antechamber. Heat rose inside her chest.

Then, as if a switch had flipped inside her mind, she stopped, sat up, and unbuckled her boots. She threw them to the side; they hit the metal wall with a thud. She leaned to the right and grabbed her iceboarding boots. She made sure to tuck her suit into them, then clipped them on, the buckles tight around her ankles. Then, placing one leg under her, she pushed up with her stiff muscles and stood. The room spun.

After several shaky steps, she bent down and grabbed her helmet. She examined it. No cracks in the visor—only a small dent on the back. She felt the axes on her hips, still firmly attached. She unclipped her empty thermos and hung it on the magnetic wall; it connected with a metallic click. Next to it hung her old chipped brown iceboard. She pulled it off, the magnets sensing the pressure and releasing it.

Kaia looked at the door that led into the living room of their tiny house made of ice with the firepit in the middle. It was a place of memories: of her dad teaching her to weld wires; of late cycles of reading old fairy tales with hot drinks; of Ingá visiting with a thermos filled with toddy, her dad laughing at her horrible jokes; of watching iceboarding clips while her dad organized their rations.

She took one deep breath, pulled on her helmet, and turned to the thick copper outer door, reinforced and insulated to keep the cold from creeping in. She didn't look back as she stormed outside, the iceboard clutched under her arm. A familiar warmth brewed in her blood, a pressure she had to release.

CHAPTER 3

Kaia leaned into the sharp turn, letting gravity pull her forward. She felt every bump and shift in the glacier under her iceboard. Her reflection twisted and distorted on the smooth ice, an image of calm—a calmness she could only achieve while iceboarding. A spray of white hit her visor as she shot through the next turn. She used the metal edge of her board to slice through the ice, carving a perfect path through the tunnel.

Iceboarding was her one escape from the monotone world of Kaldwell. This time was different, though. The board was stiff under her boots, her body slow, her mind clouded with images of burned flesh. She tried to push them away, to focus on the lines she carved through the ice, on the way her weight shifted—things she could control. But the image of her dad's bloody helmet filled her, tore at her.

She shot through the next tunnel and aimed high. The ceiling became the floor as Kaia entered the loop she had attempted to perfect for rotations. A minute of relief, of an empty mind, and then the bloody visor filled her thoughts again, enveloped her. Blinking, she lost her line and exited the loop too early. She swore, then put too much weight on her front foot and lost her speed. Why couldn't she do anything right? She bent her knees, and her speed increased.

Heat rose in her chest again. Why was she like this? She cut through another turn. Her arms burned. The air rushed past her, feeding the heat in her chest. What would everyone think of her now, the immigrant who couldn't do anything to help anyone? She swore again, and her voice disappeared behind her as she shot down the next slope. If her dad died, none of it would matter. *Nothing* would matter.

She let it loose then, the emotion she had tried to breathe away: pure rage. The vile warmth spread through her, and she welcomed it. It pulsed, filled her ears, and narrowed her vision. She smiled as it spread to her arms, to her feet. It felt incredible. Then her dad's words echoed through her. *Don't lose yourself to anger. Promise me.*

Her gut twisted. She stiffened and watched as her board caught the edge of a protruding lump of ice.

The board's safety mechanism kicked in, released her boots, and tossed her forward. With no time to react, she slammed face down into the glacier floor. She gasped at the impact. The pain was immediate. It blurred her vision as she slid across the ice, first slowly, then faster as the tunnel sloped down. Without her board, she had no metal edge, no friction to stop her from shooting headfirst down the ramp.

She grasped for her axes, her chest throbbing from the effort. The left axe wouldn't budge, but the one on her right hip unclipped. Gripping it with both hands, she slammed the longer sharp edge into the ice.

She slid past it, her body twisting around the axe, then stopped. Pain shot through her arms, but she managed to hold on. Chunks of ice and rubble slid past her. Then, with a loud *swoosh*, her board shot past her head. The sharp metal edge missed her by only a few centimeters before it plunged into the darkness below.

Face down, Kaia slumped on the ice, her helmet thudding against the tunnel floor. She didn't let go of the axe as she struggled to breathe. She couldn't be sure while the adrenaline was still rushing through her, but she didn't think she had broken any ribs. She exhaled, and a stab of pain shot through her—well, she *hoped* she hadn't. Her legs dangled behind her like slack cords. She knew she looked ridiculous. This *was* ridiculous. She should never have left the house. She was in no state to iceboard, in no condition to do anything, really.

She stared at the glacier a few centimeters from her face. Trapped inside the dark ice was a small bubble of air. It hovered there, unmoving, frozen in the moment, like she had been when she had thought her dad had died. But he wasn't dead. He still had a chance. There was still hope, and she had to focus on that.

She inhaled, her breath cut short by the pain in her ribs. That and the shock of falling had wiped out the heat inside her as if it had never existed. She exhaled, letting herself relax on the ground. She didn't have to assume the worst. Not yet. Ingá had made her a promise, and she would focus on that.

Kaia pulled her legs up to her stomach and clicked the buttons on the tops of her boots. Spikes shot out of the soles. She dug them into the ice and stood. She heaved for air, her sweat cold against her hot neck. She took one deep breath as a test. It hurt, but it was bearable. Her ribs might be bruised, but they weren't broken. Sighing, she looked at the chunk of ice she had struck. It had been decapitated.

Not feeling remorse for the chunk of ice, Kaia rubbed her hands together, trying to force warmth into them, and froze. Parts of her right glove had melted on the palm of her hand. Had she damaged it when she had slid around her axe? She examined it closer. No. There was no breach in the fabric, and it hadn't melted into her skin. She had never seen fabric melt like that before. Strange. She dragged a shaking finger across the now solid piece of plastic on her glove. It was a coincidence. It had to be. She pushed the little stab of fear out of her mind and dropped her hands to her sides.

Exhaling, she bent down and pulled her axe out of the ice. The board would have to wait. She unclipped her other axe and moved up the tunnel using both of them. The guilt still burned and churned in her, but she would focus on what she could do right now. And right now, she had to get home.

Kaia was curled in a ball on the couch, a cup of Nade in her hands, when she heard a knock. Her heart rose into her throat. This was it. She slammed her cup onto the nearby table and ran to the antechamber. She opened the interior door, and Ine walked in.

Her boots dripped water onto the floor. Her face, usually soft and pink, was drained of color. Dark circles framed her blue eyes. Her red eyebrows drooped, matching a red strand poking out from under her head covering. Ine looked ready to pass out.

Kaia searched her face. "Is he…is he…"

Ine looked blankly at her. "Lu is alive and stable. But he is still unconscious."

Air rushed out of Kaia. The room swayed, and she had to lean on the wall so she wouldn't fall to her knees. He was alive. She looked at her hands. They were steady. Then she looked up at Ine, who hadn't moved.

"Thank you." It didn't matter that Ine had broken her boots when they were younger. She was here now. "Thank you for coming here to tell me. And for carrying him up to the sick bay." Kaia's words rushed out of her.

A small smile formed on Ine's pink lips. "I was following orders. You know how Ingá is." Ine turned to walk back outside, then stopped. "So, are you coming or not?"

Kaia lifted her head, trying to keep her mouth from falling open. "You don't have to walk me there."

Ine lifted her shoulders and smiled. "I know."

Kaia ran to the steam shower, yelling over her shoulder, "Give me a minute!"

Inside the bathroom hung her thermal underwear. This time, she had made sure to turn the dryer on, made damn sure she hadn't forgotten anything. After changing into her thermals, she returned to the living room and grabbed her suit and a new pair of gloves. Leaving her axes on the wall, she followed Ine outside.

They walked in silence through the tunnels. Kaia didn't know what to say. Ine had every right to judge her. She had found Kaia frozen over her dying dad, not helping him. But Ine didn't say a word about it. She didn't make any mean jokes or taunt her. Somehow, Kaia wished she would. She deserved it, after all.

They passed another row of round houses carved from the glacier, just like hers. Kaia looked at the copper doors, the rusted chimneys, and the reflections on the sculpted ice. Between the houses stood square incinerators for burning waste. Next to them sat the batteries that provided power. Cables ran beneath the streets, leading to the geothermal plant three caves away. Green-fired lanterns hung outside. Inside, each home had a couch circling a firepit. Everything looked the way it always had, except that Kaia didn't see anyone—not in her neighborhood, and not in the next. There was no movement except for the flames, no sounds, no people. A ghost town, except for her and Ine.

When they passed the last tunnel in the road, Ine grabbed Kaia's hand. It shook. Kaia looked down at her steady hand and then up at Ine's small frame, her white face, the lines under her eyes, the tightness of her jaw. Then it hit her: Ine was afraid. Maybe fear had many faces. Still, Kaia wished she had reacted like Biorki, who had acted according to their training. Like Ine, who had followed orders despite her fear. Neither of them was a burden like her.

Kaia tried to shake off Ine's hand. She didn't deserve the warmth. Ine tightened her grip, then cleared her throat.

"I'm sorry I broke your boots." The words rushed out of her mouth, muffled by her helmet. "It's so embarrassing now. I didn't do it because I didn't like you." Ine grimaced and fidgeted with her belt with her free hand. "No, that's a lie. I didn't like you, but I didn't hate you. I did it to impress Juhán. I thought he was handsome. But you didn't deserve that."

Kaia stared at Ine. Juhán had been their classmate, a dark-haired, dimple-faced joker. Kaia smiled. "Are you still crushing on him?"

Ine looked offended. "Oh stars, no. He's such a baby. Kjartan is so much better to look at." Color returned to Ine's face, a flash of pink. "Don't tell anyone." Kaia was about to promise, but then Ine continued, "Anyway, you like Biorki, right?"

Kaia didn't know she could feel anything but guilt. So she was surprised when her face grew hot, probably matching Ine's.

She shrugged. "He is a great friend."

"Mm-hm. I won't tell anyone, I promise."

"I'm serious—we're just friends."

"Sure." Ine grinned. The smile lit up her entire face. It was the kind of smile that was contagious. Maybe Ine wasn't as bad as Kaia had thought. She smiled back, then looked at the tunnel ahead—the entrance to the main cave. Their smiles vanished as they entered.

They reached the entrance to the sick bay without speaking another word. The tall building, the largest in these caves, was also the only one not carved from ice. Gleams of polished copper shone from where it had been repaired. The rest had oxidized, making the building a pale green color. There were strange symbols above the large square metal door. No one knew what they meant or who had carved them.

Ingá had once told Kaia that the building was older than Kaldwell, that the sick bay had stood there even before the town had been carved from the glacier. Kaia's dad had laughed. "Why would anyone leave a large copper construction out here?"

Kaia had reveled in Ingá's story and had tried to think of why someone would build such a construction down here. To scope out the copper mines, perhaps? Or maybe her dad was right and it was a made-up story to entertain the children of this dull place. Still, the carvings were a mystery.

Ine let go of Kaia's hand and walked up the short staircase to the door. She grabbed the knob and twisted it. The door slid open. Screams and howls of pain rushed through the opening—an invisible wall of horror. Kaia stiffened, her mouth dry.

Ine looked down at her. "It's awful, I know." Her mouth turned into a thin line. "Take your time. You can find your dad in Ingá's office when you are ready."

The door closed behind Ine, and silence enveloped Kaia. Ready? She couldn't even move. She was stuck to the gravel on the icy ground, her body heavy and cold. She gasped for air. The world faded around the edges, then tilted.

No. She blinked. She would not let her fear consume her. She had to see her dad.

Closing her fists, she forced her right leg to move, then her left. She made it three steps before her eyes fell on something on the ground. In front of her boot were a few red stains barely covered by the gravel: marks inked on the ice by death itself. But instead of freezing up, instead of running away, she stared at the blood. It wasn't her dad's; it wasn't Biorki's or hers. And for some insane reason, the blood comforted her.

Whatever awaited her within the sick bay, her dad was alive. It was selfish, but she held on to that thought as she moved up the stairs, took one last moment of silence, and opened the door.

CHAPTER 4

Kaia drew her shoulders up as if it would protect her from what was inside the building. She flinched when the reek of antibacterial sprays, dead flesh, and sweat hit her nose. Groans of pain and shrieks of loss rattled her eardrums. She turned around, her hand on the doorknob, her back to the room of terror. She breathed through her mouth, ignoring the taste sitting on her tongue. She could do this.

After a few more breaths, she turned back and forced herself to look. Makeshift beds filled the large hall, every single one occupied. Drapes hung haphazardly between them, giving a false sense of privacy. Some people were lying on thick old blankets on the floor. Kaia stared in horror. Many were injured—so many more than she had realized.

The conscious miners howled in pain, their burns red against the gray walls. Family and friends ran between the beds, the lumps on the floor. Their desperate cries merged with the howls. But it was the dead silence, the lack of movement from some of the miners, that sent shivers through Kaia. The rows upon rows of still bodies.

At the end of one of these rows stood Ingá. She met Kaia's eyes, then turned her attention back to replacing the gauze on a woman's shin. The old gauze came away red, and Ingá stuffed the wound again, wrapping it with a wet rag. Kaia didn't know what she had expected—perhaps that Ingá would yell at her, tell her to go home, that she would only be in the way. She hadn't expected Ingá to ignore her. Somehow, this was worse.

Kaia searched the room, ignoring the growing lump in her gut, but Biorki was nowhere to be seen. He was probably still bringing the injured up from the mines. Ine was already at the bedside of a miner Kaia remembered as being a pervert. The old man groaned as Ine sprayed antiseptic on a horrible burn on his chest.

Kaia considered thanking Ine again, but she didn't. Instead, she fixed her eyes on a bolt on the wall at the back of the room and walked deeper into the building. She kept her helmet on as she moved past one row. Two rows. Five rows of beds, makeshift drapes, piles of gauze. Kaia released a deep breath. A brown door stood before her, the sick bay main hall behind her. She had made it to Ingá's office. She inhaled deeply, removed her helmet, and walked inside.

Ingá's office had been converted. Her desk was on its side, making room for three extra beds. Kaia squeezed past the first bed. It was empty. She tried not to think about who had used it and moved to the second bed. On it lay Ingá's husband, Torvald. His face was bloody, and a piece of scrap metal stuck out of his lower torso.

Kaia faltered then, almost fell to the floor. She hadn't known that Torvald had been injured. Still, Ingá had taken the time to help her dad, even when Kaia hadn't. Kaia swallowed the acid in her mouth. The lump in her gut grew. Ingá continued to do the incredible, and Kaia was useless. She would make up for it somehow. But right now, she had to see her dad.

She swallowed hard and turned to the last bed, pulling aside the old blanket shielding it. On the bed lay her dad. Someone had pulled off his helmet and wiped his face. His sharp features were soft, as if he was sleeping. A line of reddish brown ran from his nose and into his gray-and-brown mess of a beard. His arm had been straightened and splinted and lay limp by his side. His suit was cut above his thigh, revealing frostbite that circled the gaping wound over his knee. A skin graft covered the deepest part of the cut.

Kaia sighed. He would be fine. Scarred and with a limp, perhaps a weak grip, but he would live. If he woke up.

Kaia grabbed Ingá's office chair, a rusted metal thing with a brown cushion, and sat beside her dad. She stared at his chest. It rose and fell in a normal rhythm. She let her shoulders fall, her body sink into the chair, and whispered, "I'm so sorry." No reaction. "I'm so sorry. It's all my fault."

Kaia rested her head on the edge of the bed and focused on her breathing. She wouldn't cry. She filled her lungs, then released the air, as her dad had taught her. Again. And again. Each time, she whispered, "I'm sorry. I'm sorry. I'm sorry."

"Why are you sorry?" The voice was low, husky, and barely audible.

She inhaled, the scent of her dad filling her lungs. Then she heard the words again.

"K, why are you sorry?"

She snapped her head up to look at his face, the chair threatening to topple over backward. His dark crimson-brown eyes met hers. Her vision blurred with tears. She tried to wipe them away.

"It's okay. I'm okay," he said.

"I thought you had died." She fought to get the words out.

"What happened?" His voice was raspy, like his vocal cords had been rubbed against sandpaper. "Are you okay?"

Kaia took in his face, the concerned look in his eyes, his furrowed brows.

The words rushed out of her. "I'm not hurt, but there was an accident in Area Two. It looked like an explosion. The force ripped half the ceiling apart. People were buried. Some were torn to pieces. I was rappelling down when it happened. Biorki and I were first on the scene, and when I saw you lying there…" She gripped the bedsheets, looked down, and took a shaky breath. "I couldn't do anything. You could have bled to death because of me."

His still-functional hand found hers and squeezed. He lifted his head, grimaced, and set it back down. When she met his eyes, they pierced her, even now, when he was barely conscious. After being thrown through a cave he still managed to look strong, invincible.

"But I didn't. I'm alive." His eyes focused on something inside himself, like he was reliving a memory. "Sometimes, what we do is not what is expected of us."

"But if I hadn't been late to my shift, you wouldn't have been down there." Her voice cracked, tears running into her mouth and down her jaw.

He gave a short bark followed by a small laugh, which turned into a cough. "Oh, please. Ulla told you that nonsense? I was assigned that shift to help with a particularly tricky excavation. Ingá and I discussed it over breakfast." His eyes softened. "It's not your fault. You hear me?"

Kaia wiped another tear from her cheek, snot from her lips. "But I didn't help. I just sat there."

"So? You can help now." Her dad pulled her hand closer, forcing her to lean over him. "It is never too late to fix your mistakes."

Something unraveled in her gut.

His grip tightened, his face suddenly serious. "The explosion happened before you landed?"

His question caught her off guard. "Yes."

"Are you sure?" His voice was demanding, and his eyes burned.

"Yes. I heard the blast while I was descending."

He let go of her hand and relaxed back into the thin pillow. "Thank the stars you weren't there. All that matters is that you're okay."

"No, all that matters is that *you're* alive." She wiped the rest of her tears off her face. "I don't know what I would do without you."

"Oh, you would be fine. I'm just an old man." He winked. She knew he would have ruffled her hair if he could, so she ruffled his instead. The mop of straight brown hair looked nothing like hers. Did her mother have curly hair?

"Why do you always have to argue?"

"I'm your dad. It's my job to argue." He grinned.

She grinned back. "I thought that was my job."

"It is. But how would you learn if I didn't teach you how?" He winked again, his smile melting the lingering cold inside her.

Torvald choked on a breath behind Kaia. They turned in unison. There was silence, and then they heard another ragged breath. Her dad sighed and met her eyes again, no longer smiling.

"How bad is it?" His voice was slow, calm.

"It's really bad." She tried not to think about the quiet bodies. "The sick bay doesn't have enough room for everyone, and I don't know how many are still down there." She swallowed. "From what I saw, many didn't make it."

"Dritt!" he swore, the word echoing through the room, then lowered his voice. "Where did the blast originate? Did you see what caused it?"

"No, but from the scarring on the mountain and the lingering flames, I would guess it started at the cave entrance." It was a generally easy assessment for anyone trained in the mines, a survival skill.

He looked at the ceiling, his brows knitting as he took in the information. "Strange. We were still measuring the cobber quality in the cave. The explosives would have been stored somewhere else." He turned his head and met her eyes. "Are you sure it originated from the entrance?"

"I'm not sure. But it's my best guess."

And it was. The image was still burned into her mind, the way the mountain had been torn apart like gravel struck by a hammer.

"Ingá probably knows," she added. "I can go ask her." The thought of approaching Ingá made her stomach churn.

Her dad sighed. "No, she has more important things to focus on. I will figure it out later."

Kaia leaned back in her chair and breathed.

"Did you keep it in check?" It was more a demand than a question.

She knew he would eventually ask if she had kept her anger in check like they had practiced, like she had promised. She wanted to say no, to tell him about her mistake while iceboarding. But she couldn't bear seeing the disappointment on his face, and well, nothing bad had happened. She pushed the image of her burned glove out of her mind.

"Yes." She met his eyes and tried to keep her own steady.

He searched her face for a second and then, not seeming to find anything, sighed. "Good."

Silence fell, and as she listened to his breathing, she tried to make sense of her feelings. He was alive and hadn't scolded her for freezing up. But she still felt like scum. She'd been nothing but a problem. Ingá's voice was still in her head: *She will only be in the way.*

After a few more moments, she knew what she had to do. She rested her hand on her dad's shoulder, bent down, and kissed his forehead. She had never been one for physical affection, but it felt like the right thing to do. And as she pulled back, stood up, and rolled her shoulders, he smiled at her.

"I'll be fine here. Go do what you need to do." His voice gave her strength, like it always did.

She smiled even though her stomach was twisting. "How do you always know what I'm thinking?"

He grinned. "Because you and I are alike, and it's what I would do."

She smiled, left her helmet on the chair, and adjusted her suit. "I'll be back later."

And with those words, she walked out into the main room of the sick bay.

The minute the door closed behind her, the smells hit her nose, cries filled her ears, and she wanted to turn back. But instead of drowning in the moment, she clenched her hands and walked forward. *Do what you can do right now.*

She found Ingá sitting by an unconscious miner. Ingá picked at the dead skin on the woman's chest, cleaning the wounds as much as possible. Sweat ran down Ingá's pale face. Her movements were stiff but strong; she was keeping herself upright with pure willpower. Kaia walked closer, careful not to interrupt the treatment. She watched Ingá spray the burns with antiseptic, then dress the wound in a fabric dipped in a similar ointment.

Ingá wiped her brow and looked up from her patient. "Hi, Kaia. Are you feeling better?"

Kaia blinked and fought to keep her mouth from falling open. She had expected to be reprimanded, cursed, ignored, but there was a tired smile on Ingá's sharp face, her brown eyes full of warmth, of worry.

"I'm okay. Dad woke up." Kaia couldn't help but smile back. "He seems good, thanks to you."

Ingá's eyes widened, a small tear forming in the corner of her eye. "That's great news. I bet he was already grilling you about the details of the accident?"

Kaia was amazed by this woman's strength, how she could feel so much and still help everyone without batting an eye. Even knowing that her husband was injured, she was still out here.

"Of course. He wouldn't be my dad if he wasn't." Kaia helped Ingá to her feet. "Is there anything I can do to help?"

Kaia held her breath. Ingá could deem her useless, turn her down, send her home. But she just rolled her shoulders back and looked up at Kaia, who stood a head taller. "Are you sure you're up to it?"

"Yes. I can do it." Kaia rubbed her arm. This was what she had to do. She had to make up for her mistake however she could.

"Come with me."

Ingá moved through the row of beds until she reached an almost empty tray of equipment. She rubbed her temple, her lips tight, as she viewed the contents.

"We're running out of antibacterial creams, sprays, and gauzes." She picked up a pack of sealed gauze. "We've never been equipped for this kind of tragedy. Your father told us to store extra gauze, which we did, but it's not enough." Ingá held the pack out to Kaia. "I can't save those with acute injuries. We don't have enough doctors or time." Ingá's voice cracked, and her eyes slid to the door at the back of the room before she continued. "But we can try to save people from dying of infection, which means we need to wrap all burns. I need you to take down any fabric you see—drapes, blankets, sheets—and tear them into ten-centimeter-wide strips."

Kaia nodded. "I can do that."

"Biorki is running around town gathering as much alcohol as possible. When he returns, I need you to find a bucket, rinse it out, and fill it with the alcohol and fabric strips."

So that was where Biorki was. Relief rushed through Kaia, then determination. She could do this. She would be helpful.

"Got it." She noticed the stiffness in Ingá's jaw. "Will it be enough?"

"We can only hope." Ingá patted Kaia on the shoulder. "Now, let's do this!"

"Yes, ma'am."

Ingá smiled at Kaia before disappearing behind another makeshift curtain.

CHAPTER 5

Kaia had torn up half the drapes in the sick bay by the time Biorki returned. His face was red from carrying three bags full of alcohol cartridges. He dropped them next to the bucket Kaia had prepared. He looked at her once, nodded at the fabric in her hands, and began to pull the cartridges from the bags.

She was thankful for his silence. She didn't know how she would react when he finally told her how hopeless he thought she was, how she had failed him.

Without a word, they began to work together like a well-oiled machine. Kaia prepared the fabric while Biorki organized the cartridges into piles. Rescue team workers moved around them as if they didn't exist. Kaia tried not to notice when the workers carried out bodies to burn.

While Kaia tore the last drape from her pile into strips, Biorki poured alcohol into the bucket. Kaia pushed one strip into the liquid. She ensured that it was entirely soaked before adding another. When the bucket was full, they found another and repeated the process. They had filled two buckets and one box when they ran out of alcohol. Biorki looked at Kaia; she nodded, and he ran out of the sick bay to find more.

By the end of the rotation, there was no more fabric to tear or alcohol to find. After distributing the makeshift bandages, Biorki and Kaia collected old rags and used medical supplies, then piled them in buckets outside the building and burned them. Sweat ran down Kaia's back, her gloves were full of soot, and she gasped for air. But she didn't stop. She didn't take a break. No one did.

Kaia was dragging out a bloody carpet someone had used as a bed when the time tracker chimed through the hall. It was almost midsleep. Ingá's voice rang through the room. She had climbed onto one of the vacant beds in the middle of the building.

"Go home." Her voice cut through the groans, through the shouts. "We are out of supplies. There is nothing we can do until we get more."

Kaia dropped the carpet. She swayed on her feet as she listened.

"Our leaders have received an answer to their distress call. The mining union is sending a team of medical professionals with fresh supplies, but they won't be here until next cycle."

A few silent seconds passed. Then the information sank in. Tense shoulders relaxed, hands unclenched, and a collective sigh filled the air. Help would arrive in the next cycle.

Ine stood up and gestured to the groaning miners. "But what about between now and then?"

Tired eyes drifted to Ine, then rested on Ingá. Everyone was clearly thinking the same thing: *What if they don't survive?*

"There's nothing else we can do, and exhausting ourselves will not help anyone. The leaders and I will watch the sick bay in the meantime."

No one moved.

Ingá sighed, then yelled, "Go home and get some rest! Come back after breakfast. It's an order."

Murmurs filled the room, but no one protested as Ingá walked to her office.

After the initial confusion, people began to move. Some stayed behind with their loved ones. Others went home. Kaia burned the carpet and then walked to the back office. When she entered, Ingá was sitting by her husband, holding his hand. Kaia tiptoed past them.

Her dad looked better. Color had returned to his cheeks, and a smile filled his face.

"Do you feel better?" he whispered as she sat.

Kaia looked down at herself. Blood covered her gloves and sleeves, sweat made her underclothes stick to her skin, and she could barely keep her eyes open.

"Yes. I feel better."

"I figured. But you should go home and get some rest."

"What about you?"

"I'm fine. I shouldn't move my neck too much, so I will stay here. Doctor's orders." He glanced in Ingá's direction and grimaced.

Kaia smiled. Her dad rarely listened to others. Not when her teacher had claimed that Kaia was useless with the digger—he'd forced her to give Kaia another chance, resulting in her crashing it into the school. Not when the town leaders had ordered him to take on a more significant role in the mines—to Kaia's frustration, he had refused. But he did listen to Ingá sometimes.

He turned his focus back to Kaia. "You, on the other hand, need sleep in a proper bed." His eyes held hers. "You know what happens when you don't get enough sleep."

A night owl, he had once called her. She hadn't known what he meant; the word *owl* was unfamiliar. But the implications had been clear. She was an awful person in the morning—slow, grumpy, and forgetful.

She didn't argue. Her hands shook as she pulled her helmet on.

His smile widened. "See you next cycle."

"See you next cycle." She smiled and turned, leaving him behind with Ingá and Torvald.

Kaia felt better as she walked through the tunnels of Kaldwell with Biorki and Ine. She hadn't redeemed herself, but she had helped, even if it was just a little.

"Who do you think they will send here next cycle?" Ine's voice cracked with exhaustion.

Biorki looked up from the internal workings of a gadget, a small cylindrical thing he was fixing. Kaia was amazed he was able to focus on anything, let alone walk while doing it. He turned to Ine. "What do you mean? There's only one medical team in Framnes."

Ine pointed at the glacier wall in the direction of the train station. "Kjartan told me there are rumors about a new medical company offering services to the city."

"A new medical company? How would he know?" Kaia chimed in.

"Well, his dad works on the trains." Ine looked straight ahead, not meeting Kaia's or Biorki's eyes. "I trust Kjartan. He said that the leaders haven't agreed to accept their help yet, but maybe they will send them here to test them?"

Biorki looked down at the gadget in his hands. "If that's true, we might not get the help we need."

Ice crunched beneath their boots as silence fell between them. Ine bit her lip, deep in thought; Biorki resumed his tinkering; Kaia focused on her breathing. If Ine was right and the leaders of Framnes planned to send them untested help, they had to prepare for another rough cycle.

Ine waved goodbye to them at the next tunnel intersection, leaving Biorki and Kaia alone. Kaia picked at her glove, not looking up. She knew she should say something—apologize for leaving him without help, for not being the partner he needed. But the words didn't come.

"I'm sorry." Biorki's words slammed into Kaia, and she almost slipped. His eyes remained on the gadget in his hands. "I'm sorry. I shouldn't have left you alone down there." His voice was faint but clear.

Kaia gaped.

His eyes found hers and then slid away again. "I should have sent you up to launch the signal. I'm the senior scavenger. I should have gotten you out of there."

She punched him in the arm. "Are you kidding me?"

He rubbed his arm and looked down at his feet. "I mean it. I was going to apologize in the sick bay, but you seemed not to want to talk to me. I'm so——"

Kaia cut him off. "No, seriously, what are you on about? I should apologize to *you*. I froze; I left you to deal with it all alone. I should apologize, you idiot."

Her voice cracked on the word *idiot*. Biorki's head snapped up. The word lingered between them. Biorki's jaw opened, matching Kaia's earlier expression. The fans spun above them, filling the silence between them.

Then Biorki leaned forward and laughed, a warm, deep sound in a freezing world. Who could laugh in a cycle like this? Only an idiot.

She couldn't help herself. The thought was too ridiculous, and she laughed with him. Laughed at how they were idiots. How it was easier to laugh than to think about what had happened. How her dad would be okay. She didn't care that they looked like lunatics, that their voices echoed throughout the cave and their neighbors would hear.

They laughed until they couldn't anymore and exhaustion overtook them once again. She smiled up at him. "So, you're not mad at me, then?"

Biorki punched her shoulder lightly. "If you're not mad at me, I'm not mad at you."

"Fair enough." She rolled her shoulders. "See you after breakfast?"

"Of course." Biorki walked toward the street that led to his house, then turned and shouted. "Idiot!"

Kaia focused on that word, the look on Biorki's face, and her dad's words. *I'm okay.* She walked home, a small smile on her face.

Kaia sat up, her body shaking, her mouth open. The scream that had woken her had been her own. A nightmare. She swore under her breath and rubbed her jaw. Stupid dreams. She blinked repeatedly, clearing the fog of sleep from her eyes, and suddenly the events of last cycle snapped back into her mind. Exhaustion hit her again. She lay back down, her curls swirling around her head.

She stared at the ceiling of her alcove, an empty sheet of curved thick felt. It had once been filled with drawings of iceboarders, droids, and dreams. But she had torn them down when she was sixteen. Childish, she had called them. Now she missed them, missed the feeling of hope and adventure. *Damn,* she was tired. Her stomach growled under the thick thermo-blanket. And hungry.

Rubbing her face, she sat back up, her muscles stiff and protesting. She sat there, staring at nothing, eyes still unfocused. Every day, it seemed the hardest thing in the world was getting up; this cycle, it was almost impossible.

A chime filled her alcove—once, twice. It was almost breakfast time. She had to get up. A slap to the cheek and a curse later, she climbed down the ladder and went into the living room.

The familiar sound of soft fabric against the insulated metal floors followed her as she crossed the room in four strides. It was a small but comfortable home. The living room, carved out of the glacier, was a dome around her. In the center stood the firepit with an air vent above it, a long pipe set into the center of the ceiling.

They owned only three pieces of furniture. The sofa, black and octagonal, surrounded the firepit. In the pantry, there were several cupboards for storing food and drink capsules. And then there was the workbench, a flat mechanical table for fixing broken tech.

Her dad had taught her at age seven, "If you can't fix what keeps you alive, you could die. Understood?" She had nodded, and within a couple of months, she could diagnose simple CPUs.

Above the workbench sat the two alcoves, one for her and one for her dad. They were the warmest spaces in the house.

Kaia reached for her breakfast ration: two food pills, a capsule of Nade—basically water with a sour flavor—and dried salted meat. She turned, wishing she had more Sizzler capsules, and hit her knee on one of the knobs on the pantry.

"Shit." She rubbed her knee with her free hand. "Really? Again?"

With another bruise added to her collection, Kaia unhooked her copper cup that hung next to the boiler. She pushed a button, slid the capsule in, and placed the cup beneath the nozzle. The machine came to life with a hum, and steam rose from the orange water pouring into the cup. She shifted her weight from one foot to the other. The floor heater had turned on, but it wasn't warm enough yet to be comfortable in socks.

For the hundredth time she dreamed of carpeted floors. They might have an abundance of metal, rock, and water in Kaldwell, but fabric, food, and tech was only items of trade. Which made them inaccessible to most. If it hadn't been for the miner's rations, Kaia would have starved before she turned ten.

The machine quieted to a slight slurping sound, and the last drops of hot water fell into the mug. Grabbing it, Kaia inhaled the sweet scent and then carried it, along with her breakfast, over to the black sofa. She plopped down, making sure not to spill any of her precious Nade, and looked at the ceiling. It flickered, reflecting the lanterns in the room. She had always wondered if that was what the sky looked like.

She had never seen the sky, only imagined it, dreamed of it. When she had voiced her desire to go to the surface, her dad had grunted into his drink and reminded her of the poem they'd taught her in school.

The sun drifted away from Eirlys, and the world froze. The people were forced underground and built their homes under the glacier to survive. Barren and deadly, the surface is no longer a place for people. The glacier is our home.

Then he'd said, "It's too cold, the weather too violent. It's too dangerous, and it's prohibited."

She put one of the gray food pills in her mouth. The compressed nutrition was bitter on her tongue. She lifted the cup to her lips and swallowed the pill with her drink. She closed her eyes, savoring the taste of Nade, only to feel the pill catch in her throat on the way down. She coughed, took another large swig of Nade, and felt the drink drag the pill into her stomach.

Clearing her throat, she picked up the tablet she had left on the sofa the previous cycle. It had a limited range, meaning it was primarily offline, and it was old. The screen barely responded to her fingers. But it was the only way to receive messages outside of helmet feeds and to watch Stallo, to her dad's constant complaints. Although, it was an old and buried dream, she still imagined herself from time to time charging down the deadly Stallo course on her iceboard. She turned on the tablet and swiped away the iceboarding clip that popped up on the screen.

Kaia clicked on the browser; a wheel spun on the screen. She wanted to check for updates in the Kaldwell community feed, but a message popped up on the screen before that could load. She popped the second food pill into her mouth. This one slid down without any issues. She tapped the notification. The message was from Ingá.

K,

Don't come to the sick bay this cycle. Stay home.

Kaia set the cup down hard on the metal rim around the firepit. The drowsiness that had gripped her was gone. Only one person called her K. She read the rest of the message.

If anything happens, grab the bag in my alcove and run. I don't

She clicked the refresh button, but the message remained unfinished, as if her dad had been interrupted. Why would he send a message through Ingá's feed? Kaia reread it. Something was clearly very wrong. His words were too sharp, and they made no sense. Why would he tell her not to come when he knew how much helping meant to her? And what was this about a bag and running? Maybe he really did have a brain injury. She grabbed her cup again, squeezing it between her hands as cold filled her. The message didn't sound like him, except for the use of her nickname.

She tried to write back, but she couldn't get a message to go through. Damn. Why did the tablet always give her trouble? She threw it back onto the couch, chugged the last of her drink, and grabbed a piece of dried meat. She bit off a piece and stood up. Ignoring the slight dizziness from getting up too fast, she moved to her dad's alcove. Swallowing the last bit of the salty, rubbery meat, she climbed the short ladder.

She had never been in her dad's alcove before. He respected her privacy, and so she did the same. She hesitated on the last step before hoisting herself up. Inside was his neatly made bed, and behind a folded blanket sat a bag she had never seen before. It was brown and had two shoulder straps and a buckle to close around the chest. The bag was simple with no markings and just a flap covering the top. It was unlike any other bag she had seen, not made to attach to a suit or a belt. She grabbed it. The fabric was unlike anything she had touched before. It was rubbery, but it definitely wasn't rubber. Why would he hide this bag from her, and why had he told her to grab it now? There was only one way to figure it out—she had to ask him in person.

She slid down from the alcove with the bag and looked at the time tracker. It was still too early to go to the sick bay, but time be damned.

Kaia made it outside at record speed with the bag in her hand. She ran toward the sick bay, a cold feeling growing in her gut. He had to be okay, and he had to explain himself.

CHAPTER 6

Kaia brushed the front of her visor with her sleeve, her eyes wide. A large triangular building seemed to swallow the entrance of the sick bay. It had been only hours since she had walked home with Biorki and Ine, yet here stood a newly erected construction. But it wasn't the size or its sudden appearance that made Kaia stop mid-run. It was the metal it was made from. The silver surface moved with the air from the fans in the ceiling. It rippled like water, and the green glow of the lanterns undulated with it. Impossible.

She took a few steps forward. A flicker in the silver caught her eye. A symbol, partially blocked by the last houses on the street, glowed on the side of the triangle. Was this the new medical company Ine had mentioned? If so, it was nothing like Kaia had imagined. She took a couple more steps, and her view of the symbol cleared: a star within a circle within an oval. It was beautiful. The silver metal shifted like liquid around it. She had never seen or heard of metal that could move.

Miners were lined up outside the construction, all wide-eyed with surprise. At the opening stood two figures leading them inside one by one. From where Kaia stood a few houses away, she saw the same strange shimmer in the suits those figures were wearing. Like the building, they shone with a clarity that only pure metals possessed. Suits made of metal? Who were these people?

She looked down at the bag in her hand. It felt weird to bring such an old bag into such a pristine building. Also, she was afraid they might tell her to leave it outside. Something about her dad's message made her think she should hide it. She found a great spot behind one of the incinerators next to the house to her right. After ensuring it was hidden, she walked to the back of the line.

"Excuse me." Kaia tapped the shoulder of the older woman in front of her. "Do you know what's going on?"

The woman smiled, but then her gaze fell on Kaia's hazel eyes, the curls that stuck out of her head covering under her helmet. The smile fell, and a thin-lipped grimace replaced it. Kaia didn't wince; the familiar reaction was only disappointing. She was about to find someone else to ask when the woman answered, sneering. "You must live under a rock. The town leaders sent out a notice an hour ago. Isn't it wonderful?"

On the word *wonderful*, the woman smiled as if she had won a battle. As if Kaia were a chunk of ice to crush beneath her boot.

Kaia only smiled. "Yes, it is."

With a smack of her lips, the woman turned around. Kaia stuck her tongue out at the woman's back and sighed. She had forgotten to turn on the community feed in her helmet. *Stupid.* She had to learn to be more aware in the mornings. She clicked the button on the side of her helmet. The screen flickered. She hit the helmet softly, and the feed appeared in the top left section of her visor.

Like the older woman had said, the first notice on the community feed was titled solon has arrived. Below were a few sentences written by Ingá.

Framnes has sent a medical team called Solon to assist us. They have agreed to share their resources and medical knowledge with Kaldwell. During this cycle, you will see a large building erected over the sick bay. Don't be frightened. Listen to them. They are here to help.

Well, that explained who they were, but did Framnes really have technology this advanced that they hadn't shared with Kaldwell? When Kaia thought about it, it wasn't entirely unlikely. She looked at the moving metal; she had truly never seen anything like it.

Another person walked into the construction. Kaia moved forward to get a better view of the guards at the entrance. Her guess had been correct—the two men wore fully metallic suits with a blue shimmer, slim and shaped around their bodies like armor. Their helmets were drop-shaped, each one piece and clear as glass. Kaia could see their hair, their ears. But glass would shatter at this temperature. It was another impossible creation.

Another miner walked in, and Kaia stepped forward. The old woman was the only person between her and the door. Now that she was closer, Kaia could see a pattern drawn or etched into the guards' metal suits. Transfixed, she inspected the suit on the guard to her right. There was a circular symbol on the right side of his chest, and from it shot lines of white, like code patterns. The lines wrapped around his chest, legs, and arms, even creeping up onto his helmet.

Two dark eyes met hers, and the guard winked. His dark hair moved around his ears as he tilted his head to the side, examining her. His cheekbones were sharp enough to cut metal. He smiled. Startled, Kaia smiled back, smoothing the initial shock from her face. Then she looked away and focused her attention forward. Strange—the man had only smiled at her, yet she had almost reached for the ice axes on her hips.

The rude woman walked into the metal construction through a surprisingly normal-looking door. Kaia braced herself. After a few minutes, the other guard, a short and stocky man, gestured for Kaia to enter. She considered turning around, going home, listening to her insane dad. But she had to know if he was okay. So she took one last look at the shimmering construction and walked through the door.

Her mouth fell open as she took in the room before her. She had expected the space to be triangular, like the outside, but the room within was round, a massive, almost perfect globe. She walked up the steps, which led to a platform that stood level with the sick bay's door. There were no identifiable light sources, but the room was lit with a white glow, not too harsh or too dark. She couldn't figure out where it came from. It was like the metal walls themselves were emitting the light, which was impossible. In the middle of the platform stood a metal chair, and next to it was a weird square box and a girl.

The girl turned toward her, her frame thin and small. When she moved toward Kaia, she walked as if she had tightly coiled springs in her joints. A closed-lipped smile appeared on her heart-shaped lips. Kaia took a step back when she saw the girl's eyes. They were large, almost unnaturally round, cold, and intelligent. This was not a girl but a woman. How old was she? Kaia couldn't tell.

The black-haired woman held her hand out. "Nice to meet you, and welcome." Her voice was monotone, cold like the metal surrounding them. "My name is Si Vilia. I will administer a quick health inspection before you enter."

"A health inspection?" Kaia didn't know what to do with the hand in front of her.

"Yes." Si Vilia let her hand fall and gestured to the chair. "It's standard protocol. We must ensure that no contaminants are introduced to those with weakened immune systems."

Si Vilia wore a metallic suit like the guards, but the logo was on her shoulder, not her chest. She wore no helmet and carried no tablet, which surprised Kaia, because she sounded rehearsed, like she was reading from a feed. The suit shimmered as the woman walked forward, her square frame highlighted by the light. Kaia didn't move. Si Vilia's smile deepened, her eyes steely.

"Don't worry. All we're going to do is to cover you in a mist. The spray will kill anything lurking on your skin and suit. If you want to remove your helmet inside the building, I recommend removing it now. But first I will screen your blood." Si Vilia moved with elegance toward the chair. "Don't worry, it won't hurt."

Kaia shifted her weight. A blood test? Biorki had done plenty of tests for CE when he was younger. Kaia had never needed to have her blood drawn. She had been hurt, yes, but never sick enough to require a blood test.

"You don't have to get tested—it is entirely your choice—but I can't let you in without a proper screening." Si Vilia gestured to the door behind Kaia, her eyes finally matching her smile. "You can come back whenever you like."

Kaia glanced at the simple door, breathed in, and moved toward the chair. She had to talk to her dad. She wanted—no, *needed* to know what was going on. She sat down. The chair made no sound as it held her weight: no creaks of old joints, of rusted metal. Another new experience.

She removed her helmet and found that the air was warm on her cheeks; a soft aroma of metal and sweetness filled her nose. It was strangely comforting in the otherwise sterile room.

"Good." Si Vilia didn't look at Kaia, her hands already traveling across a panel on the box next to her.

She pressed something, and a screen appeared above the box. It hovered in the warm air. There was no glass or reflective surface, yet the text on the screen seemed solid. Was it a hologram? Si Vilia tapped a symbol on the hovering screen, a light blinked, and a compartment opened on the side of the box. No, not a hologram. Something far more advanced.

Si Vilia grabbed something in the compartment and turned to Kaia. "If you could roll up your sleeve for me?" She weighed the cylindrical metal device in her hand, then adjusted her grip so that a button rested under her thumb.

Kaia rolled up her sleeve, leaving a gap between her gloves and elbow. She wanted to say no, to argue that this wasn't necessary. But she only sat there as the wide-eyed woman leaned forward with the tool.

"This will sting a little," Si Vilia warned before resting the bottom of the small cylinder on Kaia's forearm. Kaia flinched when the cold object touched her skin. "I haven't started yet," Si Vilia soothed.

Embarrassed, Kaia looked away from the woman and noticed a light on the hovering screen—red, then yellow, then red again. Kaia stared at the light as it changed in the air. After a few seconds, it turned green. Then it changed again into a row of words and symbols Kaia had never seen before.

"Good. That wasn't so bad, was it?" Si Vilia straightened.

Kaia looked down at her forearm; a small red bead sat on her skin. She hadn't felt anything. She looked back up at Si Vilia and froze. The woman was staring at the screen, her already-huge eyes even wider, her small mouth open in shock. Then the expression disappeared, and she plastered on the same tight smile as before. Si Vilia continued to smile as she grabbed another tool. She dragged it over Kaia's forearm, leaving a small square of skin graft where the puncture had been. Had she imagined it, the shock on Si Vilia's face?

"There. As good as new." Si Vilia pressed a button, another compartment opened, and she dropped the cylindrical device into it. "You can roll your sleeve back down. Could you stand up for me and move to the white square?"

Si Vilia pointed to a white mark on the platform between the strange box and the entrance to the sick bay. Kaia hesitated but then did as she was told. Standing in the middle of the square, she couldn't shake the feeling that something was very wrong. "What now?"

Si Vilia's one-toned voice said, "Close your eyes and don't move."

There was a loud click, and metal poles shot up from the floor. For a second, Kaia thought she was trapped. Then mist gushed from the poles—first a soft haze, then an intense shower. She barely managed to close her eyes before cold liquid hit her face. Then, without warning, she heard the poles retract back into the platform.

When Kaia dared to open her eyes again, Si Vilia stood before her, a smile plastered on her face. "You are ready to enter. Good luck."

Kaia jumped. She hadn't heard the woman approach. Realizing Si Vilia was expecting a response, Kaia managed to croak, "Thank you."

With a nod, Si Vilia returned to the chair and turned to face the entrance. Kaia stared at her back. She expected an attack. Or something. But when Si Vilia continued to stare at the door, Kaia sighed. She was too high-strung from the last cycle. She was seeing dangers where there were none. She was too tired for this.

Kaia checked her suit and helmet and ran her fingers over her head covering. Dry. Whatever she had been sprayed with had left no visible signs. Kaia took one last look at the strange walls, opened the door, and stepped inside the sick bay.

CHAPTER 7

Kaia stared at her boots, expecting an assault on her nose, for nausea to fill her. But when she inhaled carefully, there was nothing—no burned flesh, no ash. Instead, she was embraced by the aromas of hot drinks and soups. She looked up and was met with smiles and laughter rather than screams. No, that couldn't be right. She blinked, thinking the spray might have done something to her vision. But the room in front of her remained unchanged.

Miners who had been howling in misery just the cycle before sat with large grins on their faces. They joked and chatted with their spouses, their friends. Even those still lying down were smiling, the pain and screams of the previous cycle mere forgotten memories, like ghosts. Kaia couldn't believe her eyes.

It was still early in the cycle, but the room was full of people smiling, laughing, and hugging each other. A lullaby drifted through the room, full of intricate notes and harmonies. Another deeper voice joined the lighter, softer one, both singing a song in praise of bravery. A man stood from his bed and danced. A woman joined him.

Kaia stared. She was still reeling from seeing the liquid metal, the armored suits, and the hovering screen. But this…this had to be a dream, a figment of her imagination.

"Incredible, huh?" someone said next to her, breaking the spell freezing her to the metal floor.

Snapping her mouth shut, she turned toward the voice. Kjartan, blond-haired and soft-faced, sat in a chair to her left, sipping a hot cup of energizer. It was the first time he had ever spoken to Kaia.

"I'm still trying to make sense of it all."

Kaia knew she should thank him for helping her dad and ask how he was holding up. But different words fell out of her before she could. "What happened?"

Kjartan shrugged. "I have no idea. It was like this when I got here. Solon came here at the earliest chime of the cycle. And now…well, look around. Most people have recovered enough to go back to work. Of course, some are still being observed, but yeah, it's…"

"Impossible?"

"Exactly."

They could go back to work? Images of burns, torn skin, and open wounds filled her mind. Nearly everyone had healed in less than a sleep cycle? *Impossible* might not be a strong enough word to describe it. Incredible? Deranged? No—mad. It was entirely mad.

"How?"

"Like I said. I don't know, and I don't care. The last cycle was a nightmare." Kjartan's eyes darkened a little, his gaze falling to his cup. A few seconds passed before he looked up again. "If you want to know more, you can ask those women over there."

Kaia followed Kjartan's finger. Two silver-blue figures emerged from the storage room at the back of the sick bay. In their armored suits, the women glided down the aisles between the beds, their heads bent over what looked like tablets, fingers tapping. The taller of the two wore her blond hair in a tight ponytail. She looked up and met Kaia's eyes, her hair like a whip behind her. Even at this distance, Kaia was transfixed by the woman's striking eyes of turquoise with rivers of white, like the purest ice in a newly formed glacier. They were beautiful. Kaia wished to observe them more, but the woman looked back down at her tablet. The shorter dark-haired woman bore a soft smile of boredom as she examined one of the unluckier miners. Although not sitting up like the others, the man smiled. His cheeks were pink with life, lust, or something else Kaia couldn't discern from across the room. But she could tell that the woman could throw the man over one shoulder without breaking a sweat.

Above the women hovered two small, fast drones; Kaia hadn't noticed them at first as they buzzed from one bed to another. Were they taking people's vitals? It didn't matter; she wouldn't ask. These women were entirely unapproachable.

Instead, she found a head of silky red hair a few aisles away. Ine's face lit up with laughter as she slammed a card onto the bed she sat on. With Ine sat a wispy-haired woman, her brow furrowed as she examined the cards in her hand.

There was no sign of Biorki, which was no surprise. They had agreed to meet at breakfast. She would have to apologize to him again. But there was one set of brown eyes, sharp features, and a scowl that was missing.

"Where is Ingá? I thought she would be here," Kaia said.

Kjartan leaned farther back into his chair, his eyes flickering to Ine, before answering.

"I don't know. She never showed up this morning." He took a sip of his drink. "There are some rumors that she is in discussions with the town leaders, but I honestly don't know."

Kaia sighed. There was no point in pushing him for answers when he clearly didn't have them. She looked more closely at his pale face, the darkness below his eyes, and the redness surrounding his pupils, and smiled at him. "Thank you."

"Yeah." He waved at her, his gaze falling back to Ine, a tiny smile on his lips.

Kaia walked across the room, her head spinning. If they had healed her dad like the others, then why had he send that message? Was it a glitch in the system? It didn't make sense. A drone whizzed past her head. She rubbed her elbow and squeezed her arm. It felt real, but who was she to decide what was real anymore? Maybe Ine knew something.

"Kaia!" Ine waved at her, the pink in her cheeks almost glowing. "Come here."

Kaia walked down the aisle.

"You're going to lose!" the woman across from Ine croaked, throwing down a pair of cards.

Ine looked at her cards and winked at Kaia. "I beg to differ." She countered with three of the same suit.

The woman, Kaia realized, was an older miner she had returned some lost gear to a few cycles back. Rakel scratched at her thin hair while Ine turned back to Kaia.

"Isn't it wonderful?" Ine held her arms out, gesturing to the empty beds. "They cured almost everyone within the first hour."

Within an *hour*?

Ine must have read Kaia's bewilderment, because she continued, "They have some technology that rebuilds skin, blood vessels, and nerves. Rakel"—Ine waved dismissively at the old woman, who was now swearing—"and some of the others have bad immune systems. The technology works more slowly on them or something like that." Ine leaned closer and whispered, "*She* told me." She nodded toward the blond armored woman, who leaned over an older man, tapping aggressively on her tablet.

"Is there anything for us to do, then?" Kaia gestured to the empty beds in the next row, thinking about the order Ingá had given them the previous cycle about coming to help. From what she could see, no one needed any help at all.

Before Ine could answer, a soft, melodic voice interrupted them.

"We believe our immune systems are not purely dependent on our biological resistance. Our minds and feelings are equally important. Part of our procedure is to include family and friends in people's treatment." The short and muscular woman pressed a few buttons on her tablet as she continued, "In short, we need your help entertaining them."

A wave of pure disbelief hit Kaia. They were *entertainment*? Was Solon's medical technology that good? And who was this woman who looked like she could win any fight, with a voice that reminded Kaia of warm sheets on a cold cycle?

"Entertain?" Kaia's voice cracked, the word slipping out of her before she could think.

"Yes, entertain. There is no longer any need to talk of survival, only of getting better. Isn't that wonderful?" The woman pressed a few more buttons on her tablet and walked away.

It was wonderful. So why did Kaia feel disappointed? She looked around at the people smiling, laughing. She had wanted to help, to make up for the last cycle, to be of use. And now that chance had been taken from her. She closed her fists. Guilt churned within her. Selfish—that was what she was.

She looked at Ine, who threw down a matching pair, making Rakel swear again. She guessed she could entertain people. It could be fun. The song playing became a lighter lullaby, and more people joined in. Why had her dad told her not to come?

"Go check on your dad." Ine smiled; there were no doubts in her eyes, no worries. "I'm sure he would love to see you. You can join us later if you want. Nexus is more fun with three players anyway."

Kaia smiled. "Thank you."

Ine leaned closer, pulling on Kaia's sleeve so she bent down. "By the way…" Ine fumbled with one of the cards in her hands. "Did Kjartan say anything about me?"

Kaia stared, then giggled. "No, but from how he looked at you, I would say he likes you too."

Ine's face turned bright red, almost matching her hair.

"Oh, stop thinking about boys," Rakel murmured, her eyebrows almost touching her nose with concentration. "They're only a distraction. You should have seen me when I was young. The men swarmed around me, but I focused on my job. And look at me now: the leader of the biggest mining team in Kaldwell."

Ine's eyes shone, her face still red. "Rakel, you might be the leader of L3, but you won't beat me at this game."

Rakel threw a pillow at Ine, who burst into laughter, then looked at Kaia. "Why are you still standing here? Go."

Kaia grinned back at her. Ine wasn't so bad. Maybe they could become friends after all.

"I'll be back. But don't expect me to be as easy to beat as Rakel."

"Hey! Ine hasn't won yet," Rakel croaked, trying to sneak a card from the deck without Ine noticing.

"I saw that." Ine pointed at Rakel's hand, then winked at Kaia. "I'm betting on it."

Rakel murmured something foul under her breath. She put the card back in the deck, then turned to Kaia, a huge five-toothed grin on her face. "I almost forgot—the town leaders have invited the whole town for a celebratory dinner. You will be there, right?"

Kaia stood and adjusted the belt on her hips. "I don't know. I will have to ask my dad what he thinks first."

"Sounds good." Ine smiled.

Kaia gave them a nod and walked toward Ingá's office, feeling lighter than she had in rotations.

She might go to the dinner. She and her dad usually ended up leaving such events early, when the comments and stares eventually became too much. But this time could be different. Ine and Kjartan had been so friendly, and Rakel had invited her, not batting an eyelash at who she was. Maybe this would be a good thing—a horrible but fresh start.

"Why are you here?" Her dad's voice cut through her, shattering whatever joy, whatever hope she felt.

Kaia stood in front of his bed, now the only bed inside the office. The room looked empty and cold. Ingá's desk was still pushed up against the wall, and her chair was tipped over. The warmth Solon had spread through the main hall had not reached this room.

His eyes flickered to the door behind Kaia, the whites of his eyes shining in the light. His hair had been cleaned, and his beard was no longer streaked with blood. But he looked pale as a sheet. The color he had gained last cycle was gone. His leg was wrapped neatly in a pure white bandage, and his arm was no longer in a splint, but he looked shattered. His hands twitched under the sheets, the movement sporadic.

"Why are you here?" he asked again. His eyes bore into her, then shifted back to the door. "I told you to stay home."

Cold crawled down Kaia's neck. Something about his behavior, his rapid breathing, made her cringe.

"I thought it was a joke." She didn't want to tell him that she thought he had gone crazy.

"A *joke*?" His voice broke on the word; then he lowered it. "You need to leave now!"

"Why?"

"Leave now, before they find you." Even whispered, the words came out with enough force to send spit into his beard. He slung his newly healed leg over the side of the bed; although it was better, it clearly still hurt. He grimaced as he sat up, his wild eyes darting around the room. He gripped the side of the bed, his knuckles white.

"Who? I don't understand." Kaia took a half step away from him, her hand on the hilt of her axe.

He grabbed the front of her suit, pulling her back to him. "Did they test your blood?"

Her blood? Why did that matter?

"Did they test your blood?" He pulled her closer, his breath warm on her face, his eyes burning into her.

"Yes. Why is it—" She tried to pull away from his grip, but his hands were like the claws of an excavator, like steel.

"Dritt!" The word punched through his lips as he let her go.

She stumbled back and almost tripped over the chair, the metal skidding across the floor. The screech filled the room.

Her shoulders rose against her will, her neck tensing. Her dad showed no reaction. He glanced again at the door, then back to her.

He jumped onto his good leg, grabbed her hand, and pushed her toward the exit. "You need to leave now. Go through the back door. The keys should be next to the brown box in the storage room. Grab the bag I told you about in the message. There's a map in there. Follow it. When you get to the end, someone will be there to help you."

Kaia's dad's words hung in the air, and then the sound of boots on metal reached them from outside the door. Ingá must have returned from the meeting. Thank the stars. Maybe she could explain what was going on.

Pain shot through Kaia's arm as she was pulled backward.

"Hide, and don't come out, no matter what happens." Her dad's whisper barely reached her as he pushed her toward the desk. "When it's clear, run. Don't let them catch you. Promise?"

"I promise." She couldn't argue with a madman.

"Promise me!" His eyes met hers, and her heart stopped. A tear ran down his cheek and into his beard. Her dad never cried.

"I promise." Her words sounded hollow, as if muffled by a blanket.

He squeezed her arm one last time and hobbled back to the bed.

She grabbed her helmet and ran to the desk. She had no idea what was happening, but she knew something was wrong. Either something terrible was about to happen, or her dad was mad. She slid behind the desk, her blood coursing cold and quick through her veins. The door slammed open.

CHAPTER 8

In stepped two sets of silver-blue shoes. Kaia crouched behind the desk, trying to keep her breathing steady and silent. The guards slammed the door behind them. Kaia stiffened at the sound and locked her arms around her knees. The taller black-haired guy walked into sight, the shorter guard trailing after him.

Her dad lay in bed, pretending to rest. His face was one of mock surprise as the dark-haired guard removed his helmet, a large smile on his face.

"Hi, Lu." His voice slid through the room, her dad's name like glue in his mouth. He smacked his lips together as if tasting it. "Where's your daughter?"

Kaia hugged her knees closer, making herself as small as possible.

Her dad lifted his head. "I haven't seen her since the last cycle. Why are you asking?"

The shorter guard walked around the bed and stood by the end of it, blocking Kaia's view. "Oh, stop with the games. They saw her walk in here. Where is she?" The taller guard's voice sent shivers through her.

"You shouldn't believe everything you see down here. The glacier likes to play tricks on people." Her dad coughed before continuing. "Anyway, she isn't here, as you can see. Or are you blind?"

There was a rustle of fabric, and then a grunt of pain escaped her dad. Kaia clenched her hands. It took everything she had not to jump out and punch the guard in the head.

"Don't mess around. Where is she?" The guard's voice whipped through the room.

Kaia swallowed, her throat dry as salted meat.

The shorter guard moved to the other side of the bed again, and she craned her neck to see what was happening. Her dad lay in bed between the two guards, the taller guard's hand digging into his collarbone. Kaia bit down a curse. Why were they doing this?

Her dad's eyes drifted to where she sat for a second. It was a tiny movement, just a tightness in his brow, so small she could have imagined it. But she got the message loud and clear: *Don't move.* She hugged her legs harder and held her breath.

"She is not here, and you won't find her." His voice was commanding as he looked up at the taller guard.

The guard straightened up and let go of her dad's shoulder, then nodded at the other guard and pulled something out of his pocket. Something glinted silver in his hand, and he pointed it at her dad.

"We know who you are." The guard dragged out the vowels, his voice sweet and sickly. "And you know about us. What we can do."

Kaia felt the air leave her lips, her chest tighten, and her fingers tremble. Her dad knew these people?

The guard spun the silver device between his fingers. "You might as well just tell us where she is. We will find her sooner or later." His black hair flopped around his head as he turned to the other guard. "Gin, can you confirm?"

Gin, the shorter guard, nodded, his fingers trailing over a tablet. "You're good to go, Drap."

"Good." Drap looked back down at Kaia's dad. "Any last words?"

Last words? Kaia stared at her dad, unable to look away. The tightness in her chest was a chain around her lungs. She watched as her dad sat up, his eyes almost level with Drap's.

"You will never catch her." His voice was calm and clear, as if he was describing his tasks in the mines. It wasn't a statement; it was an order. For her. She didn't understand why this was happening or how she knew, but she wouldn't let them catch her, no matter what. He had made her promise, and she would keep it. She gripped her shins and dug her fingers into them, pulling her knees closer to her chest.

Drap rested one hand on his hip, tilted his head, and smiled. "As you wish."

Drap gripped the silver device, one finger over a trigger, and pulled. A buzzing sound filled the room. The hair on Kaia's neck rose, and in the same instant, her dad looked at her. Then his eyes went blank and rolled back in his head. His mouth drooped open, and his body went slack, thumping back onto the mattress. His arms fell over the edges of the bed, one of them hitting Drap on the hip. Kaia bit down on the fabric of her sleeve so she wouldn't scream.

The room closed in on her, and white filled the edges of her vision. Even if she weren't intent on keeping her promise, her body wouldn't move. She couldn't breathe. Drap threw her dad's arm back onto the bed like a lump of ice. She flinched but couldn't look away. Gin moved around the mattress, showing something on the tablet to Drap.

"What a waste." Drap held the tablet up to his face. "But imagine what the boss will say when we show him the body. We will be swimming in the purple springs in no time. Just think about all the women we could meet there."

Gin took the tablet back from Drap. "But what about the girl?"

Drap lifted his arms. "There's nowhere to hide on this godforsaken planet. Did you see the stupid miners out there?

They will tell us soon enough. She won't be able to hide for long."

A shiver ran through Kaia. If they decided to search the room, they would find her. She was trapped. She tried to breathe in, but the motion sent tremors through her. She had to snap out of it. She had to get out of there. But how?

"What do we do with him in the meantime?" Gin gestured to her dad. "We must follow protocol. I suggest we claim he died of natural causes."

"Fine. Let's do that. Damn the protocol." Drap kicked the legs of the bed, causing her dad's limp body to wiggle.

Kaia closed her eyes and bent over as nausea rushed through her. She held it back. One breath. Two breaths. Acid on her tongue. She swallowed as Drap's voice filled the room.

"If it weren't for that damn protocol, I would kill them all and take their blood by force. It would be so much easier."

"Sure, but we follow the protocol for a reason. We need them to cooperate for the long-term goal. Yes?"

Drap sighed and turned from Kaia's dad. "Yes."

Drap's eyes slid across the room, past the crack between the wall and the desk. Could they hear her heart thumping? Could they see her?

"We should search the room. There might be some hidden passageways in the walls." Drap grinned. "And if we're lucky, the girl is still here." Drap's laugh sounded like chalk dragged across metal.

Kaia's heart dropped. They would find her, which meant her dad had died for nothing. She shouldn't have come. Gin approached the desk, the soft thuds of his boots barely audible over her heartbeat. Kaia tightened her grip around her knees.

The door slammed open, and a set of gray boots stepped inside: Ingá. They would kill her. But nothing came out of Kaia's mouth, no warning or shout, as the woman approached the two men.

"What are you doing here?" Her voice was warm but fierce. "Why are you in my office?"

Drap and Gin spun around to face her, partially blocking her dad from view. They smiled politely and pretended confusion.

"Ah, there you are." Drap scratched his neck. "We were looking for you. We thought you would be in here."

"Well, I am glad I found you. I need your help with some medical supplies outside." Ingá turned on her heel, not allowing them any time to argue.

Gin and Drap shared a look, then followed her outside.

Silence. Dead silence. Kaia couldn't move. Her arms were fused to her legs. What if they came back? She had to leave now while she had the chance. She had to get up, run out the back door. But she couldn't look away from the boots lying on the bed, the arm still dangling on one side.

"Kaia?" The whisper was like air.

Was it the guards? Had they come back to lure her out? It took everything she had, but she managed to let go of her hold on her legs. She grabbed her axes and crouched. The room spun. But she wouldn't go down without a fight.

"Oh no!" The voice cracked. "Kaia? Are you in here?"

She looked around the desk, and there he was, his eyes on the bed, on her dad. "Biorki?"

"Yes." His eyes were wet as they met hers.

She collapsed on the ground. He didn't ask her if she was okay. Instead, he moved toward her, blocked her view of her dad, moved the desk, and helped her to her feet.

"Look at me." His voice was soft, like a hot drink after a long cycle in the mines.

And although her legs shook and she wanted nothing more than to lie down, to sink into a hole, she stared back at those blue eyes.

"We need to move. Now." He held out his hand, and she grabbed it, held on to it like an anchor.

The world spun less as he pulled her behind him. Then her eyes fell on the bed, the soft beard, the brown hair, the kind lifeless face, and her legs collapsed beneath her.

Biorki caught her, pulled her arm over his shoulders, and whispered into her hair. "We don't have much time. Ingá is keeping them occupied for now, but I don't know how long she can hold them off. Can you walk?"

Don't let them catch you. Promise?

I promise.

Kaia took a deep breath, stepped away from Biorki, and slapped herself across the face. Not hard, but enough to center herself. It wasn't ideal, but breaking something wasn't an option. She pulled her helmet on and looked at Biorki, careful not to focus on the bed. If she saw her dad, she would fall again. She had to pull herself together. She had to get away.

"Let's get out of here." Her voice was hoarse, like a seasoned miner. "Out the back?"

Biorki nodded and patted a pocket on his thigh. "I have the key."

They walked out the door hand in hand. She felt hot tears on her cheek, a twisting in her gut, but his hand steadied her enough that even when they saw the silver women approaching them from across the room, she didn't flinch.

The ice-eyed woman zeroed in on them as the shorter woman typed something into her tablet, but Kaia didn't stop. Didn't stop when she saw Ine stick out a leg in front of the taller woman, causing her to fall forward. Didn't stop as Rakel shouted curses and threw a pillow at the fallen woman. Didn't stop as the woman got back up and backhanded Ine, causing other miners to rise from their beds. Kaia ran with Biorki as two friends of her dad blocked the shorter woman from reaching them.

Later, she would realize what it all meant, would understand what could happen to those who stood in Solon's way. But all she could do then was run with Biorki to the back corner of the room and out through the rusted storage door.

When they entered the main cave, Kaia skidded to a halt. "I need to get my bag. There's a map in it."

"Where is it?" Biorki wheezed next to her.

"I hid it behind the house over there. Behind the incinerator." Her voice came out breathy. She turned to run in that direction, but Biorki held her back.

"That house is too close to the Solon building. It's too risky."

She tore her hand from his, her heart in her throat. "I need it."

Her dad had told her to grab it. She had to get it. She had to. She ran, but only made it three steps before Biorki blocked her.

"If it's that important, I will get it. You should take the back way; you are less likely to run into anyone. And they are probably already watching your house. My house should be safe. Meet me there?"

She should stop him, insist on retrieving the bag herself. They had seen him run with her. What if they caught him?

But she whispered, "Okay," turned, and ran down one of the side tunnels.

She should have worried as she ran. But her mind was blank.

She made it to Biorki's house, coughing and heaving for air. No one was there—no neighbors, no Solon guards. She stood outside the door, her heart thumping in her ears. Then a figure appeared from the main tunnel, a bag in hand. Biorki. He was alone. Relief surged through her, and then something cracked inside her, shattered: her resolve. She fell to the ground, and everything went black.

CHAPTER 9

A familiar voice urged Kaia to move. Something was pressing against her stomach. It was dark. Why were they running? Who was with her? She blinked, a fog clearing. A name: Drap. It sat on her tongue, bitter and burning.

A shadow loomed beneath her, dancing across the tunnel, distorted by the curves of the walls. Suddenly, everything came back to her like a stretched rubber band snapping back into place, though not quite where it had been before.

She was with Biorki. He had her draped over one shoulder, one arm wrapped around her thighs, holding her in place. His other hand clutched the brown backpack. Her head swung back and forth in time with his heavy steps. The dark tunnel walls pressed in around them, the only light a faint glow from Biorki's helmet. It bounced as he walked, reflecting off of the slick walls, his breathing heavy under the weight of her body.

Kaia pushed herself up so her head was level with his. She felt him tense under her hands.

"Put me down." The words slipped through her lips.

She thought he hadn't heard her and was about to tell him again when Biorki's voice drifted through the tunnel. "Are you sure?"

No, she wasn't sure. She didn't know which way was up anymore. But she couldn't let him carry all the weight. She nodded, realized he couldn't see her, and murmured, "Yes."

Biorki stopped and bent down. She slid off, and her feet touched solid rock. They were no longer in Kaldwell, no longer in a glacier. They were inside a mountain passage, an old abandoned tunnel.

Biorki rose to his full height and stretched his back. He placed the bag on the ground and pulled a map from his pocket. Kaia didn't look up. Instead, she examined her boots.

"Where are we?"

The light slid to the map, then up and forward into the darkness ahead of them.

"I'm not sure. But I think we're close to a cave with hot springs. That's what the map says—the one Lu left you in the backpack." Biorki's voice was soft, neutral. "I didn't know there were any springs out here." He picked up the bag again, slung it over his shoulder, and continued forward. "Come on. I'm not sure if the guards saw us, but I don't want them to catch us in the dark."

Kaia watched him walk. That word: *guards*. Drap. A weird sound, her dad's face frozen in pain, his eyes vacant, dark, empty. She wrapped her arms around herself. It was all her fault. Biorki's steps echoed around her in the growing darkness. She should turn back, let them take her, let them kill her. But she had promised.

"Wait!"

There was desperation in her voice. Biorki slowed, but he didn't turn to look at her.

Kaia knew she should be thankful, grateful for Biorki's help. But when she reached for her emotions, all she could find was a void, empty and dark like the tunnel around her. She found herself running after him, leaving the darkness behind, at least for now. When she reached Biorki he matched her stride. The thump of their boots echoed through the tunnel as they ran side by side.

Kaia began to recognize parts of the tunnel as it narrowed.

Biorki was almost squatting by the time they reached what she was looking for. A light shone through a hole in the wall. They crawled through it, and there it was: the cave with the hot springs. A secret she and her dad had kept to themselves. Now the secret was shattered because of her.

Soft blue light flickered across the rock ceiling. It illuminated the small cave and danced inside the hot springs—bioluminescent moss, evolved to survive the harshest of climates. Dark green rock formations circled the five semicircular springs. The rocks looked little dark creatures, some hunched over, others reaching for the light.

The steam that rose from the turquoise water glowed pink. *It's the copper in the water*, her dad had explained when she had asked. Now she knew it was due to oxidation. Still, it was beautiful. And a dead end.

Kaia hunched over and puked into her helmet.

Looking at the map, Biorki sat on one of the green rocks while Kaia rinsed her helmet in one of the springs. His eyebrows grew tighter with every passing minute. They needed to move. They didn't know if they had been followed. But there was no way out of this cave.

The pain in Kaia's chest threatened to burst. So she did the only thing she could think of, what she had been trained to do—regulate her breathing. Every inhale threatened to choke her. Every exhale burned her throat.

"Kaia?" Biorki touched her shoulder.

Kaia took another deep breath and blinked. The sound of Drap's weapon still rang in her ears.

"Yes?" A whisper, a plea that her emotions wouldn't spill to the surface.

Biorki took off his helmet and turned her head to face him. Kaia looked at the ground. Her breath quickened. The buzzing sound grew higher in her ears. She gasped. The air wouldn't stay in her lungs, wouldn't leave. He raised her chin with his hand, forcing her to look at him. She was hyperventilating, shaking with each gasp. His eyes held hers, dark blue and calm.

"Cry!" he demanded. "It's okay to cry."

Something burst within her, a crack in her wall, and tears streamed down her face. Biorki squeezed her hand and sat with her as she lost herself to the pain, the fear, and the gaping hole in her chest. He didn't move or back away, even when frost bit his eyelashes. She cried until her cheeks burned, the tears freezing on her skin. The sting of pain brought her back to where they were, to what they had to do.

She blinked away the tears still in her eyes, calmed her breathing, and dried her face on her sleeve. They had to move. They had been here too long. But she couldn't shake the horrible image of Drap dropping her dad's arm onto the bed, the smile of disgust on his face. It replayed in her mind over and over again, and she knew she would never, ever forget it.

Kaia squeezed Biorki's hand. She brushed some of the frost from the dark stubble on his chin. She had never seen him without a clean-shaven face before.

"You have more hair on your face than your head." She was surprised to find that her voice was steady.

Biorki's lips curved. There was a hint of relief in his smile. He leaned closer to Kaia, his mouth almost touching her cheek. "Imagine if I grew a beard. I would look like Tom from the market."

The image of the older man popped into her head, temporarily flushing the horrible memories from her mind. Tom's beard was always braided into intricate patterns. She thought it impractical, but Tom called it art. Kaia imagined a braided beard on Biorki, and the image was so strange that she smiled. It felt good for a minute. Then guilt burned through her again, and the smile fell.

"Come on." Biorki pulled her to her feet and handed her the now clean helmet. "We need to figure a way out of here fast."

She stood up and pulled her helmet back on. "Okay, let me have a look at the map. Maybe you missed something."

Biorki assessed her while pulling on his helmet. Worry creased his brows. "Are you sure? I found it in the backpack earlier." He avoided mentioning what state she had been in when he'd found it and continued, "I think your da— It's hand-drawn."

"It's okay." Kaia squared her shoulders. This was what her dad had wanted. If she was to keep her promise, she had to become stronger. She could cry more later. Biorki had managed when his mother had died. He was proof that it was possible to be strong even if your world was torn to pieces. *Do what you can do right now.*

Kaia didn't have to explain. Biorki understood and handed the map over to her.

Thankful, she took it, unfolded it, and swore. The paper was almost blank. There was a description of the route they had already walked, a single symbol, and a word she didn't recognize: Gret-ha. Was Gret-ha the person who was supposed to meet them at the end of their journey? It could also be the name of a town or an object. There was no way of knowing.

What kind of map was this? Kaia knew her dad wasn't a very wordy guy, but this…this was of no help at all. She held back a new round of tears. And as her vision blurred, she stared at the symbol. Something about it nagged at her, like she had seen it before.

"Did you know about this cave?" Biorki looked around, taking in the steam from the springs. "We had to pass so many restricted tunnels to get here. It's not as big as the springs in Kaldwell, but it's beautiful. Do you think there's lava running under it?"

"I don't know. Probably," Kaia traced a line across the map with her glove. "My da— He would bring me here when I was a kid so we could be alone. The springs in Kaldwell are always busy, and…"

An idea formed in her mind. *No, that would be crazy.* She looked closer at the map, holding it up to her nose. She knew that symbol. It was rough and hastily drawn, but she had seen it before. *There's no way!*

She ran over to the wall farthest from the cave's entrance and dragged her gloved fingers across the moss on the dark mountain wall. There—an indentation in the stone. She unclipped her right ice axe and chipped away at the moss, careful not to damage the rock behind it.

When she had cleared most of the moss, she stepped back. She had been right. There it was, etched into the mountain too precisely to have been done by any tools in Kaldwell: the symbol on the map. It comprised two circles, one within the other, framed by a diamond on its tip. Within the smaller circle was a cross.

Her dad had rested his hand on the cross when he'd told her, *This symbol is a reminder of the old and the forgotten. A reminder of what has been lost.* He had traced the lines with his index finger. *It has many meanings to many people.*

Kaia hadn't paid attention then; she'd been too excited to continue her swimming lessons. Her gut wrenched as the memory twisted into a buzzing sound, a gasp, and a blank stare.

She pushed the memory away and traced the lines with her own gloved finger. She paused, then pressed down on its center. The cross twisted and sank into the wall. A low mechanical hiss echoed through the cave, and a handle replaced the cross. A curse slid from Biorki's mouth behind her. She took a step back as cracks shot through the mountain wall. The hissing grew louder, and within moments, a door of solid rock appeared before them.

Kaia sucked in a gulp of air. What an incredible piece of engineering, utterly seamless. A hidden door that led…where? She turned to Biorki. His wide eyes moved over the lines of the door, admiring the technology. Then he nodded. Kaia swallowed, grabbed the handle, and pulled. As expected of a solid rock door, it didn't move.

"Give me a hand." The words come out as a wheeze, but Biorki was there immediately, both hands on the handle, his shoulder next to hers.

"On three." Kaia planted her feet wide and braced herself. "One…two…"

Biorki stiffened next to her.

"Three."

They pulled. The door moved an inch.

"Again. One…two…"

They braced themselves.

"Three."

A beam of yellow light cut through the cave. Then a horrible howl filled their ears. Kaia let go of the door, and Biorki stumbled behind her.

"What *is* that?" Biorki straightened, rubbing his hands.

"I don't know." Kaia tried not to think of what could make such a sound, but it didn't matter. Whatever monster lay beyond the door, this was where her dad wanted her to go. "It's our only way out. Let's try again."

Biorki hesitated, then nodded and grabbed the handle again. "Let's do it."

With another deep breath, they pulled again, and again.

The wider the door opened, the louder the howl grew. Sweat ran down Kaia's forehead, and Biorki gasped with the effort, but there was a gap large enough now that a person could squeeze through. The howl flowed through the cave and enveloped them in noise.

"How did you know this was here?" Biorki shouted behind her.

"The symbol!" she yelled back. "My dad showed it to me when I was a kid, but he never told me it turned into a door."

"Are you sure this is the only way out of here?" Biorki's voice was steady, but she could hear his doubt. Kaia saw him clench his jaw and leaned closer to him.

"I don't think my father would send us into a monster's den. There must be a reason he wanted us to go this way." Kaia didn't feel as confident as she sounded, but a smile grew on Biorki's face.

"Like Ingá always says: always be prepared, always be ready!" Biorki yelled, and gave her the backpack.

Ingá only said that to keep people in line at the mines, but Kaia didn't correct him. Didn't tell him to go back, to leave her to face the monster by herself. She didn't ask him why he was helping her. Instead, she nodded and pulled on the backpack. Her hands shook as she secured her ice axes, then straightened. The idea of walking toward the howling made her mouth dry, but at least she didn't have to do it alone.

She looked through the gap in the door. Behind it was a staircase—long, curved, dark, and perfectly crafted. There was no monster in sight. The howl continued as they squeezed through the door.

Pulling a massive rock door open turned out to be a lot easier than pulling it closed. They tried everything, but it didn't budge; the gap remained as wide as when they'd started. Sighing, they moved up the black stairs, picking up speed as they went. They had already lost so much time. Biorki followed close behind Kaia, a comfort pushing her on.

When they had climbed for what felt like forever—about thirty minutes, in reality—the howling grew louder. The deep growl echoed off the smooth rock and the chiseled steps shaped by someone or something in the past. Something her dad had known about and never told her. Another secret.

They didn't slow. The howl drowned out their heavy breaths as they climbed. Kaia pushed against the sound, her calves and thighs burning. She welcomed it, savored it, bit down and kept moving. Biorki was at her back, ready to catch her if she fell.

Just as she thought she couldn't take one more step, the staircase leveled out. There was still no monster in sight. Kaia took a moment to catch her breath, Biorki gasping behind her, then stepped forward. At the end of the tunnel was an empty archway. As they moved closer, she saw the remnants of torn hinges but no sign of a door. Kaia looked back at Biorki. He nodded, and she walked toward the arch.

She kicked something. Looking down, she saw the rubble of torn metal and rock. So that was what had happened to the door. She stepped slowly through the arch, careful not to twist her ankle.

Biorki breathed behind her. "See anything?"

"Wait a second." Still looking down, she found a spot of solid ground, then looked up and gasped.

Thousands of white stars flew through the cave she had entered. They whirled and twisted, the crystals reflecting her headlight. *Snow.* She reached out as another howl filled the cave. The flecks of snow burst through the space in front of them and blew across her helmet, stuck to her suit. The wind was the monster, the cause of the howling.

Kaia heard Biorki gasp behind her as he realized the same thing she was thinking. She didn't look away from the snow as she said, "I think we're on the surface."

She took another step into the cave and lifted her hands. She watched the snowflakes dance between her fingers. Snow only existed in two places on this planet: in fairy tales, and on the surface.

When she had imagined going to the surface, she had thought it would be an impossible climb, that it would take weeks. They had made it in less than a cycle. The people of Kaldwell were only half a cycle away from this. It had been that easy, and yet no one in her town had ever been to the surface.

She watched as a snowflake came to rest on her glove; she closed her hand around it and squeezed. Her dad had known and never told her. Kaia took another step forward and reached out once more. Above her shone a thousand icicles, clear and sharp. They sang in the wind. Why would her dad keep this from her? Chunks of ice broke beneath her boots as she walked farther into the cave.

Biorki walked behind her. "Careful—we don't know if this cave is secured."

"It's beautiful!" she yelled over her shoulder.

She took another step, another crackle of ice under her feet. Something zoomed past her ear, and a sharp, blinding heat burst through her shoulder.

"Aaaaarrgghhh!" Her scream slashed through the howling of the wind.

"Dritt!" Biorki's hands were on her in an instant, his eyes on her shoulder. "Oh shit!"

Kaia turned her head and instantly regretted it. An icicle protruded from her monosuit at the front of her right shoulder. Embedded deep in her flesh, the clear ice acted as a magnifying glass. Bone and muscles shone through. Bile rose in her throat. She watched as blood pooled around the wound, around the icicle. Then another wave of pain rushed through her, like hot melted metal poured over her skin, burning through flesh, muscles, and bones.

CHAPTER 10

What was that horrid sound? The piercing noise reverberated through her skull. Terrible and guttural, like a wounded animal. Another heartbeat, another scream—it sounded so familiar. Why wouldn't it stop?

Drap's smile filled Kaia's mind, twisted into a grotesque mask of darkness. She needed it gone. He had to die. A vibrating hum filled her, starting in her deepest depths. With every stab of pain, it grew. Warm and horrible, it spread through her blood, her muscles, her skin, her hands, rippling through her core, a tool for her to use.

Kaia reached for it as if it were the most natural thing in the world. Held it in her mind. Shaped it. She needed to push the pain away, push that face away, push it all away. She released it, and a burst of raw energy forced itself to the surface, rippling like still water that had been struck by a rock. It breached the boundaries of her skin. And as it left her, a cry of shock and pain filled the air.

"Crap!"

She blinked, and light stung her eyes. Kaia forced them open, fighting the sudden exhaustion that filled her.

Her mind reconnected to the sensations of her body. Strange. Sizzling reached her ears. She turned, vaguely aware of some resistance in her shoulder and something warm on her face. Biorki hopped on one foot, swearing and patting his monosuit. Smoke rose from his gloves and chest. Minor burns and soot covered the patched-up fabric.

Kaia jumped to her feet, searching for signs of danger. There was nothing. They were still alone in the howling cave, a few steps away from the arch. She sighed, then grabbed her shoulder as pain ran through her again. She fell back down onto her knees. It hadn't been a dream. She looked at her shoulder, already cringing at what she knew she'd see.

She stared, her mouth falling open. The icicle had disappeared, and where there should have been a gaping wound, there was a patch of burned and twisted skin.

She couldn't believe it. She poked it. Pain crawled through her body. Yes, it was real. But how?

"What happened?" she mumbled, more to herself than Biorki, as she stared at her shoulder in a daze.

"Who knows," Biorki responded. "One second, you passed out, and the next, I was flat on my back." Kaia looked up to see him checking his monosuit for breaches or holes. He dragged his hand across a charred spot on his sleeve. "Thankfully, it's not too bad."

She looked at her hands. Was this her fault? The humming sensation was still fresh in her mind. A chill ran across her skin. Ignoring her pain, she got up and moved to where Biorki sat.

"Are you hurt?" she asked.

"No, I'm goo— Oh shit!" He pointed at her. "Your shoulder. And your suit. Your face."

"Oh, yeah," was all she managed to say.

Biorki was going to leave her now and never look back. How could he stay after this? It scared her. It should disturb him too, whatever this was.

Biorki didn't pull back. Instead, he picked up his work pack that was usually strapped to his hip. It must have fallen off on impact. He pulled out some patching tape. She grabbed his hand. She knew they had to move, but they wouldn't get far unless they patched their suits.

"You first," she said.

"But your shoulder."

Kaia ignored his protests and inspected him. There were a few breaches in his suit, but the one on his chest, right above his heart, was what sent another chill down her spine. Schooling her face, she moved on to his elbow. Bile rose in her throat at the sight of bright red skin glaring at her through a hole in his suit. Whatever had happened had burned right through both of his layers of clothing, incinerated it. By sheer luck, the skin had blistered, not fused with his clothes. She fought the sudden urge to flee, but she couldn't, wouldn't panic again. Swallowing the lump in her throat, she patched the hole.

Snow and wind whirled around them as they worked in silence, occasionally glancing at the arch. It remained empty. A few swear words escaped Biorki when he got a closer look at Kaia's wound. When he was finished, Biorki put his supplies back in his work pack and brushed off his hands.

"Done! What do you think?"

Kaia turned her head slowly and checked out the patch covering the ripped part of her suit.

"It looks great."

Heat filled her cheeks; Biorki was too close. It hadn't bothered her before, but something about his tenderness made her look down at the ground. She fumbled with the leftover gauze in her hands, then lifted her eyes to the burn on his chest, now covered by a fresh patch. "Are you sure you're okay? That burn looked bad."

"Don't worry about it. It's not my first burn." His eyes locked with hers, and he grinned, then faltered. "One more thing."

He reached out, and she forced herself to sit still. He pulled her helmet off and wiped something from her lip with his sleeve—blood. The motion made her face tingle, but she didn't look away as he put her helmet back on.

"There. As good as new." His smile stayed this time. "Looks like the nosebleed stopped."

"Thank you." She hadn't noticed the blood on her face. She looked at the arch. "Let's find a way out of here."

She searched the space. The light from her helmet danced across the imperfections of the cave. In the wall across from the arch loomed a shadow her light couldn't breach—there. Snow flew in from the darkness. That was the way out, hopefully. If the guards had tracked them, there was no way of telling how close they were, and she didn't want to find out.

Kaia pointed at the dark tunnel. "I think it's that way. Feeling up for it?"

"I haven't felt so alive in rotations." Biorki brushed some soot from his helmet and clicked something on his visor. "But let's be more careful with our headlights from now on."

She followed suit and turned her auto feature off. For now, she would leave her light on the dimmest setting, just bright enough to make out where they were going.

Biorki gestured to the tunnel. "After you."

Snow whirled around them, and the wind pulled at their suits when they made their way to the fork in the cave. This time, they kept one eye on the icicles hanging above them. They followed the white specks and turned into the dark tunnel. Kaia hoped her guess was right.

If the map was correct, they had to keep moving until they found their helper. But who would live up here? No one could survive on the surface. Then again, no one was supposed to be able to *reach* the surface, yet here they were. She watched a snowflake melt on her visor. What had her dad been thinking, sending them here?

They rounded another bend, and a bright beacon appeared before them: the cave opening. It could be a trap, but it could also be their salvation. Kaia turned off her light and charged ahead, Biorki following behind her.

Then there was nothing but snow was beneath her. It was soft and surprisingly solid under her boots. It crackled and squeaked as she pushed forward. The sound was terrific. Scents she had never smelled filled her nose, but her body responded to it all as if it was a familiar memory, a welcome home. The smell of fresh air was written in the collective consciousness of every human being. She heard Biorki inhale it behind her.

She hit something hard with her boot and barely caught herself before falling forward. The light from the cave opening burned her eyes, and she realized she couldn't see. She stopped. Biorki grunted behind her, his steps coming to a halt as well. She was blind. She knew it should scare her. Instead, it was exhilarating.

She had read about the surface. It was deadly, the texts had said. Unrelenting, barren, and not survivable for multicelled organisms. A place of storms that could cut into mountains, of cold that could freeze a body to the core within minutes. A place of ever-changing landscapes, so white you would go blind if you looked at them too long without protection.

And yet, her dad had sent them here. Where they would supposedly find help. Maybe Biorki felt the same as she did as they stood there in silence. They listened to the wind, breathed the fresh air, and waited for their eyes to adapt.

Slowly, the whiteness began to take shape. Restlessness stirred in Kaia. This was taking too long. She blinked, her mind spinning. What if Solon caught up with them while they were standing here like two statues in the snow? Another blink, and she began to see shadows. What if there was no one waiting for them at the end of this journey? Wouldn't they have seen them by now? Another blink. Why was Solon after her?

Another blink, and her sight cleared.

Kaia gasped and fell to her knees. The world before her was cut in half by a red sky. There was no end to it—no wall of ice above them, no rock, no dead ends. Only space, red-and-orange snow as far as she could see, and a small ball of white light on the horizon. The sun.

She looked over her shoulder. The cave behind them was dark but empty. She turned back to the incredible world before her.

"Look over there—the spikes on the horizon." Biorki stood

beside her now, his face full of awe. She had almost forgotten he was there. Kaia looked at where he was pointing. A ridge of dark triangular shapes lined the snowy horizon.

She stood up and lifted her hands to her helmet. "Are those mountains?"

"I don't know." Biorki squinted. "I think so."

What dangers lay waiting out there beyond the fields of snow and ice? At the feet of the closest mountain, or hidden in the shadows where the sun couldn't reach? The hairs on Kaia's neck stood on end. She shook her head. They weren't here to admire the view, as incredible as it was. They didn't have time for this.

"Do you see anyone?" Kaia turned to search the cave opening again.

"No." Biorki walked around a large boulder half buried in snow. "Do you think there are monsters out there?"

Kaia saw nothing but their own footprints. "Like the fairy tales Tom used to tell us?" She thought of the tales of giant monsters larger than cities with teeth the size of houses.

Biorki appeared on the other side of the boulder, shaking his head. "Nothing on that side. And yes. Those stories were probably just to scare us away from going to the surface, right?"

"I sure hope so." A lump had formed in Kaia's gut; there was no one here to meet them.

This was the end of the map, the last information from her dad and there was no one, nothing here. She examined the landscape for any hints of movement. But all she could see was a wall of dark clouds moving toward them. A storm. They would have to wait. But there was no way they could survive out here for long. She looked back at the cave. If they stayed in one place, they risked Solon finding them eventually. They were running out of options.

"What do you want to do?" she asked. "Should we stay here? Maybe whoever is supposed to meet us is late?"

Biorki sighed. It seemed he had reached a similar conclusion.

"Yeah, I think that's our best bet. Let's look for a hiding

spot in the cave. But it's amazing, isn't it? The sky!" Biorki looked up, the light reflecting off his helmet.

"Yeah. It's incredible." Kaia allowed herself another glance at the clouds.

"And terrifying. What do you think keeps us from falling up?" Biorki returned to her side.

"Gravity?" Kaia stepped over a small snow hill on her way to the entrance. It worked well in the mines, in the caves. It kept them all walking on the same side of the tunnels. But out here, with nothing between them and the sky? It seemed unreal that an invisible force could keep them from disappearing into the endless space above them.

Biorki grabbed a handful of snow and threw it into the air. "Gravity is only a theory, a construct, a word. I feel like there is more to it than that. Maybe if I had a spring of wire and a magnet and—"

A glint caught Kaia's eye, but before she could react, Biorki slammed into her. She flew into a pile of snow with Biorki's weight on top of her. She tried not to groan. Her shoulder throbbed from the impact. White spots filled her vision, but she clenched her teeth and stayed silent. She had seen them too—two figures in silver rounding the bend in the tunnel. Drap and Gin.

Biorki slid off of her but remained crouched. Able to move again, Kaia lifted her head out of the snow. Biorki had launched them to the right of the cave opening, far enough that they should be hidden from sight. She didn't think the guards had seen them and didn't intend to find out.

She got back to her feet, her right arm hanging limp by her side. She glanced at their footprints at the entrance; there was nothing they could do about them now. She should have been more careful. There was a lot she should have done. She should have tried harder to close the door to the hot springs. She should have told Biorki to go back. She should have listened to her dad and stayed away from the sick bay.

She exchanged a look with Biorki. His eyes were wide, his mouth set in a grim smile. He nodded in the direction of the hillside. Only one option remained. She grabbed his outstretched hand and ran into the brewing storm.

CHAPTER 11

The sun touched the mountains, throwing long shadows across the flat land—the Tundra. Kaia allowed herself to look back. She saw nothing but snow. They had lost sight of the cave entrance hours ago. If Drap and Gin had seen them, she hoped they had lost them in the storm. The wind tore around them, causing everything to blend together: the sky, the ground. It wiped out their footprints, their existence.

She turned back around and bent against the wind. Solid ice hammered against her visor. Biorki hunched beside her, a dark shadow pushing forward. They didn't dare turn on their lights in case the guards had followed them. It made their progress slow as they fumbled through the thick snow.

When they reached a barren sheet of ice, Kaia and Biorki both sighed with relief. Walking through the snow had been a lot harder than Kaia had expected. They moved onto the slick ice, their legs lighter, and Kaia triggered the spikes in her boots. They helped against the wind, which blew more strongly now, pulling at them unhindered. They had to find shelter soon. But they could see only the wall of snow and ice that whipped around them.

Which was why they didn't see it. One moment, Biorki's

shadow was in front of her. The next, he dropped into the ground, pulling her along with him. She screamed as they slid down toward a glacier rift—a death trap. Biorki looked up at her, and in that split second, she knew what he would do.

No.

Biorki let go of her hand. She tried to grab him, but it was too late. He hurtled forward, and she watched in horror as he slid into the darkness. Without his weight pulling her down, she skidded to a halt, her feet close to the edge of the crevice.

"Biorki!"

Screw the guards. She turned on her light and crawled forward on all fours. She peeked over the edge and a shaky gasp escaped her. Biorki lay on a solid ice shelf that protruded from the straight ice wall leading into the chasm below. The deep cut in the glacier spanned as far as she could see to either side of them. She couldn't see the bottom. If Biorki had slid any farther, if the shelf hadn't been there… She pushed the thought away.

Biorki rose to his feet, and her light reflected off his visor. She couldn't see his face, but his hands shook when she grabbed them. She pulled him up, and they flopped onto the ice together, gasping.

Both of Kaia's arms throbbed. Something warm and wet ran down her right shoulder, but she ignored it. There was nothing she could do about it out here.

"Are you okay?" she wheezed.

Biorki gasped next to her. She could feel the tremors in his hand as it gripped hers.

"Yeah. I'm good."

"Good."

Kaia rolled over and caught him smiling. How could he smile? He had almost died. Heat rose in her chest, and before she knew it, she was straddling him. She shook his shoulders, punched his chest, and screamed at him. "Why did you let go? I could have slowed your fall, or…or…"

She punched and shook him again, but he didn't fight back. He only looked at her. "And take you down with me? Why would I do that?"

She stopped, his words stilling her.

Why *would* he do that? Why would he do what she had done by bringing him into this, into danger? Solon wanted her, not him. He could have stayed behind, but she hadn't stopped him from coming with her. Something twisted inside her. Why hadn't she told him to stay back in Kaldwell?

Kaia slid off Biorki and looked down at her hands. "I'm sorry. I shouldn't have brought you here."

Biorki didn't respond.

"I'm so sorry," she repeated, her voice like smoke fading away in the wind.

Again, there was no response.

Kaia looked up. She didn't know what she expected, but what she saw made her freeze. Biorki's eyes were fixed on her, crystal clear and deep with emotion. And something darker. Guilt? The silly, weird Biorki she knew had changed into someone older, wiser.

Biorki blinked, and it was gone.

He sat up, rubbed his arm, and smiled. "I chose to go with you. You have nothing to apologize for." He stared at the dark rift behind Kaia and paused for a moment before saying, "Before my mother died, she changed."

Even through the hail and the snow, Kaia could see the pain in the lines of his face.

"The illness broke her. She would wake up terrified, and sometimes she couldn't remember who she was or that I was her son."

Kaia remembered hearing about Biorki's mother. She had been one of the first to die from CE when the sickness had spread through Kaldwell. But she had never thought about how it had affected Biorki, never considered it. *Selfish.*

Biorki crossed his arms and legs, a statue in the snow.

"My father was no help. I think it hurt him to see my mother like that, so he would leave me alone with her. I found out later that he spent that time at the bar."

Biorki had never talked about his past. Kaia had always

assumed he had lived a simple life, especially when he had joked with her at work. She should have asked. What kind of friend was she?

"Anyway." Biorki rubbed his gloved hands together and sighed. "In the last three weeks of her life, she would hit me and curse at me."

"I'm sorry." Kaia fumbled with the strap of her backpack. How had she not known this? Her chest tightened.

"Don't be. When she passed away, I was relieved. I felt guilty about the relief at first. But then I realized the woman who had done those things wasn't my mother, not really."

Biorki leaned back on his arms and looked at the darkness above them. The sun had disappeared behind the mountains.

"My father left for good then. But I forgave him too. People deal with loss in different ways. My father's way was to run. I had no choice but to stay."

Kaia hugged her legs with her good arm. She wasn't sure what she would have become if she had been through something like that. Maybe angry, cold, and hateful; definitely not warm, not like him.

Drap's voice filled her thoughts, and the buzz, the blank stare. She shook her head, pushing it all away.

Biorki leaned forward and put his visor against hers. Ice hammered on their helmets, an enveloping rhythm. He held her gaze. Heat rose in her cheeks. He was too close. She wanted to look away but couldn't tear her eyes from his. She noticed a small dark spot in one of his irises. Had it always been there?

"What I'm trying to say is that I understand. Maybe not everything you're going through right now, but…" He smiled, and it struck something deep within Kaia. "I won't leave you again. I promise."

Kaia wondered if Biorki had wished for that when he was younger, for someone to stand by his side. But this, the way his face gloved in the helmet light, how his eyes burned through her, saw through her. It was too intimate. She pulled back. She didn't deserve what he was offering her—unconditional understanding.

She saw the hurt in his eyes as she pulled away. If she refused his help, she realized, it would break him. Or maybe she just couldn't bear to be alone, to lose him. She grabbed his hand and said, "Thank you."

He nodded and looked back up at the sky. She was grateful for the silence. Although the wind still tore the world apart, she found quiet in that moment. Hidden by the storm, she felt safer. Biorki squeezed her hand, and she allowed herself to appreciate his presence next to her, the feel of his hand in hers. Warmth spread from her fingers to places she didn't want to think about. And then Biorki pulled his hand away.

"Well, that was tense." He tapped her helmet with a fist. "Let's find some shelter from this wind."

He had always been the best at defusing uncomfortable situations. Kaia smiled at him.

"I don't know what you mean. I'm never tense." How she was even able to joke, she didn't know. But when she reached up to knock on Biorki's helmet, pain shot through her. She hunched over, gritting her teeth.

"Are you okay?"

"Yeah, I just forgot about my shoulder." Kaia breathed out and stood. "I'm okay."

Biorki stared at her, then sighed. "We will have to take a closer look at that wound when we find…"

He trailed off as he stood, his light disappearing into the darkness ahead. They needed shelter, a medic, heat. The likelihood of finding any of those things out here was less than zero. The probability of someone finding them was even smaller. If there was someone on the surface who could help them, they had probably met Drap and Gin in the cave. She met Biorki's eyes, but she wouldn't say it, and neither would he.

Kaia brushed snow off her chest with her good arm. "We better get moving."

They walked around the rift in the glacier, taking care to test the ground in front of them before taking each step. They made excruciatingly slow progress. When they reached the end of the ice sheet, they began wading through snow again, every step harder, slower, stiffer. The wind pushed them back, blinding them. But they kept moving.

Whenever the wind relented, they caught brief glimpses of the tundra. Every hill and snow formation turned into giant creatures looming above them in the dark. Kaia had to remind herself that monsters didn't exist. Then the wind returned, and the storm consumed the landscape again.

Biorki's hand was the only solid thing in the blurry, freezing world. The temperature was dropping fast. Kaia's heat converter hummed in her ear as it fought to keep her warm. The cold out here was different, brutal, not something their suits were made to handle. They pushed on, their movement helping them maintain a safe temperature.

They had been walking for hours when Kaia's temperature gauge flickered on her visor. She came to a stop, catching her breath. Biorki stopped with her, too exhausted to speak. She tapped the screen, and the gauge came back on. She sighed with relief, then turned to Biorki and cursed. His visor was covered in frost, a sign everyone in Kaldwell knew to dread. She caught a glimpse of his blue eyes through the ice. Determination lined his face, and something else. Fear?

Biorki's headlight flickered. He knocked on his visor as if bullying his helmet into listening, and it flashed, then died. Biorki swore. Kaia stopped breathing. The light was the first thing to go when a monosuit lost power. Biorki had ten or fifteen minutes at most before losing his protection against the cold. If they didn't do something soon, he would become another permanent sculpture in the landscape. That was why they always burned their dead in Kaldwell: to release the souls from the eternal cage of death. Why hadn't Biorki said anything? Maybe he was trying to act brave, like she was, pretending they were not about to fall victim to nature's whims because they had followed a map drawn by her da—

"The bag!" Kaia shouted into the wind.

She should have checked it earlier. She swung it off her shoulders. A sudden pain rushed through her, and her knees buckled. *Dritt*, her shoulder. Forcing her head to stop spinning, she opened the leather flap on the top of the bag, untied the string securing the opening, and reached inside. She found a small cylinder-shaped pill container, a newer model of hot water canister than she had at home, and a charger for their suits' heat converters. *A charger.* She pulled it out.

Kaia clicked the button on the small oval-shaped charger. It lit up. *Thank the stars.* She waved at Biorki. He turned, and she smacked it between his shoulder blades. It snapped onto the heat converter, and a light began to pulse in its center. It worked.

Kaia sighed. Biorki would be fine. The charger would restore the suit's functions, but… She bit her lip. It was small enough that it would give only one, maybe two full charges. And in this weather…

Biorki turned to face her, a grim smile on his face. "If we take turns and keep moving, we can make it last until sunrise."

Sunrise. That was six hours away. They had six hours to find shelter or someone to help them. They should have stayed in Kaldwell. She should have handed herself in. What could Solon do to her that would be worse than freezing to death slowly?

Biorki stretched; he didn't look at her. "Anyway, that's a lot of time to find shelter. Don't you think?"

Kaia could hear the doubt in his words, could feel her optimism shatter. They wouldn't survive this. There was no shelter, no one to save them. And even if they had enough charge to keep going, they would eventually starve. Biorki knew it too. She could see it in the droop of his shoulders, the turn of his lips.

She picked up her backpack, looking at the ground. "Yeah." She pulled the bag onto her back. The pain in her shoulder didn't feel so bad this time. "Let's time the charging. An hour, then switch?"

Biorki straightened, still not meeting her eyes, and checked the stats of his suit. "Sounds good."

"Okay, then. I'll set a timer."

Biorki held out his hand without looking back. "Okay."

She grabbed it, and they walked forward into the darkness once more.

This time, Kaia let her thoughts spin. Maybe this was part of her dad's plan, sending her out here to die. It made sense. Of course there was no one to meet them up here. No one could survive on the surface. Her dad knew that. Everyone knew that. She'd been stupid to think otherwise.

She almost laughed. It was ridiculous. How could she think that about her dad? He would never do that. But maybe he would. She had believed they'd had no secrets, yet here she was, fleeing from some crazy company because of something in her blood that her dad hadn't told her about.

Kaia watched as Biorki waded into a deep snowdrift. Frost touched the edge of her visor in a beautiful starlike shape. She didn't say anything as they walked up a small hill, her legs throbbing. She watched Biorki slide on the snow before catching himself. His movements were slower now.

If her dad's plan had been to kill her, Biorki shouldn't be out here, dying because of her. The all-too-familiar twist in her gut consumed her. It hurt to realize that she hadn't known her dad at all. It hurt to think of Ingá, Ine, Kjartan, and everyone still in Kaldwell, trapped there with Solon.

She didn't say anything when her light flickered out. Didn't say anything as they reached the top of a small hill and the storm faded. Didn't argue when Biorki slumped to the ground. She just sat with him, her thoughts calming.

She wished she had entered the iceboarding contest Stallo when she still could have. Wished she hadn't dragged Biorki out here with her. Wished she had followed her dad's instructions to stay away from the sick bay. But she would keep her promise. Solon wouldn't get her…at least not alive.

Biorki sat beside her, his breath labored. His light had shut down as well, but it didn't matter. His calculations had been correct, as always—the sun was rising before them. They had made it to dawn.

The rest of the storm and the clouds disappeared in the distance, leaving them, the tundra, and the sun. There were no shadows, only gradients of red dancing on the flat frozen expanse in front of them. Small hills upon hills as far as they could see. A glittering sea of red. It was gorgeous.

Kaia leaned on Biorki's shoulder. "It's strange to think that something so beautiful can be so deadly."

Biorki didn't look down; his frost-covered visor was turned toward something on the horizon. "Sometimes the ugliest things are the most useful. That is what I learned fixing tech. A beautiful case doesn't mean the internal components are working."

As he talked, Kaia watched the spires of ice that rose from the dunes of snow.

"But this is nature. Everything has its function, no matter what it looks like. I'd rather die this way than in some human-created construction," Biorki continued.

She smiled. She had to agree; it wasn't the worst way to go.

She didn't know how long they stayed that way, and she didn't care. Nor did she care when her heat converter chimed—a little song to remind her of her imminent death.

She laid her head down on Biorki's lap. He stiffened at first, then rested his hand on her back. No, this wasn't the worst way to die. It was, in some way, a beautiful death. She should be mad that this was how her life would end, but she was too tired, warm, and comfortable here with Biorki.

Time must have moved on without them, because the sun suddenly touched the horizon. The colors changed around Kaia, and she welcomed them. The reds, purples, and pinks wrapped the world in a colorful blanket.

"Wonderful," she whispered as she closed her eyes.

Another spark of life flickered next to her. It enveloped her in a warm embrace. And then, darkness. She accepted it and let go.

CHAPTER 12

Did I pass out again?

She couldn't see anything, couldn't feel anything. There was only pure darkness. Had they slept until midsleep? But there were no stars, no lights, nothing. Now that she thought about it, there was no up or down. It was like she had no physical body. The realization didn't scare her. She couldn't quite remember what being scared felt like.

Then she sensed it: a faint buzzing. It grew and shook the dark fabric around her, warping it, a force so strong and terrible it shook her. Fear filled her then—cold, burning fear. It traveled through her, up, up, up until it reached her shoulder, and—

"OW!!"

"Stay still!" a raspy voice told her.

Whoever owned the voice needed to run away from the horrible thing attacking her. Kaia tried to move, to warn them.

"Don't you dare!" the voice growled, and a sudden sting burned her face.

Kaia tried to fend it off, but her arms wouldn't move. Why wouldn't they move? There was a stab of pain, cold and swift, different from the first. The pain was real; it had to be. Or was she dreaming? Another stab followed. It crawled within her and slithered across her bones until it settled in her shoulder.

Hesitating, she opened her eyes. Light filled her, a warm dim glow. There was no sky above her, no stars. Instead, she was looking up at a glistening white ceiling. It wasn't carved or dug out like the caves. Instead, it was made of different-sized ice blocks that fit together like a puzzle. Fascinating. She was on her back on something soft. A bed?

Her eyes caught something in the middle of the room. She turned her head: a firepit.

Crooked and unstable, the circle of black rocks rested on the icy floor. In the center was a dancing red flame. She stared at it. There was orange in it too, and white. It was magical. She had never seen red flames before. It crackled and spat within the circular pit. If spirits were real, they would look like the cinders floating up from the fire.

A sharp pain ran through her shoulder. She flinched but couldn't move. So it wasn't all a dream. She looked down at her arms. They were bare except for the restraints around her wrists and upper arms. She pulled, but they didn't budge. An unfamiliar hairy white material was wrapped around her torso and covered the rest of her body. It smelled awful.

Where were her ice axes and her monosuit? Why was she tied down? Had the guards found them? Panic flowed through her. She had to get away, *now*! She struggled against the restraints.

"Oh, do stop," a raspy voice said.

A loud smack rang in her ears, followed by a burning sensation on her cheek. The owner of the voice had slapped her. Kaia froze. A *slap*? She looked to her right. An elderly woman stared down at her. Covered in the same white material as Kaia, she looked like a wild animal.

The woman's face was dark and worn. The lines on her forehead and cheeks told the story of a hard life. A stray piece of thick black hair flowed across her shoulder from underneath a white hood. A scar ran across the right side of her face. It twisted the woman's features into a permanent scowl, but even that looked warm compared to the icy gaze directed at Kaia. She swore the woman's blue eyes could see right through her.

"So you're done fighting?" The woman searched Kaia's face. It was more a statement than a question. Then the woman turned away, returning to what she had been doing before Kaia had interrupted her.

Kaia looked back down at her restrained hands and then at the firepit. "Who are you?"

The woman didn't answer, only murmured to herself. Then, with a smack of her lips, she turned back to Kaia with a deep scowl.

"What the hell did you do to yourself, child?"

"What do you mean?" The last thing she remembered was lying in Biorki's lap. *Biorki.* "Where's Biorki?" she croaked through her dry lips.

The woman moved to the side in a casual but deliberate gesture. Kaia's eyes fell on a white lump on the other side of the room. It shifted. A small groan followed, and even though she couldn't see his face, Kaia knew it was Biorki. But why isn't he talking? She raised her head to try and see more, to see if he was okay.

"Put your head down!" the woman hissed. "Are you trying to kill yourself?

Kaia dropped her head onto the small pillow, and the woman mumbled, "Damn ungrateful…" The acid in the woman's whisper cut through the sound of the crackling fire.

Ignoring the animosity, Kaia pressed on. "Is he okay?"

The woman didn't respond. The fire snapped and popped. Finally, as a large breath of flame rose from the pit, the woman smacked her lips again.

"He is fine, considering." The woman shrugged. "He might lose sensation in his left hand, and I had to remove two toes on his right foot. He is lucky to be alive."

The woman's eyes burrowed into the lump of guilt weighing Kaia down. Down, down, down. She shifted under the restraints and instantly regretted the movement as pain shot through her right arm.

"Stop moving. How many times do I have to repeat myself?" the woman scolded. "You're going to rip the stitches."

Stitches? That was an old technique, now replaced by skin grafts. Kaia looked down. There they were: four fresh black stitches sewn into her skin. She barely managed to twist her head over the edge of the bed before she puked on the floor.

"Not again," the woman mumbled, placing a bucket next to Kaia's head. "Try and aim for the bucket next time, yes?"

Kaia nodded. The woman pulled out a brown rag and wiped Kaia's face clean.

"Thank you," She let her head fall back.

The woman grunted and walked over to the other side of the firepit. To Biorki.

Now that she was alone, Kaia became increasingly aware of her bad state. Her head pounded, her body ached, and her shoulder…her shoulder she would think of later.

Kaia traced the pattern of ice blocks in the ceiling. "Where are we?"

The woman turned back, her blue eyes once again cutting into Kaia.

"Where you are doesn't matter. It's how you got here that matters. What were you thinking, traveling on the surface? And in your condition. Absolute stupidity!" The woman's eyes narrowed farther. "If I hadn't found you…"

The memory of lying in the snow with Biorki flooded back. They had been dying, buried in the drifts. Then another memory took its place: Solon and her dad's limp arm. Guilt and grief burned through her. The woman's words sank in. *Stupidity?* The woman was blaming *her*, saying it was *her* fault they had ended up there? That her dad, that Biorki—

No. No. No.

The woman spat on the ground, turned to a pot by the fire, and mumbled something about stupid kids. Kaia felt something snap inside her. Her hands gripped the white strands from the hairy blanket; she wished she had her axes.

"Who the hell are you to judge me?" Kaia tested the rope on her left wrist; it didn't budge. "What makes you think you know what we have been through?" The hot lump in her gut grew.

The woman didn't answer as she turned and threw something dark on the fire. The fire burst into new life, licked up around the dark mass, and consumed it.

"I know you can hear me!" Kaia howled. Tears were pushing their way to the surface. She blinked them away. "Who are you?!"

The fire crackled, Biorki's breathing was loud in her ears, and the woman's voice drifted through the smoke. "I don't have a name."

She stared at the woman's back. She knew she hadn't listened to her dad. It was her fault he was dead. Her fault Biorki was injured. She knew that. But this woman had no right to judge her.

"You don't get to judge me and then ignore me. You ugly hag!"

Whack! The sound cut through the room. The woman turned toward Kaia with a broken ladle half raised in her left hand. Her eyes reflected the fire as she gave Kaia a look that could kill. If Kaia hadn't been so angry, she would have flinched. Instead, the warmth in her center spread and a vibration pulsed through her. Images filled her mind—of a burnt hole in Biorki's suit, of fabric melted into skin—and then a hum ran through her.

Kaia looked down at her chest. Panic rose in her throat. A horrible storm pushed against her skin, trying to wreak havoc on everything in her way. She had promised her dad she would control her anger. She had to make it stop, hide it. She took a deep breath, held it, and let it go, again and again, until the hum faded to nothing. She sighed.

The woman never moved, didn't say anything, as if she knew Kaia needed the space, the time. *What's wrong with me?* This woman had been nothing but kind, if rude, and she was screaming at her.

"I'm sorry." A tear ran down Kaia's face. Hands tied, she could do nothing to stop it.

The sound of the woman's dragging feet came closer. Kaia schooled her expression, focused on her breathing, looked up, and froze. The woman's face was inches away from her own, and she was smiling. Only one side of her mouth curved, the scar warping her grin. Kaia stopped herself from gaping.

"Interesting." The woman tilted her head, then straightened. Kaia watched her shift to her left leg, then squat by the bed.

Had this woman baited her? Tested her to see how she would react? Why? Her left arm tingled as the woman released her from the restraints.

"I don't have a name," she said again as she unlatched a buckle around Kaia's ankle. "I guess hag fits nicely." Her laughter filled the room, then stopped. "But I'm not ugly!"

She sat down on a rock next to Kaia and rested one knee on top of the other. The stone seemed steady on the solid ice floor.

"I don't know what came over me." Kaia rubbed her wrist as she sat up, wrapping the blanket around her.

The woman leaned farther back on her seat and pursed her lips. The wind outside was picking up speed, the sound filling the space between them.

"You need to work on your lying, girl. You know exactly what came over you." The look in the hag's eyes was insanity balancing on a fine tip.

The hair on Kaia's neck rose, her fingers suddenly cold. "I don't know what——"

"That anger in your eyes, in your soul. You need to confront it. Hiding it will only make it consume you, become a part of you." The hag pointed at her scar. "I would know."

"But I'm not..." Kaia tried, grasping for anything to make the hag stop talking. "I'm not lying."

That rage, the murmur that had been within her as long as she could remember—it scared her. Terrified her. It was different from irritation. Then there was the fear and anger that had come over her when Biorki had let go of her hand at the glacier rift. It sat in every part of her body, in every cell.

"You are lying. More to yourself than anyone else, and there's always a price." The hag uncrossed her legs and leaned forward, tilting her head.

Kaia backed away as far as the bed would allow. This woman was terrifying and too perceptive. Every cell in Kaia's body screamed for her to run, to turn away, to pretend that this wasn't happening.

The woman leaned closer, her face near enough for Kaia to feel her breath on her skin. It smelled of salt and decaying meat. "And judging by the look in your eyes, I think your price will be worse than mine. I don't know what caused your hatred, but you need to release it, or you will burn up from the inside."

Kaia's eyes grew wide. Only her dad had ever seen the hatred in her. The hatred that had consumed her as a child. That had become a part of her, pushing her to survive when others had perished because of hunger, illness, or cold. She didn't know where it had come from. It had always been there, a hidden beast fighting against her mental shackles. Even at a young age, Kaia had known not to let it out. She had created a mental wall between herself and that hatred. A mask of indifference. And her dad had helped her.

In time, she had learned to control it. She had enjoyed who she'd become. She had wanted to be carefree, a normal girl. She'd been doing fine until the explosion in the cave.

Kaia lifted her hand to her face. It was cold. Everything had changed in two cycles. Only two. The white blanket was rough against her fingers as she brushed her hand across it. The fire hissed, a tiny flame compared to the inferno within Kaia. Smoke rose into the air and escaped through a small hole in the ceiling. It was light and free, not heavy and stuck like she was.

Kaia would never be free again. She would never be that girl again. Not when she wanted to burn the whole world down, to destroy those who had taken everything from her: Drap and Gin, Solon. They all had to burn. And the one person who knew her well enough to help her, who had been the only stable thing in her life, was dead because of her. Because she hadn't listened.

The hag had taken one look at her and seen. She allowed a sliver of hatred to paint her face. Not enough to trigger whatever else was lurking within her, but enough to show how deep it ran. To show this woman what she was messing with.

Kaia expected the woman to back away. Instead, she met Kaia's gaze. A similar inferno, but calmer, steadier, and deeper, blazed in the hag's iron eyes. They were the same, she and this woman, if only in their hatred and rage.

"Aaaah, there you are." The hag's face twisted into a half grin.

She wasn't the only one. Kaia matched the hag's grin at the thought of two insane women burning together in a house made of ice. She didn't trust the hag but couldn't ignore the promise in her eyes. She knew somehow that if she asked, this woman would help her destroy the world.

CHAPTER 13

After the woman tended to Biorki again, Kaia watched the hag brew something over the fire. Whatever she was cooking smelled strange. Kaia couldn't decide if it was a good smell or an awful one. It didn't matter; she was starving.

The familiar hollow growl consumed her stomach as she inspected the blanket over her. She hadn't realized it until she sat up, but she was naked under it. The thought of the hag undressing her made her shiver. She brushed her hand over the white threads in the direction of the grain—soft and silky. Then she brushed it against the grain; thousands of stiff strands poked her skin. She pulled the blanket closer to her face. The threads connected to the gray…felt? No, it wasn't fabric; it was an animal's hide.

Kaia grimaced. The idea of wearing somebody else's skin made her own skin crawl. Although she was thankful for the warmth it gave her, she wished she had her suit.

She searched the room. It was a small round space, barely tall enough for the hag to stand up in. The stacks of white hides, scratched-up metal boxes, and piles of rusted tools made it seem even smaller. Next to Biorki stood a pair of metal skis and a large fabric pouch. On top of a particularly worn box sat their boots, gloves, and helmets and her ice axes.

"Excuse me, but where are my clothes?"

The woman pointed at the fire. "I burned them." She stirred the pot with another ladle made of a strange dark metal. "Solon put a tracker on them." Noticing Kaia's surprised face, she shrugged. "Don't worry, the magnetic field here makes it hard for them to track anything. But better safe than sorry." She nodded to her right. "You should be able to find something to wear in the chest over there."

"Wait. How do you know about Solon?" Kaia couldn't believe what she was hearing.

"I'll tell you later." The hag waved her hand dismissively. "Now, get dressed."

Kaia blinked. The hag's way of talking, her orders, and her curtness reminded her of her dad. This woman knew more than she was letting on.

"Yes, ma'am!" She stood and moved toward the stack, keeping the blanket tight around her.

The hag coughed at her response but continued to stir the pot without another word.

Kaia dug through the pile of animal skins covering the chest, each a different shade of white. It proved to be an impossible task with one arm, especially while trying to cover herself. She was growing more comfortable around the hag, but not that comfortable.

She uncovered the chest after almost dropping various hides more times than she wanted to admit. Partially hidden, it had looked unremarkable, but now she stared. It was made of a dark metal, like the ladle—a metal she couldn't name. It was beautiful. Kaia brushed her fingers over the top of the square chest. It was cold under her touch. She examined the front. Her fingers met no resistance, no cracks that indicated a lid or a handle to open it with. It was as if it were a plain, expertly polished lump of pure metal.

Kaia turned around. "How do I open it?"

"Chest! Open." The hag's eyes never left the brew.

A hiss escaped the chest, and with a click, the lid opened. Kaia had seen many mechanisms before, but not even the rock door in the hot springs had been this seamless. Where had the hag gotten it? After giving the contents a quick once-over to ensure that this wasn't a trap, she examined the lid and the frame. There were no signs of locks, hinges, or wires to explain the voice recognition. *Incredible.* Although she doubted anything could damage the chest, she was careful while rummaging through the clothes inside.

The clothes were both soft and rigid against her fingers. The fibers were strange and unfamiliar, flexible but strong. Each article of clothing seemed very precisely woven. By what, she couldn't tell. Kaia had seen this type of fabric only once before. One cycle, she had come home and found her dad clutching a white suit with a somber expression. She had never seen it again.

Kaia dropped the torn sweater in her hands and wrinkled her nose. A layer of dirt stained her fingertips. These clothes hadn't been cleaned in a long time.

She looked over her shoulder and observed the woman more closely. The hag held her head high, her back straight. Although much of her body was hidden by the big pelts she wore, she bore herself as her dad did. Had. Was she the person her dad had sent to meet her? If so, why hadn't the hag said anything about it?

Kaia awkwardly pulled on a somewhat matching gray set of underwear, thermal clothes, and socks. They were itchy but fit surprisingly well. She dug deeper into the chest and was about to give up when she saw it: hidden between two brightly colored monosuits riddled with holes was a white suit. Kaia pulled it out of the chest. Dust and dirt flew up around her. It looked exactly like the one her dad had held. No, not quite the same…but similar. This one was made for a woman.

Kaia held it up. It was a little large, but it would do. *Wait, large?* She looked at the woman. She was two heads shorter than Kaia; there was no way the suit fit her. Who had owned it? She turned to ask the woman, but then she heard a rasp of ragged breath from Biorki. She would ask her later. First, she would check on her friend.

She zipped herself into the monosuit. It was tricky with one hand, her right shoulder burning, but after a few hops and grunts, she managed. There was nothing technical about it; it was an older model. Still, the fabric seemed strong. She walked over to Biorki, every step clumsy and strange in the suit. It was like wearing a blanket that hugged her in all the wrong places.

Kaia opened the zipper again and tied the sleeves around her waist. There was no point in overheating by the fire. The thermal clothes were warm enough. She would leave the suit this way until she got accustomed to its weight. She grabbed her boots, slid them on, and crouched beside Biorki.

His chest rose and fell slowly, the fur moving with him. Kaia wiped the sweat off his forehead with her thermal sweater. His skin was cold, and she could see a hint of purple on the tip of his nose: frostbite. Kaia brushed her finger across his chin. The dark stubble tickled her skin. It was strange seeing him so still. The hag must have given him something for the pain. Kaia looked down at his feet, covered by the hide. She swallowed the lump that rose in the back of her throat. This was all her fault. She knelt and rested her forehead on his shoulder. Then, taking a deep breath, she whispered into the hide.

"I'm sorry."

She closed her eyes and breathed in. He smelled of sweat and smoke and...*citrus*. It was mixed with the scent of fur and soot, but it was there. She clenched her hands and lifted her head. She savored the lines of his jaw, the curve of his eyelashes, and the short dark hair on his usually shaved head. She tried to memorize it, like she should have done with her dad.

Kaia watched Biorki's closed eyes as she whispered, "I've known for a while, what you are to me."

She paused, but his eyelids didn't open.

"I knew the cycle we started working together, when you taught me how to use the zip line. I knew all along." Still, she had let him risk his life for her. "But I didn't want to ruin anything, so I pushed those feelings away, ignored them. I shouldn't have leaned on you. I shouldn't have… I used you. I didn't trust myself to…to do what needed to be done." Her hand shook as she wiped the sweat off his neck. "I don't deserve your help. You could have died because of my mistakes." She leaned closer and kissed his cheek. "I won't let that happen again."

A sound filled the room, deep and guttural. It took Kaia a moment to realize it was the hag singing a tune without words. A harsh melody of regret, grief, and triumph. It bore into Kaia. The hag sang of spirits, of her people, and of loss. Kaia closed her eyes. The sounds surrounded her, hugged her, tore at her. A growl filled the hag's voice, and the story changed to one of war and revenge. The hag's rich voice bounced between the walls, piercing Kaia's soul. Something warm ran down her right hand. She opened her eyes and looked down. Four red lines of fresh blood ran across her palm. Her nails had cut into her skin.

When the hag finished the song, Kaia knew what she had to do.

CHAPTER 14

The hag cleared her throat behind Kaia. She turned and saw shock pass over the small woman's face. Her eyes lingered on the white monosuit wrapped around Kaia's waist.

"I didn't know it was in that stupid box." The hag scratched a spot on her forehead. "It suits you. Here."

The hag passed Kaia a dinged-up copper bowl and turned away, but Kaia didn't miss her expression, the tear on the hag's cheek. She had seen that look on her dad's face before: a look of endless pain, something broken, something lost. She stayed quiet.

Kaia moved to a metal box between Biorki and the fire, sat down, and looked at the soup in her hands. White clouds swirled within the otherwise clear liquid. Brown specks floated on the surface. It was not the most appetizing thing, but she was starving. Thankful for the hot liquid, Kaia lifted it to her face and sipped it straight from the bowl. It warmed her mouth, her throat. It tickled her taste buds, proving it wasn't just hot water, but she couldn't quite make herself call it soup either.

The warmth spread through her and soothed some of her lingering aches. Now that she was feeling better, she decided to make her move. The hag sat on a ragged old hide draped over an ice block. She stared into the flames, her mind elsewhere, sipping from her bowl. Kaia slipped onto a seat next to her. She enjoyed the silence and the heat of her soup for a few minutes, then let her eyes wander across the flames to Biorki. She tightened her grip on the bowl.

"Thank you for saving us. For saving Biorki." The words were like glue in her mouth.

The hag grunted and lifted the bowl to her face.

Not expecting more of a response, Kaia got straight to the point. "How do you know Solon?" She looked over her bowl's rim, the steam warming her face.

The woman looked up from her soup, her blue eyes sharp. There was nothing but darkness in them.

"Solon is an abomination. That's how I know them. Filth dressed up as gold specks on a white feather. They put their noses where they don't belong, and when everything worth saving is destroyed, they leave." The hag sat her bowl down so hard that her soup splashed onto the floor. "If Solon is here, we're all doomed. And if they are after you, you run. You *run*, and you don't look back."

No soup or hot drink could melt the cold creeping into Kaia's veins and bones. Although the hag hadn't answered her question, exactly, she had confirmed Kaia's suspicions. Solon was worse than those two guards. A lot worse.

"But why are they after me? I didn't do anything wrong." She picked at her dirty fingernails.

The woman smirked, and then, after another sip, looked up at Kaia. "Did they test your blood?"

"Y-yes." Kaia choked on the word.

"There you go. That is all you need to know." The hag spat on the ground. "They found something within you that they want. They don't need any better reason than that."

"Why are they after my blood?" A knot tightened within Kaia, making it hard for her to breathe.

"I don't know exactly what is in your blood, but they won't stop until they get it." The woman served herself another bowl of soup.

Suddenly the air felt too thin, like it had been sucked from the room. Gasping, Kaia bent over and clutched her stomach. She remembered what Drap and Gin had said.

"If it weren't for that damn protocol, I would kill them all and take their blood by force. It would be so much easier."

"Sure, but we follow the protocol for a reason. We need them to cooperate for the long-term goal. Yes?"

For the long-term goal. Whatever that meant, it spoke of something far worse than what they had already done. Kaia looked down. There was still ash under her fingernails, the soot black against her trembling hands. She thought of the hum that rumbled inside her even now, that rose to meet her when she was angry. Did her anger have anything to do with her blood?

Calm down. Breathe. Get a grip on yourself.

The hag sipped her soup silently as Kaia struggled with her words. *They won't stop until they get it.* Kaia had promised not to let Solon catch her. But that didn't mean she couldn't fight back.

She straightened and braced herself. "Is there anything I can do? To stop them, to help the people in Kaldwell?" The ice in her veins throbbed with every word. *To get my revenge.*

It was a long shot. She had known from the moment she'd seen the liquid tent, the weapon in Drap's hand—Solon's technology was too advanced for them, for her. Even if they could fight back, even if the people of Kaldwell believed her, they had only ice axes and diggers.

The hag's face softened, and she turned the bowl in her hands. "You saw their technology?"

Kaia nodded.

The hag sighed. "What you saw was only what they let you see to make you all think them harmless. If you fought them, Solon wouldn't destroy only you but your town, everyone you know, with a click of a button." The hag smacked her lips, turned, and searched Kaia's face. "What did they do to you?"

Kaia's hope of fighting back disappeared along with the heat in her body. Shivering, she barely managed to choke out the words. "They killed my dad."

Because of me.

"Was your father Lu?" The hag's voice was warm, but the words cut through Kaia. It took everything in her power not to drop her bowl on the floor.

"How did you know?" Kaia had suspected the woman knew more than she let on, but this... "How do you know my dad?"

"If they have him, there is nothing you can do." The words struck Kaia in the gut. "And as for how I know him, well..."

A look of contempt crossed the woman's face. She pulled back her hood, revealing a nest of silver-and-black hair. She scratched a spot on her neck and focused on the far wall.

"Let's just say we didn't see eye to eye. The rest is not for me to say. But if you ask me, he should never have come here. He knew better than to stay in one place too long, especially considering what he did to Solon. He had it coming."

Kaia wanted to punch the hag, but the implications of what she'd just said stopped her. Her dad had known of Solon? He had done something to them? He'd never told her. If he had, Kaia never would have gone to the sick bay. No, she hadn't listened to him, and now he was... Kaia closed her eyes and breathed. What did the hag mean about him coming here?

Then something else clicked into place, pieces of Kaia's childhood. The cycles spent at the hot springs, the way he had taught her to read manuals, the breathing exercises, how he had always refused medical attention. She had thought he'd been teaching her to survive in the caves, but...had it all been for this? In case Solon had found him, them?

The sound of Drap's weapon rang in her head. She resisted the urge to scream and opened her eyes. Her hands shook around the bowl. She willed them to still. It didn't matter. Her dad was dead because of her, and she would never have the chance to ask him.

The hag's eyes were on her, catching every change in Kaia's face. Kaia held out her bowl. The hag grabbed it and moved to fill it with more soup. It wouldn't melt the ice in her heart or cool the anger crawling under her skin, but drinking gave her time to collect herself. The hag was no fool; even as she filled the bowl, she never turned her back to Kaia. *Smart.*

A cough drifted from the other side of the room. Kaia stiffened, and her eyes slid to Biorki. Had he heard them? She watched the hide over his chest rise and fall, his face slack. Guilt burned within her, and she looked away.

The hag cleared her throat beside her, and Kaia accepted the refilled bowl. After she took a few sips in silence, she looked back at the hag. "Why do you say you have no name?" She balanced the bowl on her knee. "My dad always told me that our names are guides, road maps to who we can become."

"Your dad's a fool," the hag scoffed casually, as if she hadn't already destroyed Kaia's view of her father.

Kaia gripped her bowl again and pressed her lips together. *Don't punch her—she saved your lives.*

If the hag saw her reaction, she showed no sign as she continued, "Words can create, but your actions are what make you into who you become. So don't get too caught up in the meanings of things. It can make you go crazy."

On that word, *crazy*, the hag locked eyes with Kaia and didn't look away.

"I decided long ago that seeking the meanings of things is useless, even dangerous. Knowing the meaning of something doesn't mean you're not lost. So I don't have a name. I don't need to know who I might become. I am who I am." The hag lifted her bowl and tilted the rest of its content into her mouth.

This woman was the crazy one. Kaia took another sip of the bland soup. "I think I understand, but—"

"No, you don't," the hag cut her off, placing her bowl in her lap.

Kaia looked at her hand, at the four little red arcs carved into her palm. She traced the bowl's rim with her finger. *Patience.*

"Where are we?" Kaia tried again.

The hag stared at Kaia, then seemed to decide against something and dropped her gaze. She grabbed a dirty-looking rag and wiped down her bowl. "Wouldn't you rather know how to escape Solon?" The hag wiped her mouth with the rag. "Where we are is of no importance. You need to run. Get off this planet. You can't hide from Solon for long out here. Actually, there are very few places left, even in space, where they won't find you."

Kaia clenched her jaw. The hag made a point of not answering her questions. Then the words sank in. *Space?* She had listened to stories and fairy tales about people falling from the sky, the settlers that the people of her town were allegedly descended from. But no one believed those—she hadn't believed them either. They were just children's stories, after all.

"I can help you get to Framnes. I know of someone there who can help you, if he is willing," the hag continued.

Had the hag really said she could *go to space?*

"Solon is from space?" she asked. How big must the company be if it was hard for people to hide from them there?

"Yes. You're not paying attention." The hag held out the rag to Kaia, who took it without thinking.

"How do you know all this?" Kaia watched the hag place her bowl beside the firepit. It didn't make any sense. Why would a woman surviving on the surface know anything about her, her dad, Solon? Kaia glared at the bowl in her hand and wiped its interior with the rag in slow circular motions. If anyone else had told her these things, she wouldn't have believed them. But she did believe this woman. This hag. The most annoying person she had ever met. Maybe she was crazy for believing. No, she *was* crazy. But if her dad had kept secrets from her, anything was possible.

"We're not here to talk about me." The hag sighed and took the bowl from Kaia's hands. "Anyway, that is not a story for me to tell. There's only one way you will survive this. You need to get to Framnes, and you will have to do as I say."

Kaia knew she would do anything this crazy woman told her if it meant getting away, if it meant she would get more answers. But—

"All right. Can I go to Framnes this cycle?"

She would go alone. She would leave Biorki here before he woke up so he could not argue. There was a chance that Solon wouldn't recognize him. They hadn't seen his face; he had worn his helmet in the sick bay. She knew it was a risk. But his chances were better in Kaldwell than they were with her, especially given her anger. Biorki would have no way out of this if he was seen with her again. They would hunt him too. She was sure of it.

Kaia watched him from across the fire. She had to leave him, but she didn't have the strength to tell him to his face.

The hag's eyes moved to where Biorki slept and nodded. "Yes." She pulled on her hood. "But we don't have much time before the sun sets."

Kaia shouldn't have been surprised to see how agile the hag was as she crawled through a small opening in the wall. She looked over at Biorki and whispered. "I'm sorry."

Then she pulled on the white suit, grabbed her axes, gloves, and helmet, and followed the woman through the hole.

CHAPTER 15

The wind welcomed her outside with a soft kiss that froze her cheeks and ruffled her curls. Kaia found herself standing between two mountains, though she wasn't sure mountain was a grand enough word to describe the two snow-covered shapes. They rose into the sky, touching the clouds above and providing shelter from the storms raging on the flats beyond.

The mountain to her right looked like the back of a monster. Sharp and with multiple points, it threw long dark shadows across the valley. Lines of light danced across the compact snow on the ground between two igloos, a sort of courtyard. The rounded buildings were dug into the ice below, expertly built to withstand the wild weather. Their tops were more like lids than roofs. The second igloo, across the snowy courtyard, was simpler but larger than the first. It had no pipe to let out smoke, so Kaia suspected it was some sort of storage.

She ran her fingers through the mist escaping from between her cracked lips. It disappeared as fast as it appeared. In the push and pull between heat and cold, heat always lost. Kaia pulled her helmet on and searched the courtyard. It took her a minute to locate the hag. The woman blended in with the valley, her white hides perfect camouflage. She stood by a mound of snow next to the bigger igloo.

The snow crackled beneath Kaia's boots as she crossed the yard. Her guilt grew with every step as she moved farther from Biorki. But she couldn't lean on him anymore, couldn't put him in danger because of her own fear, her own uselessness. She swallowed hard and took another step.

A deep rumble filled the air as she approached the mound. Kaia stopped and rested her hands on the ice axes on her hips. Every hair on her body stood on end. She looked around— nothing but wind and snow. But her body screamed at her to run. *Run!*

Another rumble filled the air. It vibrated through the ground, through her legs. Kaia ran forward to warn the hag. Then the mound shook. Snow cascaded down around her feet. Kaia jumped back, bent her knees, and prepared to…to do what? She didn't know, but the axes were in her hands, her right arm stiff as she tightened her grip.

The mound moved again. This time, it grew taller, blocking the hag from view. When she thought it couldn't possibly get any bigger, two enormous pointed ears popped out from beneath the snow. Kaia took another step back, broadening her stance. *Oh shit.*

Whatever it was lifted its head and shook it. White filled Kaia's vision. She swiped the snow off her visor and froze. Two large, intelligent, dark brown eyes stared down at her. Black lines ran across its eyelids, under its eyes, and across its massive snout. Kaia didn't dare move or breathe. A set of large white fangs curved from the creature's mouth, easily as long as one of Kaia's arms. She tightened her grip on her axes, trying not to imagine what those fangs could do.

She realized why she hadn't seen the creature before it was upon them. It was covered in the same white fur as the hag, as the blankets she had worn earlier. It blended so seamlessly with the snow that she couldn't determine where the creature ended and the snow began. It didn't matter anyway; from what she could see, it was massive, its head almost as wide as Kaia was tall.

Kaia's axes were toothpicks compared to those fangs. Still, she didn't back away. There was something in those eyes: a demand for respect, a promise. If Kaia showed weakness, it would be the last thing she would do. So she didn't blink, didn't move. Didn't dare try to find out if the hag was near, buried under the beast or the snow.

The creature bared its sharp teeth and growled. The noise hit Kaia like a wall. The beast lunged forward. It took everything she had not to run, blink, or flinch as she was slammed into the ground. The creature hunched over her, its eyes peering into her own, the tip of its fangs a few centimeters from her thighs, and its massive paws on either side of her body. Kaia swallowed. Her tongue stuck to the top of her dry mouth. She kept her eyes open. She would not back down, not this time.

Kaia's eyes stung. The creature looked back at her, its breath pushing against her suit. It tilted its head. One of its fangs brushed against her hip. She clenched her jaw. She couldn't blink, wouldn't. Somehow, she knew that if she blinked, the creature would take it as a sign of weakness, and it would be over. Her eyes burned. It was only a matter of time before she lost this staring contest. She had to do something fast.

Only one thing came to mind. It was crazy, but if she had learned anything in the last few days, it was that she was insane. She breathed in, then dropped the axe in her left hand. It fell to the ground, thudding softly into the snow. The creature didn't blink, didn't react. Good. Kaia tightened the grip on her other axe and reached up with her empty hand. Slow and steady. She pushed up onto her right elbow. Pushing through the instant pain in her shoulder, she placed her left palm on the creature's face. Not once breaking eye contact, she stroked the ridge of its snout. It blinked, lowered its head, and pushed its snout into her hand.

Kaia sagged and let go of the breath she was holding. After a moment, the creature sat back on its enormous hind legs. She followed, not relinquishing contact. She stood with its head still in her left hand, her axe in her right. Now what?

"Right, let's get on with it, then." The hag peeked out from behind the creature with a giant grin. "Fluff seems to like you."

Kaia had entirely forgotten the hag was there.

"Fluff?" She looked up at the creature's saber teeth. "That's its name?"

"Well, he is fluffy, isn't he?"

Kaia looked Fluff up and down. He was definitely fluffy. She watched him purr with his eyes closed. It made him seem sweeter, even cute, but the large fangs gleaming in the light told another story.

The hag patted Fluff on the cheek. "Enough cuddling, Fluff. Get your sled."

Fluff grunted in protest. The hag stared at him. With a flick of his ear and a snort, he rose to his feet. Kaia watched dumbfounded as he trotted over to the larger igloo.

"Hey! Focus. He is only a smylon. A small one, at that." The hag slapped her gloved hands together. "We have stuff to do. Or do you want to stay here until the next cycle?"

The woman's voice snapped her out of her trance. A smylon? *Small?* How big would a large smylon be? She had never heard of such a creature, or of *anything* that could survive up here on the surface. She had been told it was barren. Another lie.

Kaia glanced at the smaller igloo. No, she would not wait here until the next cycle.

"What would have happened if I had run away?" she asked.

The hag followed Fluff, who had disappeared behind the igloo. His tail was still visible as it flicked from side to side. Kaia stood, frozen to the ground, the adrenaline still loud in her ears as the hag yelled over her shoulder, "You would be lunch!"

A drop of cold sweat slithered down Kaia's spine. So she had been right. Fluff was a predator. Sighing, she put her axes back in their holsters, brushed off her suit, and followed the hag.

This was becoming a theme. She was the prey in a world of predators.

When Kaia reached the courtyard's center, she found Fluff sitting there, a leather strap hanging from his mouth. At the end of the strap stood a strange contraption. His eyes shone, and his tail waved from side to side. Excitement?

"Here." The hag appeared from thin air and dropped a pile of thick leather bands into Kaia's hands. "Put this on."

The bands were thicker than her forearm. Put them on *what*? Fluff stretched out his front paws as if on cue, curved his back, and flopped onto the ground. He lowered his head toward her. Of course they were for him.

"He's my ride?" Kaia blurted out. She had never heard of an animal being used as a form of transport. That was what trains and zip lines were for.

"What did you think you would travel in? An air balloon?" The hag's eyebrows rose past the visor of her helmet. "And before you say you can take the train, there is no way you would be able to sneak past Solon. A sled is much safer anyway."

The hag walked toward the smaller igloo. Kaia closed her mouth. The hag was right. There was no way she could go back underground.

Kaia called after the hag, "What's an air balloon?" But she had already disappeared, leaving Kaia alone with Fluff.

Not sure what to do, Kaia tried to carry the straps over to Fluff, but her right arm caved under the weight, and they flopped to the ground. Inspecting the pile of bands, she recognized the configuration of straps and metal. A harness? It looked like what she used as a scavenger, but it was older, not automatic. She looked up at Fluff, who still lay on the ground, his eyes trained on her. It was a harness—a harness for a giant predator—and the hag expected her to put it on him.

Kaia looked back at the igloo. The hag was nowhere in sight. Swearing, Kaia dragged the harness over to Fluff. It weighed a ton. She made it to the strange contraption beside him—a sled, the hag had called it. It was a capsule balanced on two metal rods. Inside was a seat covered with white hides.

Kaia didn't know what a sled should look like, but the thing in front of her seemed like it would fall apart if she stared at it the wrong way.

A low rumble filled the air, and something black was suddenly centimeters from Kaia's face. The warm air from Fluff's nose fogged up her visor. Kaia stepped back, unsure if the creature might change his mind and have her for lunch after all. Fluff lowered his face farther, his eyes now level with her head. He was trying to communicate something.

"What do you want?" Kaia's voice was low in the wind.

She felt stupid talking to an animal. Fluff blinked. He bent his neck and nudged the leather straps on the ground toward her.

"You want me to put it on you?"

Fluff nudged the harness again and leveled his eyes with her head. That was a definitive yes. Either that or she was imagining things and was about to do something really foolish.

Kaia looked around; the hag could at least show her how to attach the harness, but the woman was nowhere to be seen. A gust of wind hurled snow across the courtyard. Sighing, Kaia crouched down and inspected the harness again. It couldn't be that hard…she hoped. Fluff whipped his tail through the air, the sound loud and sharp in her ear.

Fluff's eyes never left her as she moved around him to attach the different buckles. It wasn't too hard to figure out where everything should go: four loops of leather for his legs, one for his neck, and one for his tail. Attaching it turned out to be a lot harder. Her shoulder throbbed as she systematically pulled the heavy bands across Fluff's back, shoulders, and legs. She struggled with the rusted buckles. Clipping them on while trying to avoid any sudden movements turned out to be impossible. But she made sure to remain in Fluff's sight at all times.

After connecting most of the straps, Kaia stood back. The harness looked decent, but there was still one strap left, one buckle. It had to be connected behind Fluff's front legs, across his chest, out of his sight. Meeting his eyes, she moved slowly.

Marveling at his size, she crouched under him. Fluff's heat and smell, the scent of dirt mixed with humid leather, enveloped her.

Wondering what a creature this size ate in this barren world, she snapped the final buckle shut. A howl pierced her ears, and something struck the left side of her body. The force threw her across the courtyard. She was going to die.

CHAPTER 16

Lying in a pile of snow, Kaia brushed off her white suit and looked up. Fluff was franticly licking part of his chest. The last buckle hung around his neck, the leather swinging around his ears. She must have pinched some of his fur. She looked down at herself. Nothing was broken. She rolled her shoulder. It was sore, but not any worse than earlier, and she breathed a sigh of relief. She followed a snowflake with her eyes. She wanted to fly like that, not be thrown across a courtyard by a fluffy monster.

Fluff shook his head and turned. Kaia tracked him with her eyes as he walked toward her, his breath forming a cloud of mist around his face. Was he mad at her? But something in his eyes and slow movements made her sit still. He lowered his head so his eyes met hers, opened his mouth, and licked her helmet. A line of spit ran down her visor. Kaia grimaced but relaxed.

"No, I'm sorry, Fluff. I should have been more careful with the buckle." She rubbed his nose, and a smile snuck onto her face. It felt stiff but right. She stood and brushed snow off her suit. "Let's get the last buckle on."

Kaia clipped it, careful of his fur this time, and attached the harness to the sled. She stepped back to assess her work. The harness ran across Fluff's back and looped around his limbs in a swirling pattern that matched the black lines around his eyes. The bands were thicker around his neck and chest, resembling armor. He was a damn terrifying fluffy warrior.

The hag appeared from nowhere carrying two large saddlebags. She threw them over Fluff as if they were nothing but thin blankets. Fluff let out a growl.

"Oh, hush, you're such a wimp." The hag clipped the bags to the harness. "And jumping back from a tiny pinch to your fur—*tsk-tsk.*" Kaia met the hag's eyes, and the hag winked at her. "Yes, I saw that. Such a rookie mistake."

Kaia was about to comment that the hag had left her without directions or help when Fluff snorted and shook his ears, sending a pile of snow onto the hag.

"For sky's sake," she cursed, brushing the snow off her hood. "I thought he had taught you manners."

If Kaia hadn't known better, she would have sworn a look of indignation crossed Fluff's face. He nudged the hag with his nose, pushing her to the ground. She cursed again, grabbed a bunch of snow between her hands, and threw the snowball at Fluff. It hit him square in the face. Fluff stared in shock. The hag shot Kaia a *don't you dare laugh* look as she got back to her feet. Kaia pretended to cough and looked away.

The hag crossed her arms at Fluff. "You get one new friend and you forget your old ones, huh?"

Fluff's ears twitched. The hag mumbled something under her breath and moved to inspect his harness. Kaia caught a glimpse of a smile on the hag's face before she turned her back.

After inspecting every buckle and band, the hag turned to Kaia. She grunted something about it not being entirely awful and walked back into the igloo. When she returned, she was carrying Kaia's backpack. A stab of guilt slashed through Kaia at the sight. She had forgotten all about it…or maybe she had tried to ignore it. Because even though it was the last thing she had from her dad, it was also a reminder of what she had done.

"Here—I refilled your thermos and put some food in there for the trip." The hag handed over the bag.

"Thank you."

The hag winked at her again and scratched Fluff behind the ear. "He is ready to go. Are you?" The woman held her gaze, and Kaia could see the offer in them: *It's not too late to change your mind.*

Squeezing the bag, Kaia thought about what she would miss: iceboarding, cuddling by the fire, zip-lining, Ingá's reprimands. She would miss Ine and Kjartan, and even Ulla. Well, no, she wouldn't miss her, but she *would* miss Kaldwell. The safety of the caves, the miners, the familiarity of every nook and cranny. And Biorki—she would miss Biorki more than she allowed herself to think about. But there was no going home. Solon had made sure of that, and Kaia couldn't—wouldn't—risk losing any more of the people she cared about. She had to do this alone.

She gave her dad's backpack another squeeze. It was the only thing she had left now. She looked up at the hag, who was waiting for an answer.

"I think so. But do I need a map? Or do you have some tracking device I could follow?"

The hag smiled her crooked smile. "A map wouldn't do you any good, and no compass or tracking device will work in these mountains. That's why I have Fluff." The hag rubbed him behind the ear. "He knows the way."

Remembering how the landscape had changed before her eyes, Kaia nodded. She looked up at the huge creature. "I'm putting my trust in you, Fluff."

Fluff wiggled his ears and tapped one of his back paws.

The hag patted him on his side. "It's been a while since you have seen your trainer, huh?"

He stamped his back paw again, kicking snow into the air, and growled. The sound made Kaia's hair stand up. She found him more friendly now, but he was still a wild animal. She looked at him, a ball of tension, ready to pounce. She hoped the hag knew what she was doing.

"Well, get to it, then." The hag chuckled and turned to Kaia, gesturing to the old sled. "Climb in."

Kaia took a deep breath. This was it. She grabbed her bag and moved toward the sled.

"Oh, before I forget…" The hag pulled a small round box from her pocket. "Take your helmet off."

Confused, Kaia did as the hag said, and the cold air bit her bare skin. The hag took off her gloves and opened the box. Inside was something black.

"You are too tall." The hag waved her hand.

Kaia bent down. The hag dipped two fingers in the black substance and dragged her fingers across Kaia's brow, under her eyes, and along the ridge of her nose. Seeing the question in Kaia's eyes, the hag smiled.

"Fluff has it by design." The hag pointed to the dark stripes around his eyes. "Us humans, we have to learn from nature to survive. It's to reduce the glare of the sun so you don't go blind." The hag grabbed Kaia's helmet and helped her put it back on. "Relying too much on technology can be the difference between life and death. Remember that."

The warmth in the woman's eyes as she lowered the helmet over Kaia's head surprised her. Kaia reached out on instinct and grabbed the woman's hand.

"Thank you."

The hag froze, then pulled away.

"Don't thank me. The faster you leave, the sooner I will be safe from Solon." The hag choked on her words. "Get in the darn sled."

Kaia understood. This wasn't the time to grow attached. More important things were at stake. She nodded, blinking away the moisture in her eyes, and climbed into the sled.

It felt like a tiny hollowed-out room. The seat was close to the ground and covered in fur. Sitting down, she wrapped herself in the hides, trying not to think about which friend of Fluff's she had around her shoulders. There was a leather string at the front of the sled. When she pulled it, a leather cover folded over her, leaving a small gap for her to see through. It was like sitting inside a large backpack.

She would be warm, but she felt small, insignificant, like a package. In a way, that was precisely what she was: a parcel traveling to a place she had never been, delivered by a giant beast she had just met, sent by a woman she didn't know. But it was better than taking her chances with Solon, she hoped. Hope was all she could rely on, and the word of a hag.

"Ready?" The severe expression returned to the hag's face.

"I think so." Kaia checked the bag between her feet and looked toward the igloo. "Can you please tell Biorki I'm sorry? That I'm, that I'm…" She couldn't finish.

The hag grunted, nodded, and looked into the distance, beyond the mountains.

"When you get to Framnes, you will meet Fluff's trainer. He can help you. Tell him the hag sent you. I guess that name is as good as any. He will know who you mean."

The idea of somebody meeting her at Framnes made her feel better. But then she remembered the rest of their previous conversation.

"How do I find the man who can get me to space?" The word *space* felt strange on her tongue.

The hag didn't seem to hear her. She shouted, "On it, big boy! Go to Framnes!"

Kaia knocked her head against the back of the sled as Fluff sprang forward.

Behind her, the hag yelled, "Good luck! It won't be a comfy ride. Alexi! His name is Alexi!"

CHAPTER 17

Fluff moved across the deep snow at an incredible speed. His large back paws propelled them over the rugged landscape with ease, his front paws always elegantly adjusting for the next leap. White flecks hammered Kaia's visor through the slit in the sled's cover.

The sled jerked with every leap, throwing her around inside. She felt—and probably looked—like Ulla's rag doll. She tried to protect her shoulder, tensing against every toss and bounce, her muscles complaining with each impact. When the sun dipped below the horizon, she fought to stay conscious. The constant assault on her body had drained the strength she had regained.

She didn't know when she dozed off, but it didn't last long. She woke to her right shoulder slamming into the side of the sled. She screamed from the sudden burning pain, from the throbbing in her body, from exhaustion. It had caught her off guard, and she felt tears stream down her cheeks. It was just her and Fluff against this awful cold world, and she couldn't hold it back anymore.

Kaia let her tears fall for the fear, the loss, the anger, and the pain—everything she had tried to hold back so Biorki wouldn't know how scared she had been, so the hag wouldn't see her weakness. But here on the tundra, the snow, the sky, and Fluff were her only witnesses. It all pooled to the surface, and she howled with every ragged breath, screamed and cried.

Her screams didn't echo. Instead, they disappeared into the storm around them, fading into nothing. If Fluff heard her howls, he ignored them. And maybe he understood, because he kept leaping toward Framnes while she continued to scream into the barren cold world.

By the time she couldn't scream anymore and her eyes had no more tears to shed, they had left the storm behind, and darkness consumed them.

Kaia stared, her eyes burning, as lights of different sizes painted the sky. Stars. They were beautiful. She rubbed her eyes. It was nothing like the ceiling of her hut. The stars varied in size and color, but most were white. There were thousands of them—no, millions. It was a glimpse into space. A place full of planets, other worlds, and Solon. Her only escape.

A flash of light flared across the sky. Kaia blinked, thinking she was hallucinating in her exhaustion. But no—it appeared again, an assault on the darkness. First one, then two, then multiple streaks of different colors danced across the sky like ribbons. The mountains glowed every time a band flared. Like flames carried by the wind, they burned away some of Kaia's resentment toward the world.

Then, in the blink of an eye, they disappeared, leaving Kaia to soak in the dark once again, to wonder if it had all been a dream. She pulled the furs tighter around her. She had to sleep, or she would go insane.

Kaia slept very little that cycle. The next morning, another storm raged, tore at the world, and changed the landscape again. She fell in and out of sleep as Fluff ran on, undeterred by the violent weather.

When a mountain loomed in front of them, Fluff pulled her into its shadow. Ravines and sharp edges marked the dark peak, a ragged tooth piercing the glaciers. It was a monstrosity against the otherwise flat landscape. And it seemed they were headed right toward it, moving faster and faster.

Kaia watched as a tiny light appeared before them. It blinked at the base of the mountain—a beacon. Fluff lunged forward, jumping over a ravine. Kaia had thought the first part of the trip had been horrible, but now she clung on for dear life as the sled bounced left and right with Fluff's every leap. At some points, she could have sworn she was upside down.

The mountain was no longer a ragged shape but a wall of darkness. It swallowed them. Fluff charged forward, following the blinking light. It led them through a ravine and between two huge boulders. Another leap, and the opening of a cave appeared before them, half hidden by a giant rock. Kaia would never have seen it if they hadn't been right in front of it—a perfect hiding spot.

The light disappeared, and everything went black. She felt more then saw Fluff slowing to a comfortable trot. Then he stopped.

An unfamiliar voice slithered through the dark. "Fluff, buddy, is that you?"

Kaia stiffened. She couldn't pinpoint where the voice came from. Her eyes were still adjusting to the dark. She opened the flap in one fluid motion, arranged her feet beneath her so she could jump up if necessary, grabbed her axe with her bad hand and her bag with the other. She searched the area but saw only more shadows and dark shapes.

Kaia ignored her aching joints and glanced between the different shades of black. Then Fluff began to purr, sending vibrations through the sled. Kaia watched as one of the shadows moved. Thin and tall, it moved with inhuman reflexes, jumping from one of the boulders.

"Hush, hush. I'm happy to see you too, but you know the rules." The voice was deep and sharp.

Fluff sat down and scratched his ear with his back paw, making the saddlebags on his back flap around.

The light flickered back into existence, and the speaker leaned past Fluff. "Ahh, you brought some stuff?"

Kaia saw a man swinging a lantern in his hand. Lines of white rippled across the snow-covered boulders behind him. So that's what he had led them in with. The man scratched one of Fluff's ears. "Good boy."

Fluff grunted happily and dropped to his belly. Now that he was lying down, Kaia saw more of the man. He was built like a drainage pipe, covered top to toe in a green monosuit. His helmet, the same shape as her own, was also green with a blacked-out visor. Judging by Fluff's reaction, this was his trainer or someone he knew well.

The man tilted his head in her direction. Not sure if he had seen her, Kaia let go of her bag and awkwardly stuck a hand through the opening of the sled.

"Hi."

The man's body jerked in surprise. So he hadn't seen her. Seemingly playing it off, he shifted his stance, placed one hand on his hip, and continued to scratch Fluff. Ignoring Kaia, he said, "Ahhh, so more than a delivery. Must have been a heavy load for you."

Kaia swore under her breath but stayed quiet as she untangled herself from the sled, her muscles complaining. Her joints cracked as she stood and stretched her legs. Her insides twisted as the solid ground moved beneath her. She felt like a punching bag.

When the ground stopped moving, Kaia grabbed her backpack from the sled. She sheathed her axes and approached the man. He was unbuckling the saddlebags while Fluff hummed, his tail flicking.

"Excuse me,"

The man lifted the bags from Fluff's back, still ignoring her. He grunted as the weight of them fell onto his shoulders.

"That woman never learns," he grumbled, carrying the bags to the cave opening.

When he returned, Kaia walked over to meet him.

"Excuse me," she tried again.

The man walked right past her and moved to unbuckle Fluff's harness. What was it about these people? Did living on the surface make you unreasonable? She walked around him and stood between him and Fluff, crossed her arms, and stared at him. "The hag sent me."

The man snorted. "That woman needs to start minding her own business. She lives like a hermit and still manages to mess up my life."

So Kaia wasn't the only one who found the hag disagreeable.

Kaia stroked Fluff behind the ear. "I'm so sorry for showing up here, but I need your help."

She didn't believe the man deserved her apology, but she knew one attracted more people with sweets than rocks. At least, that was what Ingá had told her once when Kaia had been in a particularly foul mood.

"I need to find—"

"Stop! Stop right there!"

Kaia flinched as the man's words whipped through the air, echoing off the mountain.

The man closed the distance between them. Looking around, he lowered his voice. "Not here."

He walked around her and reached up to Fluff's nose; the creature purred under his touch. "I will listen to what you have to say. But not here." The man's dark visor revealed nothing about his expression. "And don't expect me to help you."

Kaia swallowed hard, biting back a curse. *Don't be stupid*, she told herself. Anything was better than being left alone on the surface.

She moved to unclip the buckle at Fluff's shoulder joint. "I understand. Thank you."

"Don't thank me. Thank Fluff. I couldn't care less about your problems." He scratched the beast under the chin and unclipped the last buckle on the harness. "But it seems Fluff has taken a liking to you, so I will give you one chance to explain yourself."

The man pulled the harness off in one quick motion and dropped it into Kaia's hands. Then he turned to Fluff. "You know the drill. Rest up, and then go back to the hag."

Fluff purred, then dipped his head and moved to a pile of snow.

When Fluff had dug a snowy bed, Kaia followed the man into the mountain. She dragged the sled behind her, the harness inside. It was heavy, but she hadn't argued when the man had told her to bring it. She was glad to do something; it kept her mind from roaming through every worst-case scenario she could come up with. Following a stranger into the depths of an unknown mountain was not on her list of smart decisions.

CHAPTER 18

Their steps echoed through the tunnel as the man disappeared around another bend. Kaia tried to keep track of the turns, but after ten lefts, two rights, and another left, she gave up. Instead she adjusted her grip on the sled, her right hand now hovering over her axe.

She followed the man around the bend and jumped back; she had almost crashed into him. Standing still, he looked up at the tunnel wall. She took a few steps back and watched as he knocked on a rock. A hiss followed, and a piece of the tunnel slid aside, revealing a small entrance and another forked tunnel.

"Where are we going?" Kaia was suddenly aware that a door could be more than an entrance; it could trap her in.

The man didn't turn, his voice deep. "Somewhere safe."

He walked through the door. She hesitated.

"Come in," he urged.

Kaia looked over her shoulder. She thought she could find her way back to Fluff. But even if she managed to navigate the labyrinth of tunnels, what would she do then? Watch the snow fall? She swallowed, adjusted her hold on the leather rope that attached to the sled, and took a deep breath. She had already made the decision to go down this path when she had asked the hag for help. When she had left Biorki behind.

Feeling like a fool, she walked through the door. It slammed shut behind her and the sled. There was no turning back now. She tightened her grip on the rope. Turning back had never really been an option. Not since she had watched the life disappear from her dad's eyes. Not since she had promised him she wouldn't let Solon catch her.

"Leave the sled here." The man's order was nonchalant as he walked into the left tunnel.

She did as she was told. Leaving the harness and sled inside the entrance, she followed the man. He led her through another maze consisting of small pathways and weird rooms. Some were filled with boxes and strange-looking items. If anyone ever asked her what she had seen in those rooms, she wouldn't be able to tell them.

The man kept moving without a word or a backward glance. Her doubts grew with every step, every turn. Just because the hag had told her that Fluff would take her to Framnes didn't mean he had. For all she knew, she had been sent to a secret hideaway for thieves and smugglers. Judging by the contents of the rooms they were passing, it wasn't out of the question. She unclipped the axe on her left hip and rested her hand on its hilt. One axe should be enough to handle this man and get away, even if she had no idea where to go.

The man jumped over a crate with grace. Kaia should have noticed earlier; this man had the agility of someone trained in combat. Kaia didn't know much about combat training. Her dad had taught her only a little. But there was no mistaking the man's movements—the turn of his feet as he balanced on tiptoe, the bend of his knees as he landed on the other side of the box. She opened the clip on her right axe. It didn't hurt to be extra careful.

Just as she was contemplating hitting him over the head and fleeing, the man opened another sliding door. Unfamiliar sounds flowed through the opening. She stopped. It took her a few seconds before she recognized them—*voices*. It was impossible to tell how many. The sounds were warped as if muffled by cloth. Was that the noise of children laughing? Or was someone screaming? She couldn't tell.

The man walked through, leaving Kaia little time to think. She stepped through the door before it slammed shut.

They turned, and Kaia skidded to a stop, barely avoiding crashing into a man carrying a bag of copper dust. The man grunted something at her before disappearing into the crowd.

A crowd?

A wave of people clad in green and brown flowed between dark buildings towering around them. Kaia's eyes widened, and she pulled her bag tighter across her chest. She and the man were standing on a street lined by square buildings of different sizes. Dark green, the buildings reminded her of the sick bay in Kaldwell. However, they were coarser, not entirely square or symmetrical. Kaia dragged her finger across the nearest one. The cuts in the metal were unmistakable; these houses had been carved from the mountain.

Kaia looked up and sucked in a breath. Plateaus upon plateaus were stacked overhead, dug into the cave, each holding a row of carved buildings. The dark rock of the mountain gleamed in the green lights from the streets. Some plateaus were so high that Kaia wondered why there were no zip lines. Then she saw the towers of metal. Like pillars, they rose above the buildings and between the plateaus: elevators. She watched a box rise into the air, stopping at the third plateau.

She didn't loosen her grip on her bag, but the corner of her lip twisted in recognition as she watched this feat of engineering she had only read about, had only dreamed of seeing. She had made it. She was standing on the streets of Framnes. She stepped forward and was immediately pushed to the side by an elderly woman.

"Watch it."

Kaia stepped back and pulled her elbows tighter against her sides. She had never seen so many people in one place before. Where should she go? She couldn't see between all the pedestrians, couldn't tell which path to take. She heard someone clear their throat behind her. Then an arm grabbed hers and pulled her into the crowd. When she recognized the dark visor of the man who had led her there, she barely stopped herself from digging her axes into his flesh. He pulled her along for a minute before she tore herself from his grip.

"Let me go."

The man lifted his hands in front of him. "All right. But don't cry when you lose me in the crowd."

Kaia opened her mouth to tell him where to stick it, but before she could respond, the man began to push through the hordes of people. She lifted her hand in a rude gesture at his back and sheathed her axe. She didn't like it, but she needed his help. Losing him here wasn't an option. She knew no one in Framnes. If she asked the wrong person for assistance, they might turn her in to Solon. She lowered her face, wishing she had a hood, and followed him.

People and buildings blurred together as she walked. The man slid effortlessly through the crowd like oil in water. His height was the only thing that distinguished him from the other green-suited people. The street was muddy and wet under Kaia's boots, and she struggled to keep up. She slipped and bumped into a man with black hair and a burn across his face. Her shoulder throbbed at the impact.

"Sorry."

The black-haired man gave her a death stare before disappearing into the crowd.

Kaia looked up and swore. The tall figure had disappeared. She charged forward, ignoring the pain in her shoulder, ignoring her sore muscles as she slid in the mud.

It became harder and harder to breathe as panic rose in her chest. She pushed farther into the wave of people. She couldn't see him. How had she lost him on a straight street? Someone knocked her backward, but she caught herself and hurried on. These people moved as if the world was about to end. And maybe it was. Every expression she saw was grim and sour, a permanent scowl on every face. It seemed that moving through these streets had that effect on people; she felt her face twist into a scowl as well, her mouth pressing into a tighter line with every step. Her brows lowered and tightened every time she bumped into someone. Her breath grew faster with every slip in the mud. No one met her eyes as she ducked and twisted around them.

When she reached the street corner, the smell of sewer and rot reached her nose. She could taste it on her tongue even through her helmet's filter. She cringed. She had smelled it before in the poorest areas of Kaldwell, but this…this spoke of clear negligence, and no one seemed to care.

A message popped up on her visor. *Be aware of dangerous chemicals in the air. Decontamination filter activated.* How were these people walking around as if nothing dangerous was flowing into their lungs? Most of them weren't even wearing helmets.

They weren't wearing helmets.

Kaia stopped in the middle of the street when she realized why. There was no ice, no frosted windows, nothing to slide on except the cursed mud. It was cold but not freezing, so there was no reason to wear a helmet except for the awful smell of waste. Some people still did, though, and although a few looked curiously at Kaia's white monosuit as she passed, their eyes didn't linger.

She should have known, but it still shocked her when she looked up and saw the massive vents in the cave ceiling. She had read about them in one of her dad's textbooks. They circulated the air and heated it. But to see them in person… The article hadn't done them justice.

"Don't just stand there, move!" She didn't see the arms that grabbed her shoulders and threw her out of the road.

Kaia slammed into the door of one of the rusted houses. She groaned and pushed herself upright. She whirled to see who had grabbed her, only to find a blur of people flying past. There were no faces lit up with satisfaction, guilt, or anger, nothing to suggest who had pushed her. She cursed. This wasn't working.

Looking around, she found a little ledge on the side of the street. She scaled it and perched on top of a wall, where she had a better view of the street. Now that she had room to breathe, she saw the tents that lined the buildings: shops. Dirty and falling apart, they were stacked with strange and unfamiliar objects. She recognized some of the items. Dried meat and rows of discontinued drink capsules sat on one table. On another, she saw old helmets and boots. Then her eyes landed upon a table three houses down: weapons. Knives, laser cutters, fist-size e-bombs, hacker software, and…was that a magnetic throwing knife? A set like that had to cost a fortune.

Her stomach dropped. That knife was illegal. All weapons had been outlawed for as long as she could remember. Only objects required for survival, like her axes, were allowed in the caves. She understood now why everyone moved so quickly through these streets. Ingá had mentioned a place like this once before on a night when she'd had too much to drink, a place of illegal trades and discontinued tools. Kaia was in the black market of Framnes. And she needed to get away, now.

She finally saw the man she was looking for—the green suit and blacked-out helmet—at the end of the street, turning behind a particularly tilted two-story green building. She dropped back down to the street and ran.

Not caring if she bumped into people, she made it to the crooked building in ten long leaps. With sweat running down her forehead, she turned the corner. She found the man waving at her from the entrance to another two-story green building. Her chest tightened. Not giving herself time to consider what may await her, she followed the man inside.

CHAPTER 19

The house engulfed her in darkness as the door shut behind her. Unsure what to do, she waited at the entrance. Noises drifted from the other room: objects knocking into other objects, a crash, a grunt, feet moving across the floor.

The man shouted at her. "What are you doing? Come in!"

Rolling her eyes, she removed her helmet and walked farther inside. Boxes and bags were scattered in every room she passed. Piles lined the walls, some nearly touching the brown ceiling. She walked down what vaguely resembled a hallway. Knocking over a box, she held her breath as a stack of crates swayed above her. When it stopped, she sighed with relief. She did not want to be buried alive.

After sliding past another row of precariously balanced objects, she entered what she assumed was the living room. In the middle of the square space stood a lonely table surrounded by more piles of stuff. The man leaned over it, rummaging through one of the saddlebags. Not looking up, he waved her over. His helmet now sat on the table, revealing his neatly groomed silver hair. Kaia hid her surprise. He was a lot older than she'd thought. His green-flecked brown eyes met hers.

"You get one chance to explain yourself." He smirked; his smile did not reach his eyes. "I'm not in the habit of helping strangers." He looked Kaia over, his narrowed eyes pausing on her chest before snapping back to her face. A chill spread down her spine, but she kept her expression neutral.

"First, get out of that ridiculous suit. You don't need that here. There's a change of clothes in one of the bags over there." He pointed toward a pile of bags leaning against a rusted metal box. Without another glance, the man resumed rummaging through the saddlebags.

Calm down. You need his help. He was the only one who might be able to point her to Alexi. Kaia swallowed the foul words on the tip of her tongue and dug through the bag. The man pointed her toward the bathroom when she'd found something close to her size.

She changed into green overalls, which were too large, and a gray sweater, which made her itch all over. After folding her white suit and stuffing it into her bag, she returned to the living room.

The man had been busy. The saddlebags, now empty, were piled in the corner. Neat stacks of furs and meat lined the table. The silver-haired man had pulled up a rusted chair. He leaned back, and it creaked under his weight as he observed the goods. He scratched the dark stubble on his chin. His movements were slow, less calculated now, the image of laziness. But she caught the glint in his eye, the sharpness in his gaze as she walked into the room.

"So?" His eyes traveled across her face.

"I need to find a man named Alexi. Do you know him?" She shifted her weight. "I'm running from…someone bad, and Alexi is the only one who can help me. The hag—"

The man leaned forward, his elbow resting on his thigh, his chin in his hand. Even bent over, he looked taller than her.

"Let me stop you before you say something you will regret." His voice was like gravel, and his brows knitted together as he shook his head. "First of all, you're giving me too much information. You don't know me or my intentions. You shouldn't trust anyone."

Biting back her words, Kaia listened, ignoring her desire to slap the man across his square face. She already knew all that, but what other choice did she have? She didn't need to hear this man tell her what she was doing wrong. She needed him to tell her if he knew Alexi or not. It was a simple question.

"You didn't tell me your name, which is good, so you're not entirely hopeless." He scratched his chin. "Now, based on your naivete, there's no doubt you're from one of the smaller mining towns. Hmm…my guess is Kaldwell."

Kaia tried not to show the shock on her face. Was she that easy to read? First the hag, now this guy.

"Based on your axes and your stance, you've had combat training, so you're not another mining girl. You've asked a stranger for help, going so far as to follow me home without asking any good questions, so you must be desperate. And you've mentioned that wretched hag, so whoever or whatever is hunting you is far worse than what most of the citizens here could even imagine." He stood up and stepped toward her, his eyes locked on hers. "Why should I put myself at risk and help someone being tracked by Solon?"

Kaia opened her mouth to respond, to defend the hag—she wasn't wretched, just rude. But the words didn't come, and she closed her mouth. This man knew about Solon. If he wanted to deliver her to them, it would be easy. All he had to do was to send a message to Kaldwell, and that would be the end of her, of her promise.

Still, he had brought her here. Something in his gaze made her hope he had some respect for the hag, enough that he would help her, that he hadn't already turned her in. She was betting everything on that and the look of greed she had caught on his face when she had walked into the room.

She breathed heat into her chest, arms, and legs, then exhaled. She rested her hand on her hip and shifted her weight. She had to get a grip on herself. She tilted her head to the side, schooling her face into an expression of disinterest.

"So you know. And yet I'm in your house." She hoped she sounded nonchalant. "Which means I have some value to you. I'm also desperate enough to tell the vendors on the black market where you store your goods. I am sure they would love to get their hands on them. The things in here are secret, are they not?"

It was a risk. Threatening this man could result in more than being handed over to Solon. One thing was clear: he was not a regular miner. And she had never threatened anyone before, except for that one time she had told Ine she would break her arm if she touched her hair again.

The man's eyes grew wide. Then he slammed his hand on the table. Kaia flinched. A hiss escaped his thin lips. Kaia took a step back, startled, before she realized what he was doing. He was laughing. Laughing so hard tears ran from his eyes. He straightened and wiped his cheeks. Kaia's back hit the wall. He was clearly insane.

"I can see why the hag likes you." The man wiped away another tear; it smudged the dirt on his face.

The hag likes me? She might have tolerated Kaia, helped her, maybe even respected her, but liked? She doubted that.

"Here's my offer." The man stood up and took a step toward her, his hand stroking the table as he moved. "Leave, and I'll pretend you didn't threaten me. Or pay me, and I will find Alexi for you. And if you can't pay…" He smacked his lips. "I will give you a job." He looked her over again, and goose bumps rose on her skin. "From the look of your scrawny body, you will be great for the job I have in mind."

The man took another step forward, the table now behind him. "It's a great deal. What do you say?"

Kaia stepped to the side, her back still against the wall. "I won't work for you."

"Oh?" The man tipped his head to the side, a smile on his face.

The thought of working for this man made her mouth go dry. What did he want her to do? But he hadn't mentioned giving her up to Solon. It was the only thing that kept her standing there. Still, it was clearly a trap, and a poorly hidden one. This man knew she was desperate and expected her to do everything he asked.

All sorts of scenarios ran through Kaia's mind. She tried to remember what she had in her account. It wasn't much. She could access it through the miners' union in Framnes. But that was risky. Solon could probably track the withdrawal.

"How much money do you want?"

The man's lip twitched. He opened his mouth. Then a bell sounded from the next room. He sighed and took a few steps back, giving Kaia room to breathe. Still pressed against the wall, she watched him yawn and walk over to the door on the other side of the room. He stopped, a hand on the doorknob.

"I'll tell you what. I'm too tired to bargain with you. It's almost midsleep, and you look ready to fall apart. I don't need any useless workers anyway. If you can come up with three gold squares by the next cycle, we have a deal. If not…" The man grinned. "We will figure something out. Yes?"

Kaia's stomach dropped. Three gold squares? She had never seen or held a physical coin before. That was more than she made in an entire rotation—more than she had made her whole life. There was no way she could have that kind of money by the next cycle. Which left only one option. A chill ran down her back.

The man opened the door. "You can use my guest room."

She looked toward the exit, considering her options. She could run, take her chances on the streets of Framnes. But she had no idea where to go or how to find Alexi. If Solon was already out there, she would be an easy target. And nothing would stop this man from turning her in. She tightened her fists. She knew only what the hag had told her—she had to find Alexi.

"I'm not going to turn you in to Solon."

Kaia turned back and stared at the man, forgetting to smooth out her expression. He leaned on the open door, his head barely fitting under the frame, examining her.

"I might be greedy, but I'm not stupid." He straightened and turned his back to Kaia. "Now, come and get some food before you pass out."

Kaia opened her mouth, then closed it as the man lifted a hand over his shoulder in a mock wave. "Oh, and my name is Jonas. Nice to meet you."

He walked through the door, leaving Kaia to sort through the emotions that hurtled through her—relief, fear, desperation, and determination. This man might not turn her in, but he was dangerous. He was also her only way to find Alexi. One thing was sure: she would sleep with one eye open and her axes in her hands.

"Get up!" Jonas's voice slid through the slits in the door and pierced her ears. "We don't have time for this. Get your ass up!"

Why did he have to be so rude? He was so much like the hag. Kaia was already sitting, axes in her hands. His steps had warned her of his approach. If he had walked in, she would have slammed an axe into his gut. Sighing, she put down the axes and rubbed her neck. She was thankful she had remembered to lock the door before passing out last cycle.

"I'm up."

"Well, get on it, then. I'll be in the kitchen." Kaia heard the man's footsteps creak down the hall.

She rubbed her eyes. She hadn't slept much. The metal wiring under the thin mattress on the makeshift bed had stabbed her every time she had moved. Her aching muscles and the pain in her shoulder hadn't helped, nor had the nightmares that had woken her, drenched in sweat. Or the guilt of leaving Biorki. She had left him despite his wishes. But the main thing that had kept her awake for hours was the decision she had to make now.

She touched her shoulder softly, rolling it under her hand. It still hurt, but the pain was manageable. She felt the stitches and grimaced. Well, almost manageable. She pulled on the gray sweater and reexamined the idea she'd come up with midsleep. It was insane.

Dust and dirt filled the air when she pulled on the overalls. She coughed, wondering if they had ever been washed before. Still, she was thankful for them. They were comfortable and covered most of her skin, though she had to roll the pants up at her ankles so she wouldn't step on them.

She stuffed her dad's backpack under the bed. It wasn't the best hiding spot, but it was better than nothing. She considered bringing her axes with her to talk to Jonas but decided against it. She needed him to listen to her, and carrying weapons would only prove she was afraid. She smacked herself in the face. *Come on. You can do this.* She imagined how Jonas would react to her idea, cringed, and opened the door.

Kaia walked into the kitchen, leaving footprints in the thick dust on the floor. Jonas sat on one of the stools connected to a round metal table in the middle of the room. It was surprisingly tidy. Cabinets in different flaking colors lined the walls. His boiler—the only clean object in the room—stood tall against the wall behind him. A large square storage compartment hummed next to it. *A fridge?*

Jonas looked up from his tablet and nodded toward the other side of the table. A steaming cup of something and a metal can with a spork in it sat ready for her. She sat, and a bitter smell drifted from the can. Wrinkling her nose, she picked up the cup instead. Citrus and energizer. Memories of Biorki flooded her mind. She took a big gulp and set the cup back down.

She grabbed the spork and lifted it out of the can. A gray paste greeted her, and the bitter smell of it engulfed her. She held her breath, opened her lips, and stuffed her mouth with the goo. The gray paste had no flavor, which was a relief, but it stuck to the top of her mouth. She swallowed, and the substance slid down her throat. She grabbed her mug and chased it with her drink. Awful. But so were the food pills and most of the dried meat she had eaten.

After Kaia had finished half of the can, Jonas put down his tablet.

"So, where's my money?" He leaned back, a smug grin on his face. He knew as well as she did that there was no way she could have magically acquired three gold squares over the last few hours, or at any point in her life. He was testing her, checking her reaction. She kept her face neutral and took another bite of the gray paste. Jonas's eyes lingered on her.

She swallowed. "I don't have the money." She let the words hang in the air. Jonas didn't blink, and the crooked smile remained on his lips, but it twitched. A small movement, but it was there. She took a sip of her drink. "But I do have a proposition."

She pronounced every word slowly and precisely, then observed the subtle changes in Jonas. His shoulders tensed slightly, and a crease formed between his brows.

"I'm listening."

Kaia lifted her cup and swirled the liquid around inside. He didn't owe her anything. Her idea was a stretch. Of course he could refuse her—it wouldn't mean anything to him—and then she would have to accept his offer if she wanted help. But she was betting everything on the spark of greed she had seen in his eyes. She repeated the words in her mind again before looking back at Jonas. His eyes were slits.

"I can win Stallo for you."

Jonas's mouth opened slightly, his eyes growing wide. Then the reaction was gone, smoothed out into one of boredom. Kaia would have missed it if she hadn't been watching. She stopped herself from smiling.

"Their prize purse is ten gold squares. First place takes five, and I'm sure you could win more if you bet on me, since I'm new and an underdog."

The idea had come to her when she had dragged herself to the guest room the previous cycle. At the bottom of the stairs, she had seen an iceboard hiding in one of Jonas's piles of trash. She wasn't sure she could win the contest, but Jonas didn't need to know that. The event would take place five cycles from now.

It was a risk, not only because Jonas may refuse her offer but also because it would be hard to hide from Solon at such a public event. She had seen Jonas's face when she had mentioned Solon. He was afraid of them, but he seemed relaxed here in the city. Whatever danger they posed in Kaldwell, it seemed they didn't here…at least not yet.

Working for Jonas was a risk she couldn't take. At least at a public event, she could escape from him if he didn't keep his promise, maybe even learn Alexi's location from someone else. Unless she died in the contest, which in some ways would be better than being caught. It would certainly be better than working for Jonas and risking being locked up or ending up in some shady den full of creeps.

Jonas stood up and paced between the boiler and the storage compartment. Kaia held her breath, her heart loud in her ears. Jonas rubbed his hands together. Each step spoke of strength, careful calculation, and worry. Although his posture was terrible, he still seemed elegant. After a few turns, his eyebrows knitted together, then relaxed. He walked to where she sat and leaned forward. A massive grin spread across his face, his eyes shining with the greed she had seen earlier. He was too close. Trying to look unbothered, Kaia met his eyes even as his breath touched her face.

"I accept your offer on one condition," Jonas purred.

Kaia's stomach twisted. Perhaps the food in front of her was the culprit. She remained still.

"Your offer means you have some confidence in your boarding skills. But I have no assurance that you can win me that money."

Kaia leaned back and took a sip of her drink. *Act cool.*

"So? What is your condition?" She focused on the steam rising from her cup.

Jonas placed his hand on the table, the crooked smile back on his face.

"I will help you find Alexi and let you stay here. I'll even pay your entry fee for the event…if you pass a test."

The cup in her hands turned cold, and imagined scenarios ran through her mind. She could hear in Jonas's tone that this test would be dangerous.

"What kind of test?" Kaia kept her voice steady even as her blood quickened.

Jonas tapped the table with his fingers, his crooked smile even wider now. His teeth were a brilliant white.

"It wouldn't be any fun if I told you, would it?" His hand moved across the table as he tapped out a rhythm with his index finger and thumb. "Trust me. The test will be easy. What do you say? Deal?"

Kaia didn't trust him. But she couldn't think of any other options. The rhythm of Jonas's fingers was loud in her ears. Whatever he had planned for her, she would do it. She *had* to do it. It was her best option, her only choice. She wanted to refuse, to run. But this way, she would have some resemblance of control.

She tightened her grip on her cup and met Jonas's eyes. "Deal."

CHAPTER 20

Kaia didn't know where the test was to take place, but she was once again following Jonas. This time, he led her through a dark maze of back roads and alleyways. Lit by fewer lanterns, the streets were darker, the green glow of the buildings eerie. Feeling naked without her helmet, she rested her left hand on her hip, a finger on her axe. Although these streets were less crowded, they made her skin crawl.

Walking faster, she tried not to notice the shadows lurking in her peripheral vision. If Jonas wanted to leave her here, if this was a trap, she would be easy prey. Something moved to her right. When she turned, there was nothing there, just an empty window. She grabbed her axe. She would not go down without a fight.

Glancing from side to side, Kaia followed Jonas into another dark street lined with abandoned carved copper buildings. She was a few steps behind him when a man stepped out of the shadows to her left. She jumped back, her axe raised. Jonas, on the other hand, only straightened and nodded at the guy. The man tilted his hat in response, then disappeared down another side street. Jonas looked back at Kaia crouching behind him, a crooked smile on his lips. *Bastard.* Then he reached into his pocket. "Oh, before I forget…"

This was it. She would have to knock him over the head and—

"Here." He dropped a square piece of metal into her hand. "Make sure not to lose it. You will need it if you stay in this city."

She stared at the object in her hand. Need it for what? She turned the metal piece over. Beautiful inscriptions covered both sides, more intricate than anything else she had seen.

"Are you coming?"

Looking up, she saw Jonas standing in a small arched doorway at the end of the street. She had completely lost herself in the detailed metal carvings. *Foolish.* She ran to where Jonas stood, holstered her axe, and followed him through the door.

She had expected to walk into a small room or a house. Instead, they entered a massive hall. A sea of pale, miserable faces met them. Kaia stared as women and men wearing green overalls pushed past them. They all wore the same gray sweater she was wearing. Some turned to look at her, their eyes lingering on Kaia's face before moving to her hair. She pulled her ponytail tighter and looked down.

She took a deep breath and steadied herself. *They are only people.* But there were so many of them that Kaia could barely see the cobbled floor under their boots as they passed. She looked up, stealing herself against the overwhelming wave of faces, and froze. All thoughts of the crowd disappeared when she saw the domed ceiling.

Above her, intricate lines crossed one another to form perfect geometric shapes. The lines all met in the middle of the copper ceiling, creating five perfect arches. Polished and spotless, they were supported by an equal number of simple pillars. Lanterns hung from them, and the light made the metal come alive, contrasting with the dirty faces below. The crowd seemed oblivious to the most fantastic thing Kaia had ever seen.

Jonas grabbed her hand, and Kaia jumped, pulling away from his grip. "What are you—"

"I don't bite," he uttered through gritted teeth.

She highly doubted that. But she kept that thought to herself.

Jonas continued, "In a crowd this large, it's easy to be pulled in the wrong direction. And from what I have seen, you're not too great with people, and you're easily distracted."

Kaia was speechless. *Not too great with people?* This, coming from the guy who had called her a heavy load when they had first met. He wasn't wrong, but that was not for him to decide. And about her being distracted…well, she had to admit she had been off her game. Biting her tongue, she nodded, remembering their conversation earlier. She needed his help, and she hated herself for it.

His hand was rough, warm, and clammy when he took hers again. It felt strange not to be wearing gloves, too intimate. But she sighed and resisted the urge to pull away again as he dragged her through the crowd toward one of the arches.

On the other side was another horde of green-and-gray people and something large and metallic. A horn blared through the hall. A train? This was a train station? She looked up at the shining ceiling and then down at the cobbled floor. Not even the town leaders of Kaldwell could afford a structure like this.

When they reached the platform, Kaia shook her head in disbelief. She had seen the trains in Kaldwell; they were small, rectangular, and black, used mainly for transporting loads of copper. This train was nothing like that. It was cylindrical, each end rounded like a double-ended bullet. It was built out of different metals—copper, mostly, but there were also lines of aluminum, steel, and other alloys Kaia couldn't name. Between the driver cabs, the carriages were lined with rows of oval-shaped windows. Each had two doors.

A bell rang through the station, and the doors slid open. The corners of Kaia's mouth curved up against her will. She had never been on a train before.

After boarding, she found herself seated on a bench next to Jonas. The gray bench, stiff and uncomfortable, was one of many lining the curved walls of the carriage. The oval-shaped windows were rimmed with yellow rubber, cracked and flaking. Smaller versions of the street's electric lanterns hung from the ceiling; Kaia had hit her head on one of them as she'd slid into her seat. It swayed back and forth, throwing strange shadows across the curved walls.

She rubbed her head, waiting for the train to leave. She tracked every movement, every person inside—anyone could be in on Jonas's plan. But no one seemed to notice them. Their eyes followed a man in gray overalls walking between the benches. The other passengers showed something to the man, and Kaia pulled out the metal piece Jonas had given her earlier. She flashed it at the conductor.

"Thank you." The conductor's emotionless face resembled a ball of dough. "All good. Have a nice trip."

Kaia's cheeks burned as she nodded. She had been amazed by a train ticket. She was definitely off her game.

When the train slid away from the platform, Kaia looked out the window, soaking everything in: the train's vibration; the smell of stale socks; the city that moved past her; Jonas, who was picking his nose. Remembering how she had held his hand, she wiped her palm on her overalls.

"Where are we going?" she whispered, not wanting to break the silence in the carriage.

Jonas wiped his finger on his spotted gray sleeve before rummaging through the small belt bag that was strapped across his waist and hung over his stomach. With a grunt, he pulled out his tablet. It lit up, and a map of the city glowed between his hands.

He tapped it. "Here."

His finger touched a spot labeled Framnes Central. At the bottom of the map, a dot moved along a line, away from a place called Framnes North. Kaia's eyes nearly popped out of her head. She thought she had seen Framnes, but no, she had seen only one of the *five* sub-cities.

"Bigger than you thought?" Jonas smirked.

Realizing she was staring wide-eyed at the tablet, Kaia rearranged her face into an expression of boredom. "No."

Jonas giggled—outright *giggled*—and reached into his belt bag again. He pulled out a stick of what appeared to be brown jelly and took a bite.

"Want some?" He shoved the rest of the stick under her nose.

She turned to face the window, hoping he hadn't seen the embarrassment on her face. "No, thank you."

To her relief, he took another bite of whatever it was and returned to tapping on his tablet.

Her ears popped as the train entered a tunnel. The cabin darkened, and although there was nothing to see, Kaia stared into the darkness. The lantern above her continued to sway back and forth, back and forth.

A pinch to her side snapped her out of sleep. To her surprise, she was slumped against the carriage's side. Drool ran down her chin. She wiped her mouth and blinked.

Hot air touched her ear as Jonas whispered, "You don't want to miss this."

Just as the last word left his mouth, the train shot out of the tunnel and onto a massive bridge. Light flooded the carriage. The magnets beneath the train hissed as they connected with a hovering rail. Kaia sucked in a breath as they soared through the cave, above the houses and streets below.

She wasn't sure if she even *could* call the gigantic space a cave. It rose so far above them, she swore she could see clouds, though that was impossible. Trapped condensation? She supposed that would technically make them clouds. They would probably create snow if it weren't for the two giant turbines. The large, rusted machines were built into the rock walls, circulating the air.

Between the wonderous machines hung stalactites. They made the ones in Kaldwell look like toothpicks. They dangled from the cave's roof, and a massive metal net hung below them, stretching from one side of the cave to the other. Kaia's eyes widened. The net was meant to stop the spikes from falling onto the city.

Trying not to think about what would happen if the net broke, Kaia watched the streets pass below. They shone with polished metal and intricate architecture. Blue fires burned in the city center. Like ghosts among the living, they lined the labyrinthine streets.

"It's the copper in the air," her teacher had once told their class. "Flames can glow green or blue depending on the density of particles. Blue means the air is safe to breathe. Green means the copper dust is at a toxic level."

Her teacher had never mentioned red flames. But Kaia had to admit, the blue flames of Framnes were almost as magical as those in the hag's firepit.

Whooshing past them on both sides were plateaus like those in Framnes North. Like steps, they led up and into distant nooks in the cave. The higher the shelves sat, the greener and less elaborate the buildings became. Framnes Center looked like a well-used stew pot, dirty on the rim and shiny in the middle.

"It's quite a sight, huh?" Jonas resumed tapping on his tablet.

"Mm-hm," was all she managed to say as she soaked in the view.

She nearly thanked him for waking her, but then she remembered why they were there and kept her mouth shut.

After leaving the train station, Jonas led Kaia through cobbled streets. Unlike those near Jonas's house, these were clean, wide, and empty. After they crossed the third one, Jonas looked at his tablet. Rattling off curses even Kaia wouldn't repeat, he increased his pace. His entire posture changed as he jogged. He flowed like water, every step a continuation of the last, his body level and steady.

Kaia, however, looked far from graceful as she tried to keep up. Gasping for air, she scanned the streets and buildings, one hand on the swinging axe at her hip. She stumbled over every crooked cobblestone, slid on every loose piece of dirt like a rock trying to catch up with the wind.

Approaching a fork in the road, Jonas broke the silence. "Are you ready?"

How could she be ready? She had no idea what the test was, and he knew it; she could tell by the smirk on his face. She lifted her head and tried to control her labored breathing.

"Why wouldn't I be?"

Jonas chuckled, the smirk turning into a grin. But his eyes remained cold and sharp as ice as he walked toward one of the houses.

The house was square and unremarkable, a prime example of perfectly polished copper. The door looked like every other stainless steel door except for an X marking the silver doorknob. How Jonas knew someone with this kind of wealth was beyond Kaia's imagination.

Jonas smiled and winked at her. "You know, you really shouldn't be this trusting."

His words sent shivers down her spine, but Kaia tried to ignore the unease growing in her gut. *You agreed to this. It's the only way.* Jonas knocked once. Then, not waiting for a response, he opened the door and gestured for Kaia to enter. She straightened, lifted her chin, and walked past him without a word.

The room behind the door was spotless. Two doors were set into the dark wall to her right, and a floating set of stairs climbed the wall to her left. It led to a landing above them, framed by a strange geometric railing. A thrill ran through Kaia when she saw what hung on the wall across the room.

She left Jonas by the door and crossed the shining floor to the six iceboards. She ran her fingers across the board closest to the stairs. *Incredible—this is older than Ingá.* It was red, short, and full of scratches. She traced the bindings with her index finger. All modern boards used magnetic bindings, but this one had clip-ons. This board wasn't just older than Ingá. It was older than Kaldwell.

She walked over to the next one, letting her fingers trail along the curve of the board. This one was newer, the bindings a mix of magnets and clip-ons. It was white with X's of blue across it. It was longer than the older one, and a large chunk of it was missing by the back binding.

Kaia moved on to the next board, a black one with manual magnetic bindings. She realized then that each board represented a step in the evolution of iceboarding. She gasped. The boards people used now were longer, the metal thicker and more flexible. The shape was different too. She traced the sharp curve of the black board. These boards were historical artifacts.

"Stop that!"

Kaia jerked back while simultaneously unclipping her left axe from her belt. She had entirely forgotten where she was. Again. She whirled around, holding the axe firmly in front of her chest at an angle. Her right hand hovered over her other axe, her knees bent. The loose strands of her hair flew around her face.

The newcomer was a man, petite and younger than Jonas. He stood in the doorway to Kaia's right, a grimace of disgust plastered on his beautiful face.

"Jonas. What the heck have you brought into my establishment?"

The man's black hair, braided in a neat and intricate design, fell over his shoulder. His dark eyes—narrowed into slits—shone with intelligence. Everything about him spoke of calculated intention.

Cursing under her breath, Kaia put her axe away and straightened. She had allowed the boards to distract her, if only for a second. She looked at Jonas. His lips were clamped shut, a tight line quivering with the effort of holding back laughter. It danced in his eyes. Kaia would have thrown an axe right at him if not for the gorgeous man staring daggers at her. She forced what she hoped looked like a smile onto her face.

But before she could apologize, Jonas wiped his eyes. "Sorry, Kritan. I forgot how big of a neat freak you are."

The look on Kritan's face told Kaia he didn't believe the lie.

"How often must I tell you and your companions to remove your boots before you come in?" Kritan pointed at Kaia's boots.

Her *boots*? That was what Kritan had yelled about? She looked down. She had indeed left a trail of dirt from the entrance to the boards. *Oh.* She had assumed he was mad she had touched the boards.

Kritan sighed, his colorful vest rising and falling. "I don't know why I bother telling you. Or…" He looked at Kaia.

"Lin." They didn't need to know her real name.

Kritan's face softened. "Don't follow this guy's example, okay, Lin?" Kritan gestured to a red door. "Misam is in the dining room, as usual. You have one hour."

Kaia could have sworn she saw respect in Jonas's eyes as he bent his head to Kritan. He took off his boots and placed them by the red door.

"Come on…Lin." Jonas chewed on the word. "It's time to see if you have what it takes."

She sighed, and the lump in her stomach returned. She had no idea what meeting this Misam had to do with her test or how it would prove her iceboarding skills. But she reminded herself that she had no other choice. She gave Kritan an apologetic look and placed her own boots by the door. Jonas twisted the doorknob, and she followed him through the doorway.

A plump man sat in the dining room. When Kaia walked in, he looked up mid-bite, a broad smile spreading across his face. She was greeted by a row of white teeth with half-chewed pieces of food stuck in them. His shaved head shone in the lamplight. Markings ran from his neck to his forehead, and they scrunched up into waves when he lifted his bushy brows.

"Hi, Jonas! You brought a friend." He waved cheerfully as food fell from his mouth onto his plate.

Kaia found herself waving back, confused. She looked at Jonas, who smiled mischievously back at her.

"Lin, meet Misam. Misam, meet Lin. He is going to be your tester."

She clenched her fist, and a stab of pain ran through it. She looked down. Blood dripped from one of her fingertips. The black board's edge must have been sharper than she thought. She looked up and tried to meet Misam's gaze. She tightened her fist again. The pain was nothing compared to the dread she felt when looking into his blank white eyes.

CHAPTER 21

Sitting across from Misam, Kaia fidgeted with the metal cup Kritan had brought her, filled with a sweet drink she had never tasted before. She inhaled the smell—round, full, and unknown. The dark room was silent except for the occasional sound of Misam biting into whatever he was eating.

Colorful draperies lined every wall. They told a story of poverty and endless travels, each one a different scene detailing some exploration or horror. On the one closest to Kaia, a girl danced with what looked like a star. She was beautiful, ethereal. Jonas sat in a chair in the corner of the room, sipping from his cup and reading something on his tablet.

Not knowing what to do, Kaia took another look at the man before her. Misam looked older than Jonas, gray and worn, his eyes crowned with wrinkles. But something about his mannerisms and movements made him seem reckless and young. She inspected a small jagged scar across his cheekbone, then caught him staring at her—no, *through* her. His white eyes locked with hers, and a chill ran down her spine. She looked down at her cup. *Coward.*

She couldn't meet those white eyes again. So she sat there looking at her hands, waiting. Finally, Misam let out a big sigh, sucked his thumb, and smacked his lips.

"Kritan!" Misam's voice was soft, unlike his callused hands. "I've finished the plate. Can you bring the tray?"

How was he still hungry? The empty plate had been filled to the brim when Kaia had entered the room. Where did he fit it all?

Kritan materialized from a door behind Misam and took his plate. A few moments later, he reappeared carrying a large tray with a thick domed lid. Kritan's knuckles were white. How heavy was it? He smiled sympathetically at Kaia and placed the tray between her and Misam. Sharing a glance with Jonas, Kritan nodded, then left the room.

Misam lifted the lid off the tray. Kaia's eyes grew wide. She turned to Jonas—maybe he could explain what she saw—but his seat was empty. Kaia looked around frantically. He was gone. She turned back to ask Misam, but instead of his white eyes, she saw his back disappearing through the doorway. The lid had vanished with him. They had left her alone in the room with a tray full of...*rocks*?

Why? It didn't make any sense. This had to be a part of the test; Jonas's disappearance seemed to be proof of that. Or perhaps this had all been a scheme and he had sold her to Misam; maybe this room was a prison. But then why bring the rocks? Kaia swallowed hard and shook her head. No. There was something here, some clue. There had to be.

She looked at the tray again. Five identical rocks were spaced out perfectly in a straight line. Weird. There was nothing peculiar about them. No inscriptions, no hint of any useful information. They were just gray and plain.

After turning the stones over for the hundredth time, Kaia fell back into her seat. She looked at her time tracker. She had been in the room for an hour and had learned nothing. Her increasingly ragged breathing filled her ears. Sweat ran down her temple, and the drink had turned cool in her hands. She lifted the cold liquid to her lips. Her hands shook. When had they started shaking?

She would fail again, and Solon would find her—find her and do stars knew what with her. The feeling burned through her, churning and twisting. Acid burned her mouth and throat as she leaned to the side and emptied her gut onto the spotless floor. She tried to sit back up, but the smell made her gag again, forcing whatever was left in her stomach onto the floor.

Kaia took a few calming breaths before heaving herself back into a sitting position. She wiped her mouth on a napkin Kritan had left behind. What would he think of having to clean his floors again?

Kaia stared at the rocks. Was this it? Would it all be for nothing because of these damn rocks? She stood up. She would find Jonas and beat some sense into him.

She took a step, and something shifted. There was an unmistakable pressure in the room. She had thought it was her nerves. But as she took another step forward, her skin crawled. She took another step. An invisible blanket pressed down on her, smothering her. Something was very, very wrong.

She slowly moved around the table. There it was again—a shift in pressure, needles on her skin. So the rocks weren't so plain after all. She grabbed her cup and poured out what was left, then took two more steps. *There.* She slammed the mug upside down over the fourth rock. A noise she hadn't noticed disappeared from her head. The pressure eased, and she exhaled. What the stars was that?

This was the key…but the key to what?

Before she could consider any possibilities, her legs gave out beneath her. A door slammed open, and hands grabbed her before she hit the floor. Whoever it was kept her head steady as her body shook violently, convulsing to some inaudible twisted beat. The tremors made her limbs thrash against the floor. What was happening to her?

"Here," a voice said near her ear.

"Thank you," a voice to her right answered before a stab of pain coursed through her thigh.

Kaia pushed through the fog filling her mind. The pain in her thigh eased, as did the shaking in her body. Within a few moments, she lay slumped on the floor. Her head rested on something soft. Angry voices flowed above her. She looked down at herself and willed her foot to move. Although slow to respond, it did listen. She tried to bend her left knee. It moved. Relief flooded her.

"You let it go too far!" Kritan yelled. "And look at the state of my floor!"

"Oh, do shut up about your floor. I was right, wasn't I?" She recognized Jonas's nonchalant tone. "Anyway, Misam would have stopped me if I'd been wrong. Wouldn't you, Misam?"

"Of course."

Kaia looked up and found Misam looking down at her, smiling widely. He sat on his knees behind her, holding her head loosely between his hands on a pillow. He patted her head with his sticky fingers.

"You passed."

She pushed herself off the floor and into a sitting position. The room spun. If she hadn't already emptied her stomach, she would have puked again.

Instead, she stared hopelessly at the men circling her. They moved around each other with practiced and familiar movements. They seemed to be…fussing over her? No, that couldn't be it. Covering their bases—that seemed more likely. Kritan was already wiping the floor, and the tray of rocks was nowhere to be seen.

"I passed?" She could barely shape the words with her mouth.

"You're alive, aren't you?" Jonas's eyes gleamed.

Kritan cleared his throat and nudged Jonas, who was putting away the syringe he had used to stab her leg.

"Anyway, yes, you passed. And you will start your training early next cycle."

Cold spread through her. *I could have died? That was the test?* She looked down at her shaking hands and realized she almost had.

A warm, steady hand took hers. It was Misam's. His white eyes looked past her shoulder.

"You're safe now. The serum Jonas gave you will heal whatever damage was done." He squeezed her hand. "Don't worry." Her silence must have communicated something to Misam, because he continued, "It felt wrong, didn't it? The rock?" His voice was soft. "I did the same test when I was young."

He had taken the test too?

Misam's face softened as if he was remembering a great moment in his life. "I wasn't as strong as you, and it took my eyesight before I could figure it out. People told me I had failed, that it was a curse. But to me, it was a blessing. I see more of the world now than I did before."

Misam squeezed her hand again before getting up, leaving her even more confused. The test had made him blind? He walked across the room and grabbed the doorknob.

"Jonas, you must feed her better. She is too scrawny. And make sure she makes it to practice in time next cycle." Misam winked at Kaia and grinned.

Jonas opened his mouth, but Misam left the room before he could say anything. Maybe Misam wasn't so bad after all.

Kritan tugged at his braid and sighed. "You better not screw this up, Jonas." His voice was sharp. "We all know what happened last time."

Jonas's shoulders stiffened, and he turned away from Kaia as he answered in a hollow voice. "I will never let anything like that happen again. You know that."

Again? She wasn't sure if it was the serum they had injected her with or the knowledge that Jonas had failed before, but shivers ran through her hands. He had clearly made a horrible mistake, and she might be the next one.

Kritan patted Jonas on his shoulder. "Yes, I know. Be careful, and please take care of Misam for me." Before he followed Misam out the door, Kritan turned. "Oh, congratulations, Lin. And Jonas, do take the back entrance this time."

Jonas laughed. "Whatever you say, Kritan."

Kritan rolled his eyes before the door closed behind him.

Jonas was all smiles and laughter when they left the house through a hidden wall in the kitchen. Kaia felt strange, as if a fog had made a home in her mind. Jonas turned down an empty cobbled street. She followed, though her thoughts were elsewhere.

She had passed. But passed *what*? What did the test prove? It had nothing to do with iceboarding. And from what Misam and Kritan had said, there was more going on here than Jonas was letting on. Then there was the rock and what she had sensed. A shiver ran down her neck.

"Ah, what a fine establishment," Jonas mused, slapping his hands together. "This will be fun."

Kaia jumped. They were outside a rather shabby-looking door in a small alleyway. How they'd gotten there, she didn't know. Her body ached, and her mind was a scramble of unfinished thoughts. So when Jonas gestured for her to go inside, she didn't think twice. Or rather, didn't think at all.

Before she knew it, she found herself on a soft circular couch with a cup of buzz liquid. The room was dark and hazy and smelled of old underpants. The dust floating in the air left a strange taste in her mouth. Trying to discourage the taste from lingering on her tongue, she sipped her drink.

She grimaced. Whatever it was, it was both bitter and sweet. Unsure if she liked it or not, she took another sip. Heat flushed her cheeks, and a numbness followed. It washed away the stiffness in her muscles, her neck. It was wonderful. She had to remember to ask what it was.

She sank deeper into the couch with the drink in her hands. Squinting, she tried to focus on the heated conversation in front of her. Jonas was leaning toward another man sitting across a round table from him.

"I'm willing to bet she will do better than your other participants." Jonas tapped the scratched tabletop.

"I'm sure you think so." The man's double chin wiggled with every word. "But she has no experience with competitions. I have seen hardened iceboarders flee from Stallo. So why should I spend my money on someone like her?" The man looked her up and down with a disapproving glare.

Kaia blinked slowly. Was he talking about her? His Adam's apple bounced, and she resisted the urge to touch it with her finger. Instead, she hid behind her cup and took another sip of the clear liquid.

"Bean, you know as well as I do that adding an unknown participant throws the balance off. It will make the contest very interesting. Don't you think? Here, if that's not enough to convince you…" Jonas pulled a metal box from his belt bag and put its contents on the table. "This is my bet. Put it all on her. Whether you want to participate or not is up to you. If you win, it's all yours. But if I win…" Jonas pointed at a dirty-looking packet hanging on the wall behind the bar. "I'll have that back."

Bean laughed, his raspy voice crackling with each exhale. "Oh, but that was the first thing I won from you. I wouldn't want to give it up for anything."

Jonas leaned closer to Bean and lowered his voice. "I will consider giving you access to you-know-what."

Bean blinked and looked at Kaia, his eyes inspecting every part of her. With a last long look at her hair, Bean sighed and reached out a hand.

"It's a deal. But you better keep your word or…"

Jonas took it and smiled, a sharpness still lingering in his eyes. "Or else, I know. Don't worry about it."

Bean lifted an eyebrow, then smiled. "All right. Now that that's in order, let's have another round of drinks. It's on me."

Before Kaia could react, there was another cup before her. She looked down at the one in her hands. When had she drained it?

After a few more drinks, Jonas led Kaia outside. She walked out the door and immediately realized something was wrong. She tried to take a quick step to the left, but her leg didn't listen—it hooked itself around her other leg. She toppled forward, the cobbled street coming at her fast. She reached out with her right arm. Pain shot through her shoulder, and it gave out. She smacked her face on the ground.

"Dritt!" she yelled as a sickening crack filled her head.

This pain didn't shoot through her. Instead, it thumped against her temples. Something warm ran down her forehead. She wiped her brow and held her hand up to her face: blood. She swore again. Twisting slowly, she tried to stop the world from spinning and sat up.

"Well, that's a sight."

Kaia looked up. Jonas stood with both hands resting on his hips, a crease between his brows. "I may have bet on the wrong person."

"I didn't ask for your opinion." Kaia grumbled, her cheeks warm. "Also, what the heck was that test? I could have died. I thought we had a deal! You would help me get away from Sol—"

His hand moved so fast that she didn't see it until it connected with her left cheek.

"What the—" She blinked, her head ringing.

"Don't you ever mention that name in public. Or anywhere, for that matter," he growled, his intensity making her lean back.

The world stopped spinning as his words sank in. Kaia nodded, feeling her cheeks redden with shame. She rubbed her bruised jaw.

"Fine!" she snarled. She wasn't ready to back down yet. "But why are we here? How is this going to help me? And what the heck was wrong with that rock?"

Jonas's expression softened. Opening his belt bag, he pulled out a white handkerchief and another brown jelly stick.

"Here, since you're such a lightweight." Jonas handed her the jelly stick and crouched in front of her. Before she could pull back, he pressed the handkerchief to her forehead. She lifted her hand to swat it away, but his surprisingly gentle touch made her pause. She let her hand fall to her lap as Jonas wiped her brow. An image of Biorki patching her shoulder flashed through her mind. He should be awake and talking with the hag by now, which meant he knew she had left him behind. Guilt burned through her. She pushed it away. He would understand. He had to understand.

Jonas let out a breath, still holding the soft handkerchief to her forehead. "I'm sorry. We didn't have much time to secure your spot in the competition. I should have told you what we were doing here."

His voice was shaking. *Weird.* This new gentleness made her uncomfortable, but something in his face made her sit still, even though a part of her wanted to kick his chin.

"I was so excited, and…" Jonas sighed. He brushed her temple with the handkerchief and gestured to the door. "Usually you have to qualify in smaller contests to be considered for a spot in Stallo, even if you pay for your entry. Unfortunately, Bean is the only one who could get you in, and he requires very specific convincing." Jonas patted his now-flatter belt bag. "Let's call it an investment in your skills—a secret back way."

Kaia blinked, her head clearing slightly. She hadn't known. For all her research, she had never checked to see if she had to qualify for Stallo. She had assumed skill and money were all she needed.

She met Jonas's eyes. "And if I win, you'll make more?"

"Yes, there's that." A smile crept back onto Jonas's unusually grave face. It made her feel better for some reason.

"You should wipe your hands clean." Jonas straightened and held out the bloody handkerchief. "We have one more thing to do before returning to my house."

Kaia accepted it. It was plain except for a golden embroidered F. She wiped her hands.

"The test—that was no normal iceboarding test. Why not just test me on a course?" The buzz drink was making her either brave or stupid. "I know there was something going on with that rock. I could see it in Kritan's eyes. He was terrified."

Jonas paused, grabbed another jelly stick, and lifted it to his lips. He didn't look at her when he whispered, "I can't tell you what that rock is, especially here. But I can tell you the test is older than this city. It picks out particularly sensitive individuals. That sensitivity has made Misam the most decorated iceboarder this city has ever seen. I needed to confirm my suspicions about you, to know you were worth my time and money. To know you were talented enough to learn from Misam, especially with our time constraints." He met her eyes. "You suggested this, remember? You wanted to compete. Well, now you can."

The tension and anger within Kaia fizzled out. She looked down at the handkerchief in her hands. She *had* suggested this. Insisted on it. She wished Jonas had told her of his plan. But in all fairness, Jonas didn't owe her anything. She was acting like a child. She had passed the test, and now she could compete. A childhood dream come true.

She sighed and tightened her hold on the handkerchief. Even if she could run back to the hag, grab Biorki, and hide on the surface, Solon would catch her eventually. She would keep her promise. Regardless of the risk, no matter what Jonas asked of her, she had to enter Stallo, win, and find Alexi. She needed that spaceship.

Kaia handed the handkerchief back to Jonas. "So, what's the next step?" She let him pull her to her feet.

His mouth curved into a warm smile. "Well, first you should eat that jelly. It will help you feel better." He stuffed the handkerchief into his belt bag and skipped toward another alleyway. "Then I will show you the Stallo headquarters."

CHAPTER 22

The jelly stick did wonders for her buzzing head, though it tasted as bad as it looked. Feeling clearheaded but sore, Kaia stood in the center of Framnes. People didn't spare them a second glance as they walked across the cobbled ground. She barely noticed, transfixed by the main attraction in the city square.

Lanterns with blue fires lined a set of dark stairs. The flames fizzled and pulsed as the air circulated through the cave. At the top of the stairs stood a large square building, a structure she had seen only on her tablet: the headquarters of Stallo. Was this a dream or a nightmare?

The copper building gleamed with intricate lines. Unlike other buildings in Framnes, this one seemed to breathe with the flames, a living piece of history. There was a flicker of flame, then a dance of blue light and golden shadows. They rippled across the delicate carvings covering the windowless walls, a beautiful conversation between flame, air, and copper.

Jonas made an exaggerated gesture toward the stairs of the massive glowing building. "After you."

Remembering to blink, Kaia nodded, took a deep breath, and moved forward. Her heart raced as she walked up the pristine steps. Jonas stayed quiet, tiptoeing along next to her. What events had happened here? What types of people had walked up these stairs?

A particularly exquisite carving caught her eye, and she almost stopped walking. It shone above the entrance, but pieces of the metal had been cut or torn off, leaving the facade scarred. It looked like some giant creature had tried to break through the building, biting and slashing at it. Kaia fidgeted with the buckle on her overalls. Had it been a creature like Fluff? No, this looked like it had been something—someone—larger. Something out of the history books she hadn't read.

When they had almost reached the top of the stairs, Kaia stopped, her eyes wide. Beautiful symbols framed the triangular door in front of them. She craned her neck, trying to interpret them, and blinked—she *recognized* them. Well, some of them. They were similar to the markings above the sick bay door in Kaldwell. A matching pair of buildings, both constructed before the recorded time of the miner's union.

Kaia leaped up the last two steps and reached out. Holding her breath, she traced one of the simpler symbols made of two straight lines and a circle. But it was just that—two lines and a circle. It bore no new meaning here. She sighed. She should have paid more attention to the historical texts in the archive. Instead, she had read manuals for cooling systems.

"In challenges, we face the worst beast of all: ourselves."

Kaia looked back at Jonas, surprised. He stood a couple of steps down, staring at the building. He wore an expression she couldn't identify. He looked younger, the lines in his forehead not so deep, as if the light of the building had washed away the sadness that always lingered there. She hadn't noticed before.

His words hung between them. Could he read the symbols? Jonas stared at them momentarily, then met Kaia's eyes, his expression returning to one of mischief.

"I would be quite a difficult beast to catch, even for me. Don't you think?"

Kaia couldn't help but imagine Jonas running in circles, trying to tackle himself to the ground. It was ridiculous. The corner of her lips pulled upward, and a chuckle escaped her. A grin spread across Jonas's face. His teeth were blue in the lantern light.

"So you do know how to smile." Jonas bumped his fist into her arm below the wound on her shoulder. "Wait until you see what's inside."

Kaia realized he was right; she hadn't smiled in cycles, not really. Not since she had left Biorki behind. She tried to remember the last time she had really laughed. It had been before…before her dad…

She pushed back the tears. *Focus on what you can do now.*

Jonas took a step forward, and the dark doors slid to the sides without making a sound. Kaia took a deep breath. She had made her choice. She walked inside, Jonas following close behind.

The room beyond was nothing like the outside. Plain and practical, the walls were covered in soft draperies in muted colors. There were no embroidered stories, no carvings on the walls. Kaia would have thought it was a storage space had it not been for the labyrinth of railings on the floor. Bands of gray led to different counters, each with a sour-faced clerk behind it.

"Let me do the talking." Jonas's energy shifted again, his face suddenly serious. Then he just about *danced* through the entrance hall. His mood swings were starting to make her dizzy.

Jonas proceeded to one of the counters at the back of the room, where an elderly woman sat. The woman's expression reminded Kaia of Ulla. Well, this would be fun.

"Yes?" The word slithered out from between the woman's bright red lips.

"Hi, Morgan. How's your cycle going?" His face twisted into a bright smile, which made him look like an entirely different person. It disturbed Kaia, and Morgan's response suggested she felt similarly.

"What do you want?" Morgan's wrinkles deepened between her bushy brows.

"Ah, come on, Morgan. Don't I always bring good news?" Jonas leaned on the counter.

The crease in Morgan's forehead twitched. She ignored Jonas and looked at Kaia. Her disapproving eyes traveled from Kaia's dirty boots to her messy hair. She pursed her lips.

"You're entering *that* into Stallo?"

Kaia blinked, taken aback. She had already been stared at, prodded, and almost killed this cycle, and this woman was calling her a *that*? She was about to tell Morgan where to stick it when Jonas held out a hand to stop her. Kaia clenched her jaw.

"Yep!" Jonas grinned and slid something across the counter. Kaia vaguely remembered Bean giving it to him earlier. "I would like to pay for her entry and access to the training area."

Morgan looked back at Kaia before she took the chip and put it in her pocket. She typed something into her tablet. "Name?"

This was it. She was really doing it. She was entering Stallo. A tiny flutter of excitement raced through Kaia. Her childhood dream was about to become a reality…and no one she cared about would be there to see it. Her excitement twisted into guilt. She balled her hands into fists.

"Name?" Morgan's mouth turned down in a wrinkled grimace.

"Oh." Kaia collected herself. "It's Lin."

Morgan didn't seem to notice the little pause and directed, "Look here," pointing at a triangular object behind her. Kaia complied.

"Good." Morgan tapped on her tablet. "Okay?" She turned the screen toward Kaia.

An unfamiliar face looked back at her. The dark-skinned girl had streaks of blood running down her face. Her curly hair was gray with dirt. She still had black stripes smudged under her eyes. She resisted the urge to take a step back when she realized the picture was of her.

That's when it sank in. She hadn't washed once since she had left Kaldwell, not since the hag had drawn those lines on her face. The thought hadn't even crossed her mind, not that it mattered. It was the look in her eyes that unsettled her: empty and defeated.

"Do you want me to take another one?" Morgan's eyes told Kaia it wasn't a question.

"No. That's fine." It was not fine, not at all.

Focus on what you can do now. She breathed in, trying to loosen the lump in her chest. At least she would be harder to recognize under all that dirt.

Morgan entered some more information into the tablet. After a few minutes, she extended her hand to Kaia, ignoring Jonas. "Here." In her wrinkled palm lay a gray bracelet with a silver piece stitched into it. A number was stamped onto the metal: thirteen.

"This will be your identifier as you practice for the event. It also works as a key. It will give you access to the locker rooms and course."

Kaia reached out to grab the bracelet, but Morgan closed her hand.

"Don't lose it." Morgan's voice cut through the noise of the room. "I won't give you another."

Kaia forced a smile and met Morgan's dark eyes. "I won't."

Morgan reopened her fist. Kaia snatched the bracelet from her hand before Morgan could change her mind.

A few moments later, Kaia stood in the arena's locker room with Jonas. The room was triangular, small, and empty. It smelled of stale sweat, board wax, and something else…stagnant ice. The door to her left was plain, with the words training course written on it in white paint. Fifteen large metal lockers circled the room, each painted with a different number.

"Try the bracelet on your locker," Jonas urged. "Everything you need for the contest should be in there."

Hesitant, Kaia tapped the lock with her bracelet. The door swung open. She stepped back and felt the blood drain from her face.

Inside hung a beautiful black-and-white iceboard. On the shelf above it sat a pair of matching shoes. Kaia grabbed the board and placed it next to her. It was the perfect height and width for someone of her size and weight. She turned it around, changed her stance, and measured once more, then returned the board to the locker and snatched the shoes from the shelf. They were her size. This was not a coincidence.

She looked up at Jonas, who was grinning from ear to ear. Somehow, he had already prepared this, had known she would pass the test. A torrent of emotions ran through her. She didn't know if she was happy that he knew she would pass or angry that he hadn't told her.

Her voice shook when she finally found it again. "How did you know?"

"I would like to say I knew you would be good at boarding, coming from Kaldwell and all, but to be frank..." Jonas scratched his cheek. "Gret-ha left a note in Fluff's satchel. She told me to help you find Alexi, test you, and enter you into Stallo. She didn't explain why. So I gave you an impossible choice: pay me three gold squares, work for me, or give up. I wanted to see what you would do. If you had backed out, I'd have known you wouldn't survive Stallo, and I would have helped you hide...not that it would have done much good. But you proposed this deal instead, which worked well with my plans, and here we are."

Kaia threw the shoes back onto the shelf, slammed the locker door, and turned to face Jonas. Angry—she was definitely angry. The stream of questions and worries that had been spinning in her head pushed itself to the surface, and the words rushed out of her like water from a melting glacier.

"You were going to help me even if I refused your offer?" She had felt so alone, so hopeless. "Why didn't you just tell me after I proposed the deal? You let me believe I had no choice, that you might not help me, even *after* the test. You put me through all that even when you'd already made up your mind? Are you insane?"

Then it hit her. "And why do I have to do so much for you to find Alexi? Can't you just message him or something? What kind of person is he? You seem to have more than enough contacts in this city. Why can't you get me out of here? And who is Gret-ha?!" Gret-ha had been the name on her dad's map. She needed Jonas to confirm her suspicions.

Jonas took a few steps back. "I know I could have told you." He scratched his nose, his face apologetic. "But I still needed you to take that test. If I had told you what it was, it could have skewed the results. I needed you to go in blind with Misam…no pun intended." He tried a smile, but Kaia stared daggers at him. "Anyway, after the test, you were too exhausted, and I figured it was best to leave you to your thoughts. And after *that*…well, I needed to make sure we could talk in private. So here we are." He gestured to the triangular room.

Kaia crossed her arms and continued to stare. Jonas's face twisted as if he had just remembered something.

"Alexi is…he is the only one with a spaceship without a tracker. And he only comes out in public during Stallo. No one knows where he lives or why he hides. Stallo is the only chance we'll get to bargain with him. Gre—'the hag' was right about that. It would take me too long to find something similar." Jonas rubbed his head, and his shoulders sank. "If this had happened last rotation, we could have taken one of Framnes's cargo ship, but now…"

Jonas's voice trailed off. He walked over to one of the benches and sat down, the weight of his words draining him.

"Five cycles ago, the leaders of Framnes began negotiations with Solon. Once they make a deal with them—and they will—Solon will be everywhere on this planet." Jonas put his head in his hands. "I have seen it happen before, how Solon spreads its poison. First they promise superior medical technology in exchange for a base on a planet. Everyone is happy. The citizens see their loved ones healed. Then Solon asks for more, and people begin to disappear. People like you and me." Jonas took out the bloodied handkerchief and stroked the embroidered letter. "Like my daughter."

Kaia's breath caught in her throat. She had been ready to fight with Jonas, but his words cooled the heat in her blood. She let her shoulders fall and sat down next to him.

"I'm sorry," Her voice was surprisingly steady. "Is there anything we can do to stop them?"

It was a futile question, but she needed to hear the answer out loud. To hear someone tell her that she'd been right to be afraid, to have left Biorki behind, to have run from her dad's dead body.

"No. Nothing can stop Solon. Those that have tried are all dead or in hiding."

Jonas dragged his finger over the letter F again before putting the handkerchief away.

"Anyway," Jonas exclaimed, bouncing back to his feet, causing Kaia to topple backward off the bench. "You still need Alexi's attention and a good bargaining chip." He looked down at her as she struggled to stand. "And better reflexes."

Jonas reached out a hand, a smile on his face. Had the sadness been a trick? No, she was sure it had been real. She let him pull her to her feet.

"Focus on winning Stallo. Nothing entertains the rich and bored more than watching young people risk their lives. You'll get Alexi's attention and the money we need." Jonas's eyes shone with anticipation. "I will take care of the rest. I will convince Morgan to keep your face off the roster before the event starts. In case Solon arrives, that should give us more time." He grabbed her hand, his face a little less animated. "I won't let them catch you."

Something in Kaia shifted, softened. She believed him. For whatever reason, Jonas would help her. He knew what they were up against. It made her feel more confident and less alone.

Kaia tried not to think about the deadly hurdles of Stallo and squeezed his hand. "I will win."

Jonas let go of her hand and moved to pat her head. "I know."

She swatted it away, the corners of her lips twitching. Jonas laughed. The full and hearty sound warmed her chest.

Still laughing, Jonas walked toward the exit. "But first, you need some real food and sleep. There's no way you will win anything, let alone withstand Misam's rigorous training, on an empty stomach."

"Wait." There was still something he hadn't answered. "Was the rock radioactive?"

The idea had come to her as she'd thought about her symptoms. She had seen them before when a miner had been exposed to radon gas on a scavenger mission in the deeper mines.

Jonas turned back to her, a weird expression on his face. "Yes."

No wonder Misam had lost his eyesight. She was lucky to have survived. But maybe it hadn't been luck, and perhaps that was the point. From the look on Jonas's face, she could tell he was expecting outrage, but she was too tired.

Kaia smiled at her hands, then met his eyes. "Just to be clear, Gret-ha is the hag?"

His grimace soured further. "Yes."

She smiled and patted Jonas's shoulder, "What food are we getting? You better be paying after what you put me through this cycle, and it better not be that canned food from this morning. I'm starving."

Jonas laughed behind her as she walked out the door.

Back in the little guest room with a full stomach, she felt…better. Yes, she felt better. She was still drained and sore, but she wasn't alone. She had help, and Biorki was still safe. The tug of guilt, of loss, still churned within her. But she had a clear goal now. Something to focus on. Something to keep her from dwelling on what she had done.

Kaia rolled onto her back, the springs underneath her squeaking in protest. Cracked paint covered the ceiling, and she resisted the urge to stand up and tear off a flake.

This cycle had only been a stepping stone, the first crack into a new copper ore. She had made it through alive. She had passed the test and earned Jonas's trust. She knew she should be proud, but her nerves were raw, the food in her stomach flipping and churning. She still had to win Stallo, and she had only four cycles to prepare.

Kaia shook the thought out of her head. *Focus on what you can do now.*

She rose, flicked the light switch, and flopped onto her back again. The darkness enveloped her. Why hadn't the hag—Gret-ha—disclosed her connection to Kaia's dad? Maybe she'd wanted to protect her identity? She had done what her dad had promised: saved them and helped her get to Framnes. The reason she had not told Kaia her name didn't matter.

She turned onto her side and pulled the blanket over her healing shoulder. She thought of Biorki, of how his hand had stroked her back when they'd thought they were going to die, of how he had promised not to leave her. Her chest tightened.

She pulled her knees up to meet her stomach, adjusted the pillow so it supported her neck, and breathed in. Had he gone back to Kaldwell, as she hoped? Was he cursing her name for leaving him? Or was he still unconscious, unable to wake from the frostbite that had taken his toes? He had done everything for her, and what had she done? She had left him there without a word. Not even a goodbye or an apology. She stared into the darkness of the room. *Coward.* She exhaled. *No. You did it to save him.*

Two laughing faces filled her mind: Ine and Rakel. They had stopped the taller Solon woman, and Ingá had distracted the two guards. What had happened to them, to the other people in Kaldwell? She had left them there with an evil no one understood.

She breathed in and out. *No.* She was slipping into the past. She tightened her grip on the blanket, the course strands itching her palm. *Focus on what you can do now.*

She had to get some sleep. Based on Jonas's descriptions of Misam's training, she would need all the rest she could get. She closed her eyes and focused on what she had to do, on what she needed to be: an incredible iceboarder. If she wasn't one already, she would become one. She would do anything to succeed. She would not fail again. She would win Stallo and keep her promise. She would escape, no matter what she had to sacrifice.

CHAPTER 23

Jonas had already left by the time she woke up. *I am running some errands*, the note on the kitchen table read. *Misam will meet you at the training facility. P.S.: Don't withdraw any money from the minor's union. It's better not to leave any trace. Here are some coins. You better pay me back.* She pocketed the pouch of coins he had left next to the note.

After eating another questionable meal, she grabbed her train ticket and thermos and walked to the exit. It felt strange not putting on a monosuit. Instead, she tied her hair back, checked her overall straps, and pulled on a matching jacket. The green jacket, unlike the overalls, was too small. It made the gray sweater underneath itch even more. She let her hand fall to the empty space next to her hip. Jonas had convinced her to leave her axes at home—"You're trying to blend in, not fight monsters."

She hoped he was right, because she felt naked when she opened the door. With one last sigh, she ran into the street. The bronze coins bounced inside her pocket as she rushed to catch the train.

The ride to the Framnes city center was uneventful. She had found the same train as the cycle before and boarded it without any issues. The conductor had been equally uninteresting. Once again, she had enjoyed the view as the train had left the dark tunnel leading out of their sub-city.

Jonas had explained the function of each sub-city in the last cycle. The one where he lived was the miner's hub, which was the poorest. The people in the other sub-cities were responsible for different things, like producing food pills, equipment, and clothes, building machinery, and maintenance. Jonas had explained, along with rude hand gestures, that anyone with a higher rank lived in the city center, especially the leaders. They didn't want to live among their workers, yet they decided where the resources went and who got to live where.

"They are idiots," Jonas had said with a mouth full of food. "They used to be chosen based on their expertise, but now the positions are inherited. It's ridiculous."

Kaia had never considered these issues before. The only thing she had cared about back in Kaldwell was receiving enough coins to survive. Learning that their lack of food and medical supplies had been due to lousy leadership had only made her sigh into her drink.

Walking off the train, Kaia pulled up the dark green hood of her jacket. She didn't need the stares her hair seemed to draw. There were others here with curly hair, but still, it was a recognizable trait, one she had hated about herself as a child. It wouldn't hurt to keep a low profile, even if Jonas assured her that Solon had no base in this city yet. *Yet.* She pulled the hood farther over her head, shielding her face.

She looked at the borrowed time tracker on her wrist. Jonas had handed her the old tech last cycle. *Untraceable, but still able to tell the time.* She had arrived earlier than expected, and she slowed her pace. Still covered by the hood, she tipped her head back and closed her eyes. The breeze on her face felt terrific but unnatural. She missed her helmet.

Walking down the street, she watched shop owners roll up their curtains and open their doors. A man with red hair grunted at her as she passed. Kaia stepped to the side and saw him place a welcome sign outside his jewelry store. She had never seen the purpose of jewelry; metals were for machinery. But she had to admit some of his intricate pieces almost changed her mind.

Kaia turned a corner and breathed in. Unfamiliar, complex fragrances filled her nose. Rows of stalls stood on each side of this street, and smoke drifted up from the wheeled counters—no, food carts. Kaia watched as the owners lit their stoves and burners. More smells of mouthwatering soups and stews wafted past. She swallowed and held her breath as she walked past, telling herself, *You already ate, you already ate.* Even if it was only a gray blob of goo.

When she reached the end of the row of food carts, Kaia had to step to the side to avoid being run over by a group of kids. They giggled, their mum yelling behind them not to be late for class. A couple of old men playing cards hushed them. A blond-haired kid looked back and stuck out his tongue. A crooked-nosed man scowled and slapped another card on the table. Kaia hid a smile under her hood, remembering how she had done the same at that age.

Then she turned the next corner, and hordes of men and women appeared. They rushed out of side streets and back alleys as if on cue. Kaia looked at her time tracker; it was ten minutes till work hours began. Kaia walked among them, dodging those who were late for their shifts. To her amazement, no one looked the same. Unique faces passed her, some darker than hers, some whiter than snow. There were eyes of every color, none lingering on her. She saw hairstyles of different colors, structures, and styles. The most common seemed to be a braid—both women and men wore one or two down their backs.

The uniforms of green and gray that she had learned to expect in Jonas's sub-city seemed rare on these streets. Some people wore black-and-red overalls, others green-and-blue ones. What struck Kaia the most was the women's clothing. Dresses of every color swirled across the cobblestones. Made from thick material, the long skirts seemed to glide with the women. One exceptionally decorated woman wore a beautiful red-and-green dress. Gold circular embroidery ran down her sleeves and hems.

The woman caught Kaia staring. If looks could kill, Kaia would be a crater. She hurried forward. She probably looked suspicious with her hood pulled up, like a pickpocket or a thief. A smile crept onto her lips. She liked that idea—not being a burden or a curly-haired freak, just a thief. Simple.

When she turned the last corner before the city square, Kaia halted. A sign hung above the street with the words a blast from the past glowing on it. She walked over to the display window and lifted a hand to touch it. What a wonder it was to see glass outside of a house, used as a window. She pressed her forehead against the reflective surface. The glass was cool against her skin as she looked inside.

She blinked. *No way.* She pressed her face harder against the window. Rows upon rows of old mechanical toys lined the many shelves inside. Some moved and wiggled in repeating patterns. Others were in pieces. The neon-blue sign above them read, kit: learn to build your own. Fog filled Kaia's vision as her hot breath touched the glass. She had never seen anything like these toys, though she had read about them in an old tech magazine. Her dad had called them droids.

"Useless little things," he had said. "They never worked down here. Too cold."

They had spent hours discussing why droids were a technology of the past. The memory twisted within her, and she thought of Biorki. He would love this shop. She imagined him here, a wide grin on his face as he took a droid apart. He would examine it, figure out how it worked, and then she would help put it back together again.

Drowning in her thoughts, she barely saw the blur of movement, the shadow behind the fog. She wiped the glass with her sleeve, and two large brown eyes and a smile stared back at her. She almost jumped back as the woman waved at her to come inside.

Kaia looked at her wrist. She had fifteen minutes before the training facility opened. Feeling embarrassed to have been caught with her nose pushed up against the glass, she entered the shop. A bell chimed as the door opened and closed behind her. The shop was small, dark, and dusty. The scent of oil and grease hung in the air. Brown rusted shelves rose to the ceiling. Kaia squeezed between a pair of tilted cabinets, each full of droid parts, every piece designed to do a particular task. A note under a black part said, for planting seeds. Well, that was indeed a useless service. The woman she'd seen had disappeared into the back of the shop and was sitting on a blindingly purple pillow. Her eyes followed Kaia as she moved between the shelves.

This shop was like a time capsule, a labyrinth of old technology. Kaia dragged her finger over a red and rusted droid head. The small spaces between the shelves made her movements slow and meticulous. She read every label and looked at every part and circuit chip. She was so immersed in the parts that she didn't notice a small metal object until it zoomed past her feet.

Swearing, she stepped back, trying not to crush it beneath her boot. The sudden movement knocked her off balance. Falling backward, she grabbed on to one of the shelves. It made an awful creaking sound under her weight. Dust filled the air. Kaia coughed and blinked, trying to regain her balance. A clank of metal on metal sounded from above. She looked up in time to see one of the more ridiculous droid parts roll off its shelf. It was headed straight for the metal floor. *Shit.*

A flurry of movement, the sound of something soft being kicked, and then…*thump*. The part landed on a purple pillow. Kaia looked to the back of the shop, but the woman was no longer there. Neither was the pillow. Had she kicked her pillow from there?

A hand reached over Kaia's shoulder and touched her hair. She froze.

"Beautiful." The woman's voice was as rich as a hot stew on a cold day.

Kaia didn't dare move, her hand still gripping the shelf. She had been there all of three minutes, and she had almost broken something. An old instinct told her it was better to remain still. The woman smelled of things Kaia couldn't name, but the scent was…familiar? Like an old foggy memory of intangible figures and objects. It slipped from her mind as soon as it arrived.

The woman pulled on one of Kaia's curls. "So soft."

Kaia realized what was happening and pulled her hood back on. It must have slipped off when she lost her balance. *Double shit.* Blood pumping, she straightened and released her grip on the shelf. She took a step back from the woman; she had never liked it when people touched her hair. But this woman, whom she had never met, put her strangely at ease. Her presence was too warm, and it made Kaia uncomfortable. Kaia took another step back.

"I'm so sorry. I didn't mean to——" Kaia began.

"Oh, don't worry, it was my stupid droid. It loves to pull pranks on people." The woman looked over her shoulder. A small square droid peeked out from behind a table leg. "It's quite adorable once you get to know it. But it is quite shy."

Kaia tilted her head to see the droid better. The little square thing stiffened and scurried behind a shelf.

"See?"

The woman lifted the part that had fallen and placed it back in its designated spot, allowing Kaia to examine her more closely. Her face was soft but strong. Golden-brown eyes shone with sharp intelligence as she inspected the shelf. Her brown braided hair draped across her shoulder. Though she was head shorter than Kaia, she somehow appeared taller——a massive feat, considering that she wore oil-smeared brown overalls and an oversize sweater full of burns and holes. Still, there was an unmistakable elegance in the woman's movements, a straightness in her neck, in her posture. She could be forty rotations or twenty; Kaia couldn't tell. The woman's skin was flawless, a rich reddish-brown that glowed where the light struck the soft curve of her nose. She was beautiful.

The woman's eyes landed on Kaia. "What are you looking for? A helper droid? A builder droid? A friend?" The woman chewed on the word *friend* a little too long.

Why was she here? She shouldn't be drawing any attention to herself. Kaia looked down at her time tracker. *Dritt.*

"I'm so sorry. I really have to go." Kaia rushed toward the exit. "Thank you for letting me look around."

"Anytime," the woman called after her. "Come back whenever you want."

Kaia barely caught the last words as she ran out the door. The bell chimed behind her. She would be late for her first training session ever. How could she be so careless? Misam's face flashed before her eyes. She launched into a full sprint.

Kaia was gasping for air. The stairs had been a challenge, but she'd made it on time. She looked at her time tracker. Well, she was a few minutes late. Only Morgan and a few others were in the entry hall. Morgan looked up from her counter, frowned at Kaia, and resumed typing on her tablet. Maybe she would be alone on the course? The idea of having it all to herself made her stomach flutter.

Then she opened the door to the locker room, and the flutter became a rock.

Twelve sets of eyes looked right at her. Ten boys—or men, she couldn't quite decide—and two girls her age. No, one of the girls was older, her freckled face twisting with disapproval. On the bench closest to the thirteenth locker sat Misam. He was sucking on a straw, drinking something from a pouch in his hands. He didn't look up or acknowledge her presence, but considering his blindness, she wasn't surprised.

"You're late." Misam licked his lips, his head still turned away.

Kaia's stomach dropped. Of course he had noticed. A few of the guys smirked. Great.

"Only by a few minutes." Kaia walked over to Misam's bench.

"Late is late." Misam used his thumb to point at the locker. "What are you waiting for?"

So he wouldn't be nice to her, even after what he'd put her through last cycle. But it didn't matter. If he could help her win, she would do what he said.

She felt the eyes of the other competitors on her as she crossed the room. The younger girl caught Kaia's gaze and smiled sympathetically. She reminded her of Ine. Kaia smiled back but faltered when the older girl scowled at her. What was her problem? Kaia tried to ignore the anger rising in her chest. She was, once again, unwelcome.

She could hear Misam slurping on his pouch behind her as she unlocked her locker door. She pulled out the boots and slammed them onto the bench a little too hard. Would she be disqualified if she slapped the older girl? She turned back to the locker and paused. Preoccupied with her thoughts, she hadn't seen it at first. Now she stared at the new addition to her locker.

An old helmet with red, black, and white swirls across it sat on the top shelf. She grabbed it, turning it over in her hands. Jonas? No. She glanced at Misam. Could it be? Kaia examined the visor and padding. It had clearly been repaired recently. The visor was brand new, although the program needed to be updated.

Kaia tried it on, and the padding automatically adjusted to the shape of her head. She smiled. The feeling was nostalgic, like a hug from an old friend. She removed the helmet and turned to Misam, who was folding up his empty pouch.

"Thank you." No one had ever lent her something of that quality before.

Misam bent down and pulled out a bag sitting between his feet. He lifted it toward her and smiled, his white eyes shining.

"Well, I can't let my trainee get injured." His voice changed. "And believe me, you're going to need all the protection you can get."

Kaia didn't doubt Misam's words. This contest was dangerous. Yes, you could win housing in the city center, unimaginable wealth, and prestige. But you might not ride away in one piece. She looked at the young faces around the room. They had all resumed preparing for their practice runs. The guy closest to Kaia at locker twelve couldn't be older than sixteen. His dark brown hair swung in front of his face as he struggled to get into his brown-and-green competition suit.

There was a reason most competitors were young. Not only were young people nimbler and more energetic, they were also more likely to be reckless and fearless. Fear was more dangerous than any jump, any hurdle. Fear made you stiff, unreactive, and slow.

Kaia heard the buzz of Drap's weapon in her head. She tried to breathe it away as she looked around the room. The other competitors were all younger than her except for the freckled girl, whose disapproval was still palpable. Surely she had her reasons for being here, like Kaia. Either way, she had to be crazy.

One of the older guys with sharp features, blond hair, and blue eyes noticed Kaia staring. He smirked and winked at her. Looking away, Kaia focused on the brown fabric bag Misam had given her. Opening it, she pulled out a lump of red, white, and black material. It was soft, almost slippery, as it slid over her fingers. She found the top and held it up at full length.

She gasped. A suit—but not any suit. She had seen it many times, on repeat. Kaia stared at Misam. He raised his shoulders in reply, still sitting with his face turned away from her. It was uncanny how he always knew when she was looking at him.

"It's my old suit, the one I won my last Stallo with. I thought you would have more use for it than me. And Jonas said you might need one." Misam waved a hand. "I used to be skinny back then. It should fit you."

Kaia was speechless. She had seen that race; she had seen him win. How the rider in this suit had moved across the ice, how he had used the front of his board to launch him forward, was embedded in her memory. She had tried to emulate his boarding style, but she had never even imagined meeting him. And it was *Misam*? Her jaw hit the floor. She was holding a piece of history in her hands. And her favorite iceboarder of all time—the most decorated Stallo rider in history—was blind.

Misam pulled out another pouch from somewhere and put it to his lips. He sighed as the contents filled his mouth.

Kaia removed her outer layers and pulled on the suit without wasting another minute. It fit like a glove. Some of the other contestants stopped and stared at her, but she didn't care and paid them no attention as she pulled on her boots. She was about to fulfill her dreams with her favorite rider as her trainer. Even though the circumstances were not at all as she had imagined, she would enjoy it. She would enjoy every second of it.

CHAPTER 24

She hated it.

Misam hadn't let her go down to the course with the others. Instead, he had told her to leave her helmet and board and brought her into a connecting room. Kaia had been balancing on a moving beam for hours while Misam threw blocks at her. Another one connected with her jaw. She swore but managed to stay on the beam with a twist and a bit of flailing.

"Don't flail!" Misam yelled as he threw another hard block. "Move with the beam, not against it."

The block hit her shoulder. Wincing at the instant pain shooting down her arm, she jerked back, stepping too far to the side, and tumbled off the beam. She fell toward the pads below. The fabric-wrapped foam absorbed some of the impact, but not all, as she landed flat on her back. Kaia grunted as the air was forced out of her lungs.

"No control." Misam sighed and moved to pick up some of the items he had thrown. "You'll fall into a ravine with those reflexes. You won't even see it coming."

Kaia gasped for air; her chest throbbed. "Who are you to tell me what I will and won't see?"

The second the words left her mouth, Kaia clamped her lips shut. She almost regretted saying them. Almost. She didn't have time for this. She needed to practice on the course, to memorize the turns and jumps, not balance on a stick.

Misam threw another block at her. She rolled to the side, narrowly dodging it, and it flew past her head.

"I was questioning your ability to see"—Misam's voice was like steel—"because you're more blind than me."

Kaia got to her feet and brushed off some of her embarrassment. A slither of sweat ran down her back. She rubbed her jaw and took a deep breath.

"You might say I'm blind, but I did notice that I'm the only one with a trainer. And some of the other contestants clearly don't want me here. Why?" Kaia could guess why, but she needed to know for sure.

Misam pulled on the ropes the beam rested on. It rose above the floor, swinging precariously, a pendulum of padded metal.

"The other contestants have been practicing for months with their trainers. The only reason they are here this close to the event is to try to beat their own speed records, increase their reaction times, and to prepare for surprises in the course. Especially the obstacles the Stallo organizers will add to the course on the competition cycle. They will be as new to them as to you. That's one thing going for us." Misam walked under the beam, dodging it with a sidestep as it swung toward his head. "As for why they aren't exactly inviting, they have put rotations of sweat and tears into qualifying for Stallo. And here you are, two cycles before the contest—unknown, unproven, and with a trainer they all requested and never got. It's unheard of."

Kaia sighed. Her guess had been correct. She was already marked as an outcast. She would stand out like a sore thumb, and having Misam around made it worse. Keeping her photo out of the community feeds could only do so much. If Jonas was wrong and Solon was watching the competition preparations, this was terrible news. It made her stomach twist.

Misam grabbed the step stool, placed it below the beam, and looked at Kaia with a raised eyebrow. She climbed up onto the beam again.

"We will prove to them that you're capable of winning if you follow my instructions." Misam held the beam steady as Kaia got into a standing crouch. "But first you have to prove it to me."

Misam placed the stool against the wall and returned to where Kaia was already struggling to keep her balance. He walked to the end of the beam and smiled.

"Remember"—Misam pushed the beam into a violent swing—"breathe, focus on what's not there, and don't fall."

Kaia met the force of the swing with bent knees, her sideways stance solid, but her arms flailed again. It took every bit of her focus to stay balanced. Even breathing seemed impossible as the beam reached the end of its swing, then hurtled back the other way. How was she supposed to focus on what was not there? An object flew at her. She stepped backward, placed her boot on the beam, found her balance, and dodged the ball. How was she supposed to be learning anything when it was all she could do not to fall?

The midcycle bell rang through the room just as a ball struck her in the gut.

"Let's take a break." Misam's voice was dry after all the yelling.

"Okay," was the only word Kaia could muster as she slid down to solid ground and collapsed.

Lying on the padding, she felt her chest rise and fall rapidly. Sweat ran into her eyes and down her back, chest, and legs. Her underclothes stuck to her skin. She felt like a piece of pounded meat wrapped in plastic. Misam handed her a small towel. She wheezed a thank-you and lifted it to her face.

Squeezing her eyes shut, she sighed into the soft fabric and wiped her face. They had been at it for hours, and she hadn't made any progress. Rubbing her temples, she stared at the ceiling. What was she doing here?

Gulping down some stale air, she urged her body to move. It screamed in protest as she pulled herself into a half-slouching, half-sitting position. Everything hurt. But her legs…they were in a whole new category of soreness. She could feel her heart in her thighs. They throbbed with every beat, and her calf twitched with every movement. She wasn't sure if it was from balancing on the beam or constantly falling to the floor. She prodded her thigh and grimaced. It was probably both.

Misam cleared his throat.

"I promised Kritan I would have lunch with him. I'll be back in an hour."

Misam reached out a hand and pulled Kaia to her feet. Her legs shook with the effort of standing. The room tilted to one side, then the other. Finding her balance on flat ground turned out to be a lot harder than usual. Misam turned toward the exit, then stopped. Kaia could see him struggling with something, a tightness in his back. His shoulders rose, and he finally spun to face her.

"You're going to fail. If you can't make yourself do what I'm asking, I can't send you out there. You won't survive."

Kaia gaped at him. She had put everything into this training session even when she didn't understand the purpose of the exercise.

Before she could protest, Misam walked back to where she swayed. "Think about why we're doing this. Why are you here?"

Her own words echoed in her head. What *was* she doing here? No, she knew what; she knew the stakes better than anyone. Misam was the one who hadn't told her anything useful about the exercise. A rush of heat spread through her chest.

"I'm here to win," Kaia growled. She stepped forward. "I won't let you—"

"Then why are you holding back?" Misam's voice slammed against her, his face only a few breaths away.

"I'm not. I'm doing everything I can." Kaia shook with anger.

"Why are you holding back?!" His white eyes burned into her as spit flew from his mouth and onto her face.

"I'm not!" Kaia didn't move, even when Misam's nose almost touched hers.

His next words came out as a whisper. "Why are you holding back?"

"I don't know!" Kaia blurted out, tears building behind her eyes. "I don't know."

Misam stepped back, giving Kaia room to breathe, then took her jaw in his hand, making her hold his eyes.

"You know why." His voice was soft now, like when he held her head last cycle. "It's not going to go away. It's there; it's a part of you. Use it, or I won't let you compete."

Misam smiled softly, patted her head, and left her to crumple to the floor.

Use it? Her anger? That vile hum that lived inside her? The idea made her hair stand on end. With her knees on the ground, she bent her head to the floor, her throat closing, her breath quickening. She tried to breathe into the fabric, but the air didn't come. It wasn't a surprise that Misam knew, not after the test, but to say it out loud…that was a whole other game Kaia wasn't willing to play.

Use it, or I won't let you compete. The words spun inside her head. She had risked so much to get this far, and Misam would stop her, pull her from the competition, for not using the dark abyss trying to slither into her thoughts. No. She wouldn't do it. It felt too…*wrong*.

She hit her head against the mat. No. *Thump.* No. *Thump.* Again and again, she tried to knock the thought out of her head. No. She wouldn't use it, even if it meant being captured or worse.

Then her conversation with Jonas crept into the chaos of her mind. He had lost his daughter. *Solon spreads its poison.* Kaia banged her head again. *Thump.* Images of Biorki, Ine, Ingá, and even Ulla filled her mind. They were in Kaldwell right now with Solon. *Thump.* Would they be the next to disappear?

She shouldn't have left them, left Biorki. She had thought only of her escape—so selfish. *Thump.* There was no telling if the hag could keep Biorki safe. What if Solon found him there? She had left him, believing they were after only her. But what if there were others like her, like Jonas's daughter? How conceited had she been? *Thump.*

The sound of her head hitting the mat became a soft drum, a beat for her thoughts to march to. When it stopped, when her head cleared, she knew she had to do what Misam had said. Maybe she could fight back if she could learn to control what was inside her. Perhaps she could go back to Kaldwell and get her friends out of there. She needed that spaceship.

Fear gripped her, but she breathed it out and closed her fists. She would win Stallo, and if that meant passing the point of no return, she would do it. She would find a way to help them and keep her word to her dad.

Something warm ran down her face. The cut on her forehead had opened. She wiped her face with the towel and rose to her feet. She boxed her thighs with her fists so they would listen. She had to be ready. Her stomach rumbled. First, she needed food.

No one was in the locker room as she changed. She pulled on her hood and left the building. Feeling the weight of the pouch of coins in her pocket, Kaia walked to one of the stands she had passed that morning. The smells from the small building were otherworldly. Smoke oozed out the little window where a small man sat to serve his customers.

After standing in line, Kaia returned to walking the streets, holding a cup full of a thick and creamy soup. She tried to take a sip and immediately burned her tongue. She heard her dad's words: *When will you learn to wait?* Kaia smiled. The memory and the soup warmed her. She felt better if she didn't think about what would come next, what she had to do. But if she succeeded, she could do something for someone else.

Letting her mind wander, Kaia walked until she ended up outside the droid shop again. Finishing her soup, she threw the reusable cup into one of the recycling chutes on the street and walked in. The chime rang, and the woman's head popped out from behind one of the shelves.

"Ahh, I had a feeling you would be back." The woman smiled, and her eyes glowed with warmth.

Kaia didn't know what came over her, but she walked over and returned the smile. "Sorry about earlier. I didn't realize the time, and…well, I wanted to thank you for being so kind after I almost broke one of your droid parts."

The woman took Kaia's hand and looked up at her face with a grin. "Don't worry about it. I get very few customers, especially ones who appreciate my droids."

The woman's skin glowed in the soft light of the store. Maybe she was closer to thirty rotations?

"I must go. But thank you for being so understanding." Kaia didn't know why she needed to explain herself to this woman. Maybe it was the softness in her eyes or the kindness she had shown, but Kaia felt as if she owed her.

The woman squeezed Kaia's hand softly and nodded. "Can I be so frank as to suggest that you return next cycle?" The woman's voice was a soft wind in Kaia's ears. "I would love to show you some more of my droids. I don't expect you to buy anything; I would just love to have someone to discuss the technology with, if you're interested."

Kaia struggled to hide her surprise and delight. She could come early in the cycle before the Stallo building opened. It wouldn't take time away from her training. Also, it wouldn't hurt to learn more about this technology. Maybe this woman could teach her something about spaceships. She probably couldn't, but…

Kaia looked at the row of droid parts behind the woman. "Are you sure that's okay?"

The woman grinned and nodded vigorously, making her braid jump on her shoulder. "Absolutely! Oh, and my name is Venlá." The woman let go of Kaia's hand, which Kaia hadn't realized Venlá was still holding.

A little stab of guilt churned in Kaia's stomach as she lied, "My name is Lin. Nice to meet you."

Venlá tipped her head to the side. "See you next cycle?"

She nodded. "See you next cycle."

Kaia walked out the door, her steps a little lighter, the chime ringing behind her. Even the thought of more training didn't discourage her. She took a deep breath, held her shoulders back, and walked up the stairs to the triangular door of the Stallo building. She would prove Misam wrong somehow. He would let her compete.

Kaia's body throbbed in places she didn't know could bruise. The worst one pulsed on her left hip. Still swelling, it rubbed against her overalls, making walking to Jonas's house hard.

Kaia had failed. Regardless of her conviction, she hadn't been able to face her fear. How could she while simultaneously dodging objects thrown by Misam? He had screamed at her to close her eyes, to feel the beam, but all she had done was fall off and climb back on again over and over.

Even after working for hours, her balancing time had increased by only a few seconds. When the bell had chimed, Misam had stormed out the door without a word, leaving Kaia alone, barely able to crawl. It had taken her thirty minutes to regain enough strength to limp to the locker room. The remaining contestants had been unsympathetic, except for the young blond-haired girl who reminded her of Ine. The girl had shared a cup of cold water with Kaia and introduced herself as Sofia.

Kaia opened the door to Jonas's house. Inside, the smell of dust and plastic embraced her. No sounds drifted to meet her. The rooms were empty and dark. Kicking off her boots, she hobbled to the kitchen. No note. Sighing with relief, she dragged herself to the steam shower. She did not feel like talking, or smiling, or feeling.

Clean and fed, she crashed into her bed. Her dad's bag rested under her pillow. She had found some old blankets in one of Jonas's piles and arranged them on top of the bed to shield her bruises. It wasn't working. Too tired to care, her eyelids fell shut the moment her head hit the pillow. She had two more cycles to train, maybe less to convince Misam. But that was a worry for later.

As she drifted into sleep, her thoughts twisted into nightmares. Solon guards threw syringes at her as she balanced on a beam over a glacier crack.

CHAPTER 25

A sound tore Kaia from sleep. She jumped out of bed. If she hadn't caught herself on the only chair in the room, she would have crashed to the floor; her legs were too sore to hold her weight. The sound rang out again, and this time she could tell it was coming from her wrist. Kaia grunted. It was her crappy alarm. She had set it for early so she'd have more time at the droid shop. She rubbed her crusty eyes and dragged herself down the hall.

After a hot shower, she eased into one of the kitchen seats. The steam hadn't eased her aching muscles. Instead, it had just made her hair impossible. She tugged it into a lopsided ponytail and wiped a strand from her cheek. With a can of goo and a cup of hot Nade in her stomach, she grabbed the note on the table. Jonas must have left it at some incomprehensibly early hour.

I'm running some more errands this cycle. Misam told me you are a slow learner. I don't doubt it, but we do not have that kind of time. So get a grip and get it done!

Kaia crumpled the message and threw it in the trash. She hated mornings.

She slammed the door behind her as she left Jonas's house, her hood securely up. Why was she always surrounded by people telling her what to do? The train ride was uneventful, but her heart was in her throat when she stepped off the carriage. Her stomach twisted in anticipation as she walked down the waking street of food carts. What if she had misinterpreted the invitation? What if Venlá invited everyone to come spend time in the shop out of courtesy? Kaia stopped under the neon sign. No, this was a bad idea.

But something about the shop, the dark aisles of droids, made her step through the door. The chime rang, and inside stood Venlá, a wide grin on her face. All of Kaia's doubts disintegrated. The woman's arms were full of small droids.

"Welcome, welcome." Venlá's amber eyes shone against her golden skin. "I have prepared a little table for us in the back. Follow me."

She dropped the pile of tech into Kaia's arms and turned. Balancing the small metal pieces, Kaia followed, a smile tugging at her lips. They walked to the back of the store, where a large metal table stood against the wall. There were two tall chairs, and the wall behind it bore different droid schematics and code. Venlá pressed a button, and the tabletop lit up with a soft white light. Above it hung a round lamp on a movable frame. It was the perfect workstation.

Kaia set the droids down on the table and looked at Venlá, who had pulled out a fabric roll. She placed it on the table and untied the strings holding it together. Unhindered, it rolled open to reveal lines of different tools and gadgets. Kaia stared at the pliers, handheld plasma cutters, wrenches, pure metal pieces, files, and tools she had never seen before.

"These are for you to use." Venlá grabbed another roll of fabric. "These are mine." Seeing the surprise on Kaia's face, Venlá chuckled. "I figured it would be more fun if we worked on the droids together." She grabbed a cup and poured Kaia a hot drink. "I don't know your skill level, but some help with my commissions won't hurt. Shall we?" She handed Kaia the drink and gestured to the chair.

Kaia grinned back at Venlá and nodded. "I would love to."

Venlá turned out to be a great conversationalist and teacher. After she showed Kaia how to interlink the wires of a rotating joint, the conversation turned to more trivial things. They talked about their favorite drinks and activities, their worst food pill experiences, and which portable heat converters were best. It was nice to talk to another woman. Venlá listened and nodded along without any snarky remarks. It was refreshing.

As Kaia struggled to connect a wire to the internal circuit of an old droid, she thought of Biorki. A steady hand and a mind for details were his things, not hers. She wished he was there, then remembered why he wasn't. She bit down on her lip, refocused her attention, and leaned over the droid. A lump of hair fell out of her ponytail for the hundredth time and into her eyes. The welding tool slipped out of her clammy palm. Venlá chuckled and held out a hand. Accepting defeat, Kaia handed the droid over.

"I see the problem. You forgot to add the live wire before attaching the circuit. It's hard. Let me show you a neat little trick I learned, but you can't tell anyone." Venlá winked at Kaia, who nodded, intrigued.

Venlá rolled up her right sleeve, revealing a metal bracelet on her wrist. Flush with her skin, the almost-black metal bore no symbols or carvings. Kaia had never seen metal like it. Then the bracelet rippled. She blinked. She'd never seen metal act like that, either. Kaia leaned closer. The metal seemed to fluctuate between its solid and liquid states. *No way.* A change like that should exude intense heat, meaning it should melt other metals and burn through skin. Not to mention that it was impossible. But Venlá seemed unbothered as she smiled at Kaia, then closed her eyes.

The bracelet moved. Kaia stood, her chair creaking with the sudden movement. Holding her breath, she watched the dark metal flow up Venlá's wrist, against gravity, as if it had a mind of its own. A hum, like the rumble of boulders rolling through a cave, filled Kaia's head. The metal moved into Venlá's palm, now a shapeless blob of black liquid.

Venlá's brows tightened, and, as if instructed, the metal moved again. This time, it stretched through Venlá's fingers and into a point. It twisted in on itself and formed a long angular rod. Kaia blinked, and the metal was a solid object again.

Venlá opened her eyes. She inspected the droid with the welder tool in one hand and the strange black twisted rod in the other. After a few seconds, she pinned the red wire to the proper connection and welded it in place. When the metal had solidified around the wire, Venlá leaned back. The black rod retracted immediately, becoming a bracelet once more. She pulled her sleeve down and covered it.

"I'm not really supposed to have this, but it has helped me solve so many technical issues that I can't live without it." Venlá's voice was a whisper swallowed by the musty shelves.

"What *is* it?" Kaia couldn't look away from Venlá's wrist.

Venlá's shoulders rose, and she scratched her right ear. "That is a good question. Unfortunately, it's not one I'm capable of answering. All I know is that it is helpful to have a tool that can become anything you need, within reason."

Within reason? None of what Kaia had just seen was within reason. It shouldn't even be possible to liquify and solidify matter so quickly. And for the metal to shape itself into specific tools—that was an entirely different matter.

Venlá studied Kaia, waiting for a reaction. She had shown her this secret in good faith, had decided to trust her with this incredible thing, for whatever reason.

Kaia swallowed and eased back into her seat. "I understand. It's our secret."

Venlá's mouth spread into a smile that made her eyes glow. It was strange how that happened. "It is!" She tipped her head to the side. "Have you ever considered braiding your hair?"

"I tried to teach myself once. It didn't go so well." Kaia pulled one of her runaway curls behind her ear and shuddered, thinking about how her hair had tangled so badly that her dad had cut it short. She had endured teasing from Juhán for weeks.

"Give me a minute." Venlá turned and disappeared behind a door. Kaia could hear things being tossed around, then a shout of success. "I knew it was somewhere!"

Venlá came out holding a small brown box. A gorgeous carving of a seven-petaled flower covered the lid. It was chipped and scuffed, the flower had one broken petal, and the more intricate details were worn and discolored. It was beautiful.

"Here." Venlá gestured for Kaia to move to a lower chair by the register. "Sit."

Kaia sat down in front of Venlá, unsure what to expect.

"I think every girl should be able to braid her hair. Hair should be used to our advantage, not be a limitation. Or that's what an old friend told me." Venlá released Kaia's curls from the makeshift hairband and ran her fingers through her locks. "What beautiful hair. Your mum should be ashamed. She should have taught you how to take care of it."

Stung by the comment but not unused to it, Kaia didn't let the hurt show on her face. "I never knew my mum. And my dad…well, he barely knew how to talk to me about the monthly bleeds." Kaia's smile didn't reach her eyes. "He tried his best, though."

"I see." Venlá sighed. "Time to learn, then."

She pushed the box into Kaia's hands and pulled a comb from her pocket. Kaia inspected the box while Venlá dug into her curls. Soft against her fingers, it was shaped to fit perfectly in a hand. Lines ran through it, each a different shade of brown. The seamless layers swirled across the surface. Could it be? Kaia lifted it closer, taking in every detail and grain. It was *wood*. She had never seen wood before, or a tree, for that matter. She stroked the carvings with her finger and smiled. It was lovely.

"Open the box and hold it up for me." Venlá stopped fighting with her hair.

Kaia followed Venlá's instructions. The box had two compartments; one contained a white substance, the other a green gel. Venlá dipped her fingers in the white substance. She massaged it into Kaia's scalp and pulled it through her hair. It felt terrific.

"It's important to take care of your hair when it is dry, and it's always dry in these caves. Prep your hair with this oil, and then braid with the gel."

Venlá finished with the oil and took a dollop of the gel. She split Kaia's hair into three sections at the top of her forehead. She then braided the sections into a crisscross pattern over her head and down her back. Venlá didn't stop until Kaia's hair was tucked into one neat braid.

"There. Take a look." Venlá gestured to one of the polished metal pieces hanging on the shelf closest to them.

Kaia got up and looked at her reflection. Her face looked sharper. The curls, which had always bothered her, had been tucked away. Kaia moved, and the braid followed suit. No loose strands dared to jump into her eyes. She turned toward Venlá.

"Thank you." Kaia paused, blinking away the tears threatening to spill. "Really, thank you so much. How can I pay you back?"

Venlá chuckled and put the lid back on the wooden box. "Don't thank me; women should help each other out. Help me finish this droid, and we're square." She looked at the droid, still missing a head.

Kaia's alarm rang before they had finished the droid. She promised Venlá she would be back the following cycle before leaving the shop.

As Kaia walked to the Stallo building, she held her head high, her hood still resting on her back. She reveled in the new friendship she had made. The smoke from the food stands drifted through the air, and she breathed it all in, savoring every smell, everything about this moment. This city was all right once you got to know it.

Kaia entered the square and walked through the rush of workers. An all-too-familiar rasping cough filled the air. So CE was here too. Maybe it had started here before spreading through her hometown and killing Biorki's mother. That tragedy should have made him short-tempered or mad, but instead, he had helped people. And Kaia had left him behind.

She tugged on her new braid and let out a breath. She should warn Venlá. It could give her time to get away, a chance to fight back. But would she believe Kaia? If she didn't, Kaia would have to prove it, tell the story of how she had gotten her dad killed. How she had dragged Biorki into her mess, then left him behind. How she had fled Kaldwell, not sparing a thought for what Solon would do with Ine and Ingá, her neighbors, her schoolmates, the miners. How would Venlá feel about Kaia then?

No, Venlá didn't need to know any of that. If what the hag and Jonas had said was true, there was no escaping Solon, no fighting back. Telling Venlá now would only cause her pain and fear. Kaia shook her head and breathed. She had to focus on her mission, had to keep her promise to her dad no matter what. She had to convince Misam to let her compete. She clenched her fists and walked up the stairs.

CHAPTER 26

Only a few other contestants were there when Kaia entered the locker room. Number four, the blond guy who had winked at her the previous cycle, was chatting with number seven. Seven, a dark-haired and dark-skinned boy, looked no older than seventeen. The boy's hands moved through the air as he laughed. The older girl with the freckled nose—number eleven—was chewing on a piece of dried meat. Sofia, already dressed and ready, a number one on her purple suit, gave a little wave when she saw Kaia.

Misam was nowhere to be seen. Relieved, Kaia moved to her locker and took out the red suit. Lost in her thoughts, she didn't notice the room going quiet until someone cleared their throat.

"Hi." The blond guy moved closer to Kaia.

Surprised, Kaia turned and looked up, her boots still unfastened. "Hi?"

"Is it true that you're from one of the offshoot towns?" The guy's voice was deep and steady. Kaia guessed he was the unofficial leader of the group. All eyes were on them. Curiosity and a hint of jealousy seeped from the young faces.

Kaia had never heard Kaldwell referred to as an offshoot town before. But telling him wouldn't give much away; there were other small offshoot towns. "Yes, I am."

"Is it true that people who live there ride on scrap metal boards?"

Kaia couldn't tell if he was being serious or making fun of her. His eyes seemed earnest, but the smile on his lips wavered.

"No, not that I know of." Kaia fastened her boots. "Is it true that people in Framnes ride on boards made of gold square chips?"

Silence. Then someone burst into laughter. Kaia looked over to see number eleven, the freckled-nosed girl, bending over and clutching her stomach. Small pieces of meat flew from her mouth.

"Really, David? *That's* what you asked her?" The girl wiped her face. "Of all the things you could have asked, that's what you chose to go with?"

David's face turned white, almost matching the suit Kaia hadn't yet pulled over her shoulders.

"Oh, give me a break, Vilde." David rubbed his cheek. "My mum told me that once, and I wanted to know if it was true. I can't even imagine riding on scraps, can you?"

Vilde's brown eyes darkened. "You know damn well that not everybody here can afford new equipment."

"I didn't mean it that way." David turned to Kaia, his face now a bright pink. "Sorry. I didn't mean to be insensitive. I love boarding so much, even with the risks. I wanted to know if everyone has the same experience, you know?" His eyes didn't falter once, even as his face switched from a pale pink to a dark red.

Kaia had misread them all. They didn't seem resentful, just curious. Although—she glanced at Vilde—she wasn't entirely sure that was true of everyone.

Catching Kaia's stare, Vilde raised her shoulders. "I'm from a small town as well. I didn't have much growing up, just my board and whatever provisions we were given." Vilde shot David a look, and he closed his mouth. "When I heard about

Stallo, I knew I had to come here and compete. I took extra shifts, saved up, and came to Framnes."

Kaia swallowed. Vilde had done what Kaia had always dreamed of doing—she had made it here without any scheming or shortcuts. Her stomach twisted.

Vilde took a bite of her dried meat, swallowed, and pointed at Kaia. "To be honest, I don't like you."

"Vilde, what are you—" David started.

"But the bruises I saw on you last cycle…I can respect that." Vilde leaned back on one hand and smiled. "I think we'll all do better in this contest if we at least get along. Don't you think?"

Kaia stared at her in awe. This girl was incredible. She was willing to swallow her disdain and ignore unfairness to make the competition better for everyone. She knew Kaia had bought her spot in the contest, and she was still holding out an open hand to her.

"Thank you," was all she managed.

"Don't thank me, try to beat me." Vilde winked, a crooked smile on her pink lips. "If you can."

David's face faded back to a lighter pink, and he grinned. "Don't forget about me. I won't let you win easily either."

"Neither will I," number seven chimed in, a grin on his face. He glanced toward Sofia. "And don't underestimate Sofia."

Sofia smiled, her eyes jumping from Seven's face to the floor, her cheeks pink.

Kaia nodded at everyone, smiling, thankful, but her stomach churned. She should be happy to meet people like them, and instead all she could imagine was what would happen soon when Solon got here. It hurt.

Fighting with herself and her choices, Kaia struggled to get ready. She still didn't have her suit all the way on when Misam walked in with Kritan in tow. *Shit.*

Vilde winked at Kaia and whispered, "Good luck."

If things were different, they could have become friends. But as it was, Kaia looked up at Misam and Kritan.

"Good morning." Her words sounded hollow in her ears.

Kritan smiled, his eyes calculating but warm. "Good morning."

Misam only shifted on his feet, his eyes on the ground like a child. Kaia guessed that was just the effect Kritan had on people, because she also looked down and fumbled with the fasteners on her suit.

"So, I heard you aren't progressing in your training?" She looked up to see Kritan lift an eyebrow.

David's head turned slightly. They were all listening, even though they pretended otherwise. Now everyone knew she was failing. *Great.*

Kaia nodded, her cheeks warming.

"I'm sure you will do better this cycle." He kicked Misam's leg. "Right, Misam?"

"Yes, yes." Misam nodded unconvincingly.

"Great!" Kritan smiled, kissed Misam, and walked toward the exit. "Good luck!"

They were bonded—of course. Kaia should have known from the way they oriented themselves around each other, how Misam listened to Kritan, how Kritan smiled at Misam. It reminded her of Biorki and how his smile made her feel. She swallowed a lump in her throat and watched as Kritan left the room. Then Misam clapped his hands.

"You heard the man. Chop-chop."

Kaia did as she was told and pulled on her suit.

Back in the padded room, Misam pointed at the floor. "Sit."

Kaia sat down, her legs aching as she bent her knees. Misam's face had shifted back to an expression of determination.

"This is our last chance at getting you ready." Misam removed his gloves. "After lunch, I will send you into the course." Kaia opened her mouth, but Misam lifted a hand. "However, I can promise that if you fail this morning's training, you will not come out without serious injuries or worse. You understand?"

Kaia nodded, her heart pounding a little louder.

Misam pulled a piece of brown fabric from his pocket. "Kritan made me realize at dinner last cycle that I have been training you wrong, as if you already understand what it is like to sense the world with your body." Misam sighed heavily. "I sometimes forget that others rely solely on their sight, like you." Misam pointed at Kaia accusingly. "Although you should know better."

Kaia didn't know how she should know better; she couldn't read minds. It wasn't like Misam had told her anything about this last cycle. But she kept her thoughts to herself as he continued.

"I see your wish to succeed, but you constantly restrict yourself. You are your own worst enemy."

The words from above the entrance to this building flooded back to her. *In challenges, we face the worst beast of all: ourselves.*

Misam folded the brown fabric and held it up to Kaia. "You have to face yourself, face this challenge, without your eyes."

A blindfold. That was what Misam was holding.

"You expect me to train on the beam blindfolded?" Kaia grabbed the fabric and turned it over in her hands.

"Yes and no." Misam smiled, his teeth glinting in the light. "I expect you to ride the course blindfolded."

Kaia's heart stopped and dropped into her gut as the news sank in. Ride the course *blindfolded?* A course she had never seen?

"That's impossible." Sweat beaded on the back of her neck, cold and sticky. "There is no way anyone can do that."

Misam's grin grew wider. "I can do it. And based on the rock test, so can you. If"—Misam rose to his feet—"you can access that part of yourself before lunch."

Kaia stared at the fabric in her hands. "But how? I have tried everything. My body is bruised everywhere from last cycle. What more can I do?"

Misam walked toward the door. "Feel!" He opened it and continued, "I'll return in two hours. Don't forget to breathe!"

The door closed, leaving Kaia to her racing thoughts, her heart a fast drum against her ribs.

She didn't spare any time. If this was how she could compete, she would do it. But first, she had to figure out what Misam had meant.

Feel. Sense things with your body, not your eyes. Breathe. Kaia found one of the cubes Misam had thrown at her last cycle and sat on it. It relieved some of the pressure on her legs as she put on the blindfold. *Focus. Focus on your breathing,* a voice said in her head— her dad's voice. She took deep breaths, in through her nose, out through her mouth. Hold, exhale, hold, inhale. Her heart slowed to a steady rhythm. Her skin itched, and her elbows and legs pulsed with the pain of her bruises. She scratched her nose.

Questions rushed into her mind. *Is Biorki okay? What about Ine? Can I trust Jonas?* She answered them. *I don't know. I don't know. I don't know.* She didn't know much at all about anything. Her nose kept itching, and her legs grew numb. Nothing felt different. She was going to fail. Again.

An hour passed, and all she had managed to do was take a few deep breaths and an accidental nap on the floor. She wiped the drool off her face and sat back up, hoping no one had seen her. She hadn't gotten much sleep the cycle before due to her visit to the droid shop. Maybe that had been a bad idea after all.

Kaia slapped herself. *Focus.* The blindfold itched, but she resisted the urge to take it off. *Focus.* She allowed the air to fill her lungs. It tasted like plastic as it moved across her tongue. *Focus.*

Silence. The image of Biorki touching his visor to hers filled her. She savored the memory. Her breathing slowed once more. The air brushed against the tiny hairs on her hands, her face. Another memory surfaced of flying through the tunnels of Kaldwell, quiet ecstasy surging through her. Then the tunnel warped, engulfing her in another kind of silence, another memory.

The empty eyes of her dad stared back at her. Acid built in her throat, horror and bile rising within her. She wanted to leave these memories behind. But her dad grabbed her wrist, and she was anchored in the office. She stood by the makeshift bed, her dad sitting up, his head at a strange angle, his other arm twisted and limp by his side.

His blank eyes stared through her, and he whispered. "Promise me."

Kaia wanted to rip her arm away and disappear out the door. *Breathe. It's just a memory.* She let her tears run down her cheeks. "I promise."

His hand became fog, his eyes tunnels, as she fell deeper into them, into her mind.

"Closer, now." The words rang through her. "You must control your anger. Kaia, listen to me. Control your anger. Breathe. Push it away. Clear your… K. No. No. NO!"

Invisible arms grabbed Kaia's ankles and pulled her underwater. The dark liquid filled her mouth, nose, and ears. It tasted like sulfur and burned like melted metal, forcing itself down her throat. A soft green light shone above her. Within it was a dark, blurred shape that reached into the water. A hand pressed against the top of her head, holding her down. She struggled against it, flailed in the water. But she couldn't swim. She couldn't move. She would die.

But she hadn't lived yet. She had so much to do. Heat burst from inside her, roaring. The water around her bubbled, then boiled. She choked on it. She would drown or, worse, be boiled alive. But she felt nothing. No pain, only warmth. It didn't come from the water; it came from within. It streamed down her arms, back, and legs like tiny needles on her skin.

The surface grew closer. The water evaporated around her. Then big gloved hands found hers and pulled her out of the hot spring.

Her dad's wide eyes searched her face. "Are you okay?"

Kaia looked down. Her tiny body shook, but there were no signs of injury. Pieces of her suit had been burned off—it was black and singed at the edges. She nodded.

"Good!" Her dad gripped her wrists hard. "You can never let that happen again. Do you hear me?"

Kaia gasped and tore her blindfold off. She fell forward onto her hands and knees, her stomach threatening to purge itself. She gagged but managed to hold down her breakfast. Her body convulsed, her breathing ragged and strained. The memory raced through her like a physical blow, tearing her up from within. Her dad had thrown her into the hot springs and held her under the water. She had been seven rotations old. She hadn't understood it then, but she did now. And the truth her mind had kept from her was far worse than she could have imagined.

CHAPTER 27

Kaia was sitting on the block, the blindfold on, her chest rising and falling steadily when Misam walked in. It had taken every bit of her strength to calm down, to focus on what she had to do, why she had to do it. The memory of Biorki's face and warmth had kept her calm. She would do this for him. And if she won, if she could control what hid within her, she could save him and many others and still keep her promise.

She sensed more than heard Misam's steps across the room. He stopped right in front of her, his breathing heavy.

"Are you here to torture me some more?" Kaia whispered, not wanting to break the silence of the room.

Misam shifted his stance, and the movement made Kaia's feet tingle. A sudden movement, the flick of a wrist, and Kaia raised her arm to meet whatever was flying toward her. She caught the ball with her right hand. A flutter rose in her chest, and she exhaled. She had seen without sight. She had done it.

"Ahhh. Kritan was right." Misam chuckled. "So the silent treatment worked?"

Kaia pulled off the blindfold and stretched her legs out on the floor. "More like a loud treatment. My ears are ringing."

Misam didn't need to know about her memory or what it had done to her, what it meant. He watched her get to her feet with a grin on his face and something else she couldn't interpret.

"Yeah, silence will do that to a person." Misam picked up another ball, rolling it in his hand. "Our brains simplify things so our conscious minds can understand what we sense. If it didn't, we would probably go crazy from all the impressions around us."

Misam picked up a block in his other hand. "However, it means we become blind to things that could help us. For example, if I throw this ball on the floor, you can see it bounce off the padded mats and hear the impact. Same thing with this block."

Misam hurled the block to the floor. It bounced off the padding with a thump and flipped before landing on its side. Misam picked it up again.

"Now, close your eyes."

Kaia did as he asked, her senses still alert from the previous hour of silence. Misam exhaled quickly; then she heard something thump against the mat.

"Without opening your eyes, what did I throw to the ground?"

Without a pause, Kaia said, "The ball."

"Open your eyes."

She opened them. On the floor between them sat one of Misam's food pouches. The ball and block were still in his hands.

"It is our default to assume, and it is hard to ignore the instinct. When we act based on instinct, it can make us blind to what is actually happening. Based on the information you had, you assumed only two objects were in play. So when the sound was similar to that of a ball, your brain immediately assumed that's what I had thrown. Which means you didn't actually sense anything beyond your brain's simplified impression." Misam picked up the pouch and pointed at the ball in Kaia's hand. "When you caught the ball, you reacted to what you sensed beyond yourself before your mind could react. You were open to it, attuned to impressions beyond your eyes and ears. But to do that while moving…well, it requires enormous focus and skill."

Squeezing the ball, Kaia moved toward the beam hanging above the ground. She pushed it with one finger and turned to Misam. "And that is what this training is for?"

Misam put the pouch back into his pocket and passed Kaia a canister of water. "That, and it will make you an excellent iceboarder, among other things."

Kaia smiled. Of course, now he would expect her to balance on the beam again. But this time, she felt different. Clearer. As if an invisible blanket had been pulled from her eyes.

"Let's do this." She took a massive gulp of water before setting the canister down.

Misam nodded and moved to hold the beam steady. "First I want you to balance on the beam with the blindfold on. Then I want you to try to use the same focus with your blindfold off."

Kaia climbed onto the beam. "And focus on what's not there."

"Exactly." Misam let go of the beam. "This is your last chance."

Kaia lifted the blindfold to her eyes and tied it behind her head. "I'm ready."

The instant the darkness fell over her, she swayed. Misam pushed the beam into a pendulum swing. It jerked her backward. Sitting on solid ground and focusing had been difficult enough. This, however, was impossible.

Focus.

She tried to steady her breathing, but her focus shifted to her balance every time she reached a rhythm. It was like trying to look three places at once. Her internal and physical senses clamored for attention, while her emotions rushed through her like a torrent.

But this time, she knew what feeling to look for. And after falling off the beam three times—which felt like falling into an abyss—Kaia finally found it: the hum within her breathing. It resonated with the air around her. This was the sense she had untaught herself at the age of seven because of fear, because her dad had told her never to use it, never to show what she could do. The hum made the air feel thick, her skin hot, and her body cold.

Kaia bent her knees, solidifying her stance on the beam, and breathed. Everything pulsed around her like ripples in water. Each wave created more ripples as one touched another, an array of pulses and vibrations. The thicker and faster the vibration, the closer or more solid the object it came from. The beam beneath her neither hovered nor moved. Instead, it hummed at one frequency.

Resting on the beam, Kaia took a deeper breath and relaxed, letting her body adapt to the ripples and move with them. It was disorienting. Whenever she tried to focus on one surge, another changed its course, and then another. It was like trying to isolate a specific air bubble within a glacial river. She sensed a disruption in the air. It came from Misam. She stumbled, and every bit of her focus shattered. She hurtled forward, smacked her head on the beam, and rolled to the floor.

"Stars be cursed." Kaia held her head in her hands and rolled into a ball. "What the heck was that?"

Her head felt as if it were about to split open. Feeling the bump growing on her temple, she was surprised to find her head in one piece.

Misam didn't move. This was her challenge to overcome, to figure out. If she couldn't, it didn't matter what he said or did.

Kaia rolled to her knees and pulled off the blindfold. She wiped her forehead while trying to slow her breathing. What she had sensed from Misam had broken her concentration. Did all living things feel like that? Or was it only Misam?

When her head felt more like it had been kicked than cracked open, she got back on her feet. Fatigue rushed through her, spreading through her limbs. She fell back onto one knee. Her body wouldn't listen, like a battery at the very end of its charge. How was she so tired already? Had she hit her head that hard? But it didn't matter.

Get up!

A muscle in her right thigh twitched and danced as she returned to her feet. Slowly, she crawled back onto the beam. It was harder now, as if her body were fighting against her. She shook her arms, rolled her shoulders and head, and tied the blindfold back on. It didn't matter how much pain and discomfort she was in. Pain was only temporary. The danger of Solon, however…

Focus. Breathe, and sense what is not there.

By lunch, Kaia had managed to isolate some of the ripples. She had learned to sense Misam's arm and could dodge most of the objects he threw without falling off the beam. She had quickly realized that such intense focus was easily disrupted, making it helpful only in short bursts. It was also incredibly exhausting. When Misam had told her to try without the blindfold, she had failed.

Collapsed on the floor, she watched Misam decide her future. His head was heavy in his hands, his eyes open and staring at nothing. Kaia was too exhausted to feel anything. Her vision was blurry, her mind was foggy, and her body burned with something worse than exhaustion. Would he let her ride even if she wasn't ready? Probably not.

Her tears were about to break free when Misam sighed and walked over to where she was lying. Bending down, he picked up the blindfold Kaia had dropped to the floor. Twirling it between his fingers, he said, "Knowing that you failed, that you're incapable of sensing for longer than a minute or so and that you will most likely die down there, do you still want to compete?"

Misam stared at the wall, unblinking. Kaia struggled to open her mouth. She managed to say, her voice weak but steady, "Yes." She had already made that decision when she had suggested this to Jonas. Competing had been a long shot to begin with.

Misam put the blindfold back in his pocket. "Well, then, there is no point in training you anymore."

"But I can—" Kaia croaked.

Misam lifted a hand. "Look at yourself. You can barely move, let alone get on a board. Sending you out there now or next cycle would be stupid. If you're aiming to die, you might as well do it on the cycle of the contest."

Kaia's eyes grew wide. Was he going to let her compete?

"Don't look so happy about it. I'm sending you to die." Misam took out his canister of water and poured her a cup. "So do me a favor. Rest up during the next cycle. Study the other contestants' runs. Regain your strength. Maybe then you will walk away with your life."

Kaia accepted the cup and emptied it in one swift motion. Handing it back to him, she grinned. "So you think I have a chance?"

Misam grunted. "I think you're insane." He poured her another cup and smiled. "But I guess only insane people would enter Stallo."

Or desperate ones. She grabbed the cup again, turning it in her hands. "Is there a way to ride the course without using an additional sense?"

Misam's face slackened, and a crease appeared in his forehead. "It's possible. Most of the other contestants can't do what you and I are capable of."

Then why had she been training like this? Why was it so instrumental to her success?

"However, they have been practicing adapting to sudden changes for rotations. They have conditioned their bodies to react quickly and effectively. So although they don't have the ability to sense like you and I do, they have instincts and muscle memory that you do not have time to develop."

Kaia swallowed the water that suddenly felt stuck in her throat. "Which is why you tested me first."

"Exactly." Misam scratched his neck. "Only one capable of consciously accessing such a state could possibly improve fast enough."

But she hadn't succeeded. A lump of ice seemed to form in her gut. She was so much less prepared than she had imagined. She would die. She swallowed another sip of water, wishing it was a hot drink.

"Jonas made me promise to help you. And I will, but I need some time to think of another strategy based on your current skill level." Misam took the cup back and shook out the leftover drops of water before twisting it back onto his canister. "The best thing you can do with your time is rest up, watch the others, and learn as much as possible. You think you can do that?"

Sit and do nothing? A shiver ran through her, but she arranged her face into one of conviction. "Sure I can."

Misam lifted an eyebrow but didn't say more before moving over to the beam and lowering it to the ground. Kaia tried to get onto her knees. Resting wasn't an option. Failure wasn't an option. If he wouldn't train her, then she would train herself. It was better to die than to do nothing.

CHAPTER 28

Kaia was still slumped on the floor in the padded training room an hour later. Misam had left her alone to regain some strength. She had spent most of the time staring at the ceiling. There were forty-five bolts in the bearing beams and thirteen ventilation holes in the panels. She tried to move after counting the bolts for the second time.

Bracing her hands on the floor, she leaned forward and dragged herself onto her knees. Sucking in the stale air, she stayed there until the room stopped spinning. A muscle in her left thigh tightened and released—a cramp.

Moving onto all fours and ignoring the residual contortions of her leg, Kaia reached out for the block in front of her. Holding her breath, she grabbed it. Now for the hard part. She inhaled. Her head pounded with the effort of moving the block, but…*there*. Kaia smiled, the block comfortably under her butt, lifting her off the ground. Now that she was sitting upright, the walls settled back into solid, unmoving objects.

Closing her eyes, she found the familiar rhythm of her breathing. She concentrated on the sensation of fabric against her skin, the sounds of the building shifting ever so slightly. Her back twisted, and she gasped as the pain rushed through her body. She inhaled through gritted teeth, each hand a tight fist. She wouldn't let anyone tell her what she could and could not do. Not anymore.

Opening her hands, she allowed the air to escape through her nose. Balancing on the beam wasn't something she could do. However, balancing her mind was. Kaia found the hum, the ripples in the air. It happened faster now. She would learn to control it.

"Hey! Get up."

"Mmm. Leave me alone." Kaia grumbled.

"Girl. You can't sleep like this."

Two dark eyes stared down at her. Kaia jumped, or at least her body tried to. Instead, she found herself on her back, incapable of movement. Her eyes widened. She was still in the training room.

"What is it with young people these cycles?" It was the woman Jonas had talked to when entering Kaia into Stallo—Morgan. She clutched a pillow and a blanket in her arms. "At least get comfortable."

Kaia's muscles slackened. She let her head fall back onto the padding.

"Here." Morgan dropped the bedding next to Kaia.

Kaia tried to reach for the pillow, but her arm wouldn't listen.

"Oh, for the love of…" Morgan stuffed the pillow under Kaia's head and threw the blanket over her. "Younglings."

"Thank you," Kaia breathed.

"Shut it." Morgan rubbed her eyes. "The only reason I'm here and not at home is due to a certain frustrating guy who told me to give you a message."

"Jonas?" Kaia wasn't surprised.

"Jonas." Morgan grimaced as if the name tasted sour on her lips. "He says he needs you back at the house next cycle after training. He has some news and doesn't want you to forget to eat."

News? Kaia frowned. "What's the news?"

"How am I supposed to know?" Morgan straightened and turned toward the exit. "Anyway, I want my pillow and blanket back when you're done."

Morgan's feet dragged across the padding. She touched something by the door, and the room dimmed into darkness.

Her voice floated from the door. "And don't drool on my floors."

When the alarm vibrated on her wrist the next cycle, Kaia folded the blanket and grabbed the pillow. No drool, but her body was stiff and cold. Considering how much she had fainted during her sensory training, it was a miracle she could move at all.

Kaia dropped off the pillow and blanket at Morgan's empty counter. It was strange—the whole building was empty, no echoing steps, no whispers. She looked around; the gray drapes moved in the air from the ventilation system. They looked like ghosts. She hurried through the entry hall.

Outside, Kaia popped a food pill into her mouth and went to the droid shop. She would keep her promise to Venlá even if she was exhausted, even if it was a horrible idea. She pushed her hood back, flipped the still-solid braid over her shoulder, and walked inside.

Kaia found Venlá in the back of the shop by the workbench. Her face was twisted into an expression of concentration as she cleaned the circuit board of a square droid. Venlá looked up.

"You look like a straight mess. Did you get any sleep?"

"Is it that obvious?" Kaia rubbed her neck and walked closer.

The droid beeped as it caught sight of Kaia. It wiggled out of Venlá's grip and tumbled forward. Instead of rolling away, it tripped on a bolt and flipped onto its back. It was the same droid Kaia had almost stepped on a couple of cycles ago.

"What are you— Oh." Venlá chuckled. "I think it's scared of you."

The droid flapped its legs. Unable to flip back over, it watched wide-eyed as Kaia leaned closer. It froze. She reached out and helped it upright, careful not to touch its circuit board.

"I'm sorry I scared you." Kaia crouched before the table, her head level with the droid. "And sorry about the other cycle. I didn't see you."

The droid blinked, shook its tiny head, and spun toward the lamp on the table. It hid hiding behind the neck of the lamp, its body still visible on each side.

Venlá giggled, the sound rolling through the air. "Another brilliant hiding spot. Okay, the cleaning can wait." She patted the seat next to her and pulled out the second fabric roll of tools. "How are you this cycle? Is the training for Stallo tough?"

Kaia didn't move. "How did you know?"

"Well…" Venlá poured two cups of a sweet-smelling hot liquid. "I have lived here for a long time. And of all the people I see walking past my shop, only a few look as exhausted as you, especially at your age. And, well, Stallo is happening next cycle, so it's an easy guess."

Venlá passed a cup to Kaia, who took it and sat down. The sweet warm liquid ran down her throat. Kaia glanced at Venlá over the rim of her cup. There wasn't any point in denying it. She would be gone by the end of the next cycle anyway.

"Great guess. I'm exhausted." Kaia took another sip. "It is a lot harder than I thought it would be."

"Stallo is not for the weak-minded." Venlá smiled and patted Kaia's shoulder. "You will do fine."

A tightness in Kaia loosened. "I have a question," she murmured into her cup.

"I have a bunch of answers, but I might not have the right one. What is it?"

"How many of the contestants usually die?" Kaia's mouth felt dry.

Venlá leaned back into her chair, rubbed her wrist, and bit her lip. Her eyes focused on something beyond the ceiling. Kaia hunched over her cup and looked down.

"Only a third usually make it to the finish line." Venlá's voice was calm, a steady rumble in Kaia's ears. "Of the ones who don't make it, well…"

The chair creaked, and Kaia gripped her cup tighter. The liquid swirled. A small bubble spun around and around.

"Last rotation, there were ten contestants. Four made it, four were found alive and injured, one was found dead, and one was never found."

Kaia's knuckles were white against the dark mug. The words hung in the air. Two had died. How many contestants would make it this time?

There was a clank and a rustle, and then something cold touched her hand. She looked up, and there, stroking her hand, was the droid. Its eyes met hers, and Kaia could tell the droid understood. Another bop, and the droid rolled back and cocked its head.

"I see. You're right." Kaia leaned down closer to the droid. "There's no point in worrying about that now."

The droid nodded and rolled over to Venlá, whose jaw was open in surprise.

"That's new." Venlá stroked the droid's head. "You like her?"

The droid nodded again and turned to give Venlá access to its circuit board.

Neither Kaia nor Venlá mentioned Stallo again while they worked on the droids. The little one kept spinning between them; sometimes it grabbed a few pieces of metal and handed them to Kaia. Venlá giggled whenever the droid brought Kaia the wrong parts. It was wonderfully simple—just their hands, circuit breakers, and joint tensions. Kaia was polishing a joint when her alarm vibrated. She cursed. The hour had flown past too quickly.

Venlá disappeared into the back room without a word. Waiting, Kaia looked around the shop. It was weird how it already felt like home. She dragged a finger across one of the shelves. Dust stuck to her fingertip, a layer of gray on her dry skin. She was going to miss it, and Venlá and the little droid.

"Here." Venlá reappeared and held out a package wrapped in a dark cloth, her eyes wet. "For good luck, and as a thank-you for the help."

Kaia stared at the package.

"Take it."

"I can't accept it."

Venlá pushed the package into Kaia's hands. "Take it."

"No. I can't…" Her stomach twisted.

"Oh, for star's sake! Take it." Venlá dropped the package in Kaia's hands and bopped her on the head. "You can always return it if you don't like it."

Words got stuck in Kaia's throat. She wouldn't be back. Instead, Solon would come here, and—

Venlá wiped a tear from Kaia's cheek. "I know you probably won't be back. It's okay." Her smile didn't quite reach her eyes. "But I'm allowed to hope, right?"

Kaia blinked. How did she know? "I—"

"Now, you're going to be late." Venlá squeezed Kaia's hand. "Show them what you're made of, and make sure you win!"

Wiping her face with the back of her hand, Kaia smiled. "I will!"

Kaia spent most of her cycle sensory training. When she couldn't sit anymore, she pulled out the tablet Morgan had reluctantly loaned her. Lying on her back, she watched David, Vilde, and the others practice on the screen. The course was even more horrifying than she remembered. But what surprised her was how different the other riders' styles were.

Sofia was incredible. Her movements were smooth like water, inertia slinging her through the changing tunnels. On the other hand, David was a blur of solid blue. His muscular legs pushed him through turns at an incredible speed, throwing up clouds of ice and snow. Állan, number seven, and Vilde, who wore a black-and-yellow suit, were more technical; well-timed entries into turns and expertly executed curves allowed them to go faster.

Then there was number ten, Heaika. They had been anonymous in the locker room, gray and seemingly neutral. On a board, they were an orange monster. The solid glacier looked like powdered snow when Heaika's board forced its way through like a laser through aluminum. Kaia made a note to stay away from them the next cycle.

After hours of studying the other contestants, Kaia walked off the train at Framnes North, the package in her arms. Misam hadn't shown up, as promised, which she was thankful for. She didn't need to hear again how she would fail. She was beginning to understand her dad's constant reluctance to her competing. Kaia hugged the box as she passed the black market. At least Venlá believed in her. When she reached Jonas's house, the place looked smaller than she remembered. Kaia sighed. Jonas believed in her. Kind of.

Inside, she found Jonas talking to himself by the kitchen table. Hearing her footsteps, he waved her closer with the tablet in his hand.

"Sit, sit." Jonas didn't look up. "I made you something to eat."

Kaia placed the package on one of the towers of blankets and sat down. A can, a plate of dried meat, and a cup of Sizzler sat on the table. She cursed herself for not getting soup on her way back. The Sizzler, however, was a pleasant surprise. Picking up the spork, she opened the can and took a bite of the paste-like contents.

Kaia had finished her can and was chewing on some meat when Jonas put down his tablet. "You look absolutely dreadful." He leaned his head on his hand while looking her over. "So you ignored Misam's recommendation."

It wasn't a question. Somehow, Jonas knew everything.

"No. I did rest and watch the other contestants, like he said." It wasn't a lie, not really.

Jonas tapped a finger on the table. "And you figured sleeping in the training hall was better than here?"

Kaia shrugged and swallowed another bite of the dried meat. It was slow to go down, so she chased it with a sip of the Sizzler. Jonas leaned back and picked his nose. He must have found something in there, because he lifted his finger to his eyes and then flicked something onto the floor.

"Ready to win me some gold next cycle?" Jonas's eyes narrowed.

Kaia clutched her cup. "As ready as I can be."

Jonas's eyes glinted with something—recognition or satisfaction. Then he broke into a crooked grin.

"Good! Let's get this over with and get you a spaceship." He placed the tablet between them, displaying a map of Framnes. "We won't have much time after the contest to get away unseen. There are whispers that Solon is already here. They haven't made their presence known, though. They still haven't closed their deal with the city, and if they come off as evil. Like taking one of Framnes's citizens as a prisoner, it might screw up their plans. I think they want to catch you without an audience. Otherwise they'd be crawling all over the city." When he saw Kaia's expression, he said, "Don't worry. This is a good thing…mostly."

Kaia grimaced. "So if they catch me, no one will know. Great."

"Right." Jonas drummed a beat on the table with his fingers. "It's best for you to be in public spaces, which is why it was good you stayed at Stallo HQ last cycle. Even if they are here, they won't try to grab you in front of everyone."

"They could have followed me here." Kaia's hands grew cold, even with the Sizzler between them.

Jonas looked at his fingers, which were now tapping a slower rhythm. "I've had eyes on you the whole time. If there had been any hint of Solon, they would have protected you. So we're safe."

This whole time, someone had been watching her every move. "You had me followed? Who?" The idea left her skin crawling, but she understood why he'd done it. "Morgan?"

Jonas smiled, his eyes still on his fingers. "Yes. Morgan and a few others I trust."

It now made more sense that Morgan had brought her the pillow and blanket. A crawling suspicion took hold of her. "Venlá?"

"Venlá? The droid lady?" His fingers came to a halt.

Kaia nodded, her hand twitching around her cup.

"No, but you really should have focused on resting instead." Jonas looked at her hair. "The braid suits you, though."

Kaia sighed. She wondered how much they had learned about her, watching her cycle after cycle. Had they watched her when she was sleeping? She adjusted herself in the seat. Jonas was going to a lot of trouble to help her, but it still creeped her out.

"Anyway. After Stallo, we need to figure out a way to get you here"—Jonas pointed at Bean's bar on the map—"before the crowds disperse. There is an escape route there."

Kaia touched the healing cut on her forehead.

"When you win, go to the smallest spectator box at the finish line. I will be waiting there with Alexi." Jonas rubbed his neck. "If I can lure him out."

"*If* you can lure him out?" She interlaced her fingers around the cup.

She should thank him for believing in her, for putting so much faith in her abilities, but what if she failed? How would he feel then? She tightened her grip.

"I never said he would be there for sure, but I have heard from some contacts that he reserved a seat." Jonas scratched his nose. "Either way, we need to be ready to run to the bar after we make our bargain. Even if he won't help us, we will still have to escape."

"What if he doesn't? How will I get off the planet then?" Kaia didn't want to think about that possibility, but she had to know if Jonas had another plan.

Jonas tapped the table once and met Kaia's eyes. "I can't tell you."

She knew him better now and just stared back at him.

He lifted his shoulders. "If you get caught, I can't have you telling them all my secrets."

Kaia put her cup down, leaned forward, and rested her elbows on the table. "You can trust me. I proved that to you. I took that damn test."

Jonas grimaced. "Don't take it personally. I know that. They can extract information, regardless of your loyalty, which is why I'm only going to tell you half of our escape plan."

She leaned back in her seat and took a long gulp of Sizzler. "Fine. I understand." Understood that if she did get caught, she would probably be kept alive for her blood. But that didn't mean Solon would treat her like a sentient being. She put the cup down and traced the rim with her index finger. She caught Jonas staring at her. "What?"

Jonas cleared his throat. "I thought you would be harder to convince."

It was her turn to raise her shoulders. "I have been chased, almost eaten, thrown around inside a sled, poisoned by a rock, and beaten up by a blind guy. Having information withheld from me is nothing new. Also, it makes sense."

Jonas held her gaze, nodded, and turned the tablet toward her. "Okay, then, let me tell you what I can." He zoomed in on the map. It showed the streets between the Stallo building and Bean's bar.

"There are two ways to get there. This"—Jonas pointed at an exit at the back of the Stallo building and drew a zigzag along small crooked side streets—"is the way we will take if everything goes as planned. And this"—Jonas drew a line from the Stallo entrance straight through the square and along several main streets, the fastest route—"is what we'll do if something goes wrong."

And what if I don't win? The question hung in the air between them. But she didn't ask, and he didn't mention it as he pushed the tablet to her.

"Take it and memorize the different routes. I don't need you getting lost if you must go without me." Jonas grinned when he saw the twitch in her hand. "Don't worry, I'll be fine." He flicked her on the nose; she didn't lean back, only furrowed her brows at him. His smirk spread across his face, and he winked. "Anyway, I will tell you more after we get to the escape route. For now, I need a steam shower. See you next cycle."

After cleaning her cup and doing her best to memorize the map, Kaia took her turn in the steam shower. Her bruises had turned different shades of yellow and purple, and the cut on her forehead was a fiery red line. She touched the stitches on her shoulder; the pain was gone, the skin pink but closed.

Images of Biorki zip-lining and tinkering with his harness raced through her mind. Now that the competition was almost was here, she was glad he was far away in case anything went wrong. If she didn't win, it would all be for nothing, including her dad's death. But at least Biorki would be safe.

In her room, her face puffy, she finally opened the package from Venlá. Inside the dark cloth was an old, small, square metallic box covered in scratches and bumps. Kaia turned it over in her hands until she found a small button on one of the scratched sides. She pressed it. The box clicked and snapped. A small green light pulsed on the button, and after ten blinks, it opened.

A head popped out and tilted to the side. It was the little droid. Venlá's droid.

CHAPTER 29

Kaia woke up too early and made herself a cup of Sizzler in the kitchen. Sitting down, she stared through the door at Jonas's disorganized living room. She pulled on her braid, her callused fingers catching on a few of the strands that had escaped. Her dad's bag was packed and ready on the chair beside her, the little droid tucked inside. When she was halfway through her second cup, she heard a grunt.

"Nervous?" Jonas's voice crackled with sleep.

She looked up from her mug. Jonas was already sitting across from her, a cup in one hand, his tablet in the other. She hadn't noticed him enter, let alone make himself a drink. She took another sip, not wanting to give the obvious answer. Understanding, Jonas didn't ask again. They sat in silence, the sound of the streets waking up drifting in from the entrance.

When it was almost time to leave, Jonas stood up and rummaged through his fridge. He crawled in on all fours, and dust filled the air as he reached to the very back of the lowest shelf.

"Aha!" he exclaimed while coughing. "There it is, the little bugger."

He held out his hand. A clear vial with something pink

inside was pinched between his fingers. Jonas popped the top off the vial. A long gasp followed as air rushed back into the glass. An unfamiliar smell filled the room—primarily sweet, though it left a slight sour tingle on Kaia's tongue.

"Here." Jonas passed her the vial with a warm smile. "Leave one for me, eh?"

"Is that what I think it is?" Her eyes widened as the contents of the vial shook.

"Why don't you try it and find out?" Jonas winked and turned to grab something else from the shelves.

Using her fingertips, Kaia pulled one of the pink blobs out of the vial. She placed it on her tongue; it was soft. She let it rest there for a few moments, savoring the feeling of the sour-sweet tingling that spread through her mouth. It was wonderful. After a few more moments, she rolled it with her tongue and bit down. Powder filled her mouth. It was unlike anything she had tasted before.

Thankful that Jonas had turned his back to her, she closed her eyes. With every chew, a new rush of flavor filled her mouth. She savored every bite, and by the time she had swallowed the last of it, tears were running down her cheeks. She took a few slow breaths, wiped her face, and walked over to Jonas. He was dividing up food pills on the kitchen counter.

"Thank you." She smiled and handed him the vial.

"It's too bad you can only get fruit on the black market, huh?" Jonas grinned and popped the last pink fruit into his mouth.

She leaned on the counter, her cup in hand. "It is."

"Nothing beats freeze-dried fruit for removing nerves." He chuckled; the fruit danced inside his mouth as he spoke. Then he pursed his lips and furrowed his brows. "Now, don't let me regret giving you that." Jonas swallowed. "I don't have to remind you what's at stake this cycle."

Ice returned to her gut; it twisted and churned. His mood swings were disturbing.

"I won't fail." Kaia twisted her cup. "Not this time."

"I know." Jonas's face softened. "When you win and get to

the finish line, be prepared for anything. Don't let your guard down. I will see you then, as we planned."

The taste in her mouth turned bitter when Jonas left the room.

Kaia strapped on her boots. They had turned gray and brown from the city's dirt in the last few cycles. This was it— her final walk through the city. The bag was heavy on her back. She brushed some of the dust off her overalls. A lump bulged in one of her pockets: the pouch of coins. She smiled. If this really was her last cycle here, she might as well spend them.

Instead of walking straight to the train, she turned left toward where she had first entered Framnes, when she had still thought that Framnes North was the whole city. Where she had climbed a wall to find Jonas. She looked down the busy street and grinned.

Kaia turned the last corner before the Stallo square. She looked over her shoulder. Someone was following her. She was sure of it. But she saw nothing out of the ordinary. She pulled down her hood. Maybe she was imagining it. Either way, she couldn't get to the Stallo building fast enough. If Solon caught her out here—

Her shoulder hit something solid.

"Watch where you're going!"

The man she had bumped into rushed past her, not giving her a chance to apologize. Well, it was his fault.

She turned back toward the Stallo square and gasped. Women and men in outfits of red and green, black and white with copper embroidery on every hem filled the square. Laughter mingled with chatter about favorite contestants. The usually stationary carts had moved and now lined the square. The owners prepared their food, meat sizzling on the grills. One of the carts was filled with moving toys. Another to her right sold candy in every color. The smells of char, meat, and dust drifted past her. The rumble of wheels on the cobbled ground matched the stomping feet of the crowd.

Kaia moved past grinning faces. She savored it all—the sounds, the smells, the bright clothing. Children ran around, jumping with excitement in matching suits and dresses. Although less embroidered than their parents', their outfits were equally beautiful. Their laughter echoed and mingled with the other sounds of the bustling square.

When Kaia reached the bottom of the stairs to the Stallo building, she paused. A man and a woman dressed in the most beautiful garments Kaia had ever seen stood on either side, welcoming the spectators. The woman lifted a horn to her lips, and a clear tone filled the square. The man began to sing; his guttural and deep voice complimented the horn. The song became its own creature, growing and changing—a dance of lighter tones, then darker, then rhythmic. It was a song of Stallo, terrifying yet beautiful, sad yet ecstatic. The blue flames in the stairs' lanterns danced to the tones of victory and loss.

Kaia slid through the crowds and up the stairs. The song gave her strength, hope, and sadness about what may come, what the fate of these people may be. She breathed in the song and stored some of its energy within her. She would save this memory, never forget it, so that if everything was destroyed, she would at least have one piece of beauty tucked safely inside her heart.

She walked through the triangular entrance. The song was replaced by beeps and hurried voices. The entry hall bustled with people lining up to scan their tickets at the counters. Banners in colorful green, blue, gold, and copper patterns had replaced the gray drapes. At the back of the room stood Morgan with a large red-lipped smile. The woman shuffled people into the elevator leading to the viewing boxes and seats.

Kaia couldn't help but smile. Excitement and anticipation filled the air. It had turned Morgan into a younger woman. She stood straighter and laughed louder. And when Morgan caught her eye and gave a slight nod, Kaia returned it before pushing toward the locker room.

Kaia touched her bracelet to the pad, and the door slid open. Faces looked up, noted her presence, and then looked back down. No one was in the mood for talking. The door slid shut behind her, cutting off the room from the buzzing hall. The silence was like a slap to the face, a reality check that made ice crawl down her neck. She was not a spectator; she was a competitor. Meaning that in less than two hours, she would be iceboarding in the deadliest competition in Framnes. She gripped the straps of her bag tighter. How could she have let herself get carried away so easily? She knew what was at stake.

Only the occasional shuffling of boots and waxing of boards broke the stillness as she crossed the room. On the bench in front of her locker sat Misam. She walked past him, opened the locker, and put her bag inside.

"So, you couldn't just sit and watch, huh?"

Kaia paused with her head inside her locker. "No."

Misam sighed. "Well, let's hope it wasn't a dumb choice. Here—as promised."

Kaia turned and took the tablet he was holding out. On it was a document full of notes about the courses caves and tunnels, man-made or otherwise, and strategies she could use.

"Kritan and I made this for you. Memorize it, and you will have a better chance." Misam stood up and stared right at her. "The rest is up to you. And considering how reckless you are, you may do okay."

Kaia looked back down at the tablet. She didn't know what to say.

Misam waved his hand as if brushing something annoying away. "That's not a compliment. You will most likely die. Don't forget it. Stallo is supposed to be an impossible contest. It's supposed to showcase the best iceboarders in Framnes, which is why it's named after a creature that eats humans."

Kaia swallowed, her throat dry. So that was what Stallo meant.

Misam continued. "Kritan described some of the hurdles they've installed to me. It's one of the benefits of having a partner who works on the course. I can't tell you what they are, but remember this: snow can be forgiving, but ice is resentful. If you let your focus slip, even for a second…"

Misam let the words hang in the air. Kaia tightened her grip on the tablet. Kritan worked on the course? Is that how they met?

"I will be listening, and everyone else will be watching." Misam's white eyes met Kaia's and held them too long. Kaia nodded, her hands cold. She understood the implications. Then, without another word, Misam turned and walked out the door.

Kaia was left with her thoughts, still clutching the tablet. A slow chill seeped through her veins, restricting her movements. How was she supposed to memorize all this before the contest? Had she been stupid to practice behind Misam's back? No, she had improved. Shaking her head, she placed the tablet in her locker and pulled out the red, white, and black suit. She let the fabric slide between her fingers. Misam had given her this on Jonas's request, but she still had to do it justice.

Sitting in her suit and boots, her helmet next to her, Kaia dove into the document while swirling a food pill inside her mouth. The bitter flavor grounded her, slightly. Some of the notes were simple and rudimentary, like how to carve through a bend efficiently and how to increase one's speed on a straightaway. Those things she already knew. However, some of the descriptions were harder to understand. She bit down on her lip.

"You will be fine." The soft voice came from behind her.

It was number twelve. Kaia had heard the others talk to him earlier. Mihka, maybe? She looked up. He didn't meet her eyes as his fingers fumbled with his brown-and-green suit.

"I didn't mean to overhear…"

"Oh, get to the point, Mihka." Vilde's voice slashed through the room.

Mihka's face grew pale, his ears red behind his dark hair. He shot Vilde an angry look, and she grinned and lifted her shoulders in mock innocence. Mihka cleared his throat and whispered while looking at his hands, "Don't worry about Misam. He's worried about you, that's all. You'll be fine down there. Right, guys?" He met Vilde's eyes, and she nodded slowly. David and Állan looked up, nodded, and got back to dressing. The others either ignored him or didn't hear.

"Thank you," Kaia whispered back.

He immediately resumed waxing his board beside her, whistling to himself. Kaia returned to her studies, her shoulders a little looser, her head a little lighter.

After reading the same description for the fifth time, she looked up. She had one hour left. Kaia had expected everyone to sit quietly or do breathing exercises. Instead, David and Vilde were playing a card game. David swore at something, and Vilde grinned, her face full of mischief. Sofia and Állan were huddled together, their hands interlocked, their whispers soft in the air.

Heaika, their face neutral, was in a heated discussion with number nine, a small, muscular guy. Number two was guiding number three through a stretching routine, their backs hunched over, their hands reaching down to their boots. Did they not know that they might die? Kaia looked more closely at their faces and found tightness in their lips, their shoulders. No, they knew.

Kaia looked at number five, his dusty brown–haired head in his hands. A line of sweat ran down his forehead. Number six sat beside him, a black-haired muscular guy who was staring into space. His gray eyes were blurry, and he held a cup of something hot. And number eight, whom Kaia remembered as a large blond guy, was nowhere to be seen, his locker still closed.

Uneasy, Kaia got up. Overthinking would only make her more anxious. She opened her locker and pulled a small tin from her dad's bag. It was one of the objects she had bought from the black market. She twisted the lid off and dipped her finger in the black tar. Looking at her distorted reflection in the locker door, she dragged a thick line of black under each eye. It might not do much down in the glacier, but it didn't hurt to be prepared. She put the tin back and sat down.

Kaia startled when the bell chimed. Thirty minutes left. She pulled her helmet on, careful not to touch the camera lens above the visor. It would stream her point of view to the audience. She tried not to think about who might be watching as she attached it to her suit. The contestants formed a line in numerical order and approached the elevator. The rusted square thing would bring them down to the starting line. She stepped in behind Mihka, who fumbled with his board in front of her.

Another bell rang, and the elevator doors opened. Last in line, Kaia saw the way the other contestants jumped. Whatever they were feeling, they were all high-strung and alert. Sofia, the first in line, walked inside, her head high. The elevator—only able to carry three at a time—creaked as number three entered. David gave Kaia a wink before the elevator doors closed.

When the elevator ascended for the fourth time, Vilde, Mihka, and Kaia crammed inside, their boards resting on the nonslip floor. They stood silently as the square room descended into the caves beneath Framnes.

When the elevator groaned to a stop, they all tensed. Kaia adjusted her helmet and looked at the specs on her visor as the doors slid open. The drop in temperature was instant, the air a little lighter, less humid. Kaia lifted her hand to her face. Spotlights had been installed throughout the cave, and the light was blinding.

As her visor adjusted to the light, she stared at the illuminated dark stone roof above them. Riddled with chunks of quartz, it reflected the light in iridescent patterns. The videos she had watched as a child hadn't done them justice. She had expected to feel fear, yes. Nerves, yes. But not awe. Not before sending herself down the mouth of the tunnel.

The entrance to the course was a dark hole at the other side of the cave. It looked alive, ready to swallow them all. The mouth of Stallo led into the glacier, full of changing tunnels, ice, and water pockets. The traps and jumps had been installed late last cycle so contestants couldn't practice them before the event—a true test of a boarder's skill. Or at least that was what the announcer had said when Kaia had watched Stallo from the safety of her home a rotation earlier.

Being here, behind the thirteen metal boxes at the starting line, was a different experience. Entering this event might have been the worst idea of her life.

Vilde and Mihka exited the elevator and entered the cave. With one more deep breath, her board secured tightly in her grip, Kaia stepped onto the ice—the last to enter, number thirteen.

Small pieces of ice crunched under her boots as she made her way to the thirteenth launch box. She fumbled with the handle, opened the door, and walked into a device constructed to send her right into the mouth of the glacier. Her steps rang in her ears in the small space, a space that seemed to shrink the more she thought of what awaited her on the other side. Kaia leaned her board up against the wall and rolled her shoulders back.

The sliding door in front of her was painted with the number thirteen. Two handles stuck out from the walls. She wrapped her hand around one of them. The diamond grip of the metal bit into her gloves. Good. Underneath her boots was a patch of snow the perfect size for a board.

Reciting Misam's notes, she inspected her boots, board, suit, and helmet. Satisfied, she twisted her torso, and her spine cracked with the motion. Shaking her legs and arms, she bounced from one foot to the other. The faster her heart pumped oxygen through her body, the better. A stiff muscle, a cold joint, could be the difference between winning and—

A crackle filled her box, and then a woman spoke, her voice metallic and cold through the built-in speakers.

"Get ready."

This was it—her first challenge. Kaia dropped her board to the ground, turned the mechanism on, and stepped onto it. The magnets snapped into place, the board an extension of her body. It was a strange sensation, almost foreign; it had been too long. She should have practiced on the board when she'd had the chance. She let out a deep breath. There was no time for regrets.

She adjusted her weight on the board and jumped until she was right between the two handles. The speed would come from her hands, from the force of pulling herself out of the box. She grabbed the handles, her arms and shoulders tense. Timing was everything. Too early and she would strike the door. Too late and she would be behind the others.

Misam's note had said, "The minute you hear the second alert, brace yourself to launch. Go when you hear the little snapping sound of the gate's hydraulics. The doors will open fast enough for you to get through. Every second counts."

She had frowned at that little paragraph. She knew seconds were precious; she wasn't dumb. But to launch before the doors opened, to trust that they would slide fast enough—now, *that* was dumb. Crazy. However, crazy was what she needed.

Kaia closed her eyes and slowed her breathing. The handles dug into her palms. She could feel her board slide with every flexing muscle. The rustle of the other contestants drifted through the walls—boards against snow, magnets snapping into place.

The woman's voice spoke again both within the box and outside in the cave.

"Prepare to go."

Kaia pulled back, her arms stretched out in front of her, her board level under her. She bent her knees and shifted her weight to her front foot. She tightened her grip on the handles, took another deep breath, and let it out slowly. The air was frigid. If there had been time, if she'd had the luxury of thinking things through, she might have backed out.

The lock on the door retracted. The sound shot through her like hot iron.

Snap!

She opened her eyes, lifted her front foot, and launched forward as hard as possible. The third alert rang through the cave, and the door retracted instantly. Kaia shot through the small opening, the woman's voice trailing behind as the glacier swallowed her.

"Go!"

CHAPTER 30

The air compressed around Kaia. She forced herself forward and made herself as small as possible. She adjusted for the g-forces. Bending her knees, she sped around the first turn. The sharp metal edge of her board sliced through the glacier in a perfect carve. Her lips twitched into a smile, and a laugh escaped her. She had missed the weightlessness, the freedom.

Next was a straightaway. She made herself smaller, her shoulders parallel to the board. She could have touched the ice with her hands. Resisting the urge, she thought of Misam's notes: *A straightaway is only an illusion; expect the worst.*

The sound of metal slicing through ice followed close behind her. One, two, three, four—four of the others had caught up with her. More would follow. Seconds were precious now. One mistake and she would fall behind, or worse. A shadow on the tunnel floor caught her attention. She leaned to the side, shifted her weight to her heels, and carved up the tunnel wall. She missed the gaping hole in the tunnel floor by an arm's length. She clenched her jaw. This was no game. The sounds of the others following her carve echoed through the tunnel. She prepared for the next turn.

A red alert flashed on her visor: a cold pocket. *Crap*. The temperature dropped rapidly. One cut or tear in her suit and she would be out, frozen to death. She exited the turn and cussed. Of course—the tunnel ahead was filled with metal sheets. With no time to react, she raced between the triangular shapes. The sheets were sharp, bent, and twisted. Protruding from the ice, they rushed past her like knives. One caught board edge, one improper adjustment, and she would be impaled, a frozen piece of meat.

There was a scream behind her, a thump, and the sound of something soft hitting metal. She clenched her jaw tighter. If she wasn't careful, she would be next. She ducked and felt metal scrape the top of her helmet, then jumped over another shard at ankle level. Her board barely cleared it. The movement sent her hurtling toward another metal piece. She adjusted her front foot, the force throwing her into a turn. She passed the last shard, her arm almost catching on its edge.

The near miss cost her a perfect trajectory into the next bend. *Oh no*. There was a hiss, and a flash of purple, blue, and orange passed over her head. David's board sent a cloud of powder onto her visor. The rest followed. Vilde, a yellow-and-black flash, was in the lead. Kaia didn't see number five. Had he been the reason for the scream? *Shit*.

David, Heaika, and Sofia were already at the end of the next straightaway, a steep launch with a jump waiting at the end. Kaia's guts twisted; a drop of sweat ran down her back. The lead she had gained was gone due to a stupid mistake, a stupid turn. Her thighs shook as she squatted with her arms behind her back, her head low. The air hissed as her small shape cut through it. If there was a chance to pass them again, she would be ready.

Hoping she had gained enough speed, Kaia reached the jump. It launched her into the air, the chasm below whispering her name. She grabbed her board, and it dug into her glove, her knees almost touching her chin. Releasing the hold, she straightened her legs, twisted midair, and spotted her landing.

She met the glacier floor hard. The impact forced her into another squat, and her butt scraped the ice.

Regaining her balance, she charged into another bend. Holding her squat, she pivoted onto her toes, then her heels to find a line as the turn spiraled down and down. *Not yet, not yet.* The tunnel spiraled around once more. Then light, a sense of depth. *Now.* Kaia straightened, pushed against the force of the turn, and shot out of the spiral and into a dark cavern.

She grimaced. The dark green rugged mountain created a perfect dome. Two lines of lights ran across the rounded ceiling, throwing shadows onto the roughly cut stone. What made Kaia uneasy was the perfectly flat frozen floor. This ice was different—smoother, darker, a black mirror of perfection. It reflected everything, making it look like there was a darker upside-down world beneath its surface. Carving on black ice required skill and a sharp board edge. Should she aim straight for the exit, then slide all in one go? It would be faster—carves would slow her down. However, a set of flags zigzagged across the surface, marking a path of some sort. Sofia danced between them, the others following.

She needed to catch up. Moving straight across could do that, but… One of the notes from Misam popped into her mind: *Don't believe everything you see.* No, she would follow the others.

She carved and fell in behind number nine. When he reached the first flag, he slid off the path. The mistake sent him across the ice too fast for him to react, and before he could pull his board around, he fell into…water? The impact sent a spray into the air that immediately turned to snow. A volcanic lake: a dark and deadly illusion, only visible if disturbed. She had almost run right into it.

Kaia shivered. One mistake, and she would be in that water too—the dark, endless abyss. The image of her dad's hands pushing her under, the water filling her lungs, enveloped her, tore through her. Kaia blinked and forced her breathing to slow. It didn't work. Her heart hammered inside her skull. Her legs were suddenly weak. Spots formed at the edges of her vision. Her breath caught in her throat.

No.

Kaia lifted her left hand and squeezed the stitches on her shoulder. The icy pain shot through her nerves like an instant electrical current. She gasped at the pain but squeezed harder. The world snapped back into focus. Kaia didn't have time for fear, for doubt. She pushed it away with every ounce of willpower. She could do this. She had done it before. Rotations ago, but still—if she followed the flags and timed her carves perfectly, she could do it.

Kaia looked down, and the panic returned. She squeezed her shoulder again. *Don't look down.* She carved around the first flag, her shoulder throbbing. *Don't look down.* She focused on the last flag and the sound of her slicing board, of specific adjustments of pressure, the movements of her feet. Those sounds could be tools; if she *couldn't* look down, she would feel the path, hear it.

She held her breath and listened. A toe carve, lean to heels, lean back to toes, adjust the pressure, the weight. Arms, shoulders, hips. Too much weight to either side, and she would catch an edge, throwing her into the lake. Too little, and she would lose control, which would have the same result. Too broad a turn, and she would lose speed. Too sharp, and it would be harder to stay perfectly balanced.

The flag grew closer, closer. She passed it.

Kaia laughed, her voice cracking with relief, with pent-up fear. She sounded insane. She heard number nine struggling in the water behind her. This *was* insane, but she had to focus on what was ahead. She looked around. The other contestants were gone. Her laugh died, and she gritted her teeth.

In front of her were two tunnel openings. The trails of the other contestants led into the one on the right, clear and open. The other was almost completely blocked by snow. Once again, there was an obvious choice, but... *Remember, snow is forgiving, and ice is resentful.* She may be reading too much into Misam's words, but what other choice did she have? Even if she boarded her best on the icy path, it wouldn't be enough to win. She had to take a risk in order to have any chance of catching up. Following her gut feeling, she took a deep breath, leaned into her carve, and burst through the wall of loose snow.

The tunnel sent Kaia into a nosedive. It was dark, lit only by her helmet light. The glacier walls flew past her, a blur of twisted reflections in black and blue, the red of her suit like fire on the walls. She was gaining too much speed as she hurtled toward nothing, an unpredictable end. She would be crushed in seconds if this tunnel was a dead end. It would be an excellent way to die; she wouldn't have time to feel pain. But if it led to a fissure, she would fall to her death, and then she would have too much time to think about her regrets. She hoped it was a dead end.

The tunnel twisted once, twice, and then a light appeared at the end. Kaia braced herself, then shot out into another cave. Larger than the last, this one was filled with jumps and berms made from ice. It was a labyrinth of hurdles. But that wasn't the strangest thing about the cave. Above her hung ten big machines, five on each side of the mountain walls.

Sofia shot out of another tunnel to Kaia's right, followed by Heaika, David, and Mihka. Kaia leaned into her speed, turned, and sliced into the glacier, her body nearly parallel to the ground from the force. She dragged a hand across the ice before straightening. She fell in line behind Mihka.

Her gamble had paid off. She had to remember to thank Misam later.

Sofia entered the labyrinth. She made it look effortless as she flew, leaping from one jump to another. Then, an earsplitting sound, a flash of motion, and time slowed as Sofia's head twisted. Her body contorted, and she disappeared into the labyrinth.

An earth-breaking scream filled the cave. Had Kaia screamed? No, it had come from behind her. Állan's voice cracked, and a quiet howl followed, turning into something feral as it echoed through the cave. Kaia tried to swallow the lump in her throat. It didn't budge. Was it the weird machines that had taken Sofia out? It had to be.

Vilde entered the field of ramps: another loud noise, another blur of motion. Vilde twisted midair, the blur missing her. The projectile smashed into a ramp behind her with a spray of snow. A snowball?

Kaia bent her knees and headed straight toward the labyrinth. Her heart pounded in her ears. Another sound, another blur, this time from the other side. Vilde dodged again. A spray of snow followed. Kaia struggled to keep her focus on her board. Her body screamed at her to turn, to break from her line. David entered the field—another sound, another spray of snow.

The machines clearly reacted to movement. Even a soft projectile could kill someone if it moved fast enough. Heaika entered, Mihka at their heels. The sounds of the machines filled the cave as a relentless stream of projectiles flew back and forth, kicking up a blur of snow. The sound was so loud it was disorienting. Only a couple of seconds had passed since Sofia had disappeared.

Without time to question her choices, Kaia entered the field.

A sound, then a movement in the air. Kaia twisted, and her board followed slowly. The snowball missed her by a hair. Her suit flapped with the air pressure before she landed in a transition leading to another jump. Adrenaline pulsed through her. She focused on the memory of her training, of Misam's voice: *Let your body react for you.* Another sound, this time from the left. Kaia crouched, and the projectile flew over her head. She pulled up and stretched her legs just in time to make the next jump, spot her next path. Landing at an angle, she leaned hard to the right, her board cutting across to a berm.

Balls of ice and snow hammered down around her. Whenever she caught air and tried to spot the exit, a ball flew at her, breaking her focus. Maintaining her speed proved nearly impossible. She had to find way out now, or she would be trapped in the maze. Her legs shook with every impact, and her breath caught in her throat. Mihka's brown-and-green suit launched ahead of her, his back tight, his motions stiff, his carves too sharp. He was panicking.

Kaia's legs weakened with every second, every jump and projectile. Sweat pooled on her palms and neck. The rim of fog on her visor's edge grew, and her range of vision narrowed. She wanted to rely solely on her iceboarding skills, but time was running out, and she would crack if she didn't act now. She tightened her fists. It was a risk, but this was what she had trained for.

Ignoring her terror, Kaia took a deep breath and felt her board send her into another jump. *You can do this.* She closed her eyes. She heard a crack from her right and ducked. The air of the projectile tore at her suit, but it missed her. She drew in another gulp of crisp air, kept her eyes shut, and launched off the next jump. *There.*

At the top of the arch, she found them: the vibrations, the ripples. Each one came from a distinct source. A contestant jumped to her right. Another, with a more solid burst of ripples, moved ahead. David? The sharp, quick ripples from the snowballs pulled at her, claimed her focus. None were coming for her just then. But she kept her mind blank and opened herself.

You can do this.

A moment later, there it was. Hidden behind the chaos of contestants and snowballs, she found the duller hum of the cave, the slow ripples of solid objects: the walls, the ceiling, and the labyrinth.

Kaia breathed out and listened to the vibrations through her skin. She found them—slower but smaller than those of the cave, ripples from a hollow space. The exit.

Her eyes flew open just in time to spot her landing. She met the icy ground, turned, and relaunched herself into the air. Kaia closed her eyes again. This time, she found the vibrations of the exit within one breath. *There.* She opened her eyes, twisted away from another ball, and spotted her landing.

With every jump, she moved closer to the exit. After the fifth, she caught up with Mihka. Even through the sounds of the cannons, Kaia could hear his heavy breathing, the curses he mumbled through his gritted teeth. Kaia shot past him and launched into another blind jump.

She was getting the hang of it now—every time, she sensed the exit quicker than the last. But her legs trembled harder now, her back grew stiffer, her breath harder to catch. Then waves of that unmistakable exhaustion rushed through her, and she almost fell. Black spots floated in her vision. She blinked and shook her head. She had to make it. She bit down on her lip, and the taste of metal filled her mouth.

There. The last jump. She shot through the berm, launched, tucked in the air, and landed smoothly at the exit. A flash of blue disappeared into the tunnel. She had caught up with the lead.

She didn't smile, didn't celebrate. If Misam's notes were correct, there would be two more straightaways before the finish line, one more with hurdles and one to gain speed. *Choose your lines carefully; every carve counts.* The message was unmistakable: this was when it mattered the most. It wasn't over. She would prove to Misam, her dad, and herself that she could win this. Kaia sucked on her bloody lip, rolled her shoulders, and entered the tunnel.

CHAPTER 31

The tunnel dove down, the bulges of smooth ice warping into a blur. The shadows danced between her and the uneven walls. It was a treacherous terrain of illusions, dip and cracks invisible to the naked eye. Other lights shone ahead, David's unmistakable blue helmet a beacon. Kaia's knees ached, her ankles throbbed, and her eyes hurt from not blinking. With every new shadow, she changed her course. Her board cut through the unwilling glacier. Left, right, left.

A soft light, another turn, and there it was—the last hurdle. A massive circular tunnel opened in front of Kaia. Like a silo, it was perfectly smooth. In their path, blocking their exit, was a solid metal wall. It reached halfway to the ceiling. A narrow jump stood in front of it. She heard Heaika swear.

The jump was too small for two people to hit it at once, which forced them to make an impossible choice: push the others out of the way, or fall in line behind them. If they gave up their speed, they wouldn't make the jump. If they didn't, they would crash into each other or the wall. It was a test of precision and determination.

Kaia refused to do either.

She glanced at David. He was not too far in front of her; she could try to push him. *No.* It stung to admit it, but he was too large and too strong. She would lose that battle. Using her other sense wasn't an option either; exhaustion already gripped her. But if she didn't find a solution fast, she would be forced to slow down, which meant giving up or crashing into the wall. She tried to clear her mind, but the spotlights stung her eyes. She blinked. The white light burned as it reflected off the ceiling, the rounded ice walls.

A memory that felt like it was much older than it was popped into her mind. It had been only four—no, five cycles ago. She had failed then, but this time…

Kaia smiled and swerved hard to the left. Her board slashed through the ice. A cloud of white billowed out behind her. She could do this. Bending down, she flew up the cave wall. Right at the peak of her carve, as gravity began to pull on her gut, she stretched, turned around, and aimed down. Her legs trembled under the pressure of the drop. She raced across the other contestants' trail. Following an invisible line, she flew up the opposite wall. Her speed increased. Weightless, she pulled herself up higher, then turned again. Her stomach twisted. She saw Vilde, Heaika, and David closing in on the jump. David and Heaika seemed to be engaged in a dance, one knocking into the other. None of them had noticed Kaia. *Good.*

She cut back and forth two more times, each arc ending a little higher than her last. The compressed air pulled at her suit and roared in her ears. The colossal wall was close; one last pump, one last pull, and then she would have no choice but to follow through with her idea. She felt insane as she turned for the last time. Adrenaline rushed through her. Her vision cleared. She had one goal. *Don't flinch.* As the words filled her mind, she took one last breath and leaned into the fall.

She found the line she wanted, locked into a squat, leaned onto her toes, and raced up the side of the cave. She lifted slightly, pulled herself up with the speed, and froze into position. The carve brought her up onto the ceiling. The roof became the floor. She was upside down, and her board disconnected from the ice. She felt it slip beneath her, and fear rippled through her. Her instinct told her to abort, shut her eyes, and grab hold of something.

Don't flinch. You knew this was coming.

She had to trust her decision, her skills, her board. It was a deadly exercise. She bit down and remained in position. She shot across the ceiling. Down below, she saw the jump turn into a small box shape and the wall into a line, and then…

Her heart sank. Hidden behind the wall was a damn ravine. She had expected the sensation of falling, the loss of control, but this? It took everything she had not to react, not to move a muscle, not to flail.

She had no control over where her line would take her now. Which was an issue, considering she hadn't calculated for the ravine. If she fell, she might as well give up. She braced herself, her feet and knees meeting the force of the loop, and hoped she didn't end up in the mouth of the glacier.

She must have closed her eyes. Because before she knew it, her board scraped the ridge of the ravine, and then she shot onto the flat ground beyond. She was clear of the wall. She had made it.

"YES!"

Her line had been perfect. She laughed, her dad's proud face laughing with her.

I knew you could do it, K.

The memory of him filled her. Then she thought of Biorki urging her to enter Stallo, and she grinned. Vilde's black-and-yellow suit cut in front of her, and Kaia followed. She could hear Heakia's distinct slashes in the ice behind her. David was nowhere to be seen.

Kaia followed the next turn. Then she watched Vilde make a mistake—her board sent her too high. *There.* Turning her own board, Kaia leaned deeper into the turn, aiming to pass beneath her. A shadow, the sound of metal on ice, and Vilde cut back down in front of her. It had been a trick, and it had worked. Kaia twisted her back heel and dug her board into the ground. It slowed her just enough to dodge Vilde. Whatever extra speed she had gained from the loop was lost. *Fuck.*

Kaia followed Vilde out of the turn. There it was—the last straightaway, a bridge of ice and snow that led right to the finish line. Boxes built into the mountain wall hovered above them. Filled with people, the windows of the boxes burst with color. Two large screens sat on each side. They probably displayed the feeds from Kaia's and Vilde's helmet cams.

Kaia was right on Vilde's heels, the other girl's ice spray hitting her visor. Whenever Kaia tried to pass, Vilde was there, predicting her moves. If Kaia attempted to fake a pass, Vilde didn't react. Kaia may have the faster board, but Vilde was technical and precise. *Dritt.* Kaia did everything she could think of, but nothing worked. She began to go numb, her fingers cold inside her closed fists.

They were halfway across the straightaway when she saw it: a shadow in the bridge. She turned, but Vilde must have missed it. She rode right across it, and Kaia felt a jolt run through her legs as the bridge shifted. Then the horrible sound of cracking ice ripped through the air, and a heart-wrenching scream followed as Vilde fell through the bridge, her eyes wide with terror.

Vilde reached out for anything to grab on to as she slid into the hidden ravine. Kaia could pass her and win, meet Alexi. She could get away and save her friends in Kaldwell.

The thoughts barely registered before she leaped forward and caught Vilde's hand.

The impact tore through Kaia. Something warm spread down her shoulder; so much for her healing stitches. Vilde's eyes were hollow, her mouth open in a silent scream. Her board dropped from her boots and into the endless chasm below. Her legs dangled, and in her panic, she kicked loose more ice. The sound of the falling pieces contorted into a strange crackle that sent shivers down Kaia's spine.

Kaia sprawled on her stomach, dug her board into the ice behind her as a sort of anchor, and pulled. Adrenaline surged through her; it thumped inside her head. Her heart was loud with heightened alertness. But she could still feel the pain as her muscles tore under Vilde's weight. Kaia gasped for air. *Again.* She moved her board, stabbed it into the bridge, and pulled. Sweat ran into her eyes, and she blinked it away. Vilde's arms were almost over the edge. *Again.* Something in her back twisted as she anchored her board this time. The raw pain burned inside her spine, but she bit down and pulled.

Vilde's head made it over the edge, her eyes still wide. *Again.* Kaia re-anchored and put every last bit of her strength into the final pull. She screamed with the effort. This time, her shoulder made a sickening crunching sound. She blinked through the pain, pulled Vilde's body safely onto solid ice, and collapsed next to her.

Kaia stared into the air, the ceiling of the cave mocking her. After everything, this was what had stopped her. Her shoulder sent new pulses of twisting, awful pain. It wasn't the gash this time; something else was horribly wrong. She tried to lift her arm, and a scream pushed past her gritted teeth. She didn't dare look at the damage as she crawled back onto her knees.

Vilde was gasping in front of her, her eyes full of tears. They stared at each other. Vilde opened her mouth to say something, then tipped her head toward the finish line. She didn't have to say a word; Kaia understood. Vilde was telling her to go, to finish what they had started.

Kaia disconnected her board and stood with her right arm clutched in her left. There was only one way to gain speed without a proper launch. She kicked the board in front of her and jumped back on it, then twisted her left boot, snapping the magnets back into place. The motion gave her some forward propulsion, enough to glide down the last bit of the slope. It probably wouldn't be enough. But she had to try.

She had heard Heaika's carves when she was pulling Vilde out of the hole. The sound was loud in her ears, getting closer. There was no turn, jump, or bump that could give her more speed. Kaia leaned forward as far as she could without losing her balance while hugging her arm. She bent her knees and tucked her head to her chest. It was up to her board and the ice now; there was nothing else she could do. Her speed increased, but too slowly. The ice felt sticky. The finish line was only a couple of board lengths away. She tried to make herself smaller, to lean harder, if only by a millimeter. *Come on. Come on.*

The sound of Heaika grew closer. The line got closer.

Please.

She closed her eyes and focused on the ground beneath her. But she could barely sense anything through the pain of her shoulder, let alone breathe. Heaika's shadow loomed beside her, the finish line only half a board length away.

This is it.

Kaia shifted her weight onto the front of her board and, with strength she didn't know she had, bent it against the ground and launched herself forward. The black finish line, painted onto the glacier, passed beneath her. Unable to brace herself, she slammed into the ice chest first. The air left her lungs as she slid across the cave floor. Then, stabbing her still attached board into the ground, she stopped. Her arm twisted next to her, useless.

Gasping for breath, Kaia dropped her head to the ground. Her helmet scraped against the ice. It was over. She had made it across the finish line.

The woman on the speaker said something unintelligible. The crackling noise merged with the sound of cheering. She closed her eyes. If she didn't see or hear the results, they wouldn't be real.

"Hey." The voice sounded familiar. "Are you okay?"

It was David. He must have caught up to them.

"Do you need any help?"

Still face down on the ground, she did need help to move, to breathe. But Kaia closed her eyes and spoke to the floor. "No. I'm fine."

"You don't look fine." David's boots came closer. "Here. Let me help you up."

She didn't resist. She didn't have the strength to. David grabbed her by her uninjured arm, turned her over, and pulled her into a sitting position. Opening her eyes, she found Vilde and Heaika sitting before her. Vilde's worried eyes found hers.

"Thank you for…" Vilde's voice shook. "For saving my life. For stopping when you could have—"

"I lost, didn't I?" Kaia didn't know why she needed to cut Vilde off. No, she did know. She didn't deserve thanks. Solon would come for them all anyway. And now she had no way of getting help.

Vilde glanced at Heaika, who smiled grimly. "You beat me across the line. But…" Heaika grimaced, the words lingering in the air. They all looked at David.

"They disqualified you." David looked up at the boxes. People were leaving now that their entertainment was over.

"They what?" Kaia tried not to move her injured arm as she unlatched her board and crossed her legs.

David raised his hand to scratch his head but hit his helmet instead. "When you jumped off your board after saving Vilde…"

"If you step off your board, you…" Heaika looked over at the finish line.

"Forfeit," David finished with a grimace.

She had lost to a technicality? She felt the blood drain from her face. She looked at Vilde, who didn't meet her eyes. No, she had lost when she'd decided to save her. If Kaia hadn't jumped on her board the way she had, she never would have made it to the finish line before Heaika.

Kaia's head spun, and the world shifted in and out of focus. She looked up at the boxes. There was no sign of Jonas or Misam. Had they left her because she was useless to them now that she had lost?

Then the world snapped back into sharpness. In the second box stood a familiar figure. *Venlá?* A warm feeling spread through Kaia's chest. She had come. Then a second figure stepped forward in a shimmering suit. Kaia was too far away to see the symbol on his chest, but there was no mistaking it. Tall and horrible, Drap was here with Venlá.

Ice filled her veins, numbing her body, her shoulder. Venlá was with Solon?

"Hey." Vilde grabbed Kaia's good hand. "Something just changed, didn't it? Something bad?"

Kaia forced herself to look at Vilde. She opened her mouth to speak, but no words came out.

Vilde squeezed Kaia's hand. "Whatever you saw, does it have something to do with why you entered the competition?"

Not able to conjure up an explanation, Kaia nodded. She looked back at the box. There he was: Drap, the terrible Solon guard who had killed her dad. Venlá pointed in Kaia's direction. *Shit.* She had to get out of there now.

She tried to push herself up. Pain shot through her, and she tipped forward. David caught her before she could fall on her face.

"Not so fast."

"I need to get out of here. Now." She tried to get to her knees, but David held her down, then glanced at the others. Vilde and Heaika exchanged looks and nodded, and then Vilde moved toward Kaia.

"What are you—" Kaia started.

"Hold her," Vilde ordered.

Before Kaia could react, David's arms wrapped around her like a steel cage, trapping her good arm. Heaika grabbed her legs, leaving Kaia unable to move. Bile burned in the back of her throat as Vilde grabbed her right hand and twisted it. Searing pulsing pain clawed through Kaia's arm. She jerked back, but David's and Heaika's arms were like the claws of an excavator.

"This is going to hurt." Vilde held Kaia's eyes.

Going to hurt? How much more could—

Vilde glanced at the other two. "Three, two, now!"

She pulled. A sickening hollow sound came from Kaia's shoulder as it popped back into place. A scream left her mouth. Vilde hadn't lied—an indescribable wave of pain ripped down her arm. David and Heaika released her, leaving Kaia to bend over and breathe through the waves.

"Why did you…" Kaia gasped, her words coming out in pieces.

Vilde stood up and stretched. "You wouldn't have made it far with a dislocated shoulder. Try it. You should be able to move your arm again."

Kaia tried to roll her shoulder. It hurt, but it moved. She looked up at Vilde.

Vilde glanced at the boxes. "Don't thank me. It is easy once you know how. Now, get out of here."

Drap had made it down to the course area and was approaching them. Whatever color Kaia had regained disappeared as the blood rushed from her head.

"Is he the one who's scaring you?" Heaika searched Kaia's face.

David winked at Kaia, a soft smile on his lips. "Go. We will distract him."

Kaia's stomach dropped. Her heart threatened to leave her chest. "No, I can't let you do that. You have no idea what he can do." She stood up on her shaky legs.

Heaika pushed Kaia toward the elevator leading to the locker rooms. "Look, there are still a bunch of people down here. No matter who he is, he won't dare hurt us in front of all of them." Heaika smiled at Kaia. "Especially the winner."

"No, you don't understand," Kaia pleaded.

Drap was moving toward them, his steady gait crushing the ice beneath his feet. He was walking, not running, so maybe Heaika was right. And like Jonas had said, Solon couldn't risk making themselves known yet. And he was alone. Maybe she could fight him. Kaia blinked and shook her head. Her legs shuddered just from the strain of standing, and her arm still throbbed. No, there was no way. Maybe she could just lead him away, and then…

She reached down to her hip—nothing. Her axes were in the locker room. *Damn it.*

Kaia looked at the three iceboarders, the only other ones to have made it to the finish line, and her heart broke. It broke for Sofia, for Állan, Mihka, and all the others still lost in the tunnels. It broke for the three boarders before her, their shoulders squared with determination. They didn't know what they were offering or risking, but there they stood anyway, resolved to defend her against an unknown evil.

Vilde smiled, waved Kaia away, and turned to face Drap. "Go. We'll be okay."

"I…" Kaia managed to croak. "Why?"

Vilde looked over her shoulder. "Because you're one of us, silly."

Heaika shoved Kaia again. "Go!"

One of them. They thought of Kaia as one of them. Something tightened in her chest, and it hurt more than her shoulder, her muscles. They were willing to do this for her, someone they knew nothing about. Someone they had just met.

Kaia locked eyes with David, who grinned and turned. "Go! We've got this."

"Thank you," was all Kaia could manage. She sucked in a deep breath, opened and closed her hands, and ran to the elevator.

When she reached it and stepped inside, she looked back. Drap stood before Vilde, David, and Heaika, who blocked his path. Kaia could see his face now. The door of the elevator moved. Drap lifted the little device in his hand. Kaia tried to warn them, but nothing came out of her mouth. Drap looked up and stared into Kaia's eyes. He grinned, his face twisting into something unnatural—his eyes dark, his tongue over his front teeth. Then he pulled the trigger. David fell to the floor with a scream.

Vilde and Heaika turned. Their eyes were full of terror, their mouths open. They scrambled toward Kaia, their arms stretched toward the elevator. Kaia couldn't look away. It was as if Drap had her under a spell. He winked and lifted his device again. Heaika fell, and their helmet cracked as it slammed into the ice. The sound echoed inside Kaia's skull. Her mouth fell open, but no scream came out, only a rasping noise. She couldn't move as the elevator doors closed to a slit.

The last thing she saw was Drap grinning at her.

CHAPTER 32

The elevator swallowed her. The walls moved closer, the space suddenly smaller. Kaia tore at her helmet, her nails digging into her neck as she unclasped it and threw it off. It bounced off the metal floor. The hollow sound filled the room. She couldn't breathe. She opened the collar of her suit, her fingers struggling, her body trembling, and pulled at the fabric against her neck. The mechanics of the elevator ticked along with her gasps, the sound in sync with her choking. They had been so wrong. No, she had been so wrong. Solon didn't care who saw, not anymore. And she had allowed them to… Kaia choked on the air again.

Falling to the floor on all fours, she heaved, her chest rising and falling. Vilde's face, Heaika's helmet, David's body, and Drap's grin filled her head. She gagged, but nothing came up but slime, acid, and something pink. The fruit from this morning. How could she have been so stupid? Of course they would come after her like before. She had allowed herself to hope she could win a little contest, fly away in a spaceship, and live happily ever after.

She punched the floor. *Useless. Useless. Useless.* The darkness within her grew, a pit of bile. She was nothing but a pile of shit.

Her white glove left red stains on the floor. The elevator shook; soon she would be at the locker room.

They chose to stay, not you. The voice accompanied the images spinning in her head, twisted them. It was true—she had only followed their instructions. She gasped for air, and it tasted rancid, stale. If someone decided to sacrifice themself for her, then so be it. It was their decision. A horrible smile twisted her lips; sweat ran over them, and salt slithered onto her tongue.

They had told her to run. Her dad had too. It wasn't her fault; it was theirs.

There was a sudden stillness, an abrupt change, as if something that had once filled the room had disappeared. Kaia rose to her knees, her face slack, and wiped her mouth with her bloody hand. The smells of acid and iron hit her nose. Her blood was acid; her mind was iron. Staring at the elevator doors but not seeing them, she chuckled, a hollow and empty sound.

She pulled on her braid, wishing to tear it off. It wasn't her fault. It was Venlá's. She had shown Solon where Kaia was. Had pretended to be her friend and put others at risk, probably so she could gain something from the company. Kaia was sure of it. She blinked, stood up in one motion, and breathed. And suddenly, as if nothing had happened, Kaia's trembling disappeared, and the elevator stopped.

The locker room was empty. It looked the same, but somehow it had changed too, warped into something slimy, something cold. Kaia rolled her head from one side to the other as she walked to her locker. She grabbed her bag, opened it, and pulled out the droid box. The droid's head popped up, its eyes refocusing in the light. It turned its head to the side as if asking if everything was okay. Kaia grabbed it by the neck. Was giving her this "gift" another ploy to track her and stab her in the back?

She held the droid's body in one hand and its head in the other. Her right arm shook with pain, but she brushed it off. If she pulled a little harder, the droid's neck would snap. She didn't blink, coldness gripping her heart. The droid squirmed; its legs spun, its arms flailed, its eyes wide. Kaia pulled a little more. The neck of the droid stretched, its joints complaining. A little more, and…

No. Kaia let go of its head and placed the whole droid on her palm. It shook, the joints creaking and popping.

"I'm sorry," Kaia's voice cracked. She reached out to stroke it, but it pulled away.

Kaia fell onto the bench, the droid still in her hand. "I'm so sorry. I don't know what came over me. I just…I don't know what to do."

What had she almost done? It was not like her. Or was this who she really was, someone twisted and cold? A tear fell onto the droid. It wiped it off. Another drop, and then everything went blurry.

Her only hope was to find Jonas, and then… The rest she didn't know. But she couldn't stay here. If Drap was down in the viewing boxes, there was no telling where the rest of the Solon guards were. She had to move. Kaia lifted her head, and without wiping her face, she moved to her bag and placed the droid back on its charger. It looked up at her, wide-eyed. Kaia looked away, pressed a button, and the droid returned to sleep. She would have to deal with it, but later.

"I'm so sorry," she whispered again, placing it inside her backpack.

She attached her axes to her belt, checked the rest of the backpack's contents, and threw it over her left shoulder. She managed to wriggle her right arm through the bag's strap. It left her gasping with pain as she clipped the buckle around her chest. She left her broken helmet behind.

She turned toward the exit just as it slid open, and she froze. It was the silver woman with ice for eyes, the Solon woman who had backhanded Ine in the sick bay. Her slim frame did little to block the door, and Kaia could see the crowd leaving the building behind her. How had she managed to open the lock? The woman's mouth twisted into a grotesque smile. Her blond hair was neatly combed into a ponytail, and her beautiful eyes shone with something Kaia couldn't put her finger on.

"Hi there." The woman's voice was nothing like her face. It was cold, sharp, and twisted.

Kaia stepped back, maintaining eye contact. The woman's lips curled over her teeth, her smile growing. There was triumph in her eyes. She knew she had won, had found her prize.

Kaia stepped to the right, her jaw clenched, her hands on her axes. Her right hand trembled with the motion; she doubted she had the strength to hold the axes for long. The woman's eyes followed her like a predator assessing the distance to her prey. Kaia glanced behind her. She could make it to the training room, but that was another dead end. The elevators weren't an option. She took another step to the right. If she could make the woman move into the room, maybe she could bolt past her.

The woman's grin grew wider, and she laughed as she put her hand in one of her suit pockets. "I'm not here to hurt you." Her voice slithered between them, a hiss echoing off the walls. She stepped into the room, her hips swaying. If Kaia didn't know better, she would have considered the woman beautiful.

"Then why are you following me?" Kaia's voice came out thin and shaking. Why did she have to *sound* weak too? She took another step to her right. Her knee twisted too far, but she bit back the pain. She was way past her physical limit. She took another step.

"Because you have something I want. Something that can help others." The woman took another step, her hand still in her pocket. "Don't you want to help others?"

The woman's words were like acid as they washed over her. Kaia took another step. *Damn it*—there wasn't enough room to slip past her. Kaia glanced at the woman's pocket. She was probably holding one of those horrible devices Drap had used. The woman took another step into the room. Kaia matched the step, and white spots filled her vision.

Her eyelids felt so heavy. Maybe she should give herself up. She wouldn't have to fight anymore. She had a flash of memory of her dad and his wide grin when she had built her first CPU.

Of Biorki laughing when she had forgotten to dry her socks before her shift. She had promised her dad she would run, not let them catch her. She may have failed at winning Stallo and at everything else in her life, but she would never go back on her promise.

Someone slammed into the woman from behind. "Oh, I'm so sorry."

"What in the world are you doing?" the woman barked.

"I'm so sorry, I can't see. See?" Misam waved his hand in front of his eyes. "Is this the bathroom?"

Kaia dashed for the door. The woman tried to turn back, only to find Misam blocking her.

"Ma'am. Excuse me?" Misam turned as if confused and slammed his cane right into her knee.

"Aargh!" The woman bent over.

Misam met Kaia's eyes and mouthed, "Run."

Kaia leaped through the door. She heard the woman swear behind her as she fled into the crowd.

Kaia had made it halfway through the entry hall when a hand grabbed hers. She turned, her head spinning, her heart racing.

"Wow, relax. It's me." The hooded figure lifted his head.

Relief rushed through her like a hot drink on a cold cycle. "Jonas. I'm so sorry. I lost, and now Solon—"

"Shh." Jonas fell into step beside her. "I saw. I have found a solution to our problem. Go through the square. You remember the route?"

Kaia nodded, relieved again. There was a plan. "Get to the bar?"

Jonas nodded, then added, "And don't look back. If something happens, you keep running. Promise me."

Her dad's voice echoed inside her, and she nodded. "I promise."

"Good." Jonas lowered his head again and whispered, "See you soon." He turned and disappeared into the mass of people.

Kaia walked as fast as she could without drawing too much attention. She followed the crowd outside, trying to blend in with the waves of people. It provided her with some cover, but her suit made people turn. Some even stopped her for autographs, which she declined before hurrying on. It was strange. They looked at her with awe. In the past, she would have been grateful and ecstatic. Now she only wanted to fade into the background and escape.

When she reached the bottom of the stairs, she bolted for the end of the square. She darted between stalls, dodged children playing with miniature iceboarder figurines, and heard laughter and commentary on the contest all around her. She hugged her right arm tighter with her left. Mouth-watering scents filled her nose. Mothers lifted their children and twirled them around. For them, this had been an exciting Stallo to watch.

Kaia was a meter from the street when an earsplitting bang filled the square. The ground shook, and a heat wave singed the hairs on her neck. A chorus of screams filled her ringing ears, and a familiar terror crawled under her skin. Adjusting her footing, she twisted around, and there was the horror that had started it all—an explosion.

Blue flames and black smoke billowed out of the Stallo building. They licked the carvings and scars on the copper construction. Like a monster or a ghost, the building's golden eyes were upon them all. Out of its mouth came people, their faces painted with fear, their feet slipping on the stairs. Fathers and mothers called for their children, all the joy and celebration evaporating in an instant. Fear was nothing new for Kaia. But it shattered her to see these people scream and watch as their sense of safety disappeared in one quick swoop. The faces of Misam, Jonas, and the iceboarders flashed through her mind. She hoped Venlá burned.

She should never have come here. But she had to keep her promises to her dad and Jonas. It took everything for her to turn and run into the street. Thoughts of burned bodies and dead eyes tormented her, images that only grew stronger the farther away she got. But the tears didn't come.

Warmth spread through her instead, a crackling vile thing. With every step, it grew, twisting, eating her guilt like fuel. Hatred. It burned inside her and pushed her forward, pulsing through her body. She wouldn't let them win. She would fight or die trying.

The screams faded as she crept closer to the bar. The shadows flickered with the distant glow from the flames, and the eerily empty streets played tricks on her mind. At one point, she thought she saw someone in the shadows, but when she looked back, nobody was there. It spooked her, and she slowed her pace, sliding from dark corner to dark corner. Everything made her jump—her breath, the water drops falling from the roofs above, the sound of her boots on the cobblestones. Now and then, distorted whispers drifted through the streets. They sent shivers down her spine.

As she turned onto a tiny street, the reality of her situation hit home. She had lost Stallo. They had missed their chance to meet Alexi. Kaia's breath caught, but she released it, remembering that Jonas still had a plan. But how? What could they do without Alexi and his ship? Solon had screwed everything up. The foul, hot torrent in her gut twisted. It didn't matter. If she could get away, she didn't care about anything else.

Kaia almost collapsed when she saw the bar. She had made it. The door was as simple and unimpressive as last time, but the sight of it made her smile. Ten, maybe fifteen shaky steps, and she would be inside. Her right arm throbbed; the backpack dug into her shoulders. She was a mess. Parts of her hair had come loose, and curls hung in front of her face. What was left of her braid burned where Venlá had touched it. She itched to tear it loose. But first she had to get inside.

One step was all she could do. Then one more. Her muscles resisted, twitched, and revolted. She looked at her feet, willing them to move. *You can do it.*

"There you are."

Everything inside Kaia froze—her muscles, her breath, her mind. She lifted her head, her hair in her eyes. It took a while for the world to sharpen. A short, muscular man stood in front of her. Gin. *Of fucking course.* The heat in her gut, in her blood, bristled in response.

She pushed the hair out of her eyes. "Yes, here I am."

Gin took a step to the right, blocking her path. His strange silver monosuit and helmet shone under the street lanterns, making it impossible to see his face. It didn't matter; Kaia could remember his face perfectly as he'd stood above her dead dad. Hot needles rushed into her legs, her arms, her cheeks.

"It's great to see you." His voice was flat, emotionless.

Kaia took a step to the side. "Likewise. How is taking over our planet going? Not as easy as you would have liked?" Her voice was smooth as folded metal.

Gin's shoulders rose slightly, and his hands twitched. "So, this is where your coconspirators are staying?" He tilted his head toward the bar.

A stab of ice. Kaia didn't answer.

"I'm surprised we didn't find you earlier. It was so easy to follow you. You really should look above you when you walk around."

So that was how he had tracked her—from the rooftops. He must have been waiting outside in case the others failed. She remembered the grin on Drap's face. Maybe this had been their plan all along, Venlá's plan. The heat inside her twisted. She should have known.

Gin tilted his head to one side, and looked her up and down. Kaia's skin crawled. She stared back at him, her face emotionless.

He sighed again, took something out of his pocket, and lifted his hand. "I just want to talk."

There was a glint of silver. *Ah, the device. Of course.*

"You want to *talk*? You have a strange way of showing it." Kaia took another step to the side.

Gin matched it, keeping her path blocked. The sickening heat inside her grew. She inhaled and dropped her hands to her sides. He would shoot her before she could get close enough to do damage with her axes. She had to create an opening. She shifted her weight to her right foot and smiled.

CHAPTER 33

"If you want to talk, talk." Kaia rolled her shoulders, ignoring the throbbing pain in the right one. "What do you want from me?"

Gin stepped toward her slowly, still pointing the silver thing at her. She shifted her weight but didn't move.

"I don't want anything from you." His words were laced with something sickly sweet. "The company does."

"You don't want anything?" She clenched her teeth, her cheek flexing with the pressure. *Of course not; you already took it all.*

Something inside her cracked; all thoughts and calculations washed away like a wall, a box, a cage had split open in her mind. *Control your emotions; you can't let anyone see.* Screw that. The heat inside her folded in on itself and was sucked into that darkness, which fed it, strengthened it.

Outside the blur of her mind, she saw Gin take another step forward. She could see his face now, distorted by her eyes. He looked as bland as last time. His lips were moving, his words scrambled and faint, as if he was speaking from the other end of a tunnel. Kaia hesitated only for a moment before she closed her eyes.

She searched and found it—not outside herself, like Misam had taught her, but inside. The darkness was everywhere and nowhere. It was in her skin, gut, muscles, heart, and mind. It wasn't darkness, exactly, but no other word could describe the thing that pushed and pulled at itself and everything around it. It was solid, yet also empty space. It was a part of her. It flowed through her like waves meeting cliffs, only restricted by her skin, her mind. A boiling sea of power ready to be released onto the world, onto this man. And she wouldn't hold back. Not this time.

Gin's voice buzzed in her ears. Kaia held the image of the darkness in her mind and willed it to extend beyond her skin and wrap around her arms. It was instinctual. She was the vessel, and hatred was the key. She embraced her anger, her rage, and opened her eyes. The world was instantly sharper. Gin's face was the only thing she cared to see. She saw his expression change, the widening of his eyes, the tightness of his lips. She smiled and took a step forward. He stepped back, his gray eyes growing wider still.

Kaia stretched her arms and rolled her shoulders. The pain was gone. In fact, she didn't feel any pain at all, no soreness, no exhaustion. She flexed her fingers. The air bent around her hand like a warped mirror. She felt nothing except for a slight tingle in her hands. Why had she ever suppressed such a fantastic power? It felt incredible. Gin's hand trembled on the device. His finger wrapped around the trigger and pulled. The buzz filled the air. She grinned.

"How?" Gin's voice had climbed several octaves.

How was such a broad question. Kaia took a step forward and raised her hands slowly. The water on the ground evaporated wherever her feet touched it, sending clouds of steam into the air. Gin's frightened eyes looked almost comical. She chuckled as he took another step back.

"Do you mean how am I doing this?" Kaia flexed her fingers. The air around them moved and twisted. "Or how come your little toy there isn't working?"

Gin's mouth hung open; he seemed unable to speak. He took another step back, and Kaia grinned, her eyes steely. She hadn't felt this good in cycles. No, she hadn't felt this good *ever*. Whatever Solon was hunting her for, it wasn't this. The shock and terror on Gin's face was genuine. It made her heart flutter.

"In any case, I'm not sure." She let her lips curl over her teeth. "Do you want to test it out with me?"

Gin hit the steps of the bar with his boot, and his eyes managed to widen further. He almost fell backward but caught himself with a clumsy wriggle of arms and legs. He had cornered himself; he had been too distracted by her to notice that she had forced him back against a wall.

"Oh, nowhere to run?" Her voice sounded foreign, cold, full of gravel.

"I was only following orders. I didn't have a choice." Gin moved to the side and pressed his back to the building.

"Oh, I'm sorry." Kaia lifted her hands in mock surprise. Gin's eyes followed them, unable to look away. "So killing my dad and my friends was okay, because you were just following orders."

Kaia took a step forward, her hips swaying, the air rippling. Gin didn't move. His face pale, his hands rose between them. She wanted to see his eyes empty, like her dad and friends.

Gin opened and closed his lips, then opened them again. "I-I didn't—"

Kaia launched forward and grabbed his neck. She squeezed. Gin let out a gurgling scream and tried to grab her arms and tear them off of him. Her arms burned him, singed him even through his gloves. She smiled as the suit around his neck tried to fight the heat of her hands. If he were wearing regular fabric, it would have burned already.

This fabric seemed alive. It pulsed and moved to meet the pressure and heat flowing from Kaia's hands. She had never seen anything like it except for Venlá's bracelet. She squeezed harder as she stared into Gin's eyes and smiled. He met her gaze. Horror lined every line of his face, a plea in his eyes. Why had she ever been afraid of him?

She focused on her arms, the vibrations streaming through them, and then Gin's suit folded back. Unable to withstand the pressure and the heat, it melted under her bare hands—her gloves must have burned off. Gin's mouth opened to scream. His legs kicked her shins, and his arms flailed by his sides. A gurgle left his lips. The smells of burned flesh and metal filled her nose, and she sucked it in. She watched his eyes grow unfocused as his life slipped away.

A sound filled her ears, so twisted it almost made her let go. It was evil, a promise of death, and it had come from her. *Her?* She was suddenly watching herself as her hands glowed with heat that seared through Gin's neck. His skin bubbled under her touch, his neck breaking under the pressure she exerted. Her hair was a wild thing; some of it burned from the heat coming from her body. Her face was twisted into a horrible smile. Then she saw Gin's face. Tears streamed from his wide eyes as his last breath left his lips. *No.*

In that second of doubt, a shadow passed behind Gin, knocked him over the head, and pulled him out of her hands. Confused, she hesitated, the vibrations faltered, the heat dissipating, and then, in a rush, it all turned inward. A pain Kaia had never experienced ran through her like the cords of a mining drill. It carved into her fingers, her hands. It shredded her nerves and splintered her muscles. She gasped, unable to move or escape as it tore through her.

She stood there, frozen in pain, as the dark figure moved closer. *No. Not now.* She had to fight back. She had to—

Green and gray blurred together, and then familiar images floated into her spotty vision. Dark hair, longer than she remembered. Blue eyes above a sad smile. Two warm hands touched her cheeks.

"Hi." His voice was soft and rough and something else. "Hi, Kaia."

His voice reset something in her mind. It cooled and warmed her, and the vibrations and darkness fled back into their cage. She fell to the scorched ground and looked up at his face. He crouched in front of her, never letting go of her face or breaking eye contact.

"Biorki?" Her voice sounded small, nothing like it had a minute ago. "Is that really you?"

He pulled some burned hair from her face and tucked it behind her ear. His touch left lines of heat behind, but it was nothing like her internal inferno; it was healing, soft, and right.

She tried to reach up and pull her fingers through his hair, but her arms wouldn't move.

"Yes, it's me." Biorki leaned back, and his hands left her skin.

She swayed forward. *No, don't let go.* But he was already back on his feet, moving toward the bar door, and she could do nothing to stop him.

A rasping sound filled her ears. There was a gasp, then more rasping. It was the lump of blue that had been Gin. His chest rose and fell, but barely. So he was still alive. She was surprised to feel relief rush through her.

Biorki bent down in front of Gin, a grimace of disgust on his face. He rolled Gin onto his back. Had he seen what she had done? What she had been about to do, would have done if he hadn't come? She looked at the stiffness in Biorki's shoulders. Yes, he had seen.

Her gut twisted, and nausea rolled through her, sending an ache through every fiber of her body. It was a different kind of pain, not sharp or acute like the fire that had carved through her. It was a slow, creeping cold that wormed itself into the deepest parts of her. She had crossed an invisible line. She had let her anger control her and had almost killed a man. She *would* have killed him if it hadn't been for Biorki.

CHAPTER 34

After Biorki pulled Gin's body into the bar, he returned for her. Kaia let him drag her to her feet, and with one arm over his shoulders, he walked her into the building. Neither of them said a word. Kaia struggled to stay conscious. She sat in one of the booths while Biorki waved his arms to get Bean's attention. She felt her head droop. The next thing she saw was Bean pulling on a backpack, the body of Gin nowhere to be seen. She drifted off again.

She woke to solid arms around her, a chest against her back, and wind pulling at her hair. Two rusted lines disappear into the darkness ahead. A loud whine surrounded her, like the sound of a dying animal.

She blinked and squinted against the exhaustion. It wasn't an animal but old, rusted wheels gripping the train tracks beneath her. She sat in a roofless makeshift cart that shook as it sped along the abandoned rails. She hoped they were abandoned, anyway; if they met a train down here, they would be crushed. The cart didn't even have a proper light. She watched the lantern tied to the front rattle as the cart dipped and turned in the dark tunnels.

The aroma of citrus enveloped her. Even the wind blowing past couldn't erase Biorki's scent. He held her tight against him. She assumed it was a precaution so her unconscious body wouldn't fly off. Still, dread and realization flooded her at his touch. She moved against his arm, and he loosened his grip.

"Welcome back." Biorki's warm breath brushed against her neck.

She didn't know what to say. She had almost killed someone in front of him. No, she had *almost* killed someone in front of him. Her throat tightened; air wouldn't flow through it. Suddenly, his arms were like a corset. She tried to pull at them, but she was too weak.

Biorki released her and took her right hand in his. She stopped moving, her breath still catching. He traced a circle on her palm. His breath was warm on her ear as he leaned closer and whispered, "You did nothing wrong."

Kaia had forgotten how good he was at reading people, at cutting straight to the point. She exhaled, but that iron taste was still on her tongue.

"He deserved it. I would have killed him myself if you hadn't gotten to him first. I was going to. Then I saw you, and…" Biorki's finger on her palm paused, then continued. "I couldn't let you become a killer. Not when it was my fault he found you."

"Your fault? What do you—" *Wait.* Jonas had said he'd had her followed. Biorki could have traveled with Fluff and met him. But Jonas would have said something. Wouldn't he? Her stomach flipped as the cart took another turn too fast.

"You were the one following me this whole time?"

Biorki stiffened and leaned closer. "I can't tell you now."

She looked behind them. Bean sat on the other seat in the back of the cart, a grin on his face. He winked at Kaia. Something crawled down her neck, and she turned back to face the dark tunnel.

"I will explain everything later." With a last squeeze of her hand, Biorki let her go and scooted back in the seat.

Cold enveloped her, and although she was happy to sit

alone with her thoughts, she wished he had held her longer. No such sentiment showed on Biorki's face, his head low as he rummaged through his bags.

Jonas hadn't told her the entire escape plan for a reason. But it still hurt to know that he had kept from her that Biorki would be involved. If she had known, would she have acted differently? Would she still have tried to kill Gin? Maybe, maybe not. She shrank into her seat.

The cart shot up and turned. Without Biorki to support her, Kaia had to grip the seat. Needles of pain slithered over her arms, along with something else. Her palms itched, and her skin was numb. The cart shot out into a straightaway, and she lifted her hands to inspect them. They were wrapped in medical gauze from her elbows to her fingertips. Why would she need—

She looked behind her and caught Biorki's eyes. He looked away. That stung more than her arms. Then he looked back up, his eyes laced with worry. He leaned closer and whispered, "You got burned when you…"

When she had tried to kill Gin.

She turned back around before he could finish his sentence. She stared at the mountain walls rushing past, her arms uselessly hanging at her sides. Everything hurt, but at least she could brace herself with her thighs. She would deal with her arms later, and Biorki and Jonas…if Jonas had made it. Her stomach flipped again.

She lifted her head and sighed. She could do nothing now as they plunged deeper into the unknown mountain, even farther away from everything she knew. Right now, she would allow herself some rest, some much-needed emptiness. She would worry when they arrived at the next step in Jonas's secret plan. Until then, she would ignore the tightness in her chest, the bile in the back of her throat.

They reached the end of the tracks hours later. When the brakes initiated, Kaia was sure the cart would fall apart and send them flying onto the tracks. Instead, sparks flew up around them as metal scraped against metal. Bolts rattled, and joints shook. They all sighed with relief as the cart stopped on a small abandoned platform.

"You said this was safe," Biorki snapped at Bean, his voice demanding. Kaia flinched. She had never seen Biorki act like that before. He didn't seem to notice her reaction.

Bean raised his arms. "Relax. I never said it was safe. I said it would get us here, and look, here we are."

Biorki mumbled something under his breath and turned to Kaia. He looked exhausted, his skin pale and tight over his bones. Purple shadows lay under his eyes. She hadn't noticed them earlier. Still, there was a fire in his eyes, and they lit up even more when they found hers. He smiled, his lips a tight line. She probably looked worse.

"Let's get moving before the cart breaks apart." Kaia tried to smile and failed.

Biorki grimaced and shot Bean a sour look. "Yeah. The faster we get off this thing, the better."

Kaia couldn't do much with her arms wrapped in gauze, so she stayed out of the way. After unloading a few boxes from the cart, Biorki pulled her dad's bag from a crate. She made a little noise of gratitude, and he helped her put it on. For a moment, it almost felt like they were back in Kaldwell, getting ready for a shift. But then Biorki turned again, and the coldness between them seemed to grow. He had lied to her. Well, not directly, but he had chosen to stay away and had left her to struggle alone. And she had left him behind without an explanation.

Bean and Biorki stacked the boxes on a metal sheet they had placed on the platform. By the time they finished, the pile was taller than she was.

Bean wiped his red and sweaty forehead. "Jonas better keep his side of the bargain."

"Don't worry. He will."

Biorki bent down and lifted the last box out of the cart. It was darker than the others, and he set it behind the sheet, away from the rest. He the box, then pushed a button on it. It unraveled into a gravel hauler, attached itself to the sheet with the stacked boxes, and lifted it off the ground as if it weighed nothing. Then it hauler rolled underneath and clicked into place.

Kaia looked at Biorki. "One of your inventions?"

A smile she hadn't seen in a very long time spread across his face. "Of course." He rubbed his head, his black hair a mess. "Let's hope it holds."

She couldn't help but grin back at him at the memory of all his failed experiments.

"Oh, get a room." Bean walked past them. "Or get moving. We don't know if that Solon guard managed to message his team. And if he did, it won't take them long to find this tunnel in the back of my bar." Bean stared at Kaia, his eyes slits. "Thanks to you, I can't go back home!"

She already knew it was her fault, knew she had led them to Bean. She was already blaming herself, and now this man was judging her? Her bandaged hands closed into fists. She could still land a punch. It would hurt, but it would be worth it.

Biorki stepped between them.

"Bean, you have plenty of other establishments. That bar isn't even your main venue. So leave it alone." Biorki crossed his arms over his chest. "Not only that, but your deal with Jonas is worth much more than that run-down bar."

"Oh, come on. It was my favorite run-down bar." Bean noticed the look in Kaia's eyes and sighed. "Fine. I'll let it go. However, that doesn't change the fact they will find the tunnel any minute."

Biorki looked at Kaia. "Let's get moving, then."

At his words, the gravel hauler rolled into the tunnel. The boxes shook on its back as the three of them followed behind it.

They walked together in silence, the sound of the gravel hauler echoing around them. Its metal chain treads made a repetitive jarring sound against the stone floor. When they had walked for an hour, Kaia turned to Biorki.

"Where are we going?" She hated that she had to ask. She wished Jonas had told her. Wished Biorki had told her he had been in Framnes this whole time. Wished she didn't feel so lonely, so ignorant.

Biorki didn't look up from his tablet, which displayed a map of hundreds of passageways. "We are going to the power facility of Framnes. It's one of the few ways out of the city that doesn't require us to go through a checkpoint or travel by train."

Kaia thought of the path Jonas had led her along from the surface, the many tunnels filled with smuggled goods. She nodded at Biorki before falling silent again, lost in her thoughts.

They were entirely reliant on Jonas—his word, his promises. Yet he had withheld so much from her. The more she thought about it, the more frustrated she became. Why hadn't Biorki let her know he was there? She wouldn't have trusted Venlá if he had, and the other contestants wouldn't be dead. Then again, Kaia had left Biorki behind without a word. Her mind spun and twisted to the beat of the hauler-bot.

Biorki cleared his throat, and the hauler-bot stopped. A broad brown rusted door stood before them in the otherwise empty tunnel. On it was a triangular sign that read, danger ahead—no trespassing.

A gasping ball of sweat, Bean rested his hands on his knees and chuckled. "Welcome to the powerhouse of Framnes, where few get to go and fewer return."

"Don't be so melodramatic." Biorki sighed and turned to Kaia. "From what I have heard, it is a difficult place to work, but most come back alive."

Kaia raised her eyebrow. "Most?"

Biorki adjusted the boxes on his droid so it could pass through the door. "It's like any mining gig in Kaldwell. There's always a risk of not coming back."

Kaia was under the impression that every town and city on this forsaken planet ran on geothermal energy, and none who worked in the Kaldwell plant would have called it risky. Instead, it was considered a post for the weak-hearted. What was so different about this plant?

Biorki gave the bot a verbal command and pulled the handle on the door. It didn't budge. He uttered something under his breath, pushed down the handle again, and yanked. His muscles flexed under his gray sweater. The door swung open with a loud crack.

Kaia had expected something grand or terrifying. Instead, the door led to a large but otherwise plain room. It was empty except for the dust covering the brown floor. Two doors sat on opposite sides of the room. Walking in, Kaia ensured that her steps were quiet. Bean stomped behind her, his dark boots kicking up dust. Kaia narrowed her eyes at him.

"What?" Bean gestured to the doors. "No one is going to be here this cycle. They were all watching Stallo. I'm sure they are still dealing with the aftermath."

Kaia flinched and turned away. The word *Stallo* was like hot metal. It burned through her.

"You made me a richer man, losing like that." Bean's voice was shrill. "You should have seen Jonas's face when you jumped off your board. Valiant effort, throwing yourself over the line even after being disqualified. Admirable."

Kaia closed her fists, the pain like daggers in her skin. Her hands and shoulders shook. If he didn't shut up, she would make him. The thrill of seeing Gin's eyes, his life slipping away in her hands, thrummed within her... *No.* She lifted her hands to her ears.

"And your iceboarding friends—what a group of idiots, losing to someone like you. It was such a relief when number ten crossed the line and—"

A loud crack echoed through the room. She turned to see Bean fall on his butt, Biorki staring down at him, his hand in a fist.

"What the..." Bean rubbed his cheek.

"Keep your mouth shut." The cold in Biorki's voice startled Kaia; his eyes burned. "Remember that your deal with Jonas only applies if I tell him you were helpful. Are you being helpful?"

Bean's eyes widened, then narrowed. "Sure, but I could always go to Solon and get a better deal."

Kaia took a step forward. Of course he would sell them out.

Biorki leaned on the hauler-bot. "And tell them what, exactly? That we're here? They probably know that already. And what could they give you that Jonas hasn't already offered? You don't seem like someone who would risk your underground business for a bad deal."

Bean's narrowed eyes flicked to Kaia, then back to Biorki. "Oh, come on." A smile suddenly appeared on his face. "I was kidding. Relax. I won't mess with your girlfriend. I promise."

Kaia stole a glance at Biorki. His shoulders were straighter, and his voice was sharper. She wasn't the only one who had changed.

Biorki caught her gaze, a sadness in his eyes. Then he turned and spoke to the hauler-bot.

"Let's get ready." Biorki pulled a suit from one of the smaller boxes on the droid. "Bean and bot, you know what to do." Biorki grabbed a box off the hauler-bot and walked toward the smaller door. "Kaia, come with me."

A shard of ice stabbed at her insides. There was no warmth in those words.

CHAPTER 35

Once again, silence fell between them like an invisible wall, unbreachable and unmoving. Kaia followed Biorki through a maze of smaller rooms. Some contained switchboards. Others had rows and rows of power cells. The buzz of the room's air vents made the silence bearable. Well, almost bearable.

"I—" The vowel got stuck in her dry throat.

Biorki's back stiffened slightly, but he didn't slow down.

"I'm sorry I left you behind. I just…" She didn't know if any words could properly explain why. If the right ones existed, they didn't present themselves to her. So many things had happened; so much had changed since then.

"I couldn't…" she began again.

Biorki's shoulders flexed as he shifted his hold on the box. He looked over his shoulder.

"You couldn't let me die because of you?" he finished, his voice sharp.

Kaia nodded, then breathed in. "Yes. That, and I had to do it by myself." She hadn't understood it then, but she did now. "I had to prove to myself that I could do it alone."

"And how did that work out for you?" His voice wasn't cruel, but the words cut through her like daggers. Her stomach twisted, and she had to stop to catch her breath. Biorki walked on. Maybe things would have turned out better if she hadn't left him.

"It was my problem, not yours. You should have gone back to Kaldwell." Her words flew out of her like a whip, the consonants bouncing off the metal walls of the room.

That made him stop, but he didn't turn to look at her. "I wish you had talked to me before you left. There were things I needed to say, that I still need to say. But before I can, we need to find Jonas."

If Jonas survived the explosion. The unsaid words hung between them.

Biorki adjusted the box in his arms and resumed walking. Kaia followed, her eyes on his back. He was right; this wasn't the time to talk.

After walking in silence through another room, they entered a gray corridor. A row of lamps lined the ceiling to their left, glowing with a bright white light. To the right, the corridor was dark. Biorki took a few steps into the dark tunnel, and the lights above him came to life. So they reacted to movement, which meant… Kaia looked to the left. Someone had walked down this corridor recently.

Biorki turned left, his steps as steady as before. It was eerie to walk through this empty corridor. Kaia wondered what it would look like full of workers. Did they wear the same green overalls as people did in Jonas's sub-city? What did they do here?

Before she could think too much about it, Biorki stopped before a silver door. The sign on it read control room.

"Here we are." Biorki placed the box on the floor and reached into his pocket, presumably for a key.

The door slid open before he could unlock it. A familiar figure stood in the doorway, a crooked grin on his face. *Jonas.* Relief rushed through Kaia.

"I knew you would make it." Jonas looked at Kaia's bandaged hands, grimaced, then looked at Biorki. "Though it seems things didn't go entirely to plan, hmm?"

Biorki picked the box up from the floor. "It was your plan, not mine. I followed it. It's not my fault you miscalculated how fast Solon would get there."

"Yeah, well, someone tipped them off." Jonas glanced behind Kaia, who stood wide-eyed and bewildered. "Bean is holding up his part of the bargain?"

"Yep. He might be greedy, but he would never risk losing his business. He is preparing the vehicles now."

Kaia stared as Biorki followed Jonas into the room. They acted like coconspirators. Neither of them acknowledged her presence as she followed them inside.

Biorki placed the box on a table in the middle of the room. Behind the table, along the room's back wall, was a row of switchboards and screens, a seat at every screen. On the other side of the room sat a drink dispenser. Next to it stood a small rack of capsules.

Kaia needed a drink. She walked over to the machine. The voices of Biorki and Jonas bounced inside her head as they argued about something by the table. It was as if she didn't exist. She knew she should pay attention, but she felt drained, like an empty shell. She looked through the capsules.

A brown capsule on the bottom read energizer plus. She grabbed it, found a cup, and popped the capsule into the machine. She pressed the button. *Please work.* The hiss of water filled her ears. *Yes.* She placed the cup underneath, and colorless liquid filled it.

So, Biorki knew Jonas—fine. But based on the way they spoke, they'd likely known each other before this whole mess, and neither of them had told her. It pissed her off.

Kaia grabbed the cup, sat on a the bench, and watched them. Biorki was animated, gesturing wildly at the box and at her. Jonas was calm, seemingly amused by Biorki's outburst. She felt like she was watching an instructional tech video from her childhood, the kind her dad had downloaded to her tablet to teach her how to weld and fuse wires. Back then, Kaia had thought the way he acted was just a dad being a dad. But it might have been something else, something more intentional.

She took a deep sip of the energizer. It burned her tongue. She didn't care.

"What do you think, Kaia?"

The two men turned toward her—one handsome, whom she had thought she knew but obviously didn't, and one older, a liar she had believed she could trust.

So now they finally saw her? It didn't matter. She didn't care anymore. She ignored their question and took another sip. They exchanged a look. Had *everyone* kept something from her? Her dad, Biorki, Jonas, Venlá—

"Oh no!" She pulled the backpack off her shoulders and placed it on the cracked counter.

Biorki and Jonas looked at her but stayed quiet as she took out the droid and clicked the button on the charger. The droid's head popped out of its box, but this time it did so slowly, assessing her. It was still scared of her. She didn't blame it.

"Hey, little one." She tried to keep her words soft, even though everything inside told her to rip the droid open. "I need to check something in your CPU. Is that okay?"

The droid looked around the room and then up at her face. It stared her down, its eyes moving in and out of focus. She didn't move, just stared back. Finally the droid nodded.

Kaia carefully lifted it from the charger box and placed it on the bench. The droid turned around and unlocked the hatch to its CPU compartment. Kaia sucked in a breath. Inside was the wooden box of hair gel and a note scribbled on a metal plate. She removed the box, careful not to disturb any internal wires, and then the note. It was tricky with her bandages, but she did it. Kaia examined the droid from top to bottom, charger box and all. No false wires, no transmission ports, no trackers. It was clean. The note lay on the bench, writing side down.

Kaia chugged the rest of her energizer and popped another capsule into the machine. This one said energizer—red. The water that came out of the machine was clear, but if a smell could have a color, this one would be red. She stared at the back of the metal note while the machine hummed. Why would

Venlá have left her this box if she was going to hand her over to Solon? It didn't make sense. None of this made sense.

Kaia turned to Biorki and Jonas. They were observing her.

"Jonas, you mentioned that someone tipped off Solon. Do you know who?"

Jonas's smile faltered, and his eyes darkened. "All I know is that the message was sent from someone outside Framnes. The code was too scrambled to extract any more information."

So maybe it wasn't Venlá? But she had seen her with Drap. Kaia grabbed the metal piece with her bandaged fingers.

Dear Lin, I want you to have little Fuse. Fuse can be troublesome, but it needs to see more of the world than my shop. It seems to like you, and I thought, why not? I could see it in your eyes when you walked in. You will do good in this world. I believe it. And the hair gel—you need it more than I do. Anyway, I want to thank you for spending time with little old me. You made droid building feel fun again. Good luck on Stallo. Yours, Venlá.

Kaia stared at the note, her hands suddenly cold. There was no threat, no code, nothing to indicate that Venlá intended to turn her in. The familiar darkness flickered within her, her skin a tingle of needles. She swallowed and breathed. She couldn't allow herself to lose control. Not again.

Venlá hadn't known what Solon was; Kaia hadn't told her. They could easily have tricked her by asking what seemed like an innocent question. That was what Solon did, after all. And Kaia had wanted innocent Venlá dead, for her to burn in the Stallo building. What if she had? She clutched her stomach.

Biorki was by her side in a blink. She held an arm out. "Don't touch me."

Biorki stopped and let his hands fall to his sides. Kaia breathed in, then out, then in, until an icy calm fell over her. It was easier now to push her feelings away, to become numb. However, her anger was still too close to the surface. She hated feeling so useless, like she had no control over her emotions, over her own life. She hated it.

Who had tipped off Solon? Whoever it was had caused so many unnecessary deaths. If she ever found out, they would burn.

Kaia lifted her drink and took a sip. It didn't help. The burning ball of guilt and anger still roared to be let out. But Fuse did not need to see that. She placed the note back into Fuse's compartment, put the hair gel in her bag, and set the charger box next to Fuse. She closed the CPU compartment and patted the droid's head. "So, your name is Fuse?"

The droid turned to face her, nodded, and tilted its head to one side.

"That's a great name. You better get some sleep. It will be a long cycle."

Fuse waved and rolled into the box. She clicked the button, and it went to sleep.

Kaia spun to face the men; she didn't meet Biorki's eyes. "Now, you better tell me what the stars is going on, or I will force it out of you." She flexed her arms.

Biorki didn't move, his eyebrows pinched into a scowl, but Jonas took several steps back. Ah, so they knew about her power, and it scared them. Good.

She walked over to the table. "Spit it out."

Several emotions passed across Jonas's face before it settled into his usual crooked smile, but it didn't reach his eyes. He sat down by the table. He gestured for Kaia to sit as well, but she didn't move. He sighed and pulled his hand through his messy silver hair.

"I understand that you're mad…"

Kaia almost punched him in the face then and there. Jonas shifted his weight, and Biorki shot him a sharp look.

"I mean, I'm sorry I didn't tell you everything. I had my reasons." Jonas's smirk faltered. "We don't have much time before Bean finishes preparing the snow rovers. But I will explain why I have lied to you and why Biorki is here."

"Go on," she ordered through gritted teeth.

"First of all, my name is not Jonas. Well, it is in Framnes. But my real name is Alexi."

Cold, sharp realization cut through Kaia's rage, and she had to stop herself from sitting down. How had she not seen it? She was so stupid. Of course there was no Alexi who was only reachable through Stallo. She had been too fast to believe, too quick to trust. It had all been a lie. Anger rose inside her again. This time, she struggled to hold it back.

"So when the hag told me to find Alexi, she meant you?" Kaia rested her hands on her hips.

Jonas—Alexi—cringed at the mention of the hag and pulled his now-clean handkerchief from his pocket. He dragged his fingers over the embroidered F.

"Yes and no." Alexi sighed. "The Alexi Gret-ha used to know is gone. The person she needs me to be isn't around anymore."

Kaia raised an eyebrow.

"What I mean to say is, Gret-ha and I used to be linked, bonded, married, tied together. Whatever you want to call it." Alexi placed the handkerchief on the table. "We used to be a part of a secret organization that saves people like you from Solon."

Kaia tightened her grip on her cup.

"I left that organization when they failed to save our daughter. But Gret-ha dove deeper into the work and became obsessed. I couldn't be around that anymore." He rubbed his brow and looked at Kaia. "I still send her supplies with Fluff from time to time. It had been rotations since I had talked to Gret-ha when she sent you and that note to me. To make it worse, you were wearing our daughter's favorite monosuit."

Kaia had seen the anger in his eyes when he had seen the suit. He had told her to change. Some of the heat in her chest evaporated, and she sat down. "What happened to your daughter?"

Jonas—no, Alexi—seemed to struggle with his words, his eyes turning watery. "Flora was like you: strong, kind, and a little crazy. And she could do things others couldn't. She could heat water with her hands. The organization found us shortly after she turned sixteen. They tracked us to the planet we lived on."

Alexi was from another planet? Kaia swallowed some Energizer Red and listened.

"They told us that a company would soon come to our planet and offer to heal those who were sick, that they would give everyone a blood test, and that we should run before it was too late." Alexi locked eyes with Kaia. "We didn't believe them. Three cycles later, Solon came. They tested our blood, and something changed when they tested Flora's. They asked us to bring her in for a check-up, that something was wrong with her, but we knew they were lying. Flora was never sick; that was one of the weird things that made her different. So we contacted the organization. With their help, we managed to flee the planet. That was when we joined."

Alexi looked at Biorki and continued, "At first, the organization helped us, sheltered us. But in return, we had to help them find others like Flora, and we did. We saved a few too. Then Solon found us; they had tracked us from our hometown. Gret-ha and I were on a mission at the time, and when we returned to the hideout, everyone was dead. Flora and the others were gone." Alexi's voice broke on his daughter's name.

"When you showed up in the sled, I knew you were like my daughter, and I couldn't handle going through it all again. I had also gambled away the key to our spaceship, so even if I wanted to, I couldn't use it. Then you suggested entering Stallo, and it gave me an idea. I could test you to see if my suspicions were correct, and if you passed I could get my key back by entering you into Stallo and gamble on it."

"The radioactive stone?" Kaia leaned back in her chair. "And Bean had the key?"

"Exactly." Alexi smiled softly. "You passed. That's when I knew I had to get you out. You already knew me as Jonas and agreed to the plan. I figured the less you knew, the better. And there's also this."

Alexi reached for her left hand. She allowed him to take it even though she was still angry. He unraveled the gauze slowly, and Kaia gasped when the last piece dropped to the table. Biorki sucked in a breath next to her. Her arms were lined with crooked white burns that ran from her fingertips to her elbows.

They looked like the burns she had seen on miners who had accidentally touched electric wires. However, these scars were neater, straighter. They twisted and crossed up her forearm.

"This is why the secret organization tries to keep people like you away from society. You're not only in danger from Solon—you're a danger to yourself and everyone around you."

CHAPTER 36

Kaia stared at her arms. She should have been doubled over in pain. Instead, the burns only hurt if she moved them, and only about as much as if someone had squeezed her arm. Her instincts had been right: whatever lurked within her was dangerous. She looked up at Alexi, and he looked at Biorki.

"Your turn." Alexi rewrapped her arm while Biorki cleaned his throat. She didn't look up at his face. *This better be good.*

"Do you remember when I told you about the cycle my mother died?" Biorki's voice seemed different, uncertain.

Kaia nodded, still staring at nothing. "Mm-hm."

"Well…" Biorki walked over to the wall across from the drink machine. "There's something I didn't tell you. I completely lost it that cycle. I was about to…to kill myself."

She opened her mouth, then shut it again.

"I walked to the older caves in the glacier; you know, the ones that can collapse at any minute?" She could hear the torment in his voice. Alexi pretended not to listen as he bound her arm. "Well, I was about to jump into one of the fissures when your father found me."

She snapped her head up, her eyes wide. "My dad?"

Biorki's shoulders seemed to droop with the weight of the memory. "He saved me, helped me get food, and even cleaned my home. He knew that if he left me there, I would try again. So he gave me a task: to watch over you whenever he wasn't around. He didn't explain why back then."

So her dad had known all along. The realization didn't shock her. Instead, it made her feel even more alone. He had known and kept it from her. Her life was built on lies. He'd made her promise to run but had never told her why. Why she was different. Why she was so angry all the time. Why she had to hide it. Why they had moved to Kaldwell.

It all made more sense now—Biorki's sudden change, his coldness. He had helped her out of duty, not because he cared. And she had read into his attention, leaned on him. She bit down on her lip. *Stupid.*

"Then, last rotation, he told me he was a part of a secret organization. He asked me if I wanted to join. I said yes." Biorki's voice turned into a whisper. "I didn't know then that—"

Alexi cut him off. "To summarize, Biorki is part of the organization and has been working with your dad to keep you safe." He scowled at Biorki. "He showed up with Fluff a cycle after you arrived and told me to keep his presence secret. And here we are."

Kaia stared at Biorki. "Why didn't you tell me? Why did you let me believe that…that…"

She couldn't finish the sentence, say the words out loud: *that you cared about me.* She had been so stupid. It had all been á part of a plan she wasn't supposed to know. Hot needles ran up her back, across her arms. She shook her head, pushed it down.

"Your father swore me to secrecy, and when he died, it felt wrong to tell you. It also felt wrong *not* to tell you, but I didn't think I should say anything. Then we almost died on the surface, and that changed my mind, but when I woke up, you were gone." His eyes found hers. "Gret-ha helped me. Then I learned that you had made plans with Alexi. I figured it was better if you didn't know I was involved."

"You figured?" Kaia stood up and kicked her chair. "You figured, and *you* figured!" She pointed at Alexi, who had taken a few steps back. "My father figured I didn't need to know. That I couldn't handle the truth. Is that it?!" Whatever cool she had managed to keep evaporated. "You figured!"

Smoke rose from the gauze on her hands, and the pain returned. Biorki and Alexi exchanged a look.

"I would never have let Solon test my blood if I had known. I wouldn't have entered Stallo if I had known. I wouldn't have—" Her gauze burst into flames.

Biorki took a step back. "We were going to tell you. But your dad wanted you to live a normal life. It was a mistake. By the time your dad figured out that Solon had arrived on the planet, it was too late. He messaged me that cycle, telling me to find you at your house before you went to the sick bay. But you had already left. I ran to the sick bay and saw you walk in. I should have told you. Instead, Lu died, and I didn't know what to do except get you out of there."

Tears ran down his face. They washed the dirt off his skin, leaving light lines across his cheeks. Kaia's gauze dropped to the floor, the cinders floating like black snow. Something had sucked the anger out of her, and now there was just a hollowness, a void. She breathed, relaxed her hands, and sighed.

"Whatever." Kaia turned to Alexi again and lifted her hands; the lines glowed through the burnt gauze. "So, can someone explain what this is?"

Alexi stood up, and with practiced hands, he lifted the lid off the box on the table. He pulled out her white helmet, a pair of gloves, a pack of food, and a little brown box. Alexi placed the brown box carefully in front of Kaia. His eyes lingered on it before meeting her gaze.

"We don't know much." Alexi let his hands rest on the box, his fingers tracing a pattern. "The only one who really understood it was your father."

Kaia shot Biorki a look.

"He never told me anything," Biorki sighed. "I swear. I wish I could tell you…I…"

Kaia ignored him and turned back to Alexi. "What can you tell me? What about Misam?"

Alexi didn't look away from the box. "Misam is like you but different. He can sense things others can't; that is his ability. But as far as the organization is concerned, he is not valuable." Alexi changed the pattern he was tracing. "Sensing more than other people is only the first step in what you can do, in what is happening to you. Which is why I had Misam teach you."

Kaia had already figured as much, but it didn't explain why Solon was after her. Or why, unlike Misam, she seemed to burn around the edges. She picked up her mug and listened.

"I figured if Misam could teach you how to sense the world, it would help you control your power." Alexi looked up at Kaia, his eyes full of worry. "Turns out I was wrong."

She remembered the moment she had uncovered the memory of her dad holding her underwater, the look in Gin's eyes when she had let her power out. Alexi hadn't only been wrong; he might have unknowingly unleashed a monster. She was a monster.

"No shit!" Kaia gestured to the ceiling; more charred bandages fell to the floor. "Why didn't you ask the organization? They should be able to tell you what is wrong with me."

Biorki grimaced. "Lu was my only direct contact. Only those at the very top know anything useful."

Kaia shot him a burning look. "I didn't ask you."

Biorki closed his mouth and turned around, his shoulders tense.

Good.

"Biorki is right. They never told me anything either, only that what we were doing was for the good of the individuals we were protecting." Alexi's lips twisted. "I know, why would I follow orders I didn't understand? I have been asking myself that ever since my daughter disappeared."

Alexi's fingers drummed on the box. The sound reminded Kaia of an old song she had heard as a child.

"I think I did it out of desperation. Out of hope that maybe they could help me understand my daughter and keep her safe." Alexi glanced at Biorki. "We all have our reasons for our actions. In the end, they taught me two things. First, you can only trust yourself to keep someone safe. Second, whatever energy is within you is destructive." Alexi slid the box toward her. "Which is why I brought this. Open it."

Kaia stared at the box. She narrowed her eyes.

"You just told me to trust no one, and now I'm supposed to trust you?" Kaia pulled the rest of the gauze off her arms. "You have lied to keep me safe from myself—or so you say—but you know nothing about why I have this power or how to control it. You even triggered it." Alexi didn't look away from her arms. Kaia put her hands on the table and leaned forward. "Whatever this is, it isn't what Solon is after. They didn't even know what I could do until—"

"Until you tried to burn Gin to a crisp?" Biorki's voice cut through the tension of the room.

Kaia flinched. She could feel his eyes on her face.

"I've had suspicions since they tested my daughter's blood." Alexi crossed his arms. "My guess is that whatever gives you this ability is tied to what they want from you—maybe something in your DNA. But I have never seen Solon hunt anyone like they're hunting you. It means something. But you're right, I don't know why."

Kaia was about to respond when she heard a crackling sound. Alexi pulled something off his hip and placed it on the table. He pressed a button on the side of the weird object and spoke. "Status?"

He let go of the button, and another crackle followed. Then Bean's voice filled the room.

"Diggers are full, and gear is packed."

The object was a communicator—ancient, from the look of it.

Alexi pressed the button again. "On our way." He returned the device to his belt.

"Diggers?" Kaia straightened. Why would they need diggers?

"I will show you in a minute." A smile crawled onto Alexi's face, but he turned it into a scowl. "We don't have much time." He pushed the box toward Kaia again. "I know you don't have any reason to trust me. But I could have turned you away. I could have kicked you out on the street. Instead I have risked everything to help you. I ask only that you trust me one last time."

She already knew this, but it didn't make her feel any less betrayed. She opened the box, looked inside, and turned to Alexi, confused.

Within the box sat a pendant. The oval shape bore no markings, but silver strands twisted along the dark metal. She lifted it. It was attached to a black chain that rippled and moved like water, like Gin's suit. She almost dropped it. She looked at Alexi, her eyes wide.

"That…is my daughter's pendant." Alexi's voice cracked a little. "It was given to me by the organization to help her gain control. I never had the chance to show it to her. The cycle I received it was the cycle that…"

Alexi moved around the table. Kaia dropped the pendant into his outstretched hand.

"Anyway. I think I was meant to meet you so I could help you and give you this." Alexi's eyes found hers, and suddenly she didn't feel so hollow. He held up the pendant. "May I?"

She let Alexi move behind her. Despite it all, there was no denying that he and Biorki were there to help her. It was the only reason she said, "Yes."

"Ready?" A crooked grin filled Alexi's face. He wore the same monosuit she'd seen him in the first time they met. His dark-visored helmet was still under his arm. Kaia nodded.

When they had told her to get dressed, she had pulled the white monosuit out of her backpack. Alexi had nodded, and that was that. With her arms rewrapped, she had squeezed into the monosuit. It barely fit over the new gauze. The pendant hung cold against her chest, a reminder that Alexi was here to help her, regardless of his questionable methods.

Biorki, dressed in his patchy monosuit, waited by the door. He looked miserable, and she had no intention of changing that.

"As ready as I can be. So, what's next? And don't lie to me this time." Kaia glanced at Biorki, then Alexi.

"We need to get to the spaceship." Alexi walked over to the switchboards. "I hid it in a silo in an old mine. There used to be a direct line from Framnes, but it caved in five rotations ago. Now there's only one way to get there."

Alexi pressed a large button on the switchboard, and with a click, the wall behind it moved. The metal shields slid up to reveal a thick layer of tempered glass. Beyond it was a cave almost as large as one of the sub-cities. Kaia stared open-mouthed. Two enormous turbines were built into the cave opening. Between the large gray wings was a white blanket— snow. They were on the surface. Framnes ran on wind power? The revelation shook her foundation yet again. Turbines required maintenance and constant supervision, which meant that people were on the surface all the time. Maybe not for leisure activities, but going there was certainly possible. It contradicted what all her teachers had told her. The leaders knew, and yet they let their miners die underground in ignorance, in darkness, never to see the sun, the sky, or the stars.

Her dad had known otherwise, yet he too had maintained the lie. He had known about the hag, about space travel, and still he had held her back and kept her in a cage of lies for reasons she didn't understand. Warmth billowed in her chest, in her arms. She closed her fists tight and breathed.

A small figure waved up at them from the cave floor: Bean. Next to him stood three modified diggers. Painted white, they stood on six chain-linked wheels. The usual gaps in the chassis were sealed, and an antenna protruded from the roof of each digger.

"So we're crossing the surface?" Kaia leaned closer to the thick layer of glass.

Alexi grinned. "Isn't it exciting?"

Kaia shared a look with Biorki. He tightened his fists, and she tried not to look down at his boot where he was missing two toes. *Exciting* wasn't the word she would use to describe it. Kaia swallowed the lump in her throat and looked back at the turbines. The fans were still spinning in the snowy wind. There appeared to be no door to the surface except for a small one on the side of the left turbine.

"How are we going to get those outside?" She pointed at the diggers.

Alexi leaned on the switchboard. "By doing this."

He typed in a code. A red light appeared, a warning. Alexi ignored it, typed another line of code, and pressed enter. A green button blinked on the board.

"We will have five minutes." Alexi pushed the button before they could respond.

A deafening screech hit Kaia's ears. The turbine on the right disconnected from the engine, and the automatic brakes on the fans clamped shut. Rocks and icicles fell from the roof, some leaving dents in the diggers. Bean threw himself inside one of the machines, barely dodging a large piece of ice. It broke into a thousand pieces where he had been standing. The device on Alexi's hip crackled.

"How about a warning next time?" Bean's angry voice snapped.

Alexi twisted the knob that controlled the volume, and Bean's voice disappeared.

"What are you waiting for?" Alexi yelled from the door. "Move!"

CHAPTER 37

Swearing, Kaia ran with Alexi and Biorki through the corridor and a few rooms, down a set of stairs, and through a red door. They burst into the cave at a full sprint. Kaia was breathing heavily by the time they reached the machines. The diggers, which had looked tiny from up in the control room, were larger than she remembered. Made for carving tunnels through solid mountains, the drills on the front were two meters tall.

The cabins on top of the chain threads were angular, and each could fit only two individuals; after all, digging through mountains was usually a one-person job. The rest of the chassis were built to protect the engines' batteries. Next to these incredible machines, Biorki's hauler-bot looked like a child's toy.

Kaia fought the wind and jumped into the cabin of the second digger. The interior was old and cracked. Rust lined the levers that controlled the machine, the colors faded, the metal handles worn and smooth. She grabbed one of them, flicked the right lever's top open, and pressed down on the button. The digger came to life but almost immediately choked. *Fuck.* This was different from the one she had trained on.

She was about to find Alexi when Biorki climbed up and joined her.

"Forgot that you're horrible at driving diggers?"

Biorki had seen her during miners' training. He'd watched as she had crashed her digger into an electrical panel. It had been months before they had been able to resume classes.

"You know my instructor sucked." Kaia got up to leave. "I'll sit with Alexi."

"I know you're pissed at me, but we don't have time. Look." Biorki pointed at the turbine.

The fans were moving. Although they were slower than before, they were still spinning. Kaia looked closer. The wind had picked up, and the joints in the center of the turbine were bending.

"If the wind gets any stronger, it will restart its cycle to reduce the chance of the engine breaking." His words rushed out of him. "A safety mechanism of sorts, which means—"

"Which means we have less than five minutes," Kaia finished.

"Exactly."

Kaia sighed and moved back into the flip seat. "I understand. You know how to drive this, right?"

Biorki grinned, sat down in the cockpit, and pressed a button on the left lever. The cabin door closed, protecting them from the elements. A screen lit up before Biorki, showing the exterior angles of the digger.

"Of course." Biorki shifted his foot on one of the floor pedals, tilting it forward. "My mother was a digger, after all."

He thrust the right lever forward and the left one back. The digger turned to the left. Biorki pushed both levers forward. The digger jolted and charged onward. Kaia tucked her bag and helmet underneath her seat and strapped herself in. The buckle clicked over her chest. They moved closer to the turbine. It rose above them, both a door to freedom and a chopping block.

Inside the cockpit, they would be blind if it weren't for the machine's sensors and cameras, which showed only their immediate vicinity. This machine was built for close-quarters digging, not surface adventures. Using them must have been Alexi's idea. Only a crazy person would convert them for long-distance transport.

The blade of the turbine cut in front of them. The wind pulled at the digger. The newly installed anemometer on the roof rose from yellow to orange. The wind was picking up fast. If the meter reached red, they were screwed. Biorki pulled back on the levers. The rear camera showed Alexi and Bean following behind in their diggers.

Biorki slowed the digger. Another blade passed in front if them, the pressure almost lifting them off the ground.

"One, two, three, four, five, six, seven, eight." Another blade. "One, two, three, four, five, six, seven, eight." Another blade. "Now!"

Biorki leaned forward on the levers, his foot pressing hard on the pedal. Kaia gripped the seat in front of her. The screens showed the open path between the turbine blades.

"One, two…"

They were at the edge of the turbine.

"Three, four…"

The chain tread hit the edge where the blades touched.

"Five, six…"

Biorki groaned as he put every bit of his strength into the digger. They had almost passed out of the blades' path.

"Seven."

The rear camera showed the blade zooming down.

"Eight."

The blade cut through the air behind them. For a second, Kaia felt it pulling them backward. Then the chain tread gripped the snow, and they were outside.

Silence.

"Dritt!" Kaia and Biorki exclaimed in unison.

Biorki turned back to look at her, and they burst out laughing. Biorki had done the impossible.

"That was insane." Kaia tried to breathe through her laughter. On the screen, they saw Alexi make it past the blades.

"Honestly. When I imagined being a digger as a kid, this was not what I had in mind." Biorki pushed the lever in his hand.

"I don't think we could have imagined our future at all." Kaia leaned back and fell silent.

Bean made it through, but not without losing one of the winches attached to the back of his digger. The blades shook, red lights blinked all around the cave, and with a loud screech, the brakes released. The blades picked up speed, and within seconds, they blurred together, sucking in snow. No one mentioned how close they had come to being chopped meat.

The ancient communication device sat silently on the dashboard as they moved forward. They rolled over piles of snow and hills of ice. The sun hovered just above the horizon, the cycle at its end. Snow whirled around them, catching the dying light. It looked gray under the dark clouds that gathered above. If Biorki hadn't adapted the sensors and cameras to self-clean, they would have been blind in the storm.

Biorki pulled a fob from his pocket when the turbines had disappeared behind them. Plugging it into the digger's computer, he watched as a map popped up on the center screen. It looked like a child had drawn it. A line of black twisted and turned until an X marked the spot between two triangles. It looked ridiculous.

Kaia squinted at the map over Biorki's shoulder. "Alexi's drawing?"

Biorki rubbed his chin. "He said it would explain where we had to go."

Kaia sat back and hid her smile. Of course it was Alexi's drawing. Who else would draw an unreadable map when their lives depended on it? Then her dad's map came to mind, and her smile fell. She gripped the belt across her chest.

Biorki picked up the ancient communication device Alexi had given them—*untraceable*, he had called it. He clicked the button on the side. "Alexi, what the heck is this map?"

Silence. Biorki pressed the button and repeated the question, then released it.

Crackling filled the small space, and then Alexi's laughter bubbled around them. "I couldn't help myself. You were so adamant that I give you a map. So I made you one."

Biorki cursed while Kaia covered her mouth, trying to hold back her laughter.

"How the stars do you intend to find anything out here without a map? We can barely see in this thing."

"Don't worry. Click the second file on the fob."

Kaia could imagine the crooked grin on Alexi's face, the satisfaction in his eyes. Biorki clicked something on the screen. The map disappeared, and a radar display replaced it.

"Do you see it?" Alexi's scratchy voice crackled around them.

"Yeah," Biorki grumbled.

"I had Bean install radar in these things a few cycles back. It's set to find a certain frequency only I know. It will lead us to where we need to go."

There was a bright red dot on the screen, which must have been the target. Below it moved three black dots: the diggers.

Bean's thick voice joined them. "It was such a pain in the butt too. You better pay me extra."

"Yeah, yeah. Remember to keep your lights off. The infrared cameras should be enough. We don't know how close Solon is. We should reach the silo in two hours. Enjoy the ride."

Biorki swore, then sighed and returned the communicator to the dashboard.

"Why is his name Bean, anyway?" Kaia blurted out.

Biorki glanced over his shoulder, a smile on his face. "It's his wife's nickname for him." His smile widened. "Because of how he's shaped."

Kaia couldn't help but chuckle. She had never seen a real bean before, but from what she had read about them in her agriculture lessons, his shape was indeed similar.

After Biorki swore he would never work with Alexi again, they fell silent. The only noise was the occasional beep of the radar. Kaia rested as well as she could on the hard seat. She was exhausted and happy not to have to cross the landscape on foot. The digger dipped and tipped, causing them to bounce around on their seats. The citrusy smell of Biorki grew more potent as sweat formed on his neck. He strained against the levers as he drove the machine over the rugged landscape.

Dusk fell as they entered a vast, flat, frozen plain. Spears of ice rose from the snow. Formed by the wind, they stood at an angle, sharp and solid. At one point, Biorki got too close to a cluster of spikes. Kaia expected them to break against the massive machine. Instead, they cut into the side of the digger drill and, from the sound of it, tore parts of the metal to shreds.

Progress was slow after that. Crossing the plain turned out to be a serious headache. The spears caused Biorki to loop back around more than once, Alexi and Bean close behind them. What should have been a two-hour trek proved to be much longer. As Kaia was massaging her legs for the fifth time, two triangular mountains rose before them.

She looked at the mountains on the screen and was surprised by the grief that rose in her chest. She should be relieved that this was almost over, but all she felt was loss. She had to leave the only place she had ever lived, everything she had ever known: the people, the music, the drinks. She wouldn't miss the food.

Then it hit her—Alexi had said he would go with her. "Someone has to steer the thing, after all." But...

Kaia looked at the back of Biorki's head. "Are you coming?"

Biorki remained focused on the path ahead. "You mean to space?" His voice was calm. "I don't have anyone waiting for me at home. No family. The only person who took the time to help me is gone, and I promised to keep an eye on you, to keep you safe. So yes, I'm going."

Kaia let out a small breath. Biorki was still following orders. It was similar to the promise she was keeping, she understood, but it still hurt. It hurt that her feelings still bubbled to the surface when she looked at him, that the flutter in her chest was still there. She was a fool, and perhaps she always would be, because even after everything—the lies, the betrayal—she was happy he was coming. Also, sitting alone in a tin box with Alexi for weeks or months sounded horrible.

"Did it mean anything to you? Our friendship? The promise you made to me last time we were out here?" Kaia gestured to the barren landscape, remembering his words.

It was stupid to ask. Of course it didn't mean anything to him. He had only sacrificed himself because of his promise to her dad. But she needed to hear him say it so she could let it go.

Biorki inhaled, and she saw him clench his jaw in the reflection of the main screen. He opened his mouth. Then a groan left his lips as the digger jolted hard to the left.

She screamed. The digger slammed into the ground. She struggled to catch her breath before they were once again slung through the air. Kaia managed to grab her bag and helmet before they hit the ground again. Had something crashed into them? No. She watched the tilted image on the monitor. The glacier beneath them had cracked. Sheets of ice moved around them. Another crack appeared, and the sound shot through the digger as the ground ripped apart underneath them. An earthquake?

Biorki's expression twisted into one of horror. He pulled on the levers. They had to get out of there fast, or they would tumble into the glacier. Another push and another turn, and they moved up toward the only solid piece of land they could see. The end of the ice plain was right in front of them, a mountain of solid rock. Biorki pressed the digger as hard as he could. The engine pulsed under them; the joints protested as he pushed the machine to its limits. *Faster. Faster.* The ground behind them shifted like a wave, pulling them backward. *No. No.*

The digger's chains spun in the air. Then they struck something solid, and the ground flung them forward. Kaia hugged her bag and helmet tightly and bent her head. For a moment, there was no gravity, only her seat belt, which dug into her chest.

The digger struck the ground with a sickening crunch of metal. Kaia slammed back into her seat. She felt her spine popped under the pressure. Her helmet struck her shin. After a second, she opened her eyes. Her bag was still in her lap, the helmet intact. She straightened. Her back, to her relief, seemed to be fine, but her shin throbbed. Biorki gasped in front of her. Something must have struck him, because blood ran from a cut below his ear.

Biorki didn't wait. He slammed the levers forward again. Kaia held her breath. The engine hummed around them; it still worked. She leaned forward as if it would make the digger go faster. Then the ground leveled, the world no longer tipping on its axis. They had made it to solid rock.

Seconds later, Alexi's digger crashed onto the rock beside them. He must have been on their tail. Then silence. No tremors, no movements in the rock beneath them. Kaia tightened her grip on her bag. They should still feel motion on solid ground if this was an earthquake. Something was very wrong.

"Pop the hatch. Now!" Kaia pulled on her helmet.

Biorki was already securing his own helmet. He opened the hatch. Cold air filled the space around them; snow flew through their field of vision. They jumped out and turned to look at the ice plain.

Kaia had felt fear before, and desperation, but what rose before her made her bones shake and her blood freeze. Out on the glacier was a towering creature—a creature from ancient tales, from the stories told by the old folk of Kaldwell. Horror stories of monsters the size of cities, of long-ago massacres. Stories meant to scare children.

The image of the Stallo building flashed into Kaia's mind, the slashes and cuts on the exterior, like those on the sick bay in Kaldwell. The buildings were so old, no one remembered when they'd been built. Then, words Ingá had said to her when she was nine rotations old slithered into her mind.

Who is to say the stories aren't true? Just because you haven't seen the monsters doesn't mean they don't exist.

CHAPTER 38

The monster's long neck rose up from the frozen plain. Its skin, oily and spotted, was covered in thin black hair. A dark shadow loomed below the dark ice: the creature's body. It twisted, and the familiar sound of a glacier fracturing filled the air. The hairs on Kaia's neck stood up as the sound traveled through the ice. The monster shifted again, and another fissure opened.

Wide black eyes found Kaia, then slid away. She tried to step back, but her body wouldn't listen. The creature swayed from side to side. Its eyes rolled, searching for something. They found her again and, like before, slid away. Cold gripped her chest. It didn't see them. She recognized what it was, because she had felt it herself: blind rage. Unhindered, uncontrollable rage.

The creature shook its head, and that was when she saw it. Between its massive teeth was the third digger. Bean. The creature flipped its head up and threw the digger into the air. The machine somersaulted before the creature caught it again. Kaia flinched as the chassis warped and cracked. The creature bit down again and shook it back and forth.

"Damn the stars!" Alexi's voice barely reached them over the creature's howls.

The sound sent a new wave of fear through her. She would not freeze up again. She bit down hard on the scabbed cut on her lip. It tore open, and warm liquid ran into her mouth. With the taste of metal on her tongue, she turned to Biorki. His eyes were wide, his mouth open.

She shook his shoulder. "We need to do something. Now!"

Biorki didn't move, didn't blink.

Kaia turned to where she had heard Alexi. He was searching through the boxes on the back of his digger. She ran toward him and yelled, "What can I do?!"

The creature's growls drowned out her voice. She tried not to look at the beast thrashing through the glacier behind her.

Alexi pulled one of the boxes off his drill. "Grab the black item inside the box, click the button, aim, and shoot!"

Kaia tore the lid off and threw it to the side. More ice and metal cracked and broke behind her. Bean screamed through the communicator. Kaia found the black item: a pulse weapon. It was old. She grabbed it and ran back to Biorki, who hadn't moved. She rested the weapon on her injured shoulder; she needed her best shooting arm for this. Her dad had taught her to handle weapons. Now she knew why.

She pressed the button to activate the energy core. It didn't work. She pushed it again. The monster was entirely out of the ice now. Its massive, oily body bore dark spots and old scars. Its four legs were more like fins with claws, and its long black tail slammed into the ground behind it as it thrashed, the digger still in its mouth.

Bean's screams stopped. Now Kaia could hear only the crackling of the communicator over the creature's roaring. She pressed the button again. Alexi was already shooting at the beast from somewhere behind her. The pulses struck the neck of the monster, and though the impact sent small ripples through the fat beneath its flesh, it didn't even flinch.

On the fourth attempt, Kaia's weapon lit up. She pulled down the trigger handle, rested the front of the gun in her left hand, and held the trigger with her right. She aimed, tightening her muscles, and relaxed into the weapon. She breathed slowly in, then out, and squeezed the trigger. The buzz tore at her eardrums. The blast made her stagger back, but her aim had been good. The pulse hit the monster straight in the eye.

It recoiled, opened its mouth, and lost its grip on the digger. The lump of metal crashed to the ice on the far side of the monster. The beast blinked, a third eyelid sliding across from the side: once, twice. Its pupil dilated, then became a slit as it found her. *Shit.*

Kaia punched Biorki in the arm. "Move! Move! Go get Alexi and try to grab Bean!" The wind howled and pulled at her suit. "I will distract it!"

She worried he hadn't heard her. Then the life returned to his eyes all of a sudden. He found her face. She smiled, and he nodded. Biorki ran toward Alexi, who was still firing at the creature.

Kaia didn't need to look back to know it was coming for her. The ground shook, and the monster's growls reverberated through her skull. She could almost sense its hatred. She made it to the digger in two shaky leaps, pressed the hatch lock, and turned the thing on. Watching Biorki had paid off. She didn't have to be a good drill driver. She just had to make the machine move and distract the creature long enough for them to get to Bean. She would figure the rest out later.

The drill made a strange chirping sound. Something was wrong with the engine. She pulled on the left handle and pushed on the right one. The pedal squeaked under her foot. She screamed at the machine. Then, with a sudden jerk, it moved. She leaned into the left lever and turned the digger toward the monster.

It came at her. The creature slithered through the glacier like it was water, mouth open. Kaia pushed both levers forward and groaned as she charged at the beast. The radar on the screen blinked. The second black dot was moving toward the third black dot. *Good.*

She took a steadying breath and opened the small red switch lid on the dashboard. The beast leaped out of the ice, its teeth illuminated by the light from the digger. She flipped the switch. *Come on. Come on.* The drill came to life. *Yes.*

The beast halted, confused. In that moment, Kaia stomped down on the pedal and turned the drill down. She would be easy prey if the creature caught on to her plan. She dug into the glacier and under the monster. Its screech reached her through the layers of ice and metal. She aimed the digger back up, right at the belly of the beast. If only she could get there in time.

It dug its claws into the ground, and just as she breached the surface, it pulled itself out of the way. *Dritt.* How could something that size move so fast? She had underestimated it, assumed it would be confused and slow. And now she was back out of the glacier and vulnerable.

The beast pounced. Its teeth came at her, and before she could react, it tore the drill off her digger. She held on to her seat belt as the digger flipped and jerked. Warning lights flashed on the dashboard. She focused on the moving black dot on the radar. It was closing in on the red dot. They had made it. *Thank the stars.*

The screen blinked once, twice, and the dashboard died. Everything was dark and…quiet? A breath left her lips. Two breaths.

Then a horrible noise cut through Kaia's eardrums as large yellow teeth passed through the metal above her head. With a roar, the roof became the sky, and two large evil eyes found her. She curled into a ball on her seat. The creature bent down, ready to pounce. It was so close she could see the pattern on its tongue and the dark color of its gums. Ropes of drool hung from its teeth. This was it. This was how she would die.

This time, the darkness within her didn't respond. Maybe it was because she didn't feel anything—no anger, no grief. She slumped back into her seat. She had fought. She hadn't been a burden. She had tried, and in a way, she was keeping her promise. Solon couldn't catch her if she was consumed by something else first.

Then a different howl filled the air. Kaia straightened, and a blur of white charged across her vision. She was imagining things. The black creature twisted to the side, and instead of teeth, a fin of claws cut toward her. Kaia slid down in her seat and dodged it by a hair's breadth. Maybe she wasn't ready to die. Or perhaps it was that familiar roar that had changed her mind. She stared. In front of her stood Fluff, and on his back sat a small figure in white and black: the hag.

The woman raised a hand and pointed. Fluff leaped, his powerful back legs launching him up in the air and onto the creature's back. He dug his claws into the oily skin, barely holding on as the creature twisted again, trying to throw them off.

Two more smylons like Fluff charged from the snow. The largest aimed for the creature's neck and missed. The other slashed through its tail. Fluff bit down on the creature's back and tore off a chunk. Blood flew everywhere, instantly freezing into red beads of ice that bounced off the hard frost on the plain. The creature twisted its neck. Fluff jumped, and the creature's jaws snapped shut exactly where he had been.

The smylons regrouped, and they followed Fluff and the hag as they began to circle the beast, drawing it away from the mountains. Entirely forgotten by the monster, Kaia resumed breathing. Its frenzy was now focused solely on the pack. Shaking her head, Kaia unbuckled her seat belt and slid to the floor of the digger. Panting, she grabbed her bag, which by some incredible luck was still tucked under her seat. She confirmed that the creature was still charging away from her, then jumped out of the shredded digger and ran.

The sound of flesh tearing, screams, and roars followed her as she stumbled over the cracks in the ice. A battle cry of blood and ash began—the hag was singing with joy as she fought. They had come to save her.

Kaia made it to the edge of the plain, the mountain towering above her, the darkness almost upon them. Two lights moved toward her. It was Alexi in the digger. He popped the hatch.

"Get in!"

Kaia looked back, the sound of the hag's song twisting and turning around the growls and yells of the monster. One of Fluff's companions limped, blood pooling beneath it as it paced around the creature. Fluff and the hag were on the monster's neck, tearing at anything they could reach. Something silver shone in the hag's hands. She dug her knife into the creature's neck and climbed. Fluff dodged the beast's snapping mouth. A pile of red-and-white fur lay beyond the fight. It didn't move.

"We need to help them!" Kaia yelled.

The creature launched at Fluff. Its teeth found his tail. Fluff screamed, a howl so earsplitting that Kaia almost fell to her knees.

"We must go. Now!" Alexi tried to grab Kaia, to pull her inside.

Fluff twisted, and with his right front paw, he clawed the creature's eye. The beast released him with a yelp. Kaia could see the unnatural angle of Fluff's tail. The hag continued to sing as she climbed. She was almost at the top of the monster's neck.

"But I—"

"Gret-ha and Fluff will be fine. This is not the first tibilos they have fought." Alexi pointed at the horizon. "We need to go. NOW!"

Kaia followed his gaze. Three hovering lights moved across the ice plain.

"Are you shitting me?" Kaia jumped into the digger.

"Nope. I'm sorry to say I am not shitting you. Solon always shows up at the worst possible times." Alexi leaned on the levers.

As they moved, the darkness swallowed the monsters and the hag, the roars fading behind them. She hoped Alexi was right about Gret-ha, about Fluff.

Alexi and Kaia left the digger outside. There was no point in hiding it if Solon had tracked them here. They hurried to load the boxes through the rusted door built into the mountain wall, and then Alexi locked it behind them.

"This won't hold them off for long." Alexi's voice echoed within the room.

After running under an open sky, the room felt claustrophobic. Kaia had never felt that way before. She tried to slow her breathing.

"What was that thing?" Kaia's voice shook with adrenaline.

Alexi ran to the middle of the room, where Biorki crouched over Bean, a small lantern beside them. "That was a tibilos." He placed the box he was carrying on the floor and popped the lid open. "What do you think Fluff eats out here?"

Kaia placed the box in her arms next to his. "But why would it attack us? I know the fairy tales, but…"

Alexi pulled out a small pack and kneeled next to Bean. "Don't believe everything you're told."

Kaia bit back a retort.

"Tibilos are usually dormant. I haven't heard of any active ones in rotations. Maybe it was the disturbance of Solon flying over the surface, trying to find you, that woke it. I don't blame it for lashing out; how would you feel if someone interrupted your sleep?"

She grimaced. She knew exactly how that felt. Alexi had interrupted her sleep once, and she had almost put her axe through his skull.

Alexi opened the lid of the small box; inside sat four vials and an injector. Bean grunted.

Kaia moved closer. "How is he?"

Biorki patted Bean's shoulder. "I'm no healer, but from what I can see, he was knocked unconscious, and his leg is broken." He snapped a vial into the injector. "He's lucky."

Seeing what Alexi was about to do, Biorki rolled up Bean's suit to expose his forearm. Alexi pressed the injector to Bean's pale skin and squeezed the trigger. Bean spasmed, his arms jerked, and with a deep, raspy breath, his eyes snapped wide open.

"What happened?" he grumbled. His voice was weak.

"You were a tibilos's chew toy." Alexi gestured to Kaia. "She shot the thing right in the eye. It dropped you, and we got you here."

Bean blinked a few times, then looked at Kaia. "Where's Solon?"

Alexi placed the injector back in the little box. "They are about to reach the mountain."

Bean cursed. "Then why are you still here? Go! I can figure something out."

Biorki looked down at Bean's crooked leg. "Your leg is broken."

"And? Where's my pulse gun?" Bean stared at Alexi, his eyes narrowed.

"It's still in your digger." Alexi smiled.

"Damn. I liked that thing." Bean waved at Alexi. "Give me yours, then."

Alexi grabbed the only gun they had salvaged from the tibilos attack. "What will you do if I give it to you?"

Bean threw his arm up, then winced. "I will hold them off! It's the only thing I can do to repay you. I know you don't like me, but a deal is a deal."

"That's not true." Alexi grinned and moved back to Bean's side. "You make some damn good buzz drinks. I like you for that."

Bean chuckled, then bent over as coughs tore through his body. After a few short breaths, he whispered, "I knew you were a pain in my butt. I should have guessed you hung around for the drinks."

Kaia didn't move. She just watched as the old rivals smiled at each other.

"Anyway, I need to have a word with those bastards. They threatened my customers and ruined my business." The hatred in Bean's voice was unmistakable.

Alexi tilted his head toward the back wall. "Kaia, Biorki, help me move him."

They did as they were told and propped Bean up so he faced the door.

Bean grunted through gritted teeth. "Thank you." Another round of rasping coughs tore through him. They all saw the blood on his hand before he closed it, but no one said anything. They knew what it meant.

"What are you waiting for? Grab your stuff and go!" Bean grinned, his eyes sharp. "I can't wait to hurt those bastards."

Biorki opened the last box. "Here." He threw climbing tools to Kaia and Alexi. Kaia placed a harness on her chest and clicked the center button. The straps shot out and wrapped around her. Biorki and Alexi followed suit. With her backpack on her back, her ice axes on her hips, her harness secured, and a grapple gun in her hand, she was ready.

"I'll follow you soon." Bean grinned, the pulse weapon in his hands pointed at the door. "And then you can give me what you promised, Alexi."

Alexi smiled, his eyes soft. "I'm betting on it!"

Bean winked. Alexi turned and walked into the hallway at the end of the room. Kaia couldn't think of anything to say. She met Bean's eyes, tipped her head, and followed Alexi and Biorki through the door.

CHAPTER 39

They made it through five crumbling tunnels before the sound of Bean's weapon reached them. Biorki found Kaia's eyes in the dim light, and without thinking, she grabbed his hand. It was stupid; whatever was between them was a lie. But she needed it, and from the look in his eyes, so did he. At least here in the dark, she could allow herself that much. The distinct sound of a laser bounced around them. Bean was holding his ground, at least for now.

Alexi waved at them. His scanner showed no hidden fissures ahead. They ran until he stopped them to take another scan. It was slow and frustrating. Every scan halted their progress, but Alexi insisted on doing them. "I would rather take my chances with Solon than be buried alive."

Kaia felt no such sentiment, but she kept her thoughts to herself. She was too tired to argue. Or maybe she wanted Solon to catch up so she could confront them. Hurt them.

They had just reached the first shaft when silence wrapped around them, louder than any laser. Alexi punched the wall. Ice and gravel hit his helmet. The scan finished with a beep.

"Go," Alexi whispered.

Kaia stared at the darkness of the mine shaft above them. She turned on her helmet light. The shaft was a mix of rock and ice and looked like it would collapse any minute. She pointed her grapple gun, held her breath, and squeezed the trigger. The hook shot into the dark. It struck something, and the wire slackened. She grabbed it and pulled. A screech filled the tunnel, then stopped. She hoped it had hooked onto something solid. She threaded the taut wire through the belay device on the front of her harness. Then she angled the grapple gun, flipped the switch, leaned back, and squeezed the trigger again. The wire retracted back into the grapple gun, pulling her up the shaft.

She eased into her ascent, testing the wire. Satisfied it would hold her weight, she squeezed the trigger harder. She shot forward and ran up the wall. When she reached the top, she pulled out her axes and dug into the ice. Using the tension of the wire, she pulled herself over the edge. Her right shoulder threatened to pop out of its socket, but to her relief, it held long enough for her to scramble away from the shaft.

On her feet, she released the hook from the rock. At the same time, a new hook flew out of the shaft. Kaia tapped the belay device twice to signal the hook was secure, and Biorki made his way up the shaft. By the time he reached the top, Kaia had put away her grapple gun and axes.

Biorki moved out of the way, and they signaled again. Within seconds, Alexi launched out of the shaft. But instead of his usual grin, he was wearing a grimace when he landed. There was no mistaking that look. Solon was too close.

Alexi pulled out his scanner and looked at the tunnel ahead, then back down at the shaft. He pulled a small round object from his belt bag and stuck it to the back of the scanner. "Run."

Biorki's eyes widened. "But what about—"

Alexi clicked a round button, and a red light flashed in its center. "I've changed my mind." He threw the scanner down the shaft.

Kaia grabbed Biorki and pulled him after her. She didn't know what the round device was, but from the look on Alexi's face, she did not want to be near it long enough to find out. She broke into a full sprint. Biorki matched her speed. After two heartbeats, Alexi flew past them, his long legs propelling him forward, a curse on his lips.

Kaia had just reached the tunnel bend when the world exploded. Something slammed into her back and threw her forward. She landed awkwardly in a squat as a wave of dust burst past them. Then an earsplitting boom rang through the mountain walls, and her visor glowed red with a warning: "325 decibels detected. Sound muffling initiated."

She looked up to see a fissure opening in the mountain. It shot past them, releasing more dust into the tunnel. She covered her head as rocks fell around them. Ahead, Alexi waved at them to move; she couldn't hear him, but she understood. With Biorki by her side, she launched forward. She stumbled over a large chunk of raw copper but kept running.

She ran and didn't look back to watch the tunnel crumble behind them. She would have run right past the next shaft if Alexi hadn't held out a hand. She stopped, her breath catching as she tried to regain some composure.

Biorki swore next to her. "You could have warned us. We could have been buried alive."

Alexi pulled out his grapple gun. "But we weren't."

"Do you think it will slow them down?" Kaia pulled out her own grapple gun.

Alexi looked back behind them. There was nothing to see, only red dust. "Not for long."

"Dritt." Biorki patted his suit. "That ship better be there, Alexi, or we're trapped in this mountain for nothing."

Alexi shot his hook up the shaft. "Don't worry, this is all a part of my plan."

Biorki met Kaia's eyes. This had definitely not been a part of the plan. Kaia lifted her shoulders, and Biorki sighed. "Okay, so what is the plan now?"

Alexi hooked himself to the wire, leaned back, and grinned. "We get to the ship before Solon." He shot up into the shaft.

Kaia tracked Alexi with her eyes. "In other words, there's no plan."

Biorki threw his hands up. "He's insane."

She didn't know why Alexi's words made her calm, why they made her feel sharp and focused. She should have been annoyed, scared not to know what came next, but instead it sent a thrill through her. She felt a smile tug at her lips.

"We're the ones following him." Three knocks reached them from above. "What does that make us?"

When they reached the fourth and final shaft, voices filled their ears. Alexi was the last to climb, and when he popped out into the tunnel, his eyes were wild. A hook flew out of the shaft immediately behind him. He kicked the hook loose and turned. "Run!"

As she ran, Kaia pulled off her harness with shaking hands. As planned, she dropped it, along with the rest of her climbing equipment. The lighter they were, the better. Beside her, Biorki tore his own harness off, his face red with exertion. Alexi was a whirlwind of movement as he caught up to them. The sound of flying metal rang through the tunnel as they reached the end.

Clutching her axes, Kaia turned the corner. She almost slipped as the icy ground turned into slick, polished rock. Adjusting her footing, she focused on the metal door at the end of the arched tunnel; cut from a massive natural slab of malachite, it was a funnel of green lines and waves. Her heart pounded in her ears as she pushed forward, Biorki gasping behind her.

Alexi reached the door first, and his hands immediately began to move over the keyboard. "Work. Work. Work."

With a click and a woosh, the gray door slid open. Then steps echoed behind them, and they turned.

Kaia's heart dropped, and cold ran down her spine. At the other end of the tunnel stood Drap and the two silver women. They wore their shimmery suits and clear helmets, clutched the silver devices in their hands. Drap grinned. The women bore stone-cold expressions. When the blond woman met Kaia's eyes, she bared her teeth. Drap tilted his head and tapped the silver device on his helmet.

"Now, what's the point of this?" Drap's voice slithered off the polished walls. "Alexi—that's your name, right? I did some research when I realized she had help. You of all people should know there's no point in running. We always get what we want."

Drap's grin widened, and Alexi twitched behind Kaia. She tried to step forward, but Biorki grabbed her shoulder, stopping her. She tightened her grip on her axes. She wanted to smash that grin off Drap's face.

Alexi stretched behind her, and in a barely audible whisper, he hissed, "I need you to buy me some time."

Then, as if nothing had happened, he rolled his shoulders and answered Drap. "I'm sorry, but I don't know you. All Solon guards look the same."

Biorki squeezed her shoulder. She understood. They would do this together somehow. First she had to pull focus away from Alexi, which shouldn't be too hard—she was the one they wanted, after all.

Drap's grin faltered for a second; then he raised the device in his hand. "Whatever. They will give me—us—a great reward for bringing you in."

Taking a deep breath, Kaia holstered her axes, dropped her bag on the floor, and stepped away from Biorki. Drap's eyes fell on her, and a shiver ran down her neck. *You can do this.*

"You!" Drap narrowed his eyes. "You nearly killed Gin. How did you do it?"

She walked to the side, putting a larger distance between her and Drap. Now what? She couldn't use her power. If Alexi was right, the pendant would restrict her. And even if she could access it, she couldn't risk hurting Biorki. She doubted she could take them on without it, leaving her only one choice: keep them talking. Schooling her face, she crossed her arms.

"He refused to answer my question." She stepped to the side, blocking Alexi from view. Even if she knew how to describe what she had done to Gin, she would never tell Drap. "So I will ask you. What do you want from me?"

Drap tilted the silver object to the side with a sheepish grin. He knew she was trying to buy time, but he played along. *The prick.*

"Gin didn't tell you?" Drap took a step forward, and the women followed. "My boss wants you."

Kaia put her hands in her pockets. Fear crawled under her skin, but she cocked one hip and smiled. In her peripheral vision, she could see Biorki following her movements.

"You didn't answer my question. What do you want from me?" Kaia kept her voice steady, but she wanted to scream, to spit at them, curse at them.

Drap waved the silver device as he spoke. "We want your blood."

"You already have my blood." Kaia clenched her jaw, heat rising in her chest. All of this for her blood? The prickly warmth rose inside her, but her power stayed out of reach. The pendant was working.

The blonde laughed. The soft sound made Kaia's hair rise on her neck. "Oh, darling. One vial is not nearly enough. Has no one ever taught you biochemistry? How sad."

Kaia clenched her hands in her pockets and breathed. She took a step forward, keeping herself between them and the door.

"We have answered your question. Now answer mine." Drap aimed the silver device. "How did you hurt Gin?"

Biorki fell into a defensive stance beside her. So he wasn't scared of real monsters. She hoped that whatever Alexi was doing wouldn't take too long, because her next idea was insane.

Kaia winked at Drap. "Why don't you come and find out?"

A glint of joy passed across Drap's face, and a grin spread over his lips.

"I thought you would never ask." He tensed his hand.

Kaia whipped her hand out of her pocket. The small metal blade she threw struck Drap on the elbow and forced his hand up. The pulse from his weapon missed Kaia's head by a thumb's width. She pulled at Biorki. Her elbows throbbed as they slammed to the ground.

The white pulse of energy bounced off the wall above the door, then ricocheted and struck the blonde on the shoulder. Her suit absorbed the impact, leaving other parts thin. Then it reshaped itself into an even layer. The blonde rolled her shoulder, but her expression didn't change. If one runaway shot can do that, what would happen if they kept shooting?

"You're crazy," Biorki breathed next to her, his voice a whisper. "How did you know that would work?"

"I didn't." It had been a gamble. Kaia hadn't expected the pulse to hit the taller woman—that had been a bonus. But the way the suit had reacted gave her another crazy idea. She pulled her feet underneath her.

Drap sighed and placed his device on his hip. Seemed he'd reached the same conclusion she had. Their silver weapons were too big of a risk to use here. The women followed suit. Rolling his neck, Drap pulled something from his chest pocket.

Kaia jumped to her feet. "Do you have a weapon?" she asked Biorki.

He smiled and nodded, his face tense. "Lu taught me some fighting skills too."

Kaia ignored the stab of pain his words elicited. She dropped into a wide stance. *Focus.* Biorki flicked his wrist, and a metal staff appeared in his hand. At the same time, the shorter woman pulled two black sticks from behind her back.

Kaia clicked the button on her left palm. The silver blade spun through the air from Drap's right, and with a metal snap, it found the magnet on the back of her left wrist. Lying flat against her skin, the knife vibrated from the impact, ready to be thrown again. She had bought the throwing knife at the black market before Stallo. She had intended to hit Drap's wrist with it, but her right arm was still too weak.

Kaia grabbed her axes and clicked the handles—a sharp blade extended from each head, turning the climbing axes into double-edged weapons.

Drap and the blonde pulled something black and solid over their wrists: bracelets that weren't bracelets. Kaia swore under her breath. She had seen this tech before in Venlá's droid shop. She tightened her grip on her axes as pure cold fear rippled through her.

The dark liquid metal flowed over Drap's hand and twisted. It lengthened, then flattened into a black barbed blade the length of her forearm. Drap grinned and pointed it at her. She heard Biorki swallow behind her and felt her own mouth go dry as sand. Without the silver devices in play, she had thought they had a chance. Big mistake.

She glanced at the blond woman; her right knuckles were covered in black metal that took the shape of a knuckle dagger. The woman's face twisted into something grotesque as she moved forward.

"Oh, you thought you could fight us and win?" the taller woman snickered. "How cute."

"Moira, stop playing with them," the shorter woman sighed. "Let's get this over with so I can go back and check on Gin."

"You're such a drag, Criola. You know I've been wanting to test this out for months now." Moira slammed her left hand into her right palm.

Criola lifted her shoulders and sighed. "Whatever. Just be quick."

Alexi, where are you? This was not a practice match; this was three against two. Drap moved forward next to Moira, excitement on his face. Criola stayed behind. Kaia observed their steps, their arms, and their movements. Drap moved to the right, Moira to the left.

A memory of steaming hot springs and bruises flashed through her.

Gauge your distance. A punch is only as powerful as the movement you put into it.

They were trained fighters. They knew to leave enough space to move, meaning they could only fit two side-by-side in the tunnel. A calmness fell over her, a sharpness.

"Biorki, I have an idea," Kaia whispered so low she wasn't sure he could hear her.

There was a tug on her belt. He'd heard her. Good.

"Did my dad ever teach you the shadow blade?"

It was a shot in the dark, but Biorki tugged on her belt again and moved so that he was right at her heels, like her dad had done rotations ago. She'd thought this maneuver was a secret between her and her dad—a lie. But right now, sharing it gave her strength. Biorki gave her strength.

With her heart in her ears, she tensed and took two steps toward Moira. Biorki followed like a shadow.

"What are you waiting for?" Kaia forced the words out, locking eyes with Moira. "Are you scared?"

Moira's blue eyes widened, then narrowed. She rolled her shoulders. Then, quicker than Kaia had anticipated, she launched forward.

Kaia ducked as Moira's metal fist punched the air above her head. It scraped the top of her helmet with a high-pitched screech that rattled through her teeth. Kaia twisted and threw her blade at Drap, forcing him back as Moira tried to punch her again. The swing left Moira open, but only for a second. Biorki's staff punched the air over Kaia's shoulder.

The staff struck Moira straight in the chest, pushing her back. A pure tone of hollow metal rang through the tunnel. It gave Kaia the second she needed. Biorki's staff flexed against Moira's suit, which thickened at the point of impact and left other parts of her suit thin. Moira's eyes widened. Kaia was already mid-swing.

She felt everything as her axe tore through Moira's weakened suit, then her flesh, muscles, and tendons, to lodge in her thigh bone. The force traveled up Kaia's arm and into her weak shoulder. Moira shrieked with pain. Kaia pulled, but the axe didn't budge.

A force slammed into Kaia's ribs. She felt her bones cave under her skin as Moira's fist struck her body. She'd been too slow. Pain shot through her hip, elbow, and shoulder as she crashed to the floor. She coughed. Drops of blood spattered her visor. Something sliced through the air, connected with Moira's head, and sent her into the wall.

Kaia struggled to blink, to breathe. Moira groaned before she slumped against the cave wall. Biorki stood in front of Kaia, staff out. They had done it—together they had breached Moira's defenses with their rapid successive attacks.

Kaia's relief turned to horror as a gleaming form rushed forward. Biorki twisted as Drap's horrid knife sliced through the air where his shoulder had been. Kaia placed a hand on the ground and pushed. The effort sent her into a coughing fit, and pain blinded her as she crumpled back onto the floor. *Damn.*

Drap was a blur as he dodged Biorki's staff. His twisted knife was light in his hand, an extension of his arm. She swore she glimpsed a smile on Drap's face as he danced around Biorki, who stood stiff, his movements strong but hesitant.

Kaia pushed herself up again. She coughed more blood. Moira's body lay collapsed a few meters away from her. *Good.* Drap's knife sliced at Biorki's chest, and Kaia's heart stopped. But Biorki drove his staff into the wall, launching himself in the other direction, barely dodging the blade.

Where was Alexi?

Biorki staggered, his chest rising and falling, his eyes wide with concentration. Drap grinned his steps light and calculated. He stabbed, missed, and then danced back as Biorki swung his staff. Kaia saw it then. *No.* Biorki's suit was full of gashes, exposing him to the frigid air. Drap wasn't missing his target. He was playing with his prey. If the fight went on much longer, Biorki would freeze to death.

Kaia got to her feet. The pain almost drove her back to her knees, but she bit down and stood. Her breaths were pure hot pain. She glanced to the side. Criola looked bored, her sticks resting on her shoulders. Biorki dodged another knife swing as Drap burst into laughter. The sound sent ice through Kaia.

She clicked the button in her palm. Nothing; her blade didn't come. She looked at Criola. There it was, under her boot. *Damn.* Criola scratched her back with the end of her right stick. She met Kaia's eyes with a humorless look but made no move to join the fight.

Drap stepped forward, this time faster. Biorki was still recovering from his last staff swing. He wouldn't be able to dodge Drap's weapon. Ignoring the burning pain in her chest, Kaia moved closer and swung her axe. It met Drap's knife on the downswing. Kaia's heart dropped as the blade moved *through* her axe. No, it moved around it like liquid. She watched in horror as the blade's edge struck Biorki's helmet, shattering his visor.

Biorki staggered back, his gasps loud in her ears. *No, no, no!* Kaia moved toward him, but before she could do anything, a shadow slid into her vision and hit her in the back. Body-crumpling pain tore at her muscles, her nerves. She screamed, her limbs twisting beneath her. Millions of needles moved under her skin. They sliced at her insides, her muscles. Then it stopped, and she lay still on the ground.

Criola hovered over her, returning her sticks to her back. The woman's face was blank. "Can we leave now?"

"Oh, let me have some fun!" Drap's voice was full of laughter.

CHAPTER 40

Kaia wanted to scream, to rip Drap's eyes out of his head and plunge her axe into his skull. Instead, she watched helplessly as Drap lifted a helmetless Biorki by the collar of his suit. Biorki groaned and dropped his staff. Blood covered his face. Drap sighed and took a deep breath. The knife in his hand became liquid once more.

Kaia tried to move, to gather enough strength to lift her arms, to do something. But her body wouldn't listen. Whatever Criola had done, it had numbed every nerve in her body. A whimper left her lips as the liquid moved from Drap's hand to Biorki's neck. His eyes bulged as it entered his mouth, nose, and ears. Kaia couldn't look away as Biorki convulsed, struggling for air.

Drap looked delighted, his eyes bright, his face glowing.

"Please stop," Kaia croaked.

Biorki's eyes found hers; in them was pure fear, a pleading terrible fear. He knew he would die and she would have to watch. Why was she so weak?

"Please stop. Please—"

A crackle filled the cave. Kaia thought it was her mind breaking.

"Move out of the way!"

Drap's smile twisted. Criola looked around. It was Alexi. Something in his voice broke here paralysis. She had to do something, and she *could* do something. She closed her eyes. A spark, then darkness. It was harder to find her power now, a conscious effort, but she pulled at it. A trickle at first, then a sticky stream. It removed the numbness and filled her muscles with heat, with fire.

The crackle of Alexi's voice filled the room. "Get up! Move!"

Drap turned toward Alexi. "What the heck is that?"

Kaia braced herself and watched Criola turn. *Now.* She pounced from the ground, her elbow connecting with Criola's helmet. Criola stumbled and stepped off Kaia's knife. Kaia grabbed Drap's hand and sent all her hatred into her arm, her palm. It was nothing like when she had tried to kill Gin—so weak, so slow. She hoped it would be enough. It had to be enough.

Drap's suit glowed and rushed to where she touched him, to protect him. *Come on. Just a little more.* The smell of burnt flesh filled her nose, and Drap cursed. He jerked his arm away, lost his grip on Biorki, and the dark liquid returned to its master. A gurgling gasp came from Biorki as Kaia held her left hand up and pressed the button on her palm. The knife lifted off the floor and struck Drap in the shoulder, where his suit was still weak. He screamed and bent forward. Without looking back, Kaia pulled Biorki toward the door with her. Somehow, he was still moving, limping on.

When she looked up, Alexi stood at the door, an enormous weapon on his shoulder. "Run!"

With Biorki's arm over her shoulders, Kaia focused on her breathing, her last bit of energy. Biorki groaned against her. Her legs shook. A curse came from behind them, a growl of pain, but they didn't turn. A few more steps and they would be at the door.

Something shot through the air over her head. It crashed into the frame of the door and fell to the floor. It was one of

Criola's sticks. Kaia's lungs burned; Moira's punch must have broken her ribs. She tried to summon more power, but it was fading fast, slipping from her grasp.

A lump of brown slumped to the right of the door. Her bag—she had forgotten it in the chaos. She pushed Biorki toward the door, ran to the bag, and grabbed it. It was stupid and reckless, but it was the only thing she had left of her dad.

"You won't get away!" Drap's voice cracked with pain, yet it was cold and inhuman.

Kaia spun on her heel and saw Biorki beside Alexi, gasping. Thank the stars. She took one painful breath and charged toward the door herself. One step, two steps. Her bag bounced on her back. In her peripheral vision, she saw Drap and Criola break into a run.

She reached the opening. Alexi leaned into the scope of the weapon, closing one eye. She ran past him and was barely through the door when a shock wave sent her to the ground. Kaia twisted, trying to take the impact with her good shoulder, but it didn't help. Her chest contorted, and raw, searing pain tore at her lungs. She coughed up more blood.

On the other side of the door, the mountain shattered. Screams mingled with rocks hitting rocks. Kaia smiled as she heard Drap shriek. Dust and pebbles swallowed her as the tunnel they had just escaped collapsed. *Die, assholes.*

"You need to get up!" Alexi pulled her to her feet.

"How's Biorki?" Kaia winced from the effort of breathing.

"I'm fine." Biorki's weak voice came from her left.

Kaia looked over. He was gasping on his knees on the green mineral floor. His suit was riddled with holes, but his face was even worse. Blood ran from multiple gashes on his cheeks, forehead, and nose. He was alive, but he wouldn't last long in the cold. She had to get him somewhere warm.

"The ship. He needs to get to the ship," Kaia wheezed.

Kaia took in the vast room—the silo, as Alexi had called it. It was perfectly circular, carved from malachite. The walls rose above them until they became dark mountain rock. It was hard to see through the dust, but she swore she could see a massive hatch above them.

What stole her breath was not the patterns in the malachite glowing in their helmet lights. Nor was it the strange old crates and boxes, clearly from a different world, stacked along the walls. It was the large teardrop-shaped object in the middle of the room. The spaceship?

It was made of completely smooth silver metal—no bolts, no joints, only faint surface lines that suggested it had been assembled at some point. How it had been built was beyond her understanding. Not only that, it hovered above the ground. Kaia could see everything in the room reflected in that silver: Alexi beside her, his weird weapon on the ground, her white suit, covered in soot and blood, Biorki struggling to get up. They looked terrible and insignificant.

Alexi pulled her arm over his shoulder. "The rocks won't stop them for long. Get in the ship. It needs time to initiate."

Could the Solon guards survive a tunnel collapse? Kaia tried to turn and look, but Alexi placed his arm on her back and pushed her toward the ship.

Kaia tried to shake him off. "Help Biorki. I can get myself there." The motion made her hunch over in pain.

"Don't be ridiculous." Alexi dragged her forward. "Biorki already made his choice."

Kaia looked up at the spaceship. Something was wrong; Biorki had disappeared from the reflection.

She twisted out of Alexi's grasp and spun around. Her eyes widened, and her heart sank. Biorki stood at the tunnel entrance. One of the rocks from the collapsed tunnel had stopped the door from closing. Kaia moved toward Biorki, but Alexi grabbed her arm hard.

"Let me go!"

Alexi only squeezed her arm harder. "This was always a risk. Why did you think he came here? He made his choice."

Alexi tried to pull her back, but she didn't budge as his words sunk in. The only way to close the door was to move the chunk of malachite, which rested at an angle on another loose piece from the collapsed tunnel. The green rock looked too heavy to push up the other rock and that only left one option. Kaia felt her airways close. To move the rock someone had to do it from the other side of the silo door. Dread filled her as Biorki lifted the communicator he held to his lips, eyes full of emotion.

"I'm sorry I couldn't keep my promise." Biorki's voice drifted to her in a daze.

As if in slow motion, Biorki leaned into the rock and pushed. The piece of malachite tipped, then fell forward. It broke into a million pieces skittering across the silo floor. The doors slammed shut, and the last she saw was the smile on his face. Alexi's communicator crackled again.

"K, you idiot. You need to live!"

Everything stopped—her heart, blood, and brain—as if time refused to go on without him. *Not again.*

A tiny whisper left the device. "I love you. Now, go!"

Not again. Not again. "NOT AGAIN!"

She tore out of Alexi's grip and ran toward the door. She didn't care that she couldn't breathe. She didn't care that Alexi screamed at her to come back. She would never let someone sacrifice themself for her again. Biorki had lied to her. He said he would go with her. He said he would never leave her. He'd promised.

Fury rose within her, a bubbling vile hot thing. It burst from every cell of her body. She pulled at the door. It wouldn't open. She slammed the keypad. Nothing.

She reached outside herself and felt the vibrations, the empty space where Biorki should be. Then she closed her eyes and turned inward. A thousand needles of heat crawled through her. She found her darkness, but she didn't pull this time. Instead, she walked inside it and let it consume her.

She opened her eyes, and it exploded from her body. With a loud boom, a wave of pure energy burst out of her.

Radiant near-invisible lines of heat bubbled through the air. They pulsed in time with her heartbeat—exploding, retracting, then bursting again. She focused on the door and willed it to be gone. The metal turned from a light gray to a hot glowing orange. The alloy turned into liquid in front of her eyes. Her suit melted away, and embers floated through the air.

Something moved around her neck and squeezed.

A current raced through her nerves, and her body erupted into pain. She was still conscious and aware, but she couldn't move. She could only watch as cold and blinding pain devoured her, only watch as her body crumpled to the ground.

No.

She hadn't made it through the door. The pure energy slipped from her grasp like smoke. Without it, she couldn't fight the shards of pain tearing her apart from the inside. She tried to scream, to claw at her neck. Nothing. She couldn't even blink.

She watched as Alexi picked her up like a bag of gravel. She screamed and screamed inside her head for him to stop, for the pain to stop. But he couldn't hear her. Alexi ran with her body like dead weight in his slim arms. She couldn't close her eyes or look away as he initiated the ship's startup sequence. A door appeared on the side of the ship.

No. Not without Biorki.

She couldn't cover her ears as what was left of the tunnel door blew from its hinges and Biorki's scream filled the silo. Couldn't do anything as Alexi lifted her into the spaceship.

He bent down and whispered, "I'm so sorry. I didn't want it to end like this." She couldn't feel it, but she saw Alexi place something in her burned palm.

Then Alexi turned his back to her. *No.* He walked away from the ship with a strange weapon in his hand. *No, don't leave me.* Beyond his slim frame was Drap. Covered in blood, he limped toward the ship, blind rage twisting his face. Alexi's back stiffened.

"Initiate launch." His voice was calm, steady.

Please! Don't leave me alone!

"Launch initiated," an unfamiliar voice responded.

The doors closed, and Kaia was swallowed by darkness and pain.

CHAPTER 41

Kaia didn't know how much time had passed. Hours? Cycles? Rotations? The sound of her ragged breathing was the only clue that she was still alive. She hated that sound. The pain had stopped, but she still couldn't use her limbs. At some point, her body lifted from the hard floor and slammed into the wall. The darkness seemed to move. New shadows appeared as her eyes adjusted. The shapes were ominous, looming above her helpless body.

Another endless minute, hour, or cycle passed. Then needles crawled over her skin. Not the hot, searing kind her power caused, but cold, painful ones. They crawled through her toes and fingers, then up her arms and legs until everything throbbed. She welcomed them. Anything was better than the numb emptiness she had been trapped in.

When the needles reached her neck, her locked muscles released, and she sagged to the floor. The invisible cage was replaced by her throbbing ribs, bruises, and convulsing muscles. Her eyes felt like they had been dragged across sandpaper. She could ignore her physical pain; so what if one of her ribs might have punctured a lung. It was the emptiness inside that pulled at her, drowning her.

After another endless measurement of time, she tried to move. She didn't want to, didn't want to live, but curiosity won out. She had to know what Alexi had placed in her hand. It had disappeared into the darkness when she had slammed into the wall. She focused on her fingers first, then her hands, her toes, her knees. Her muscles felt off, her joints foreign, like her nerves were fried beyond recognition. Based on the pain she had felt, they probably were.

It was a slow and frustrating process, but she eventually made it onto all fours. She placed a hand on the wall and stood with shaking legs. That was progress. *Where is that thing?* She leaned on the wall and dragged herself forward.

Brilliant, blinding light flooded the small room. She squinted. *Light sensors—great.* The room was unlike anything she had seen before. She didn't care. *Where is that thing?*

She dragged her feet over to where she had seen it slide. A white wall stood before her, full of see-through compartments for storage. *Whatever.* Looking down, she found the object beneath shelves full of what looked like packs of freeze-dried blood. It was small, flat, circular. A chip? It took everything she had to bend down and pick it up.

She turned it between her fingers. Silver like the ship. Was it a key? On the back, it read, for kaia. So, not a key?

She walked over to the smaller door in the room. The one Alexi hadn't abandoned her at. There was no button or handle. Voice recognition?

"Ship, can you open the door?"

Her voice was flat, unrecognizable. She felt ridiculous talking to a door. But then the door answered.

"Name?"

She sighed. "Kaia."

"Full name?"

Kaia blinked at that. This was the first time anyone had ever asked for her full name.

"Kaia'Rin."

"Acknowledged. Request?"

Of course this ship knew her full name. "Open the door."

The door slid soundlessly to the side. "Would you like to automate the doors on the ship?"

Kaia breathed, her rib protesting. "Sure, whatever."

"Door automation confirmed."

She walked through the door and into a white corridor. It turned, so she couldn't see the end. She stopped. "Ship, where can I find a chip reader?"

The voice filled the corridor. "My name is not Ship."

Kaia tightened her fist. "Then what is it?"

"Directive 103-BE32 at your service, but you can call me BE3."

"BE3. Where's the chip reader?"

A row of lights appeared on the ceiling. Kaia followed them.

Her footsteps echoed in the empty corridor as she passed many doors. This chip had to be important. Why else would Alexi have given it to her? She took a few more steps before something twisted so deep within her that she had to stop. Hunched over, she tried to breathe. The rasp of her windpipe stroked the slick walls. The chip dug into her palm. *Find the chip reader.* She straightened and limped forward.

After a few more turns, the lights led her toward another indistinguishable door. It slid open as she approached. Inside, in the middle of a room, stood a table with six matching white circular chairs. The walls were clean, empty and white. No lights, no fixtures, just an oval room with a table and chairs. It smelled like everything else in this place: sterile.

"BE3, this is not a chip reader. Where is it?"

"If you're too dumb to figure it out, then so be it," BE3 snapped.

She gaped. So BE3 wasn't just a primary directive.

"Show me the damn chip reader!"

Silence.

Kaia inspected the room more closely. Maybe BE3 wasn't messing with her. In that case, the chip reader should be here. She moved toward the table. Nothing, just a clean white surface. But what if…

She placed the chip on the immaculate surface. The whole room lit up. The walls turned into screens, the table into a computer. It should have amazed her, but she was too exhausted. She scoured the walls and found a file. She dragged her finger across the table and tapped it.

A face filled the wall. Kaia slammed the table, and the face disappeared. She took a deep breath, her ribs aching, and pressed it again.

On the screen was flowing black-and-silver hair, a dark face, and blue eyes—the hag. Gret-ha's face was solemn, her eyes insistent. She sat in her igloo, the white walls curving around her. A white mist left her chapped lips when she breathed.

"If you see this, Kaia, it means I succeeded." The grave voice, not as powerful in a recording, filled the sterile room.

Gret-ha grabbed the device in front of her and turned it toward a white shape with curly hair sticking out. It was her, Kaia. Then Gret-ha turned the camera back to face her. The hag smiled.

"It's finally happening. You left that awful place, Kaldwell." Gret-ha pulled a strand of hair from her face. "You must know that I didn't intend for your father to die, but he didn't listen. Said that he wanted you to have a normal life, to live it out under the glacier." Gret-ha spat on the ground. "I knew you were meant for more. There were prophecies! I thought they referred to my daughter, but when I saw you at the hot springs and the water disappeared…that's when I knew."

A terrible feeling fell over Kaia.

"So I made plans. I contacted the leaders of Framnes. Told them about Solon's free advanced medical care. They wouldn't listen to an old woman, of course." Gret-ha scratched her cheek. "Then CE spread. They changed their minds, and I helped them contact Solon. Once they made it here, I knew Solon would start slow and gradually work their way up to take everything, as they always do. It would force Lu to act."

Kaia hadn't thought she could feel any worse. She'd been wrong. A hollow coldness shot through her. It had been Gret-ha—all of it.

"Although, I didn't expect them to take seven rotations to get here. When I received word of their impending arrival, I let Lu know. But that darn stubborn man still refused my help. He said that if Solon was on the way, he had a plan to keep you safe. So I made it impossible for you to hide. Once I heard the first ship from Solon landed in Framnes I placed an explosive in the mines. It worked beautifully. The leaders of Kaldwell did as I expected—they asked for help, and Solon was ready. That's when I shut down your father's communicator so he wouldn't be able to warn you. Somehow he managed anyway, but you still went to the sick bay. Stupid girl.

"It all went to plan until the Solon guards followed you inside. Usually they have a protocol not to kill, but of course those bastards decided to act on their own authority. It wasn't my fault Lu died. At least he did one thing right and got you out of there."

Bile filled Kaia's mouth; acid was in her throat. Gret-ha had killed so many people.

Gret-ha grinned. "I followed you on the surface—I wanted to see if you had the will to fight. And now you're here. I will send you to Framnes, to Alexi, and he can get you on that ship and away. He might be a loser, but when Alexi meets you, he will help you. Then you can fulfill your prophecy and destroy those who destroyed my daughter."

The clip ended. Then another smiling face appeared on the screen: Alexi. Sadness filled his eyes, his smile not reaching them.

"Gret-ha sent me this chip to give to you. I'm so sorry. I didn't realize what she was doing. If I had known, I would have put a stop to it. Lu was an amazing man. He was right to give you a normal life." Alexi's voice was warm, and tears fell from his eyes. "You know, Lu saved me once—saved me from myself, from my loss. I'm sure you know what kind of man he was. Kind, selfless, and strong."

Alexi wiped his eyes. "I know I can't change what Gret-ha has done, but I will make sure one of your dreams comes true before more of your life is taken from you. Lu told me you dreamed of entering Stallo, so I entered you this morning. You're quite a stubborn person, you know. Gave me no choice in the matter." Alexi smiled softly. "Like father, like daughter."

Kaia sat there, her emotions unreachable, an empty numbness where her heart used to be.

More tears fell from Alexi's eyes. "If you see this, Solon got to us, and you are alone on BE3. Remember, you're not to blame. I knew the dangers. Your father knew the dangers. Please don't listen to Gret-ha; there is no prophecy. You can make your own destiny. You are free to do anything, to travel anywhere. But stay safe and hidden. Solon is still out there, hiding around every corner. I have given the ship coordinates to a safe place. You should be able to hide there for now. The rest is up to you."

The screen turned black, silence filled the room, and the walls faded back to white.

Too much. It was too much. Kaia couldn't breathe, and it wasn't because of her ribs. It wasn't her broken body but her mind. Panic, fear, and guilt raged through her. She closed her eyes and screamed. The torrent of emotions shattered her. She screamed until she had no voice, until her lungs gave out, until she lay on her side on the floor, clutching her head.

"Rapid bodily decline detected. Please move to the cryo chamber." BE3's voice faded into the background. "Rapid bodily decline detected. Please move to the cryo chamber."

White spots filled her vision, and she curled in on herself.

"No reaction. Rescue activated."

The door slid open, and in the corner of her foggy vision, she saw something moving toward her. She woke to walls and doors blurring together. Then it all went black.

EPILOGUE

Alexi brushed the dust off his suit and placed his weapon back in its crate. What a mess. Thank the stars he had built a secret storage room under the ship. Looking up at the stars, he found no sign BE3. Nonetheless, he stared into the empty dark. It had been too close. He needed to figure out a way to block Solon's tracking tech if they were to have any chance of standing against them in the future. Hiding shouldn't be their only option.

He had survived this time by using a distraction. The launch of the ship had sent shock waves into the air. When they had squashed him and the Solon guard into the ground, he had dropped into the hidden hole. It was sheer luck that they hadn't found him afterward. Biorki, on the other hand…

Stupid boy. He should have tried harder to die. The guards had taken Biorki away with them, which meant he was alive. That was a fate worse than death. Alexi shook his head. It was safe to assume the guards were returning to their ship now. They would try to follow Kaia, but they wouldn't find her as long as she didn't do anything stupid.

Rubbing his neck, Alexi sighed. *Gret-ha, what the heck did you do?* Kaia wasn't ready. If the prophecies were true, which he highly doubted, she would need more than a grumpy ship to survive. And if she failed… He shook his head. The signs of Solon's influence were already there, in Framnes, in Kaldwell. The next wave of guards would come soon.

He crouched and picked up a piece of burnt fabric, twirled it between his fingers. He hoped he had made the right choice to stay behind, to let Kaia decide for herself what her life would be. It wasn't his place or Gret-ha's to decide her future. Their daughter was gone; that wouldn't change. But Kaia had escaped.

He closed his fist around the fabric and squeezed. Soot fell from his glove. The only thing he could do now was to prepare for the next wave of guards. And hope. Hope that they would find a way to fight.

Alexi walked to the large box he had picked up at M-Base 325. He had to get this to Kritan, or they would never survive the war to come.

SIGN UP FOR REBEKKA'S NEWSLETTER

Be the first to learn about Rebekka Strand's new releases and
receive exclusive content.

WWW.REBEKKASTRAND.COM

ACKNOWLEDGMENTS

When I sat down to write Shattered Ice in November 2020, I had no idea what I was in for. Yet, through it all, on the nights I cried full of doubts or on the days I wouldn't shut up about new book ideas, my husband, Jeromy, has been nothing but incredible. You pushed me on when I wanted to curl into a ball and give up. You never let me tell myself I couldn't do it. You supported me when many others would have doubted me. Thank you for giving me the courage to pursue my dream.

To Mamma, the woman who surrounded me with wonderful stories when I was a child. The woman who showed me the wonders of books and the words on a piece of paper. I don't remember a time in my childhood when there weren't books around me. From when I joined you at your job at Gyldendal in Norway to every nighttime story before bed. You never told me what I could and couldn't read, letting me explore the world of stories independently. For that, I am forever grateful.

To the man who introduced me to the world of sci-fi, Pappa. You have inspired me to do what I love regardless of others' opinions. To get up again when things get tough, to move on when life gives you lemons. Thank you for the many phone calls where I could blabber to you about my story.

Thank you for the art you made for me and the time you spent helping me with this novel. Your insight has been invaluable.

Jim, the man, the myth, the legend. You gave me the space to write, the room to dive into my imaginary worlds. You read my very first draft and motivated me to keep going. Thank you for supporting my insanity and listening to my many crazy book ideas.

To my dear friends and family who kept asking me about my novel, even though it had been years since I announced I would write one. You are the most incredible supporters, and I know you will brag about my novel, even if you think it is terrible. And I love you for that.

To the woman who read my novel when it was, simply described, a total mess. Thank you, Mcara Lee, for spending those hours out of your day to help me stitch my first draft together. I don't know what this novel would have been without you.

Nothing is more terrifying than sending your first manuscript out and into the world. A huge thanks to my Alpha readers: Kim Hillmer, Deana M VanCura, Nicholas L James, Leah Burks, and Steffen R. M. Sørum. For caring for my artistic heart and being the best help and motivation to carry on. And for becoming my friends in the process. You have been the most amazing support.

To my Developmental Editor, Emily Klopfer, who confirmed my suspicions and made great suggestions to plot and changes to my first manuscript. The story would not be as well-developed without you.

To my fantastic Beta readers: Elizabeth Orthman, Cassandra Petrich, Caitlin Gerardy, Kaden Donnelly, and Kevin Michaud. For your honesty and your love for the craft of writing. You taught me a lot about myself and my story.

Although only stopping in a few times, The Mysterious Galaxy Writers Group took me in with open arms and asked me important questions about my craft. I still ask myself these questions occasionally, making me a better writer.

To my cousin Mira Nordin, thank you for lending me your snowboard expertise when I was writing the iceboarding action scenes.

Being bilingual is both an advantage and a curse. Thanks to Alison Cherry, my copy editor, my book will be free of weird sentence structure. Thank you for taking on my large manuscript and refining it to what it is today.

Ethemos, you are an incredibly talented concept artist, and I can't wait to see how far you will go. Merci pour tout. I am so proud to share my book cover thanks to your art.

To authors and writers out there. We do not have to be perfect. We do not have to do it all ourselves, even in self-publishing. We do not have to be literary geniuses. What we need is a story and persistence. Keep going and ask for help when you need it.

And to all the people on the internet supplying independent authors with the help they need. For answering questions we never asked but needed to hear, and for sharing your knowledge with the world. Thank you for making so many writers' dreams possible. You know who you are.

GLOSSARY

Alexi [uh L EH K s ee] – The name is an abbreviation of Alexios of Greek origin, meaning: Defender of Humanity.

Állan [AL Uhn] – Number seven in Stallo.

Bean [b EE n] – A nickname that is what it sounds like.

Biorki [B or Key] – The name is a made-up abbreviation of Birk of German origin, meaning: Birch; The Protector.

Criola [Kree Ow Lah] – Solon nurse 2. The name is of Portuguese origin, meaning: of American birth but European descent.

Cycle – an Eirlys day. A set 24-hour cycle of time, unrelated to the sunrise or sunset. The 24-hour cycle follows the biological clock and not the rotations of the planet or sun.

Cystic Effusion (CE) – An incurable illness that will make a person go mad before dying of lack of oxygen.

David [Day Vid] – Contestant number four in Stallo.

Drap [D R uh P] – Solon guard 1. The name comes from a Norwegian word that translates to Murder.

Dritt [Dre T] – A swear word of Norwegian origin, meaning: Shit.

Eirlys [AY R L ih s] – The name of the planet. The word is of Welsh origin, meaning: snowdrop.

Fluff [FluF] – A smylon who belongs to Gret-ha.

Framnes [F ram n uh s] – The capitol of Eirlys. The name is a combination of the name of the ship used in expeditions of the Arctic and Antarctic regions by the Norwegian explorers in 1893, Fram, and the Norwegian word Nes, meaning a small and pointy piece of land sticking into the ocean.

Fuse [FYOOZ] – A droid.

Gin [j IH n] – Solon guard 2. The name is an abbreviation of Eugene of English origin, meaning: Well-born; Noble.

Gret-ha [Grea T Ha] – The name is an abbreviation of Margareta of Persian origin, meaning: Pearl.

Heat-converter – A piece of technology that filters and heats the air inside of a monosuit.

Heaika [Hike Uh] – Number ten in Stallo.

Ine [EE n uh] – The name is of Scandinavian origin, meaning: The Only; Clean.

Ingà [ING uh] – The name is an abbreviation of Inga of Scandinavian origin, meaning: The Goddess of Fertility; The Daughter of a Chief.

Jonas [jo Naas] – The name is of Hebraic origin, meaning: Due.

Kaldwell [K AW L D w eh l] – The town's name is made up of the Norwegian word Kaldt, meaning Cold, and the English word Well, meaning: Cold Well.

Kaia [Ka ee ya] – The name is of Scandinavian origin, meaning: Pure; Life; The Sea.

Kjartan [Char T uh n] – The name comes from the Irish King Myrkjartan, meaning: Sea Warrior.

Lu [L U] – Kaia's father. The name is of Latin origin, meaning: Famous Warrior; Light.

Midcycle – Refers to the hours of a cycle for activity and work.

Midsleep – Refers to the hours within a cycle for sleeping; it can also mean Midnight.

Mihka [Me Kah] – Number twelve in Stallo.

Misam [M ih s uh m] – The name is of Arabic or Indian origins, meaning: Happy; Smiling; An Innocent person.

Moira [Moy R uh] – Solon nurse 1. The name is of Irish origin, meaning: Bitter.

Monosuit – A multilayered one-piece of clothing that covers all of the body. Designs can be wary, but the fabric should be loose enough to maintain air between the body and the suit to generate heat and tight enough not to be dangerous when working with big machinery.

Rakel [Ra Kel] – An older miner. Leader of L3.

Rotation – A time measurement to describe the planet's full rotation around the sun. However, the people of Eirlys only know it as measuring a defined number of 24-hour cycles. Over time, the measurements have become less tied to the rotation of the planet and more to the number of cycles.

Si Vilia [Sea We Le Uh] – The tent attendant for Solon.

Smylon [SmI Loh n] – A predator, a huge saber-toothed cat, who can hunt in packs or by themselves. Native to Eirlys, Smylons' have evolved to withstand sub-zero temperatures and travel far distances. Smylons' can survive on moss, growing inside the mountains, or on raw meat. If necessary, a Smylon can go without food for rotations as they hibernate.

Sofia [SOH Fee Uh] – Contestant number one in Stallo.

Solon [SOH lun] – An intergalactic company with unknown ambitions and goals. The name comes from the Athenian politician and lawmaker Solon (638-558 BC), who is credited with having laid the foundations for Athenian democracy.

Stallo [Stal Loh] – The name of the iceboarding contest in Framnes. The word comes from the Sámi peoples' folklore. A Stállo is a large, human-like creature who likes to eat people. I encourage you to learn more about the native people of Scandinavia and their history.

Tibilos [Tea B Loh S] – A lonely predator. Tibilos are highly territorial, but if one does not disturb them, they will keep to themselves. Very little is known about their eating habits or their life cycles. One text from the old folklore describes them as the guardians of Eirlys.

Torvald [Thor wall duh] – Ingá's husband.

Ulla [Uh la] – The name is of Scandinavian origin, meaning:
   Willpower; Determination.
Venlá [When L Uh] – Owns a droid part store in Framnes.
Vilde [Will D Uh] – Contestant number eleven in Stallo.

Rebekka Strand taught herself to read English by reading Harry Potter. She was six.

Born in Norway in 1992, Rebekka grew up among frozen hills and hot stews. She learned to build fires in school and cross-country skied on the weekends. Then, she found skateboarding and, through it, her husband.

After graduating with an M.D. in Behavior Analysis, she moved to San Diego, California. Surrounded by sand, palm trees, and spicy foods, Rebekka found the contrasts inspiring. Unable to leave and unable to work, she had too much time on her hands. And so, stuck in a foreign land, she began writing her debut, Shattered Ice.

You can visit her online at www.rebekkastrand.com, Instagram (@rebekkacwstrand), or TikTok (@rebekka.strand).

A WORD FROM REBEKKA

Dear reader.

Thank you for taking time out of your day to read Shattered Ice. If you have made it this far in my novel, you deserve a hug and to hear what inspired me to write my debut.

It was on a late night in November 2020, when the sun had set, and the darkness crept into my bedroom window that the idea of Shattered Ice sort of fell into my mind. At the time, I was waiting for my green card to process, which had been delayed by Covid. This meant I could not work or leave the country, and I hadn't seen Norway for over a year. It was the longest I had ever been away from my birthplace, family, and friends. Needless to say, I missed it.

Looking back at that day and now reading Kaia's journey, the way she is torn from everything she knows, I can see that it represents how I felt at the time. I experienced so many new wonders in California. I met many incredible people and saw many fantastic places, yet I still missed everything I had left behind.

What I have learned is that going on a journey has two sides. The side that is thrilled by the new experiences and the adventure it promises and the side that mourns what was left behind. Although the pain can sometimes be overwhelming, To gain something, you might have to lose something else. Is it fair? No. But it is up to you if you are willing to take the chance.

If you like the novel (I am guessing that if you made it this far in the book, you do), then please leave a review on Amazon or Goodreads.

PS: I am working on Book 2 in the series. We will get to see Kaia's adventure in space as she seeks her revenge. But Solon has their grip in the most unlikely places. One wrong step, and Kaia will have fled for nothing.